THE HEART OF A HERO

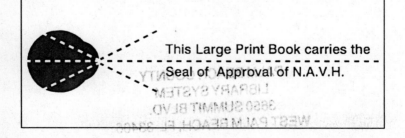

SPELLBOUND FALLS

THE HEART OF A HERO

JANET CHAPMAN

KENNEBEC LARGE PRINT
A part of Gale, Cengage Learning

GALE
CENGAGE Learning·

Detroit • New York • San Francisco • New Haven, Conn • Waterville, Maine • London

GALE
CENGAGE Learning·

LIBRARY OF CONGRESS CATALOGING-IN-PUBLICATION DATA

Chapman, Janet.
   The Heart of a Hero / by Janet Chapman. — Large Print edition.
      pages cm. — (Spellbound Falls Series) (Kennebec Large Print Superior Collection)
   ISBN 978-1-4104-6190-2 (softcover) — ISBN 1-4104-6190-4 (softcover)
   1. Hero (Greek mythology)—Fiction. 2. Police, Private—Fiction. 3. Mountain resorts—Maine—Fiction. 4. Maine—Fiction. 5. Large type books. I. Title.
   PS3603.H372H43 2013
   813'.6—dc23   2013020196

Published in 2013 by arrangement with The Berkley Publishing Group, a division of Penguin Group (USA)

Printed in the United States of America
1 2 3 4 5   17 16 15 14 13

To Raymond Byram.
You've always been a soft place
to land, big brother, but your wisdom
and grace make you a truly amazing
family patriarch.
(You will, however, always
be Dipsy *to us.)*

CHAPTER ONE

Watching through the windshield of his truck, Nicholas studied the three young men getting out of the late-model pickup on the far side of the employee parking lot at the base of Whisper Mountain. But the more the man sitting beside him explained why he'd asked him to come down here today, the more confused Nicholas became. Rowan was second in command of Nova Mare's security force and quite capable of dealing with this sort of problem on his own.

"And the reason you didn't simply intervene?" Nicholas asked. As he watched, one of the three young men lifted a bicycle out of the pickup and leaned it against a tree in front of the older, mud-splattered truck they'd pulled up beside. "They're on resort property, Julia Campbell is an employee, and last time I checked, keeping our staff safe was in your job description."

Apparently not the least bit intimidated

by the growl in his boss's voice, Rowan shook his head with a soft snort. "If I've learned anything living in Spellbound Falls this past year, it's that Mainers don't particularly care to have strangers butting into their business — especially family business. Her brother's the one with the peachfuzz beard." Rowan scowled at the young men lighting up cigarettes as they leaned against the shiny red truck they'd arrived in. "And I didn't intervene last week because I was afraid it would make things worse for Julia when she got home. Here she comes," he said when the bus shuttling employees down from the mountaintop resort halted in the middle of the parking lot.

Nicholas reached over and stopped Rowan from getting out. "Let's sit and watch for a while. You say he's here every Friday waiting for her to get off work, and that it's obvious he's hitting her up for money?"

Rowan nodded. "She usually has it in her pocket and just hands him some folded bills. Only last week he apparently wanted more than she was offering and grabbed her purse. They got in a small tussle, she lost, and he dug out her wallet, pulled out a fistful of money and tossed the wallet and purse on the ground, then got in his truck and left. The punk couldn't even be bothered to take her home, but left her to ride her bicycle in the rain. There, that's her in the red wool jacket and black pants, carrying those empty feed sacks," Rowan said, nodding at the worker stepping off the shuttle bus.

Nicholas saw the woman in red hesitate when she spotted the three young men leaning against the pickup, then watched her square her shoulders and head toward them — her brother straightening at the sight of her.

Julia Campbell was taller than average for a woman and somewhat on the thin side, with a thick braid of light brown hair hanging halfway down her back that Nicholas suspected would spring into a riot of curls when let loose. It was dusk and starting to snow, so he couldn't make out the color of her large eyes set in her oval face on top of a gracefully long neck. Her posture was intrinsically feminine, her stride filled with purposeful energy despite it being the end of her workday. "She's older than I was expecting," he said, assuming she'd barely be out of her teens, judging by the age of her brother.

"I asked the shuttle driver her name after that little tussle," Rowan said, "then went back up to your office and checked her employee file. She turned thirty last month, has been married but is divorced. And even though I've since learned her mother's dead and that she lives with her father between here and town, she listed a sister as next of kin to notify in an emergency. The empty sacks she's carrying were full this morning. Her family owns a cedar mill, and Julia supplies the resort with kindling and pinecones for the fireplaces to supplement her wages and tips. She works housekeeping Tuesday through Saturday, and from what I've gathered from quietly checking around, she asked to always be assigned the same eight cottages."

Nicholas glanced at him, arching a brow. "Any particular reason you've become an expert on one of our female employees?"

"I'm *concerned*," Rowan growled back. "Sweet Prometheus, man, I'm old enough to be her father." He suddenly grinned. "And yours, sir," he drawled, just as Julia Campbell reached her brother, her hand already emerging from her pocket holding some money. "I don't like interfering in family business," Rowan continued. "But I also don't like seeing a woman being harassed. That's why I asked you to come down here today and help me decide what to do — if anything."

"Our authority ends at the resort's property lines, which means it's not our place to interfere in —" Nicholas stopped in mid-sentence. Julia had just handed her brother the money, then twisted away when he made a grab for her. She stepped around him and pulled a set of keys from her pocket as she headed for the older pickup, but halted again when the other two boys moved to block her path.

Nicholas was out of his own truck and halfway across the parking lot when he saw Julia's brother start dragging her toward the bicycle while trying to wrestle the keys away from her. "Come on, Reggie, it's *snowing*," she said as he dodged employees walking to their vehicles. "Give me a ride home."

"I'm not heading back to town," the punk said, still dragging her. "Dad's drinking again, so I'm spending the weekend at Corey's camp." Finally getting hold of the keys, he gave her arm a shake. "You were supposed to leave the keys under the mat so I could get the truck this afternoon. I had to wait four freakin' hours in town."

She yanked her arm out of his grip. "I kept them so you'd give me a ride."

"Not happening, sis. Pedal fast and you'll beat the storm. And while you're at it, you can figure out how to lug your kindling on

11

your bike from now on, because you're not getting my truck again."

"Is there a problem?" Nicholas asked from directly behind the boy.

"Not that I know of," the kid snarled as he pivoted, only to stumble back when he found himself glaring at a broad chest. "Who the hell are you?" he asked, taking another step back.

"Director of security for Nova Mare," Nicholas said, matching him step for step. He looked past the boy at Julia. "You in need of some help, Miss Campbell?"

Her eyes widened, apparently surprised that he knew her name, before she dropped her gaze and shook her head. "No, everything's okay."

"I'm outta here," the boy said, reaching for the door of his truck.

Nicholas placed his hand on the door to hold it closed. "I believe your sister asked you for a ride home."

"No, that's okay," Julia said as she headed for the trees. "I've decided I'd rather ride my bike." She set her sacks and purse in the basket attached to the handlebar, nodded at Nicholas with a forced smile, then walked the bicycle along the tree line before veering into the parking lot several vehicles away.

Suspecting Rowan was right about their

interference creating more problems for her, Nicholas turned to the boy. "I catch even a whisper that you've laid a hand on your sister," he said quietly, "on *or off* the resort grounds, you and I are taking a long walk in the woods together, you got that?"

"Are you freakin' *threatening* me?"

Nicholas leaned in, crowding the punk against the mud-splattered door. "Yes," he said succinctly. He turned and walked to his pickup. "Take the shuttle back up the mountain," he told his second in command when the man fell into step beside him. "I'm giving Miss Campbell a ride home."

"So much for not interfering," Rowan said on a chuckle as he headed to the bus with a wave over his shoulder.

He'd *had* to interfere, Nicholas decided as he got in his pickup, because he couldn't stand seeing a woman being harassed any more than Rowan could. He started his truck, but then had to wait for several cars to idle past before he was able to pull out behind them. And why was Julia Campbell letting some fuzzy-faced punk half her age push her around? If the little bastard wanted money, he could damn well break a sweat for it, not bum it off his sister.

Nicholas unclenched his jaw and turned on the windshield wipers to clear the swirl-

13

ing snow. "It's none of my business," he muttered, finally pulling onto the main road behind the procession of exiting workers. "I'm just going to make sure she gets home without breaking her lovely neck."

He'd been working at Nova Mare over a year now and still couldn't get a handle on the locals, which was confounding, considering there wasn't a country or culture he hadn't studied at length — some quite intimately. But Mainers appeared to be a breed unto themselves; maddeningly stoic, stubbornly self-reliant, and highly resilient. They were also deeply proud, especially the women.

Nicholas scowled out the windshield. Not only were the women proud, some of them were really quite bold when it came to pursuing something — or *someone* — they wanted. And apparently several of them wanted Nova Mare's unusually tall, blue-eyed director of security. Which was becoming a real problem, as he didn't particularly like being considered Spellbound Falls' most eligible bachelor — a title he'd heard whispered around. By the gods, some of the women's antics were bordering on brazen.

Not that he had any intention of living like a monk if a lovely lady happened to catch *his* interest. He just preferred to be the one doing the pursuing.

So how had the decidedly lovely Julia Campbell escaped his notice?

Nicholas saw the vehicles in front of him swerve across the center line, allowing his headlights to land on Little Red Riding Hood walking her bicycle down the side of the darkened road in the nearly blinding snow. She'd pulled her hood over her head and was struggling to keep the bicycle's snow-caked tires out of the ditch, making him wonder why none of her coworkers were offering her a ride.

Tempted to hunt down her brother and take the punk on a *one-way* walk in the woods, Nicholas had to make himself relax his jaw again as he drove past her and pulled to the side. He got out of his truck, but then had to snag the bicycle's seat when Julia merely veered into the road to go around him. "Take your purse out of the basket," he said as he grabbed the bike by the frame. "I'm giving you a ride home."

He lifted the bike when she didn't move — which made her snatch her purse with a startled squeak — and set it in his truck, but then had to grab Julia's arm and hustle her out of the road as several vehicles swerved around them. She opened the passenger door, but then just stood there staring at the chest-height seat.

She gave another soft squeak when he caught her around the waist and lifted her into the truck. Nicholas closed the door before she could see him grin at the realization that Julia Campbell's eyes — their long lashes littered with snowflakes — were a rich hazel-gold. Feline eyes, he decided, with the potential to be warmly inviting one minute and stubbornly aloof the next.

And wasn't it interesting that he happened to like cats?

After walking around the front of the truck, he slid in behind the wheel, checked his side mirror, and pulled back onto the road. "You'll have to tell me where you live," he said into the silence broken only by the thump of the windshield wipers.

"Just a few miles on the right. Um, thank you."

"You're welcome." He pulled off one of his gloves with his teeth and turned up the heater fan, then held out his hand to her. "Nicholas."

She hesitated, shook his hand without taking off her own glove, then went back to hugging her purse to her chest. "Julia."

What Nicholas liked most — and, ironically, least — about cats was their fierce independence, while he considered their most endearing quality to be their general lack of vocalization. And although he only suspected Julia Campbell could be stubbornly independent, judging by her determination to walk home in a snowstorm rather than ask a coworker for a ride, she was also proving to be a woman of few words. "How long have you worked at Nova Mare?"

"Since May."

Only six months. "And before then?"

"I waited tables at the Drunken Moose weekends and worked at my family's cedar mill through the week."

Wow, a whole sentence. "So were you living here when the mountains moved and the earthquake turned Bottomless into an inland sea three and a half years ago?"

"No, I was living just north of Bangor. But we felt the earthquake down there."

"You work in housekeeping, don't you?"

"Yes."

Nicholas felt his jaw tightening again with a whole new appreciation of the women who complained that talking to him was like pulling teeth, and tried to decide what about this particular woman was bugging him. "You enjoy working at Nova Mare?"

"Very much," she said, adding a slight nod when she obviously heard the edge in his voice. "Mrs. Oceanus is a wonderful boss.

17

That mailbox is my road." She reached for the door handle. "You can drop me off here. I live only a short ways in."

Nicholas turned onto the road and kept going, stifling another grin when he heard his passenger release a barely perceptible sigh. "With this weather, it looks as if your days of riding a bicycle to work are coming to an end. You don't own a car?"

"I . . . It's being repaired."

Must be quite a major repair, since Rowan had told him Julia had been biking to work for months now — except on Fridays, when she apparently borrowed her brother's truck to bring her kindling and pinecones. And the woman's idea of a "short ways" was an understatement, considering he'd already driven down the rutted forest road over a mile without seeing any signs of a house yet.

And he still couldn't figure out what was bugging him. It wasn't anything she was saying or *not* saying, just that something was . . . off. Not that it was any of his business, since he was only making sure one of their employees made it home without getting run over by a snowplow.

She really was as quiet as a cat, and just as . . . That was it; Julia Campbell wasn't *moving.* She didn't fidget, hadn't pushed back her hood or even wiped the melting snow off her face, and had managed to avoid any real eye contact with him. Nor had she questioned his showing up to give her a ride or protested his manhandling.

Nicholas knew that the first defense an abused woman learned was how not to draw attention to herself — especially unsolicited male attention. For the love of Zeus, she'd let a virtual stranger toss her in his truck without even so much as a scowl.

Granted, everyone who had anything to do with Nova Mare knew him on sight, and Julia probably figured that if she couldn't trust her employer's chief security guard then she couldn't trust anyone, but she should have at least questioned why he'd intervened in the parking lot today and taken her home without even asking.

So, did Julia Campbell simply pick her battles or was she afraid of men?

Not that it was any of his business.

He finally spotted the house sitting *two miles* off the main road, and pulled up behind a fairly new pickup that was as muddy as her brother's. He shut off the engine when he saw the porch light come on, then quickly reached over when Julia opened her door. "Wait and let me help you down," he said, getting out and walking around the front of the truck, not surprised when she didn't protest. "I've been meaning to have a set of running boards installed," he continued, guiding her to the ground. "Careful, there's ice under the snow. Let me get your bicycle out and I'll walk you —"

"Julia! That you, girl?" a heavyset man called out as he came down the porch steps wearing slippers and no coat and carrying a tall glass in his hand. "Who's that with you? You send him away and tell the fool we close at noon on Fri—"

"Daddy, be careful!" Julia cried, bolting for the house when the man missed the bottom step.

Nicholas dropped the bicycle and ran after Julia as her father stumbled toward a tree only to end up sprawled facedown in the snow — pulling Julia down with him when she tried to break his fall.

In what was starting to feel like a comedy of errors, Nicholas found himself in a small tug-of-war when the man tried using her to pull himself up before Nicholas finally wrestled Julia free and stood her out of the way. "Let me help you," he said, catching the man under the arms and lifting him to his feet.

"I told that Christless girl to spread the

stove ashes out here this morning," the man grumbled, staggering forward to hug the tree he'd missed earlier. "And where in hell is she, anyway? She's supposed to come straight home from school and cook me supper." He pointed at Julia as she straightened from picking up her purse. "It's your fault. Ever since you gave her that truck, she ain't never home."

Julia shot an uneasy glance toward Nicholas, then walked to her father. "Trisha told you she had band practice this afternoon," she explained just as a small SUV pulled up beside Nicholas's truck. "There she is now. Come on, Daddy, let's go inside and I'll cook you some eggs and pork."

Her father batted her away. "I spilt my drink," he growled, pointing at the empty plastic tumbler on the ground. He then glared up at Nicholas. "And I ain't going nowhere 'til I meet your boyfriend."

"Jules," a young woman said, rushing up only to grab Julia's arm when she slipped on the ice. "What's going on? What's wrong?"

"Both you girls are due for an attitude adjustment," their father snarled, his eyes narrowed against the swirling snow as he pointed an unsteady finger at them. "And don't you think I won't do it, neither, just 'cause it's been a while."

Nicholas forced himself to unball his fists as he stepped up to the obviously inebriated man. "Let me help you to the house, Mr. Campbell," he offered, his grip — and likely his size — squelching any protest.

"I expect a man wanting to date my daughter to ask me first," he muttered as Nicholas maneuvered him up the steps.

"I'm not dating Julia, sir. I just gave her a ride home from work."

The man yanked to a stop at the door and pulled free, the porch light revealing his bloodshot glare. "You think you're too good for my Julia, is that it?"

"Dad," the woman under discussion protested as she opened the door.

"Come on, Daddy," her sister said, pushing on her father as Julia pulled. "Let's get you inside before you catch a chill."

Mr. Campbell shrugged off both girls, then grabbed Julia's arm and gave her a shake. "This is why you can't get another man," he growled. "And why you lost the good one you had. How many times I gotta tell you to show some gratitude when a man's nice to you?" He pushed her in front of Nicholas. "I say driving you home in a snowstorm deserves a kiss."

Julia and her sister gasped in unison, and

Nicholas stiffened at the realization the man was serious. And if Julia's father had placed her in an untenable position, he'd put Nicholas in a quandary. If he simply turned and walked away, the drunken idiot would likely get angry at *her*.

"And not some shy peck on the cheek, either," Mr. Campbell continued, nudging his frozen daughter hard enough that she stumbled forward.

"Daddy," her sister growled, grabbing Julia's jacket to tug her back.

Well, hell. Nicholas pulled Julia into his arms, lowered his head as he lifted her onto her toes, and kissed her — making sure to linger just long enough to satisfy the bastard that she was properly grateful. "You're welcome," he murmured as he released her and straightened away. He gave a slight bow, then turned and walked down the steps, got in his truck, backed around, and drove out the road.

Definitely not his business, he decided as he touched his tongue to his lips — which he noticed now held a taste of peppermint.

CHAPTER TWO

His expression effectively conveying that he wasn't in the mood for conversation while he washed down his supper with a couple of beers, Nicholas sat at a small table with his back to the wall, watching the eclectic assortment of patrons enjoying the only bar in Spellbound Falls. Vanetta Quintana, proprietor of the family restaurant next door named the Drunken Moose, had opened the livelier and definitely louder Bottoms Up six months ago, hoping to wring a little more money out of the tourists visiting what was being referred to as the ninth natural wonder of the world.

The Bottomless Sea had formed three and a half years ago when an earthquake of epic proportions had brought a subterranean river surging in from the Gulf of Maine, surfacing in six lakes in Maine and one in Canada before spilling back into the Atlantic via the Gulf of Saint Lawrence. Having been the state's second largest freshwater lake at forty miles long and nine miles across at its widest point, Bottomless had become an inland sea complete with tides and all manner of marine life, its length added to when several mountains had shifted to create a twelve-mile-long fiord at its northern end.

Well, the earthquake was considered epic by mere mortals and baffled scientists, but Nicholas knew it had been only a minor miracle for Maximilian Oceanus, a powerful wizard who also happened to be married to Nicholas's boss. Although Mac had turned the state of Maine on its ear simply to satisfy his need to be near salt water, it was Olivia who actually owned and ran the five-star resort on the summit of Whisper Mountain named Nova Mare — which, appropriately, was Latin for *New Sea.*

And so, looking forward to some peace and tranquility and many lazy days fishing in his boat, Nicholas had become Olivia's head of security just over a year ago. It was a far cry from his former life as a mythological warrior, but it was past time that he settled down and started a family. Now all he had to do was find a lovely lady who enjoyed long stretches of silence, who liked cats, and who had the physical as well as mental energy, and the courage, to love him.

Thinking of cats — and feline eyes in particular — the problem with staying out of other people's business, Nicholas knew from experience, was that he inevitably got right in the middle of it anyway. And if there happened to be a woman involved . . . well, he'd like to blame the Oceanuses for instilling in him a sense of duty to champion the weak, but suspected his love of a good rousing battle had more to do with his genetics than upbringing.

Not that anyone seemed to know what those genetics were, since he'd been only a few days old when a crusty old whale named Leviathan had spewed him onto a beach on the equally mythical island of Atlantis. He'd been taken in by the island midwife and her husband, and shortly after Nicholas's seventh birthday, Titus Oceanus had moved him and his parents into the palace, with Maude becoming the Oceanuses' family healer and Mathew their royal gardener, while Nicholas had been given the questionable honor of becoming baby Carolina's personal bodyguard.

That should teach him to fall in love with a screaming minutes-old princess, seeing how his devotion to Lina had involved thirty-one years of traveling across time to more centuries and countries than he cared to count. But the Oceanuses weren't exactly ordinary royalty, as Titus and his son, Maximilian, were actually theurgists — more accurately known as divine agents of human affairs.

Titus had built Atlantis upon which to cultivate his Trees of Life — which contained all of mankind's knowledge — in order to protect earthbound mortals from the warring mythical gods. But when the gods had discovered that mankind's champion had also trained a small army of drùidhs to protect the Trees, Titus had been forced to scatter his mystical Trees and drùidhs all over the world, then sink his little kingdom into the sea before the gods could destroy it — and him.

Funny, Nicholas thought as he downed the last of his beer, how Titus and Mac had complete access to all that knowledge, yet the wizards couldn't seem to find out where the mysterious babe on the beach had come from. Or rather, they *claimed* they couldn't, which Nicholas had always suspected was only half the truth. Not that the circumstances of his birth mattered all that much to him, since he'd experienced nothing but love and generosity from his adoptive parents and the Oceanuses. Still, when you're five years old and nearly a foot taller than your buddies, as well as the only blue-eyed person on the entire island, it would be nice to know *why.*

By the age of fourteen, when seven-year-old Princess Carolina had finally been allowed to run wild outside the palace walls, Nicholas had stood six feet tall, weighed a good hundred and eighty pounds, and rode a horse and wielded a sword with the skill of a battle-hardened warrior. But just last year, at age thirty-seven, he'd suddenly found himself unemployed when he'd happily handed Lina over to Alec MacKeage — may the gods have mercy on the brave bastard's soul.

So having decided he liked all the amenities of the twenty-first century, as well as this rugged corner of the world, Nicholas had promised Olivia that he would keep her guests and employees as safe and happy as he'd kept her sister-in-law. He'd so far upheld that promise with some fancy technology and two dozen men, four of whom were elite warriors he'd brought from Atlantis. And come spring he'd be adding several more guards when Inglenook — a family-oriented resort sitting right on the shore of Bottomless — finished being refurbished and started taking guests.

Nicholas had found this last year pleasantly relaxing compared to keeping a head-strong princess safe and happy, but his new job was still exciting enough to get him out of bed every morning, since some of Nova Mare's patrons actually hailed from past centuries as they came seeking Mac's magical services. And twice now the theurgist had asked Nicholas to do a little time-traveling for him; once to squelch a senseless war before it really got started, and another time to right a perceived wrong between a jilted bride and a drunken idiot king.

So considering all he'd lived through — and survived — Nicholas figured he couldn't complain that it was taking him a while to find a lovely lady he'd be interested in sharing the rest of his natural life with. But Zeus's teeth, at this point he'd be happy to find one he liked well enough to bed. Preferably a woman who didn't talk incessantly about nothing, who didn't view him only as a titillating prize, and who thought waking up to find a few cats burrowed under the covers with them was endearing.

He wondered if Julia Campbell liked cats.

Nicholas placed enough money on the table to pay his bill as well as a generous tip, then stood up, slipped into his jacket, and settled his wide-brimmed hat on his head of short dark hair. He gave a nod to the harried waitress as he headed for the door, feeling somewhat disheartened that Julia probably wasn't the lady for him. If she truly did fear men, then she'd likely run screaming in terror if she found herself being romantically pursued by a six-foot-seven, two-hundred-and-thirty-pound former warrior.

Nicholas stepped outside and turned up his collar against the rain with a sigh. Such was the fickleness of early November weather in Maine in the mountains, he guessed as he walked along the slush-covered road to his truck parked in front of the church. He'd just reached the driver's door when he spotted the two women coming out of the woods on the far side of the building and immediately recognized Julia's red jacket. Her sister — Trisha, he believed her name was — was wearing a bulky backpack and had her arm wrapped around Julia's shoulders as if supporting her.

He shifted to stay hidden behind his truck as he watched them suddenly scurry into the bushes when someone exited the Bottoms Up and crossed the road. Nicholas waited while the person drove off, his patience rewarded when the two women, still huddled together against the wind-driven rain, emerged from the shadows and hurried down the driveway leading to a parking lot at the rear of the church.

He silently followed, more concerned than curious as to why they were skulking around town in the pouring rain — every scenario he came up with darkening his mood. He stopped at the corner of the church when they reached the back basement door of the building, and decided Julia definitely was hurt when he saw her slouch against the granite foundation while Trisha yanked on the door.

"It's locked," he heard Trisha say.

"No, it's just stuck," Julia said, awkwardly adding her own efforts. "Reverend Peter never locks anything, not even the poor box."

The door suddenly popped open, making Trisha bump into Julia, which in turn made Julia hiss in pain. "I'm sorry," Trisha said, wrapping her arm around her sister and ushering her inside. "What if your ribs are cracked? Maybe we should go . . ."

Nicholas lost the rest of the conversation when the door closed. With a look back to make sure no one else was around, he walked over and took off his hat, then pressed his ear against the door to hear their footsteps retreating up a set of stairs. He straightened and put on his hat, grasped the knob, and splayed his other hand on the swollen wooden door, then simply imagined it silently opening. He stepped inside and gently pulled the door closed. He attuned his senses to the century-old wood beneath his feet to avoid any creaks as he silently walked up the stairs and once again picked up the thread of the women's conversation.

"I swear, I don't know who was more surprised," Julia said, "me or Dad that he actually hit his target." Nicholas heard her groan at the same time wood squeaked. "It's been *years* since he's caught me off guard like that."

"I heard the crash all the way out in the driveway," Trisha said, "and dropped the ash pan and ran inside just as he was taking another swing at you. No, let me help you take off your coat."

"I'm okay, only sore. I told you, the crash was the microwave falling when I knocked it over trying to get — ohh."

"I'm sorry," Trisha said, just as Nicholas moved into the shadowed hallway to see the two women at a front pew — Julia sitting turned sideways with Trisha standing and helping her out of her jacket. "Maybe we should have gone to Tom's instead."

Julia sighed and started unbuttoning her

blouse. "He'd just find some reason it's our fault Dad's gone off on another bender."

Trisha dug in the backpack, pulled out a flashlight and sat down, then carefully slid Julia's blouse off her shoulders.

"Well?"

"Oh, Jules," Trisha murmured, aiming the light at her sister's back. "No blood, but you've got a nasty welt. Are you sure your ribs aren't cracked?"

Nicholas silently shifted, then stiffened at the sight of the angry-looking mark.

"I can breathe okay, and it only hurts if I move too quickly."

Trisha set down the flashlight and unhooked Julia's bra. "I'll call Nova Mare first thing in the morning and tell them you won't be in."

Julia carefully slid her arms out of her sleeves, then gathered the blouse to her chest. "I'm not calling in sick tomorrow. Saturday is when most everyone is checking out, and I don't want someone else scoffing up the tips I spent all week earning."

"But I thought whoever cleans on your days off has to give you your share, because they can't keep seven days' worth of tips after working only two days."

Julia snorted. "Like they'd be honest about how much they find. And I don't want them to realize I get tipped almost twice what the other housekeepers do." She looked back at Trisha. "Can you hand me that heavy fleece you packed?"

"They still haven't found out you give the guests in your cabins your employee cell number?" Trisha asked, digging through the pack. She stood up to slip the fleece over Julia's head. "Didn't you say when you were given that little phone that they told you it was only for employees to communicate and for emergencies?"

"That's what I was told," Julia said from inside the depths of the fleece. There was enough light coming from the flashlight sitting on the pew for Nicholas to see that she was smiling — rather smugly — when her head popped out. "But giving my guests a card with my name and number is what doubled my tips. And that's another reason I have to go to work tomorrow. I need to collect all those cards before the Sunday housekeeper finds them. Come on, let's toss some of these pew cushions on the front platform," she said, her smile vanishing when she stood up and grabbed the back of her waist with a groan. "The last thing I need tonight is to roll off one of these narrow pews."

"What are we going to do, Jules?" Trisha

asked, walking across the aisle and gathering up some of the long, thin cushions. "We need to move out of the house *now.*"

"You've survived almost eighteen years of Dad's binges," Julia said. "You can make it a couple more months. Although up until a few years ago we both had mom running interference for us, and I had a reprieve while I lived in Orono."

"Some reprieve," Trisha muttered. "You spent six years supporting Clay, and he divorced you the moment he graduated. Then the bastard told everyone you'd slept with half the guys in the fraternity house where you cooked to put *him* through school."

"Hey, no swearing. You want to be treated like a lady, then —"

Trisha snorted, cutting her off. "Yeah, yeah. Then *talk* like one." She dumped the cushions on the platform. "I hope you know Clay's sister is even worse than he is. Remember my new friend Kimberly? Well, her mom says that whenever you stop at the bank, Vivian starts talking nasty about you just as soon as you leave. Forget that everyone thinks you're a slut; she's saying you're also stupid for moving back home."

"I told you, all that matters is that you and I know the truth," Julia said, walking to the platform. "As for Clay and Vivian, I refuse to stoop to their level. Because all that *really* matters," she growled, clasping Trisha's shoulders, "is that you're going to college in September to become Maine's prettiest, brightest marine biologist. And I'll get that guest liaison position at Inglenook this spring, and together we'll show all those idiots that the Campbell sisters don't have one stupid bone in our bodies."

Trisha gently turned Julia around and started undoing her braid. "Do you really think Olivia will give you the job without a college degree?" She sighed. "Too bad they don't give diplomas to people who sneak into classes and read whatever textbooks are lying around a frat house. Heck, you actually helped some of those guys with their papers. And Clay's master's degree should have *your* name on it, not his."

"Don't forget I used to work summers for Olivia back when she ran Inglenook for her ex-in-laws," Julia said. "So I'm hoping I can persuade her I'm as valuable as any applicant with an honest education." Julia ran her fingers through the riot of curls that had erupted the moment they'd been set free, and turned to Trisha. "I have to get that position because it comes with housing. And since it seems I can't stop Reggie from turning into another belligerent Campbell male, I can leave home without feeling guilty. And you'll be a legal adult next month, so Dad can't stop you from moving out. I'll ask Olivia if you can live with me until college starts and also spend your summer and winter breaks with me." Julia clasped Trisha's face and touched their foreheads together. "Just a couple more months, little sister, and our lives will finally be *ours.*"

Nicholas heard Trisha sigh as she turned away and spread their wet coats over the pews. She then pulled some clothes and a heavy quilt from the pack, walked to the platform, and balled up a couple of shirts as pillows. She helped Julia get settled on her side on the cushions and covered her up, then started unlacing her sister's boots.

Nicholas dropped his chin to his chest with a silent curse as he remembered wondering why no one had offered Julia a ride home. Did everyone in town truly believe she was stupid for moving back in with a drunken father after her failed marriage? Had no one considered that she might have returned for her sister's sake after their mother died?

Because personally, he thought Julia might be one of the toughest women he knew. She was pretty damn smart, too, for stealing an education — even if she didn't have the degree to prove it. But then, he also knew a little something about seizing opportunities when they presented themselves. Like her use of the phones, which had a range of only five miles, that he'd persuaded Olivia were needed so he could send out a blanket alert if there was trouble; Julia certainly hadn't hesitated to use his security program to her advantage, he thought with a grin.

Seeing that both women were finally huddled together under the quilt, Nicholas started to leave, only to be pulled up short by Trisha's softly spoken words.

"I nearly fainted when that guy kissed you," the girl whispered. "I mean, jeesh; he just gathered you into his arms and kissed you. And you just *let* him. Except for Olivia's husband and Mr. MacKeage, I don't think I've ever met anyone as big and formidable-looking as that guy tonight. I can't believe you didn't panic."

"I didn't panic because it was obvious he was only trying to help me. Oh, Sis," Julia said, touching one of Trisha's short curls. "Please tell me you're not afraid of men. Not all of them are like Daddy and Clay; most are actually nice. And some might even be smart," she drawled. "Nicholas probably just figured kissing me was the easiest way out of the mess he'd gotten himself into for giving me a ride." She chuckled, although it held no humor. "The guy obviously didn't know he was kissing the town slut."

"But what happens when you see each other at Nova Mare? What are you going to say to him?"

"The only times I've even been within fifty feet of Nicholas were when he and his men were giving instructions on resort security during a staff meeting. And we don't exactly run in the same social circles, so I probably won't come face-to-face with him for another six months, and by then he'll have forgotten all about it."

"But how come he gave you a ride home to begin with?"

"I think he just happened to be in the parking lot when Reggie started acting like a brat again, and he came over to see if I needed any help. It's his job to worry about employees, and he apparently takes it seriously." She snorted. "Really seriously. You should see him standing there while his men give the talks at our staff meetings; I swear they're preparing us for an invasion or something."

Trisha giggled. "If Nova Mare is ever invaded, promise that you'll run and hide behind him. The guy looks like he could turn back an entire army single-handed."

Nicholas scowled, undecided if he'd just been complimented or insulted.

Julia laughed. "I'd have to get in line behind all the female workers — single *and* married. Really, Trisha, you should hear them in the locker room talking about 'the mysterious man with no last name.' Apparently size *does* matter to a lot of women."

"Well, you all but disappeared in his arms when he kissed you," Trisha said. "It certainly shut Daddy up. At least until he got a few more drinks in him and started in again about us girls sticking our noses in the air when it comes to men, and how we can't catch ourselves a husband if we're not properly grateful for *any* male attention."

"I'm sorry Clay's lies about me ruined your reputation, too. But once you get to college, I promise you'll find yourself a really nice young man."

"Ah, yes; the dreaded 'slut by association,' " Trisha moaned, making Nicholas grin when the girl pressed the back of her hand to her forehead — her angst ruined by her laugh. But then she sobered. "Tell the truth, Jules: Did you like it?"

"Like what?"

"That kiss tonight. What does it feel like

40

to be pulled into the arms of a big strong man and kissed like that? It wasn't a quick peck, either. I mean, it looked *real.* So what was it like?"

Nicholas stopped breathing.

"You really want to know?" Julia whispered, to which Trisha immediately nodded. "Well, it was a good thing he stopped when he did," she said with a nod, "because I was one second away from kissing him back." She gave a snicker. "Why do you think he all but ran to his truck? He obviously felt me getting ready to knock his socks off."

Nicholas barely stifled a snicker of his own. He'd stopped because he'd felt Julia getting ready to panic. Then again, maybe she'd been getting ready to slap his face.

"You kissed him back?" Trisha squeaked in surprise.

Nicholas heard Julia sigh, and saw her reach out and gently touch Trisha's cheek. "I *almost* did. But apparently it's been so long, I've forgotten how." She dropped her hand. "But if you swear never to tell a soul, I will admit I did like getting a little taste of passion."

"Because it reminded you of when you and Clay were first married?"

Julia suddenly choked on a laugh. "Good

heavens, no. I realized a long time ago that what I felt for Clay was just dumb teenage lust, combined with the excitement of being married and getting out of this sleepy town."

"Well, Spellbound isn't sleepy anymore." Trisha gave a loud yawn. "Not since the earthquake."

"No," Julia agreed, rolling onto her stomach with a groan. "For once I'm glad I don't have any boobs, so I can sleep on my belly tonight — unlike you, Miss Curvy."

"You had boobs when you weighed more. You don't eat all day because you're too cheap to buy lunch at the resort, and Daddy won't let you pack one unless you start paying him rent."

"I'm not paying rent when I wash his and Reggie's clothes and cook their meals and clean up after them. I am going to have to dip into our savings and finally get that old pickup fixed, though, even if it does mean throwing good money after bad."

"I can go back to riding the school bus."

Julia lifted her head. "No, you can't. You need to stay after for extracurricular activities. They're important for college. And besides, if you start coming home at three, Daddy and Tom will put you to work, and I swear I'll burn that mill to the ground before I'll let you break your back stacking

42

pallets of shingles." Nicholas saw Julia yawn and settle her head back on the rolled up shirt. "Come on, let's go to sleep. I think the aspirin I took is working, and that shot of rum is finally kicking in. I'll be back in fighting form come morning. Night, little sister," she said. "Sweet dreams."

"Night, Jules."

Nicholas stood rooted in place, trying to decide how he felt. On the one hand, he wouldn't mind paying a late-night visit to the Campbell homestead, yet he was also in awe of Julia and Trisha's resiliency. Hell, he didn't know many *men* facing what these two women faced every day who would keep fighting like they did.

He waited until their breathing had evened out in sleep, then quietly exited the church back down through the basement. But instead of heading to his truck, he turned and entered the woods. As he'd expected, he found Trisha's dark green SUV parked down an overgrown path far enough to be hidden from the main road.

Which suggested this wasn't the first time they'd sought sanctuary in the church.

Pulling his hat lower on his brow, Nicholas nevertheless found his mood lifting as he walked back to his truck. But instead of getting in when he reached it, he stood staring through the rain at the church and actually felt a grin threatening to form at the realization that far from being afraid of men, Julia Campbell was merely fed up with them. Well, most of them, anyway, he thought as his grin broke free, as she apparently didn't mind getting a little taste of passion from a giant trying to help her.

But before he got too excited, Nicholas decided as he climbed in his truck and headed toward Nova Mare, he really should find out if the woman liked cats.

CHAPTER THREE

Julia took three aspirin, chased them down with a long swig of water from her work-issued aluminum water bottle, then wiped her mouth on the back of her hand with a fortifying breath. "There is no problem," she said out loud, unwrapping a peppermint candy and shoving it in her mouth as she looked around the main room of the cabin she was halfway through cleaning. "Olivia just wants to tell me that I'm in the running for the Inglenook position." Yeah, Julia decided as she carefully slipped on her coat; she'd turned in her application two weeks ago, and Olivia just wanted to set up an interview.

That was why she'd called and asked Julia to meet her at Foxglove Cottage, and *not* that Nicholas had told their boss what had happened last night when he'd given an employee a ride home, so Olivia was *not* going to ask why her top security guard had been forced to *kiss* his way out of a humiliating situation.

Julia locked the door behind her and walked down the steps to the compact electric cart fully equipped with everything she needed to service her cottages. She loved driving around the forested paths that led to the various-sized cabins scattered over the east side of Whisper's summit — each cottage named after a local wildflower. The most secluded cabin that she cleaned was almost half a mile away from the resort's common green, and every day Julia felt like the luckiest girl on the planet to be working in such a beautiful setting while taking care of the priciest, prettiest cabins in Maine. But she couldn't help wondering what it must have cost to build Nova Mare and also completely refurbish Inglenook, because it appeared as if Olivia's funds were as substantial as the inland sea sitting nearly two thousand feet below — especially considering it was rumored that Olivia's husband, Mac, had also bought up all the timberland around the fiord all the way to Canada.

But even though Nova Mare commanded an entire mountaintop and catered to the very wealthiest people in the world, Inglenook had its own charm for being right on the shoreline. Julia had biked up the Inglenook road on one of her days off a few weeks back and had been blown away by the renovations being done to the old family camp where she'd worked summers from high school up to four years ago. Where crooked old leaky cabins had once stood there were now charmingly rustic but very modern two- and three-bedroom cottages. The old dining hall had been torn down and replaced with one that included a state-of-the-art commercial kitchen and a dining room large enough to seat a small army. The main lodge had been completely refurbished and the old grounds-keeper's cottage spruced up — including a new fence surrounding it and a new brass bell standing sentinel at its gate.

Remembering Olivia's rule that no one was allowed past that gate into her private sanctuary when she'd been running Inglenook, it was apparent the woman was keeping that rule intact for the new guest liaison — which would be *her,* Julia hoped and hoped and hoped. "Please let this be about that job," she said almost as a litany as she drove to Foxglove. She stopped beside Olivia's shiny green personal cart, swallowed what was left of her peppermint candy, then climbed the stairs and went inside.

"Hey, there you are," Olivia said, walking

out of the bedroom — which Julia knew was spanking clean because she'd just finished here not an hour ago.

"What's up?" Julia asked, slipping off her jacket and hanging it on a peg by the door. "How's the place look?"

"Honestly? *Better* than I remembered." Olivia gave a small laugh, shaking her head. "Between running Nova Mare and racing to get Inglenook finished in time for our first guests in May, I just realized I haven't set foot in any of these cottages in months." She motioned toward the table. "Come sit down, Julia, and let's talk."

Julia nervously brushed down her jersey and walked over and sat down, mentally repeating her litany that this was about the job.

"First off, I want to say that I was surprised to see your application for Inglenook's guest liaison," Olivia said, sitting at the small table diagonally from her, "since the posting I put up in the locker room to give employees first dibs said I was looking for someone with a bachelor's degree — preferably in hospitality."

"But I have plenty of experience, a good deal of it with you."

Olivia gave a nod. "I said I was surprised, but I'm also pleased you didn't let that little

48

requirement stop you. I don't have any doubt you could take care of my guests, based on our past experiences together." Olivia's smile faltered, however, as she reached in her pocket and pulled out a small card, which she then set on the table and slid in front of Julia. "As well as from what I've been discovering about you these past two weeks, since I started looking into why some guests are specifically reserving any cottage *you* clean based on suggestions from their friends who have stayed here."

Julia felt all the blood drain from her face as she stared down at the card with her name and employee cell phone number on it. "I can explain," she whispered.

Olivia gestured around the room they were in, her hand stopping to point at the hearth. "And you know what's funny? I don't remember furnishing any of the cottages with old chamber pots to hold kindling, or wooden crates for the pinecones, or deer and moose antler sheds to display on the mantels. And I could have sworn the furniture was set up differently in here." She reached for the basket sitting in the center of the table and pulled it closer, then started poking through the acorns, pieces of birch bark, lichen, odd-looking pebbles, and dried autumn leaves before she picked up the note card that had been leaning against it. *"Keep an eye out during your walks,"* she read, *"and add your own unusual finds to this woodland treasure trove for the next guests to enjoy."* She looked at Julia. "And I can't for the life of me remember coming up with this idea."

"It . . . This is one of the family cottages," Julia said, dropping her gaze to the basket as she felt the blood rushing back into her cheeks. "And I thought sending the kids on a treasure hunt might help the parents entertain them." She looked Olivia directly in the eyes. "And I know the phones are for employee use only, but I always make sure to introduce myself to my guests, and they like having someone they know show up when they need help starting a fire in the hearth or have a question about what to do in the area."

"We have a concierge desk for that, Julia. Why, when I checked before coming here, is the table in Thistledown set with candles that look an awful lot like the ones in our restaurant and a bouquet of fresh cedar boughs and elderberry twigs?"

"I . . . um, I heard the couple coming in from Japan is on their honeymoon."

"You mean when you *checked* with Reservations this morning to see who would be staying in your cottages this week, like you check every Saturday before you start your rounds?"

"I thought it would be nice to set up the cabins specifically for whichever guests are staying in them."

"And this?" Olivia asked, reaching in her pocket again and pulling out a small cloth sack tied with jute string and a little card attached that described its contents.

"I can explain."

"Good. Because I'm dying to know why one of our guests asked how come our gift shop doesn't sell any of the 'pretty little tree-shaped soaps' we have in our cottage bathrooms." Olivia untied the string, pulled out the soap and held it up to her nose, then set it on the table between them with a snort. "Which got another guest in the shop all huffy, saying she was in one of our expensive suites and *her* bathroom didn't have any tree-shaped soaps."

"I was . . . It's just an experiment. I wanted to see if people would even use goat soap before I approached you about supplying the cottages with them."

"They're obviously homemade."

Julia nodded. "I found them at the town's Columbus Day craft fair, only they were just square chunks. Regan Coots makes them.

You know Regan, don't you?"

"Doesn't she live on the Spellbound-Turtleback town line and have, like, ten kids or something?" Olivia asked with a laugh.

Julia found her first smile since walking in. "She's got at least ten kid *goats* and twice as many nannies, but most of the human kids you see her with belong to other people. She also runs a day care."

"Did you buy the soaps from Regan to put in our — or should I say *your* — cabins?"

"No," Julia said with a shake of her head. "I asked Regan if she'd find a small cookie cutter shaped like a fir tree and cut the soaps, then give me a few samples to try out on the guests. I told her if they were popular that you might consider buying more from her, just like you buy your kindling and pinecones from me."

"Only our cottages and pavilions have wood-burning fireplaces, Julia, so you don't have any problem keeping up with demand. But Nova Mare goes through an awful lot of soap in the course of a year, especially if I wanted to supply all fifty hotel rooms and sixteen cottages. Can Regan fill that kind of order?"

"I wasn't intending for them to be the only soaps we supply; just an added little touch of Maine. That's why Regan scents some of them with balsam."

Olivia arched a brow. "Like the balsam sachets you've tucked up out of sight on all your closet shelves?"

Julia fought down her blush again, although she couldn't stifle her smile. "I wanted the closets to smell woodsy, but they've been lugging off those little pillows faster than I can sew them." She leaned forward, clasping her hands together and resting her arms on the table. "I'm sorry for not running my ideas by you first, but I wanted to make sure they were popular." She shrugged. "Some tanked, but the majority of them were well received. And I have a ton of other ideas for Inglenook when it opens." She stood up. "In fact, I have a notebook full in my cleaning cart. Let me —"

"Hold on," Olivia said, jumping up with a laugh and grabbing her arm — only to quickly let go when Julia flinched away. "What's wrong? Julia, are you hurt?"

"I . . . I wrenched my back yesterday. I'm okay; it only hurts when I forget and twist or move too fast."

"At work?" Olivia asked with obvious concern. "Did you hurt yourself here?"

"Oh, no," Julia rushed to assure her. "Last

night. At home. Let me go get my notebook so I can show you what a good guest liaison I'm going to be."

"It can wait," Olivia said, carefully ushering her back to the table and motioning for her to sit down. She then reached in her pocket for a third time before sitting down again. "As well as the cottages you've already cleaned this morning, before calling you I also checked out the ones you haven't gotten to yet." She set some folded money on the table, but left her hand on it. "And when I saw the size of your tips," she said, tapping the money with her index finger, "I decided I should probably hand-deliver them." She then unfolded the small wad and tapped the top bill. "It's a really good thing I know you personally, because another boss, particularly if they happened to believe town gossip, might wonder why a single male guest staying in our most secluded cabin leaves his housekeeper a three-hundred-dollar tip."

Julia jumped to her feet with a gasp, even as she grabbed at the sharp pain that spiked through her back. "They're lies, every one of them! Olivia, I'm not —"

"I know. I know," Olivia rushed to say as she also jumped to her feet. She guided Julia back to her chair, then sat down again with a heavy sigh. "Damn, I'm sorry, Julia. That didn't come out the way I intended."

"Clay told everyone I'd slept with half the men at the fraternity house where I'd worked," Julia said, hating that her voice was shaking, "so he wouldn't look like a jerk for divorcing me after I spent six years putting him through college." She set her elbows on the table and hung her head in her hands. "But people would rather believe the worst about someone instead of hearing the truth, especially if it involves the daughter of the town drunk." She lifted her head. "Clay's the *only* man I've ever slept with. And from where I'm standing, it looks like he's going to be the last." She straightened and gestured toward the window looking out over Bottomless. "Not that I wasn't given plenty of chances the first year I moved home in disgrace, with every Tom, Dick, and Harry figuring I was easy pickings." She shook her head. "I swear I was pinched and groped more often than those fresh watermelons Ezra gets in at the Trading Post."

"I'm sorry," Olivia said, her own cheeks darkening.

"No, *I'm* sorry for overreacting just now." Julia waved at the money on the table. "If I were running Nova Mare and saw those kinds of tips being left to the cleaning lady, I'd be all over her like flypaper."

"Well, okay," Olivia conceded with a wince. "I did think the worst after finding your . . . ah, calling card. But then I found an even larger tip at a family cottage you hadn't cleaned yet, so I took a nice long look around the ones you've already gotten ready for tomorrow's arrivals. It was then that I started putting the gift shop incident together with your reservation inquiries, as well as the fact that guests were asking for your cottages in particular, and finally realized what you were up to."

"The bigger tips are actually a by-product," Julia said, carefully relaxing back in her chair. "I was just trying to make everyone's stay memorable so they'd go home and tell their friends that Nova Mare is worth the exorbitant prices you charge."

Olivia arched a brow.

Julia arched a brow back at her. "A one-week stay in your *small* cottages would pay in-state tuition at the University of Maine for an entire semester."

Olivia dropped her gaze and smoothed down the front of her fleece. "Our hotel rooms are more reasonably priced," she murmured. But there was a gleam in her eyes when she lifted her head and shrugged one shoulder. "It's apparently true that the more you charge for something, the more people simply *have* to have it." She gestured at the window facing Bottomless just as Julia had. "If they want *quaint* instead of five-star, they can go stay at Silvia Pinkham's camps down in Turtleback. Um, you do know that if Nicholas finds out you've been handing guests your number," she said, nodding at the card on the table, "he's probably going to give you a two-hour lecture on resort security." She suddenly tapped her forehead with her hand. "What am I saying? He'll make one of his men give the lecture, because three sentences appear to be that man's limit."

Julia felt her face draining of color again, and Olivia leaned back in her own chair with a laugh.

"I'm kidding — at least I hope I am. Let's just agree not to tell him, okay, and you'll stop handing out the cards?"

Julia looked down to hide her scowl. Darn it, those cards made her tips.

"How about," Olivia said, leaning forward and reaching across the table, "if I instruct the front desk to send the specific house-keepers to the cottages and hotel rooms they're assigned?" She tilted her head. "I guess I should have questioned why you asked Bev to always give you the same cabins each week." Olivia shrugged. "She and I thought it was because you liked zooming around in our little housekeeping carts instead of doing the hotel rooms. But I think you're onto something here, Julia. I like the idea of our housekeepers feeling proprietary toward their rooms week after week, and I'm going to tell Bev to make that a new policy." She leaned back and crossed her arms. "So, what else have you got?"

"Ah . . . got?"

"Your ideas to make our guests deliriously happy to pay the *exorbitant* prices we charge. You said you have a notebook full, so give me a couple of examples."

Julia went back to scowling at her lap. "Well, I thought we — I mean *you,*" she said, looking up with a grin, "might like to get some pull wagons. You know; the big metal wagons with the all-terrain tires? I found one in a yard sale in Millinocket that I use for collecting my pinecones at home. Anyway," she rushed on, "I think if you parked one on every cottage porch, the parents would take longer walks on the foot trails since the toddlers could ride when they got tired. And you could get some for each of the hotel segments, too. When I'm looking for cones up here, I never see

58

families more than a mile out, but some of the best views of the fiord are two and three miles away."

"We're on a *mountain,*" Olivia said with a laugh. "The wagons wouldn't be here a week before we started seeing them racing by full of older kids looking for a thrill ride."

"Oh. I hadn't thought of that."

"What else?"

Okay then; instead of Olivia wanting to set up an interview, it appeared they were having it now. Too nervous to sit any longer, Julia stood up and walked to the large front window. "Well, I remember that at Inglenook you used to have —" She stilled when her cell phone started ringing and snapped her gaze to Olivia.

"Gee, I wonder who that could be," Olivia drawled. "You have guests staying over in Pine Tassel and Elderberry, don't you?"

Julia nodded as she pulled out her phone. "It's the front desk," she said with a frown as she answered it. "Julia Campbell. Wait, slow down. What?" One minute later she snapped the phone closed and headed to the desk on the far wall. "A woman just called the resort and said something about my father and Trisha. They said she was screaming and not making much sense," Julia added, picking up the cottage phone, but then just looking at it. "What number do I dial to get a direct line out?" she asked, turning to Olivia. "Don't I need a guest code or something?"

Olivia walked over with her hand out-stretched. "My cell phone will be quicker."

Julia then stood staring down at the cell, which was nothing more than a solid black screen. She thrust it back at her. "I don't know how to use this. I have to go home, Olivia." She rubbed her forehead, trying to clear the black fog that had descended when the receptionist had mentioned Trisha. "Okay, look; I didn't wrench my back last night," she finally admitted. "Dad's on one of his binges, and when he came at me last night I didn't duck in time. That's why I need to get off this mountain and make sure Trish is okay. I have to go home *now.*"

"We have a plan for that," Olivia said, working her finger across her cell's screen. "I'll have someone drive you. Nicholas," she said into the phone, smiling when Julia gasped, "I need you to pick up one of our staff at Foxglove Cottage and drive her home. She has a family emergency. No, wait; she hurt her back, so run up and get my truck. It'll be easier for her to get in and out of. We'll be waiting out front. Foxglove," she reminded him, touching the screen again and slipping the phone in her pocket. "Come on, let's get you in your jacket and wait on the porch. He'll only be a minute."

"Is there someone else who could drive me?" Julia whispered as Olivia helped her into her coat. "Please?"

Olivia stopped with the sleeves halfway up Julia's arms. "You have a problem with Nicholas?" she asked in surprise.

"He gave me a ride home from the parking lot yesterday." Julia pulled her coat all the way on, then looked down to button it up. "And he . . . um, my father insisted that I kiss Nicholas to thank him for the ride, and he . . . he . . ."

Olivia pressed her hands to Julia's flaming cheeks and lifted her face. "And he what?" she whispered.

"He kissed me. To shut up my father, Nicholas pulled me into his arms and kissed me, then said 'you're welcome' and drove away."

Olivia encircled Julia's shoulders and headed for the door. "Well, the man is rather astute when it comes to reading situations, and no one could ever say he's not fast on his feet — or with his lips, apparently," she added with a chuckle. She stopped on the porch. "I bet you nearly fainted."

"I was humiliated, and he was appalled. The guy had to *kiss* me to escape."

"Or he could have simply turned and walked away."

"I don't need to embarrass myself to him twice. Can't someone else drive me?"

Olivia gave her a tender smile. "Let it go, Julia. You don't have a monopoly on embarrassment. And don't forget, he got a *kiss.* And when have you known any man to have a problem with that?" Olivia slipped her arm through Julia's when they heard a vehicle coming up the cart path, and led her down the stairs. "Trust me; Nicholas is the man you want backing you up if there's trouble at home."

Julia blew out a resigned sigh. "Do you have any idea what it's like to be thirty years old and still have your father embarrassing you? Most girls outgrow that by their late teens, but I'll probably still be blushing when they're throwing dirt on my grave."

"If any of the female workers hear that Nicholas finally kissed one of you ladies . . . well, let's just keep this our little secret, okay?" Olivia said, her eyes gleaming. "And I promise not to ask if your insides clenched and your palms started sweating and your heart started racing so fast you thought you might faint, if you promise to let it go.

Deal?" she said with a laugh when Julia just gaped at her. Olivia sobered when a pearl-white SUV pulled up beside them and stopped. "Now go see what's going on at home. I'll finish your cottage. Nicholas," Olivia said when he came around the truck as she led Julia to the passenger's door. "The front desk just got a call that something's going on at Julia's house. I believe you know where she lives?"

He stilled after opening the door and snapped his gaze first to Olivia, then to Julia, then back to Olivia. "Ah, yes, I do."

Feeling as if her cheeks were about to blister, Julia slid in and fastened her seat belt, folded her shaking hands on her lap, and stared out the windshield. Darn it, why was Trisha even home? The girl was supposed to hang out with Kimberly today until one, when Duncan MacKeage was going to pick her up at the Nova Mare marina and take her across the fiord to babysit his and Peg's little tribe of heathens tonight and all day tomorrow.

So what was she doing home? And who had called the resort in a panic? Their sister-in-law, Jerilynn? Then that meant Trisha had called Tom for help, which meant the girl must be in some pretty bad trouble.

CHAPTER FOUR

"What's going on at home?" Nicholas asked, returning the guard's nod as he sped past the booth at the beginning of the road that descended the mountain.

"I don't know. Somebody called the resort and said Trisha's in trouble with my father. She's my sister that you . . . met last night."

Nicholas pulled his phone from inside his jacket and held it out. "Does she have a cell? Call her. Or call your house," he added when Julia didn't take it.

"I don't know how to *use* those phones," she softly growled.

"Yes, you do," he growled back, sliding his thumb across the screen to unlock it. He held it out to her again, even as he slowed to make a hairpin turn while watching for oncoming traffic — specifically a silver Lexus he'd been told had been the only vehicle through the lower gate in the last half hour. "Use your finger. Touch the phone icon and dial, then touch send."

She took the phone just as he exited the turn, and Nicholas sped up again as he also kept an eye out for the stretch limo he'd been told had left the summit about thirty minutes ago but hadn't arrived at the lower gate yet. Every driver traveling the resort road was given a radio they would then turn in at the opposite gate, so his guards could give updates about road conditions. It was a program he'd implemented within a month of taking over as director of security, and it had already proven invaluable during several winter storms last year, a number of accidents, and two ambulance runs. And just like all of his guards, Nicholas knew the road's every twist and turn to the point he could make today's run in about twenty minutes — assuming his passenger had an iron stomach.

Julia apparently figured out the phone and held it up to her ear, only to lower it a minute later. "She's not answering her cell," she said, dialing another number, then holding the phone to her ear again. "Jerilynn! What's going on?"

Nicholas heard a frantic female voice on the other end, although he couldn't make out what she was saying. "She locked herself in her bedroom?" Julia said, also sounding frantic as she grabbed the handle above her door when he took a corner without slowing down. "Did he hit her?" she whispered tightly. "Look, just make sure Tom keeps him away from her. I'll be there in — Jerilynn! *Hello?*"

Julia lowered the phone to her lap. "She hung up. Or she dropped the receiver and it broke. I heard a loud crash." She handed him back the phone. "My brother Tom is there. He won't let anything happen to Trisha. Jerilynn said she called the sheriff."

They passed the Lexus parked in a scenic turnoff just as the road grew less steep, and Nicholas pushed down on the accelerator. "Can your brother handle himself in a fight?" he asked. "Your father's not exactly a small man, and last night he appeared to have the strength of an ox — even inebriated."

"Tom's at a disadvantage size-wise, but he's strong. Um . . . about last night," she whispered. "I want to apol—"

"Let's agree that you won't apologize for something you had no control over," he said before she could finish, "and I won't apologize for getting involved in your business in the first place." He grinned in her direction. "And we'll also agree not to feel awkward when we run into each other at work."

He saw her take a deep breath — which ended abruptly when her expanding lungs pressed against her sore ribs, apparently. "Works for me."

They both fell silent with their deal struck, Nicholas figuring Julia had quickly agreed because she didn't think she'd run into him for at least another six months. She was wrong, of course, but he saw no need to enlighten her. They sped past the limo pulled off the road next to a timber bridge, the driver leaning against its front fender and giving Nicholas a wave on their way by. Several minutes later he shot past the lower gatehouse with a nod at the grinning guard, then slowed to a less reckless speed now that he had no control over the traffic for the remaining mile of resort road.

"I wondered why we only saw two cars," Julia said, glancing over her shoulder at the three cars waiting at the entrance gate before looking at him, her large hazel eyes widened with surprise. "You called ahead and had the road closed?"

He nodded as they passed the resort's entrance to the Nova Mare marina. "I also had the guards at both gates tell me the number of vehicles already on the road so I could watch for them, although the drivers were warned by radio to pull off and wait until after we passed," he explained, gesturing at the radio permanently mounted on the dash of Olivia's truck. He stifled a grin when he heard his passenger sigh as she stared out through the windshield again. "I'm impressed, Julia. You didn't scream once."

She snorted. "I'm pretty sure that's why it's called *frozen in fear.*"

Nicholas checked his watch when he pulled onto the main road, pleased that he'd made it down the mountain in nearly record time. They soon reached the Campbells' mailbox, and he saw Julia stiffen when they passed Trisha's SUV parked on the edge of the long driveway halfway in from the main road.

"Stay in the truck," she suddenly said into the silence when they reached the house. "Better yet, just leave."

Nicholas jerked the vehicle to a stop and looked at her, incredulous. "You expect me to sit out here while you walk in *alone* on a drunken man in a rage?"

The woman unfastened her seat belt and looked at him, her eyes narrowed and direct. "This isn't your business, so stay in the truck *or leave.*"

She was out her door and halfway to the house before he recovered enough to scramble out and chase after her. By the gods, if he wasn't in a bit of a rage himself, he'd be tempted to laugh. He turned stone-cold sober, however, when he saw Julia grab a stout stick leaning against the house before she yanked open the door and stormed inside. He scaled the steps and slammed inside behind her, only to pull up short when a heavily pregnant woman spun toward him with a startled scream.

"Oh, thank God you got here fast, deputy," she cried, rushing over and pulling him toward a staircase at the far end of the kitchen. "My husband's up there but he's hurt, and the girl's father is trying to break down the bedroom door with an ax. Where's your gun? Aren't you supposed to have a gun?"

Nicholas took the woman by the shoulders and sat her on one of the kitchen chairs. "Stay put," he growled, rushing up the stairs just as something struck wood with enough force to shake the house, followed by a muffled scream — which was followed by an outraged feminine growl. He rounded the corner in time to step over a body and snatch the stick away from Julia as it was descending toward her father, then pluck the startled woman off her feet and set her behind him just as her father wrestled the ax out of the door and swung it toward him.

Nicholas caught the ax in midswing and yanked it out of the bastard's hands, effectively pulling him off balance as he drove a shoulder into the man's stomach hard enough to knock the wind out of him. Nicholas then straightened with him over his shoulder, turned and strode past Julia, stepped over the fallen body, and walked down the stairs past the gaping woman, through the kitchen, and out the front door. He walked down the porch steps and deposited his heavy load on the ground next to the same tree the bastard had been hugging last night, ironically catching the man's head just before it slammed against the trunk.

A sheriff's cruiser sped in the road, its lights flashing but no siren blaring, and Nicholas straightened to see a large gold SUV speeding in behind it. Julia *really* wasn't going to be happy, he decided when Olivia opened her door before Mac even brought the vehicle to a complete stop, because "this isn't your business" was apparently about to become her boss's.

"Damn, Nicholas," the deputy said as he walked up, one hand on his weapon despite his grin. "I love it when I find you at a scene. It always means I'll be leaving with all my teeth."

"Jason," Nicholas said with a nod as he stepped aside.

"Christ almighty, Vern," deputy Jason Biggs muttered as he crouched in front of Julia's gasping father. "What have you gone and done this time?"

"He was using an ax on a door trying to get to his youngest daughter," Nicholas said, seeing how Vern Campbell was too busy trying to breathe to answer.

"Where's Julia?" Olivia asked, rushing up to Nicholas. "Is she okay? Is Trisha okay?"

"I haven't seen Trisha, as she was behind a locked door, but Julia's okay. A man and another woman are also in the house." Nicholas looked at Jason when the deputy stood up from cuffing Vern Campbell's hands in front of his big belly. "There's a man lying on the floor in the upstairs hallway, out cold."

"That's probably their brother Tom," Olivia said, stepping closer to Nicholas when Vern Campbell rolled onto his side and started throwing up.

"Could I get you gentlemen to keep an eye on this idiot while I go see if we need an ambulance?" Jason asked, already heading to the house.

Olivia turned to her husband. "Do something," she softly growled, gesturing at Julia's father, "before he kills somebody."

Mac shook his head. "You know the rules, wife," he said quietly.

"Then *I'll* do something," she snapped, pivoting and storming to the house.

The wizard folded his arms on his chest as he watched her run up the steps, then looked over at Nicholas. "She doesn't always agree with my protecting free will when it's someone's will to harm another."

Nicholas snorted. "Can't say that I disagree with her." He walked to the stairs and sat down on a middle step, then rubbed his face in his hands. "Zeus's teeth," he growled when Mac sat down beside him. "The bastard had a double-edged felling ax, and Julia ran inside armed with only a stick." Still holding his head in his hands, he looked over at Mac. "She told me to stay in the truck because it wasn't my business."

"You've been living here over a year now and that surprises you?" The wizard visibly shuddered. "I break into a cold sweat when Sophie or Ella gets their mother's stubborn look in their eyes and I picture them out in the world beyond my reach."

"I'm never having daughters," Nicholas muttered.

"Good luck with that, my friend," Mac

said with a humorless chuckle. "You figure out how to persuade Providence to give you only sons, and *I'll* give you a bottomless satchel of money."

"Your father already gave me one for putting up with your sister for thirty-one years." Nicholas straightened, shooting Mac a threatening scowl. "So quit asking me to babysit Ella, because my answer is and always will be *no.*" He went back to hanging his head in his hands just as Vern Campbell started snoring, apparently all tuckered out from his rage. "The bastard struck Julia in the back yesterday, likely with the very stick she tried using on him today." He glanced at Mac. "She and Trisha spent the night in the church. And she was at work this morning, even though she was badly bruised."

Olivia came outside with her arm around Julia, who had her arm around Trisha — who looked shaken but unscathed. "Drop the pride, Julia, and be practical," Olivia whispered tightly, guiding her past Nicholas and Mac when they stepped out of the way. "You and Trish are taking one of our rooms until you can find a rental."

"They can't leave, Livy," Jason said, following them out of the house, "until I get their statements."

Olivia kept the two women walking. "You can take their statements up at Nova Mare," she said without looking back.

Nicholas grinned when Jason gave a heavy sigh, the deputy obviously having learned that when Olivia Oceanus was on a mission, wise men got out of her way and fools argued at their peril. "I believe it was novelist Robert Heinlein," Nicholas drawled, "who said that 'women and cats will do as they please, and men and dogs should relax and get used to the idea.' Come up the mountain, Jason, and I'll treat you to dinner at Aeolus's Whisper."

Jason Biggs immediately perked up at the mention of the five-star restaurant with a million-dollar view of the Bottomless Sea. "I suppose it doesn't matter where I take their statements." The deputy didn't even try to hide his grin. "And I can hear your version of what happened while I'm stuffing my face with surf 'n' turf."

Olivia came running to the porch. "You drive Trisha's truck back," she said, handing Nicholas a set of keys. "And later today, I'd like you to bring Julia and me back here to pack up their belongings." She looked at Jason as she gestured toward the tree. "He will be in jail, won't he?"

The deputy nodded. "At least for tonight,

and maybe longer if I can get Tom to press assault charges." But then he shook his head. "I've never gotten him to in the past, though, and probably won't this time, either. Not with Jerilynn expecting their first child. Vern is the one holding the purse strings, and if he goes to jail he'll close the mill just to spite everyone."

Olivia glanced toward Vern Campbell and sighed, apparently not surprised by what Jason was saying, then looked at her husband. "Yeah, well, he's not controlling Julia's purse strings, and I'm letting her and Trisha stay at the hotel until they can find permanent housing, even if it takes a month."

"My apartment is available," Nicholas said. "Or it can be as of tomorrow. My house is finished enough for me to start staying there."

"Oh, that's perfect." But then Olivia's smile vanished. "Assuming Julia's pride doesn't get in the way, knowing our staff housing is for international workers. Never mind, I'll figure it out," she muttered, turning and running to her truck.

Nicholas immediately followed, going to the rear passenger door and opening it, then leaning inside. "I would see for myself that you're okay," he said as he gave Trisha a visual inspection. Satisfied she was only shaken, Nicholas slid his gaze to Julia. "You might reconsider ordering me to stay in the truck from now on, as it appears that size really does matter," he said before straightening away to hide his grin — and also to keep from acting on his urge to lift her jaw when it slackened. He shut the door and walked back to Mac, his grin disappearing when he remembered Julia racing into the house alone. Far from fearing men, the woman apparently not only thought nothing of ordering around one twice her size, but wasn't afraid to go up against one while being armed with nothing more than a stick and one hell of a temper.

But then his mood lightened again when he pictured her squaring off against a small herd of bossy cats.

"I'm sorry I went back, Jules," Nicholas heard Trisha say for the third time since they'd all started back down the mountain just before one o'clock. "I really needed my book bag to take with me to the Mac-Keages', and I thought I could sneak in without Dad's knowing. I even parked down the road."

"Peg said you don't have to babysit tonight," Julia told her for the third time.

"But they've been planning this trip to

Bangor for weeks. And I'm okay. Really. That is, if you're okay staying alone tonight," Trisha whispered.

Nicholas glanced at the rearview mirror in time to see Julia hug her sister. "Are you kidding?" she whispered back. "I've got cable TV and room service."

Not that she'd use the room service, Nicholas guessed as he pulled into the marina to see Peg MacKeage standing at the top of the dock ramp. She immediately ran over and had the back door opened before he'd even shut off the engine.

"Oh, Trish," Peg said, pulling the girl out to hug her. "Are you really okay?"

"I'm fine, Mrs. MacKeage. I locked myself in my bedroom and pulled my bureau in front of the door."

Apparently not quite ready to stop hugging her babysitter, Peg looked past Trisha's shoulder as Julia climbed out of the truck. "You can both stay with us for however long you need."

"They're going to take Nicholas's apartment for now," Olivia said. "Just as soon as he moves out his stuff and we burn up two vacuums sucking up all that cat hair," she added, shooting him a scowl as he stood grinning at them over the top of the truck. She looked back at Peg. "And Julia's commute to work will only be three minutes long."

"Well, the offer stands," Peg said, releasing Trisha to wrap an arm around the girl and start toward the dock. "I'll bring her back around six tomorrow night, okay, Jules?" she said past her shoulder. She urged Trisha to keep going as she stopped and turned. "Or she can stay over and get on the bus with the kids Monday morning."

Julia shook her head. "Thanks, but I prefer she take her truck to school. Trisha?" she called out when the girl climbed in the speedboat tied to the dock. "You remember our room number, right? You call me tonight after the kids are in bed, just . . . just to talk," she added when Trisha nodded. Julia then softly groaned, turning to Olivia when Peg climbed in the boat and shoved off. "I thought my worries would be over if I could just get Trisha safely settled in a dorm room in Orono, but now I'm afraid I'll be even more of a basket case when she's over a hundred miles away."

"Hey," Olivia said, touching Julia's shoulder. "Trisha's a sharp, mature young woman, and she'll do just fine at UMO. You told me yourself that she's maintained a three-point-eight grade point average despite losing your mom and putting up with your father. She's resilient and determined." Olivia opened Julia's door with a laugh. "Listen to me; I'll be worse than you — no, I already am worse — and Sophie's only in middle school."

Instead of getting in the truck, Julia gave Olivia a hug. "Thank you for being such a good boss."

"Hey, we're *friends,*" Olivia said thickly. "And neighbors. We take care of one another up here. Now come on, let's go pack your stuff."

Nicholas looked around the marina that had once been Peg's gravel pit before the earthquake had cut a fiord practically up to her front door, his gaze stopping on his fishing boat tied in a slip between a day sailor and small cabin cruiser.

He wondered if Julia liked to fish.

With a sense of déjà vu to be acting the errand boy again — although for a much, *much* younger Mrs. Oceanus — Nicholas slipped on his sunglasses with a sigh, got back in the truck, and once again drove Julia Campbell home. *But this time to pack her belongings and move her only half a mile away as the crow flies,* he thought cheerfully. It was farther by road, though, as the home Lina had designed for him — that Duncan MacKeage's construction crew and a bit of Mac's magic had built — sat a little over a mile down the winding resort road from the summit. He'd chosen the site for its proximity to Nova Mare in case he was needed in an emergency, while still being far enough away to afford him plenty of privacy. He also hoped it was too far for his cats to want to make the trek to the restaurant's kitchen twice a day for gourmet handouts.

"Nicholas."

"Hmm?" he murmured.

"I said," Olivia drawled as he pulled up next to Vern Campbell's pickup and shut off the engine, "that we'll let you know if we need you to carry any heavy stuff to the truck. We should only be about an hour."

"Take your time," he said, getting out and looking around, his gaze stopping on Julia as she walked up the porch steps and disappeared inside. She was definitely a lovely-looking lady, he decided as he slid his hands in his pockets and wandered toward what he assumed was the cedar mill set behind the house. She was also quite fearless, although maybe to the point of recklessness. And his size didn't seem to be an issue for her, although she hadn't seen him naked . . . yet. She definitely wasn't chatty, she appeared to have an excess of energy, and she was smart, resourceful, and obviously determined to get herself and her sister settled into new lives.

She did seem to have a powerful pride, though. But he didn't consider that a bad thing, as he rather liked a woman who was a bit abrasive, since he admittedly had a few rough edges that could use some polishing. She was also on the thin side, but then, his cats hadn't exactly been butterballs when they'd each first come to him, so he figured it wouldn't take him any time to have Julia . . . well, no longer able to sleep on her belly.

Nicholas stopped and peered inside the building at what he decided was the shingle manufacturing section of the mill, considering the strange-looking saw nearly buried in sawdust and the pallets of shingles stacked against the far wall. He continued on to another door, stepping inside to study the variety of lathes surrounded by curled shavings, and he realized the Campbells also made cedar rail fencing. He skirted the ancient-looking machinery to reach the open back wall of the building and looked around the muddy yard stacked with cedar logs.

Spotting the rusty metal wagon half-filled with pinecones sitting in front of another small building, Nicholas headed down the well-worn path through the trees toward it. He wrestled open the door and peered inside, and grinned at the realization he'd found Julia's workshop. He glanced back to see the mill was blocking his view of the house, then took off his sunglasses and stepped inside.

The first thing he saw was a large chopping block with two hatchets driven into its center and two smaller blocks on either side of it serving as seats. He grinned again, picturing Julia and Trisha chatting away as they split the short cedar log ends stacked nearby into kindling. He continued snooping and saw some sacks full of pinecones — which were excellent fire-starters for the resort's fireplaces — leaning against the back wall. He then turned to the bench that ran the length of another wall and dipped his fingers into a bowl of evergreen needles. He held up his hand and sniffed, then brushed the needles back into the bowl and picked up one of the small burlap pillows already filled and sewn closed. He set it down, picked up an even smaller pouch made of a more colorful material, and slid its contents into his hand with a frown.

Soap, he guessed as he ran his thumb across the tree-shaped cake. He held it to his nose to find it also smelled of balsam, which he liked well enough to slip it in his pocket before he plucked a different colored tree from a nearby box. Finding it smelled of lavender, he tossed it back into the box and picked up another one, which smelled like roses. Another one smelled . . . hell, it could be any one of a dozen plants, because what did he know about scents? It had been centuries since he'd stopped to smell the flowers.

He set down the soap and looked around again, only to realize that Julia was about to lose access to her supply of cedar. She could collect pinecones on Nova Mare land and dry her balsam needles and package her soaps in her new apartment, but he suspected the kindling was her most lucrative product.

And since there didn't appear to be anyone around to stop him, Nicholas pulled out his cell phone to call some of his men to come load up a couple of pickups with the cedar, because what fun was there in bringing a small team of elite warriors with him from Atlantis if they couldn't do a little neighborly raiding to keep life interesting? It wasn't like they were attacking Carthage or anything; they'd leave all the buildings and equipment and any stacked stones intact.

And they'd grab the chopping block and hatchets and pinecones while they were at it, along with the soaps and pillows and balsam needles, and simply move Julia's little cottage industry up the mountain — which should make the order-issuing, stick-wielding woman deliriously happy that he'd butted into her business.

But Nicholas suddenly slipped the phone back in his jacket with a snort. It was obviously longer than he remembered since he'd found himself interested in a lovely lady, as he'd apparently forgotten the finer points of a romantic pursuit. Though similar in some ways to mounting a war campaign, he wanted to *capture* this particular target, not overpower her. And last he knew, women balked at a full-speed, head-on attack, but usually responded quite nicely to a more subtle approach.

He took one last look around, then walked out and pulled the door shut. How convenient that he happened to have a workshop at his new home that was filled with scraps of lumber he'd intended to cut up for kindling. He also happened to know where several large stands of pines teeming with cones stood, some of the groves requiring a slow, lazy boat ride to reach. Well, slow if they happened to be dragging a couple of fishing lines behind them. And what woman wasn't attracted to a man who enjoyed long walks in the woods?

No; he'd never been accused of *not* taking advantage of a situation, especially when the prize was a lovely lady he wouldn't mind finding curled up in bed beside him one morning very soon.

Nicholas made it back to the house in time to grab two large trash bags just as Olivia set them on the porch. "Let me carry anything down from upstairs," he said, heading to the truck with what felt like clothes.

He made five trips inside, up the stairs and down, carrying several more trash bags full of Julia's and Trisha's belongings. His last trip to the truck, however, found him carrying a large plastic bin of carefully packed items Julia had pulled off the walls and taken from a china cabinet in the living room. Apparently worried she wouldn't be allowed back in the house, it appeared the woman was taking some of her mother's more precious possessions.

"I . . . There's one more thing I need to get," Julia said as she set a half-filled trash bag in the rear seat and turned to Olivia.

"You can wait here," she added, heading at a stilted run toward the mill. "I'll just be a minute."

Nicholas decided he was going to have to get used to Julia's concepts of time and distance, however, when ten minutes went by and she still hadn't returned.

"Let me go see what's keeping her," Olivia said, heading for the mill only to stop halfway there when she realized he was following. "I think I should go alone, Nicholas. Julia's still pretty embarrassed about what happened today and . . . last night." She shook her head. "I would have come alone with her this afternoon, but I wanted you here in case Vern suddenly showed up." She smiled. "And to lug the heavy stuff." But then she sobered and touched his arm. "Don't take it personally, okay? Just try to understand that it's . . . well, it's humiliating for a grown woman to have a man see her throwing all her belongings in trash bags as she runs away from home."

Nicholas shoved his hands in his pockets and turned away to hide his scowl. "I'll wait at the truck, then. But call me if there's a problem." Only he hadn't even gotten the driver's door open when Olivia called out to him from the mill.

"Nicholas, we need you," she shouted

before disappearing again.

He ran through the mill and practically beat her back to the shed. "What's wrong?" he asked, following Olivia inside to see Julia cradling a hand wrapped in a rag as she sat on one of the chopping stumps. And if he wasn't mistaken, she'd made a valiant effort to rub away the evidence that she'd been crying.

"She was trying to pry up that board," Olivia said, pointing at the floor where he specifically remembered bags of pinecones had been but were now shoved to the side. "When the hatchet slipped and cut her hand."

"The wood is swollen stuck," Julia said, her voice husky with restrained tears. "But I can't leave without the box hidden under it."

"I'll get it for you," Nicholas murmured, crouching in front of her. "After we decide if you need stitches."

"I just skinned it, and the bleeding's already stopped," she said, even though she allowed him to take her hand and peel the rag away. "It's mostly my back that hurts. I must have . . . I guess I wrenched it again prying on the board."

He shot her a grin. "I'm worried you're a bit of a walking disaster, Julia."

That certainly wiped away those threatening tears. It got rid of the defeat in her eyes, too. He let go of her hand and turned away before she saw his triumph, and grabbed the raised end of the spongy floorboard and popped it free.

"Apparently muscle also matters," he drawled as he reached in the cavity and pulled out a plastic container. He turned still crouched to hand it to her, arching a brow when he saw her eyes suddenly narrow. "Not a very creative hidey-hole, though," he added, taking the box back when she started wrestling with the lid — which he popped off before handing it to her again. "Or safe from a fire if this —" He snapped his mouth shut when she pulled out a large plastic bag stuffed with money.

"Julia," Olivia said on a strangled gasp. "What on earth are you doing hiding that much cash under the floorboard of a shed?"

Her face draining of all color, Julia darted a worried glance at him, then looked at her boss. "I can't . . . It's my and Trisha's savings," she whispered.

"But why isn't it in the bank?" Olivia asked just as softly. "There must be thousands of dollars there."

"Almost eight thousand," Julia confirmed, her voice having grown husky again. "And I can't keep it in the bank because Clay's sister works there, and I don't want him knowing I have this kind of money." She darted another glance at Nicholas, then took a deep breath that squared her shoulders as she looked Olivia directly in the eye. "I'm still paying off a credit card bill he stuck me with."

"But Julia, bank employees can't talk about customers' accounts."

She looked down at the bag and merely snorted.

Olivia sighed. "Then give it to Nicholas to put in the safe in my office until . . . well, we'll figure it out." She looked around the workshop and picked up the box of little soaps. "Is there anything else in here you want to bring? I suppose we could come back for the cones and whatever kindling you've already split. But what are you going to do for a source of cedar now?"

"I've been paying Reggie to save the butt ends from the mill and stack them in here for me, so I might be able to get him to bring them to the resort. That is, if you don't mind. I can keep them out in the woods and just cover them with a tarp."

"We'll make it work," Olivia assured her. "You're my only source of kindling, and winter's coming. Maybe we can set you up in the woodshed out behind the barn."

And that explained Julia handing her brother money every week, Nicholas decided as he finally straightened to his feet. He reached down, but instead of taking him up on his offer to help her stand, Julia plopped her entire savings in his outstretched hand, then grasped a wall stud and slowly pulled herself up.

"Who is Clay?" he asked, tucking the bag inside his jacket.

"My ex-husband," she said, avoiding eye contact with him by looking around the workshop. "Nothing else is worth coming back for." She gave Olivia a sheepish smile. "The balsam pillows are a wasted effort if they're just going to keep lugging them off."

"Or we can make the guests *buy* them in our gift shop," Olivia said as she headed out the door carrying the soaps. "We might as well get going then, if you're sure you have everything you want."

Julia took one last look around, used her uninjured hand to grab the hatchet driven into the chopping block, and followed. Nicholas closed the door and followed the women with a scowl at the realization that his plan to give Julia his scrap lumber had been thwarted — only for his mood to lighten again when he remembered she still needed a source of pinecones.

CHAPTER FIVE

Julia woke up to a pounding headache from having cried herself to sleep the night before, the rising sun streaming through the floor-to-ceiling windows making her roll over and bury her face in her pillow with a groan. She wished she still cussed, because if ever there were a time she needed to have a blistering tirade, it was now.

She'd never been so humiliated in her life, not even when Clay had started those nasty rumors about her. Despite most everyone believing them — she *was* the daughter of the town drunk, after all — the knowledge that they were lies had still allowed her to hold her head up. But yesterday Nicholas had seen the stark, naked truth about her, and it hadn't been pretty. She might as well have been wearing a sign that said *Julia Campbell is an utter and complete failure.*

But really, what should she care what Nicholas thought about her? He was just another too tall, too blue-eyed, too maddeningly gorgeous guy. No, the really sad truth was she'd humiliated herself in front of her boss, and Olivia would have to be crazy to entrust the well-being of her Inglenook guests to someone who couldn't even keep her personal life out of the ditch.

For crying out loud, she was thirty years old, and all her worldly possessions were sitting in trash bags in the second bedroom of Nicholas's apartment. That had been Olivia's idea, thinking they might as well not move her stuff twice. Julia had quickly agreed, since she really didn't want any of her coworkers seeing her lugging a bunch of trash bags from her high-priced hotel room to her temporary apartment after Nicholas moved all of his worldly possessions — most likely neatly packed in boxes — to his likely even more maddeningly gorgeous home.

Yup, she was a failure with a capital *F.*

No, she was a *walking disaster.*

Julia rolled over again, threw back the goose-down-filled, seven-hundred-count, Egyptian cotton-encased comforter and sat up with another groan. For as much as she'd love to continue wallowing in self-pity in this luxurious room, she really needed to get up and get going; certain if she just kept moving, the humiliation demons couldn't bring her down and gobble her up completely.

Yeah, what did she care what Nicholas thought? She wasn't interested in catching his interest, partly because men were more trouble than they were worth, but mostly because she didn't like standing in lines. And Nicholas had a really long line of interested females.

Heck, just last week, Wanda Beckman had been bragging to anyone who would listen that the director of security had *personally* driven her down the mountain when she had missed the shuttle. But what Wanda had left out of her story was that she'd actually hidden until the bus had left. Julia knew, though, because she'd watched the divorced mother of three change out of her waitress uniform, contort herself into a tight pair of jeans and low-cut jersey, spray her really impressive cleavage with cologne, then take a magazine and walk into the maintenance room to wait.

Julia got out of bed with a groan, willing to bet all her worldly possessions that Nicholas had made the trip down the mountain in half the time it had taken him to get her down it yesterday, even as she'd wondered what Wanda had . . . offered the man for thanks. Julia stood in the middle of the hotel room and tried to imagine what it was like to be a walking, talking chick magnet.

Not that Nicholas seemed to notice. Or if he did, not that he seemed to let any of the chicks ever . . . stick. Since he'd shown up in Spellbound Falls a little over a year ago, Julia had never seen Nicholas in town with a woman. He used to come into the Drunken Moose on the weekends she worked, but always with one of his guards, or with Mac or Duncan, or often alone. She remembered he was a good tipper, but she also remembered that when any of the waitresses had tried flirting with him, he'd either politely brushed them off or pretended not to notice.

Guessing nobody's life was perfect, not even walking, talking chick magnets, Julia headed for the bathroom with every intention of trying out the luxurious marble soaking tub. She stopped when she heard a knock on the door — only to spin around when she realized it had come from the *rear* entrance to the room.

Even though she cleaned the cottages, she knew about the corridors carved into the granite that ran behind each of the five hotel segments, as well as the tunnels that joined the segments together so the rooms could easily be serviced during the winter months.

In fact, there was an entire warren of caves connecting the hotels with the pool, conference pavilion, and restaurant, which the guests were also encouraged to use during foul weather. Not that the corridors *felt* cavelike, since some of them were actually large enough to drive a cart down and the myriad glass-topped reflective tubes flooded them with natural light.

"Who is it?" Julia called out when the knock sounded again as she looked at the bedside clock, wondering why housekeeping was so *early.* Dang it, she really didn't want any of her coworkers knowing she'd spent the night here, figuring it would be bad enough when they found out she'd been given an apartment.

"Room service," a heavily accented male voice answered.

Really? "Just a minute," she muttered, sprinting into the bathroom and grabbing the plush robe off the back of the door. She walked back into the room as she belted the robe closed, then opened the rear door a crack. "I didn't order room service," she said to a man she didn't recognize holding a tray of covered dishes. "Oh, is that coffee?" she asked, opening the door wider, only to shake her head. "Never mind. You must have the wrong room. I didn't order anything," she repeated.

The guy glanced to the left of the door, then stepped inside. "Numeral seven," he said, walking over and setting the tray on the table in front of the windows. He pulled an envelope from his pocket and handed it to her. "For a Mademoiselle Campbell?"

Julia pulled out the card and frowned at the handwritten note.

Consider this a blatant attempt to persuade you to accept a proposition I have for you, Julia, although in no way should you feel obligated. I'm afraid Olivia was correct in stating that my apartment is in need of a good vacuuming, and if you were to consider performing that particular task, I would enjoy treating you and Trisha to dinner at Aeolus's Whisper this evening.

— Nicholas

How . . . lovely.

Well, he knew she worked in housekeeping, after all; but dinner at Aeolus's? Either the man really hated vacuuming or he'd just discovered there was enough cat hair in his apartment to stuff a king-size mattress. The smell of coffee tickled Julia's nose, and she realized the waiter had poured some into

97

the delicate china cup on the tray and was now looking at her . . . expectantly.

Oh, he was waiting for his tip! "Just a minute," she said, going to her purse on the bureau. Dang it, how much did she tip a five-star room service waiter? She pulled out a ten dollar bill, folded it in half, and walked back and handed it to him. "Thank you," she murmured, opening the *front* door of the room and smiling at him . . . expectantly.

He stuffed the money in his pocket, returned her smile with an added nod, and left. Julia closed the door behind him and locked it, then ran over and grabbed the cup of coffee, blew on it briefly, and took a sip. She gave a hum of pleasure and took another sip, figuring there was nothing like caffeine to cure a crying hangover. Another sip, then she lifted the larger of the domes on the tray and actually laughed. Oh yeah, there must be *a lot* of cat hair, she decided as she sat down and pulled the tray in front of her, if the size of this breakfast was any indication.

She ate the perfectly cooked eggs Benedict, all six slices of crisp bacon, both thick oat-nut toasts — that she slathered with both tiny jars of jam — most of the hash browns, and every last piece of exotic fruit while washing everything down with what was definitely fresh-squeezed orange juice.

"Okay, Mr. Nicholas," she said with a laugh, saluting the window with her third cup of coffee and leaning back in her chair with an overstuffed sigh. "I guess your blatant bribe worked. I'll vacuum up your cat hair for just the price of breakfast."

She was not, however, having dinner with him — even if her sister was included — at Aeolus's Whisper. Not at the risk of being seen dining with Spellbound's most eligible bachelor, because she didn't want to be found dead on a cart path tomorrow morning after being run over by Wanda Beckman or any one of a dozen female workers. And besides, people *dressed* for dinner at Aeolus's, and her only decent outfit was crumpled up in a ball at the bottom of a trash bag at the moment.

Nova Mare's international employee housing sat back in the woods beyond the resort's horse barn. The two-building complex consisted of ten apartments on the ground floor with male and female dorms running the length of each building above them. The dorms were usually filled with young men and women from all over the world during the resort's busy summer season, while Julia believed the apartments were occupied year-round by a few of the nonlocal security guards, some of the reputedly fearless road maintenance crew, a husband and wife horse wrangler team, and several restaurant workers. There were only four children residing on Whisper Mountain: Olivia and Mac's three — twelve-year-old Sophie, ten-year-old Henry, and two-and-a-half-year-old Ella — as well as the horse wranglers' teenage son.

Nicholas's apartment — now temporarily hers and Trisha's — was an end unit with two bedrooms and two baths, a well-appointed kitchen, and windows on three sides. None of the apartments or the dorms had a spectacular view, but then, everyone spent their days looking down at Bottomless and were probably all viewed out, anyway.

"Didn't I tell you Nicholas was fast on his feet?" Olivia said with a laugh as she watched her top security guard drive away. She set Ella down and turned to Julia, even as she gestured toward the window. "I just have to show up with Princess Hugs-a-lot, and he vanishes faster than a cat at a rocking chair convention."

"He doesn't like children?" Julia said in surprise, bending to pick up Ella when the toddler started tugging on her pant leg and holding up her arms, making Julia chuckle when the girl lived up to her nickname by immediately giving her a fierce hug.

"No, just the opposite," Olivia said. "Nicholas loves children."

"Then why vanish?"

"Because the last time he fell in love with a baby princess, he ended up spending the next thirty-one years as her bodyguard."

"Excuse me?"

"Mac's sister, Carolina," Olivia explained. "You've met her, haven't you?"

Julia was forced to merely nod since Ella was now clasping her face, trying to get Julia to look at her instead of Olivia.

"Well, Nicholas's mother was the midwife at Carolina's birth, and when Rana suddenly took a turn for the worse, Maude apparently handed the minutes-old infant to him — Nicholas was only seven at the time, I've been told — and he refused to give her up for the next three days while everyone focused on saving Rana." Olivia smiled crookedly. "Actually, he refused to give Carolina up for the next thirty-one years, until he decided Alec MacKeage deserved to spend the rest of his life dealing with her." She gestured at her daughter, who had forgone clasping Julia's face in favor of fingering the elastic on Julia's thick braid of hair. "And that's why he beats a hasty retreat whenever Ella heads for him with her arms raised, afraid of being saddled with another Oceanus princess for thirty-one more years. It's also why he swears he's only having sons." She snorted, even as a gleam came into her eyes. "Assuming he can find a woman willing to marry him."

Julia decided she wasn't touching that little comment with a ten-foot pole. "So Nicholas was a bodyguard before he came to work for you?"

"Among other things," Olivia said vaguely, walking down the hall. "You don't have to clean this apartment yourself, Jules," she continued as Julia followed carrying Ella. "I can have Bev send over some of her staff, and they'll have this place spit-shined by the end of the morning."

What, and have them see all my worldly possessions in trash bags? "Thanks, but I'd rather do it myself," Julia told her. "And for a bachelor, Nicholas was a pretty good housekeeper. Other than a little extra vacuuming, it won't be any different than giving one of my cottages a good cleaning between guests."

Olivia plucked Ella away from Julia and replaced the child with a set of keys. "Well,

it's all yours for however long you need it."
She touched Julia's arm. "Please don't run
off and rent the first place you find out of
stubborn pride. This apartment will just sit
empty all winter, so you might as well take
your time looking for something that's nice
as well as affordable." She canted her head,
that gleam returning. "Then again, who
knows what exciting surprise might be waiting just around the corner for you?"

Julia caught her breath on the hope that
Olivia was referring to the Inglenook posi-
tion. She nodded. "Okay, I won't. But
Trisha and I are paying rent, right?"

"For an apartment that's going to sit
empty all winter anyway?" Olivia said with
a laugh, heading back out to the living room
carrying Ella.

Julia followed her down the hall. "We're
not living here for free."

Olivia turned with her daughter clasping
her face trying to get her undivided attention. "Then how about if you stop by my
office and ask Lucy to show you my babysitting schedule, and you sign up to chase Ella
around for a few hours each week?"

"That's it? You want me to babysit in
exchange for housing? Heck, I'm not afraid
of falling in love with a princess. I'll take
her anytime."

Olivia gave an ominous little snicker as she headed for the door. "We'll see how you feel after your first session, when you find yourself peeling her off anyone she can coax into picking her up." She opened the door and looked back, shaking her head. "Even the horses aren't safe. And now that she's found out where the chickens live, they're not safe, either."

"*Gallinae!*" Ella squealed, bouncing in her mother's arms. "Go tee *gallinae!*"

Olivia gave a groan and headed for her cart. "According to my head chef, hens apparently think being chased by a two-year-old trying to hug them is the same as being chased by a fox trying to eat them, and they quit laying for a week."

"*Gallinae!*" Ella growled, twisting against the straps as Olivia buckled her into the safety seat on the passenger side of her cart.

Julia was confused — or else Ella was. "Why is she calling them *gallinae?*"

Olivia straightened with a tight smile. "Because my dear sweet husband is teaching her *Latin.* Once you unpack your swimsuits, you and Trish feel free to use either of the saltwater pools. The outside pool is also heated, and they're both open to employees from ten to midnight and four to six every morning." She waved toward the parking lot separated from the complex by some trees. "If you're worried about Trisha driving the mountain, she can leave her truck down below and hitch a ride up on the shuttle. And in the morning she can ride down with me or Mac when we take the kids to the marina to catch the school bus with Peg's tribe."

"Thanks. I like that idea, especially with the weather turning."

"You have studded snow tires on the truck?"

Julia nodded. "I had new ones put on a couple of weeks ago."

"Since I finally caved in and had the road paved," Olivia said, "the crew promised me they can keep it passable all winter now, and we'll only have to use the snowcats *during* storms if there's an emergency." She shook her head. "I'm not really sure how I let Mac talk me into building a resort on top of a mountain, much less keep it open year-round." She snorted. "Now he's talking about stringing a cable across the fiord for scenic gondola rides."

"That's not all that far-fetched, is it? There are gondolas in the Alps."

"It's over *a mile* across." Olivia waved toward the fiord. "And this is *Maine,* not the Alps, and sure as hell not Disneyland."

She took a deep breath and gave Julia a sheepish smile. "Sorry. I've got a lot on my plate right now."

"Just right now," Julia drawled, "as opposed to *always*?"

"Yeah, always," Olivia said with a sigh. She slid into her shiny green electric cart — that Julia knew had been altered to go faster than the others — and set her hands on the steering wheel with a wince. "I can't believe I'm saying this, but I actually miss cleaning cottages." She suddenly gave Julia a cheeky smile. "How about you and I switch jobs for a week?"

"Not on your life," Julia said with a sputtered laugh.

"Gallinae!" Ella screeched, leaning into her harness, trying to reach the steering wheel. "Mum, go tee *gallinae.*" She looked at Julia, her huge, striking green eyes filled with impatience. "Bye," she said with a surprisingly regal wave, apparently hoping her mother would get the hint. "Go tee *gallinae* now. *Bye,*" she repeated, this time aiming the wave at Olivia — who reached down with a loud sigh and put the cart in reverse.

She backed up, slipped the cart into forward, then looked at her daughter. "Okay, we'll stop by the chicken coop on our way to go find your father, because you know what?" she said, widening her eyes at Ella. "Daddy wants to take you *riding.*"

"Equus!" Ella squealed, clapping her hands in delight. "Wide *equus* wit Daddy."

Olivia rolled her eyes and silently zoomed off toward the barn with a wave over her shoulder. Julia stepped back and closed the door, then blew out a loud sigh of her own as she gazed around her temporary, fully furnished apartment.

"Okay then," she said as she headed for the kitchen. "Things are looking up in the walking disaster department. Trisha and I are living in the safest place on the planet thanks to my generous boss, I don't have to bike to work anymore, and I'm apparently still in the running for the Inglenook position." She opened the cupboards under the sink to check for cleaning supplies and found only a mousetrap.

Wait, hadn't a couple of cats lived here? Then what idiot mouse would think this was a good place to spend the winter? Unless . . . Julia shivered and closed the cabinet doors. Unless the cats snuck in mice as future entertainment for when the boss was at work all day — which is exactly why there had never been any cats in the Campbell home. Well, *inside* the house, as there were always several semi-feral cats prowling the mill, thanks to their mouse and bird diets being supplemented with table scraps.

Julia spent the morning cleaning — one full hour vacuuming — and the afternoon unpacking all of her and Trisha's worldly possessions, until she found herself staring into Trisha's closet with a stupid smile on her face. She touched the ankle-length green wool coat, heartened to know her sister would be going to college looking quite sharp thanks to Peg MacKeage's beautiful hand-me-downs.

Julia had met Peg — then Peg Conroy — their first day of kindergarten, as the both of them had stood pressed up against the school building watching the horde of children on the playground, both still shaken from the hour-long bus ride to Turtleback Station. Julia remembered whispering that it felt like they'd traveled clear across the world as Peg had inched closer and pulled a small rock out of her pocket, saying her mom had given it to her to rub if she got scared, and that they could share it for the day and she'd ask her mom if she could bring one for Julia tomorrow.

That had been the beginning of a quarter-century friendship that had seen them through way too many outrageous pranks and disastrous romantic crushes, marriages and births, deaths and divorce and widow-hood, and everything in between.

Peg was actually a year older — which she liked to lord over Julia — but had been in the same grade because her birthday was October 19, making her miss starting school the previous year by four days. Julia's birthday was October 1, so she had techni-cally still been four years old that first day.

Julia closed the closet door and walked out of the room, down the short hallway, and into the kitchen just as her stomach gave a hungry gurgle. More from wishful thinking than optimism, she opened the fridge hoping Nicholas had forgotten to pack his cold food, only to find a bottle of wine sitting beside a tray of dome-covered dishes with an envelope propped between them. She pulled out the tray, set it on the counter, and started to close the door, but then reached in and grabbed the bottle of wine. She set the wine on the tray, picked up the envelope, and pulled out the note written in bold, familiar handwriting.

A little something to tide you over until dinner tonight.

— Nicholas

His phone number — which was seven

digits, indicating it was his personal cell rather than an employee phone — was written below his name, along with a PS stating to give him a call when Trisha got back and he'd come pick them up.

Dang, she'd completely forgotten about dinner. Why hadn't she told him they wouldn't be going when she'd first arrived at the apartment just as he and another man had been loading the last box into his truck? Although in her defense, since he hadn't asked if she'd enjoyed her breakfast or mentioned her vacuuming, she'd thought he might not want Olivia to know about their deal, so she hadn't said anything, either.

Julia lifted one of the domes to find a club sandwich large enough to choke a horse wrapped in plastic to keep it fresh, a small bowl of potato sticks, a dish of pickles, and a tiny jar of mayonnaise. She found a decadent-looking piece of cake large enough to choke an elephant under another one of the domes, and what looked like apple-filled pastries under the last one.

Heck, forget the sign saying she was an utter and complete failure; she must be wearing one that read *Julia Campbell will do anything for food.*

She tucked the note between the plates

and started opening drawers until she found a corkscrew. She then opened cupboards until she was pleasantly surprised to find two wineglasses, only to frown when she realized there were only two tumblers. She reopened the cupboard with the dishes and saw two plates, two bowls, and two coffee mugs, then opened the silverware drawer again and counted out four forks, knives, and spoons.

She closed the drawer with a snort.

Nicholas had filched half the dishes and eating utensils.

Julia set the wineglass on the tray with a smile, liking that she had a little dirt on Nova Mare's director of security. Granted, it wasn't exactly felony dirt, she guessed as she carried everything into the living room, but it could nevertheless come in handy someday. She set the tray on the small dining table in front of the window, sat down, and picked up the card again with a sigh, figuring she might as well break the news to him now. She looked around for a phone but didn't find one.

Dang, she was going to have to get herself a cell phone. She'd gotten one for Trisha when she'd given her the truck, not wanting her baby sister on the road with no means of communication if she broke down or got in an accident. But every penny they'd both been scrimping and saving was needed to make up the difference between the cost of college and what financial aid Trisha had managed to get, so Julia had drawn the line at having her own phone.

The one exception to dipping into their savings was Trisha's upcoming trip to New York City, when Turtleback's school band got to play in the Macy's Thanksgiving Day Parade. Trisha did a lot of babysitting for Peg and Duncan, and Julia had promised her sister that if she saved enough to pay her share of the trip's cost, she would then match it with spending money.

The girl had lived up to her end of the bargain, and one week from today, Julia was putting Trisha on a bus with her bandmates for a seven-day trip to the Big Apple — which was twice as far as Julia had been from Spellbound Falls. She'd only made it to Boston on her honeymoon, and then only so Clay could check out Boston University's master degree programs.

That should have been her first clue the jerk was going to renege on their deal that she support him while he got his bachelor's degree, after which she was supposed to get her teaching degree. In the end, Clay had stayed at the University of Maine for all six years, gotten his master's in engineering, and gone to *work* in Boston instead — newly married to a woman Julia later found out he had cheated on her with for the last three years of their marriage.

Realizing she'd crumpled up the note with Nicholas's phone number, Julia calmly smoothed it out on the table, slowly folded it in quarters, and leaned over and slipped it in the hind pocket of her jeans. She'd stop at the registration pavilion when she left to go pick up Trisha at the marina, and have the front desk give Nicholas the message that she and her sister couldn't have dinner with him because . . . well, she'd come up with a believable lie by that time.

And then she'd get back to her routine of cleaning cottages and *not* seeing Nicholas except at staff meetings — and then from the safety of the back row. And, Julia decided as she unwrapped the sandwich, she would remember this three-day *walking disaster* as nothing more than a really bad dream. Well, except for those heavenly few seconds on her porch Friday night, because who knew when she'd ever get pulled into the arms of a big strong man and be kissed like that again?

CHAPTER SIX

"Jules. Jules, wake up," Julia heard Trisha whisper as she felt her shoulder being repeatedly nudged. "But don't move."

"What's going on?" Julia asked, opening her eyes to find the hall light spilling into her bedroom as she tried to sit up, only to have Trisha press down on her shoulder.

"Don't move," her sister hissed.

"W-what's wrong?"

"There's a giant lynx or bobcat or something curled up against your leg," Trisha continued softly. "And I really don't think we should startle it."

Julia realized the girl was holding her clarinet like a baseball bat, apparently ready to sacrifice her beloved instrument to save her big sister. She also realized there *was* something warm and heavy pressing against the length of her thigh, and she slowly lifted her head and looked down.

Yup, that sure looked like a lynx or bobcat

to her, its huge eyes staring unblinking at her from a long-whiskered face, its hair-tufted ears also trained on her. "It . . ." Julia ran her tongue around her suddenly dry mouth, breaking her gaze with the eerily silent creature. "It has to be one of Nicholas's cats," she said, slowly trying to slide away — only to go perfectly still when it reached out one of its massive paws and snagged the blanket over her thigh.

"How do you suppose they got in here?" Trisha said in a whisper, sounding a bit relieved at the prospect it might actually have an owner.

"I don't know, but judging by that paw, maybe it just turned the doorknob. Wait, what do you mean, *they*?"

"I made sure both doors were locked when we went to bed. But you might be right about it belonging to Nicholas, because I woke up to a cat curled up in bed with me, too. Only it's not nearly as big as this one."

Julia glanced toward the hall. "Where is it now?"

"Still on my bed. I came in here to tell you about it and found *him*. Or her," she said softly, gesturing slightly with the clarinet. "Do you think Nicholas raised it from a kitten, so it's tame? It's not purring.

My cat was purring. That's what woke me."

"Where's your cell phone?" Julia asked.

"I can't find my house charger, so it's plugged into the one in my truck."

That's because Julia was pretty sure the house charger was still sitting on the counter back home. "Okay, I'm going to try to slide —" Julia barely stifled a shriek when Trisha's nocturnal visitor suddenly jumped up on the bed as quiet as a . . . cat, walked across her belly, flopped down beside its buddy, and started purring.

Big Cat started washing Small Cat's face, even though Julia was pretty sure they weren't related, as the black-and-gray big one was long-haired, stout-boned, and had an eerily humanlike face, while the smaller one was short-haired, sleek, and solid gray, with huge round eyes that appeared orange in the hall light.

"What are we going to do?" Trisha whispered.

Julia once more tried sliding away, but stilled again when Big Cat stopped in mid-lick and, without even looking at her, curled its paw resting on her thigh into the blanket deeply enough that she felt its claws snag her pajama pants. "Um, how about you go to the kitchen," she softly suggested, "and take the meat out of what's left of the sandwich in the fridge and bring it back here? Maybe we can coax them off the bed and then lure them outside."

Trisha slowly extended her clarinet toward Julia, causing Big Cat to stop licking again when she slowly pulled her hand from under the blanket, took the instrument, and held it lying across her chest. "Okay, go. *Slowly.*"

Trisha backed out of the room and halfway down the hall before she turned and sprinted toward the kitchen. Julia looked back at the two cats and softly sighed as the big one resumed washing the smaller one's face. She wasn't normally afraid of cats, but there really wasn't anything *normal* about either of these. Big Cat had to be at least part lynx or bobcat, because she didn't believe house cats got that huge. And she'd actually seen a lynx once while out walking in the woods, and it had been just as silent and had had an equally spooky face. Heck, this one's eyes appeared to be ringed with black eyeliner, and the tufts sticking out of its ears gave it a devilish look. As for its buddy; Julia hadn't known cats could have orange eyes, and its fur was a ghostly shade of bluish-gray. But at least it purred like a normal cat.

They had to belong to Nicholas, because

now that she thought about it, he really wasn't all that normal, either. Whoever heard of anyone not having a last name? Well, other than rock stars. And he didn't appear to date; how did a man that maddeningly handsome not have women hanging all over him?

He certainly kissed like he'd had plenty of practice.

And the guy had a weird sense of humor, like calling her a walking disaster when she was right in the middle of an emotional breakdown. And what was up with that "size matters" comment, anyway? Did he have the staff locker room bugged or something?

Where in heck was Trisha? Was she *eating* the sandwich?

Big Cat suddenly stopped licking again, its whiskers twitching as it lifted its nose in the air not two seconds before Trisha came sprinting back into the room. "Slowly," Julia hissed as both cats suddenly stood up — the big one straddling Julia's body.

Trisha skidded to a halt and started backing away when they both jumped off the bed and started toward her. "Jules," she squeaked, speeding up. "Help me."

"Oh, for crying out loud," Julia growled, tossing back the blankets and getting out of bed. "They're cats, not mountain lions." She rushed past them and headed for the door — although she was still holding the clarinet. "It's not like they're going to eat us."

"Yeah, well, I didn't see *you* shoving them off your bed," Trisha muttered as she backed out the door Julia had opened. The girl immediately stepped to the side and lobbed the handful of meat halfway down the front path, watched the two cats pounce on their prize, then scurried back inside the apartment.

Julia slammed the door closed, turned and leaned against it as she bent to rest her hands on her knees, and started laughing just as Trisha plopped down on the arm of the couch and also burst into laughter.

"Aren't we fearless women?" Julia said with a snicker. "Afraid of two cats."

"Did you see the size of that big one?" Trisha said, sobering. "I swear it must weigh twenty-five or thirty pounds."

Julia straightened, shaking her head. "It has to be all hair," she said, despite remembering how heavy it had felt on her bed. "Considering I vacuumed up about three pounds of cat hair today — I mean yesterday. What time is it?"

"I think it was almost five when I went into your bedroom. How do you suppose they got in here?"

"There must be a cat door somewhere in the apartment." Julia walked to the window, lifted the pleated shade, and looked outside. "They're gone," she said, turning and looking around the apartment. "But I didn't see a cat door when I cleaned today. If Nicholas had one for them, wouldn't he have fit it into a window rather than cut a hole in the wall or door of a rental?"

Trisha walked to the kitchen. "I noticed a bottom cupboard was open when I came in to get the meat. Maybe he hid it inside a cupboard so no one would see it."

Julia followed just as Trisha snapped on the light, and saw the cupboard next to the back entrance was indeed ajar. Trisha got down on her knees, opened the cupboard all the way, then sat back on her heels as she pointed inside. "There it is." She blew out a sigh. "That makes me feel better. I was starting to imagine all sorts of weird ways they might have gotten in here."

"Does it have a lock on it?"

Trisha leaned inside the cupboard. "Yup," came her muffled reply. She backed out and sat up again, brushing her hands together. "There; we won't be waking up to find them in bed with us again." She waved at the cupboard. "It's a neat little door and looks professionally installed. But Nicholas really should have told us about it, before we found ourselves waking up to raccoons going through our frid— oh!" Trisha shrieked when a loud rattling came from inside the cupboard, making her scramble away and bump into the trash can.

Julia slammed the cupboard door closed and held her leg against it. "You're sure it's *locked*?"

Trisha took a deep breath and got back on her knees with a scowl. "It has little metal pins on both sides that slide into eyelets on the door. I closed both of them," she said, grabbing the cupboard handle. She nodded. "Okay, move away and I'll check and make sure they're both still in place."

Julia stepped away, then watched as Trisha slowly opened the cupboard and peeked inside just as the cat door rattled again. "Go home, you brats," Trisha said into the cupboard, making the rattling stop. "You don't live here anymore. You moved down the mountain." She grinned up at Julia. "It was probably a mistake to feed them."

"A well-aimed bucket of water might change their minds," Julia drawled.

Trisha closed the cupboard and stood up. "They'll eventually get bored and leave. But Nicholas really should have told us about the cat door, or at least thought to lock it, expecting they'd come back."

"He was too busy escaping from Ella to tell me," Julia said on a laugh. She walked over and started looking through the boxes Trisha had brought back from the Mac-Keages' — that Peg had thoughtfully filled with food staples for their new apartment. She hoped her friend had included coffee for the coffeemaker Nicholas wisely *hadn't* filched. "Apparently our big, strapping director of security is afraid of little girls," she continued, sighing in relief when she found a can of coffee. She started digging through the boxes looking for filters. "Oh, by the way, Olivia said I can work off our rent by babysitting Ella, and you might as well sign up for a shift or two yourself."

"Sure," Trisha said, grabbing the carafe and filling it at the sink. "Mrs. MacKeage can give me a reference if you think it'll make Mrs. Oceanus feel better. And Sophie and Henry know me quite well, since they spend a lot of time at the MacKeages'."

Julia slid the drawer closed with her hip after pulling out the can opener and started opening the coffee — savoring the sound of the air rushing into the can when she pierced the lid. "Don't you think it's time you started calling people by their first names like Peg keeps suggesting?"

Trisha spun toward her. "Mom would roll over in her grave."

"You're an adult now, Trisha." Julia gestured around the kitchen with the can opener. "You're living almost on your own, you earn your own money, and now you'll be able to deposit the social security checks you started getting when Mom died into *your own* checking account."

"Do . . . do you think Dad's going to let me? Those checks are the biggest reason he dragged me home the last time we tried to move out."

"You'll be a legal adult in a month, so he can't force you to live with him anymore, and we'll go online and have Social Security send them to *your* checking account the moment you turn eighteen." Julia waved at the apartment again. "And even drunk, Dad wouldn't have the courage to come up here and drag you home at two in the morning — assuming he could even get past the bottom guardhouse." She touched Trisha's shoulder. "You're free now, little sister. Dad's not going to start anything this close to your birthday."

A slow smile spread across Trisha's face, her eyes filling with the knowledge it was finally over. "No more drunken tirades and sleeping on church pews, and no more embarrassing public scenes in town or at school."

Julia started spooning coffee into the filter. "Sorry, sis, but the embarrassment doesn't end with emancipation; it just changes." She started the coffee brewing, then turned with a smile. "But you'll survive by holding your head high and thumbing your nose at anyone who tries to knock you down. Oh, and it helps to keep moving," she added with a chuckle. "So you can stay one step ahead of the humiliation demons." Julia pulled her sister into a hug. "And you begin as you intend to go on, and that includes calling people by their first names."

"Even . . . even Mrs. Richie?" Trisha whispered. She leaned away, her eyes now dancing with amusement. "I really don't want to be responsible for sending an eighty-four-year-old woman into anaphylactic shock by calling her Christina."

"Have you ever heard *me* call her Christina?" Julia said on a laugh, giving her one last fierce hug before stepping away. "But everyone else by their first names, including Ezra at the Trading Post, okay?"

"Um . . . Mr. Oceanus?" Trisha said, already shaking her head. "Duncan I can probably do, but not Olivia's husband. He's just . . . he's too . . ."

"Big and scary?" Julia finished for her. "Yes," she said with a curt nod before heading down the hallway. "You put on your big girl panties and call him Mac."

Trisha followed with a heavy sigh. "Why is growing up so scary? I'm freaked out just thinking about riding a stupid bus to New York City with *friends.*"

"You think calling people by their first names and visiting a big city are scary?" Julia asked, stepping into the bathroom and turning to arch a brow at her. "You just wait until the boys at UMO get a look at you next September and you find yourself having to beat them off with a stick."

"I'm not letting any stupid boys distract me from my studies. And I've decided I'm not trying out for band, either."

Julia stepped back into the hall, making Trisha step back in surprise. "Being distracted by college boys is part of your education," she growled. "And so are extracurricular activities. You've been living like a nun all through high school," she said softly, touching Trisha's curls. "Please don't hide in your books at college, too."

Trisha gave a sad smile, even as she lifted her chin. "I've only been following your example. When was the last time *you* went on a date?" She in turn tugged on a lock of

Julia's wild mess of hair. "I'll start dating when you do."

"I don't have a campus full of men to choose from." Julia waved toward the living room. "And unless we suddenly have an explosion of frogs and I start running around kissing them, there's not much chance of finding Prince Charming in Spellbound Falls."

"Then move to Orono with me."

Julia sighed and stepped back into the bathroom. "We've had this discussion before, and my answer is still no." She leaned against the half-closed door. "I'm still holding out hope for Reggie, and Jerilynn's pregnancy seems to be having a positive effect on Tom, especially the closer she gets to her due date. And besides —"

"And besides," Trisha said, cutting her off as the girl headed for her bedroom — that had its own bath, because Julia had figured a teenager needed more mirror time than a thirty-year-old who'd given up trying to impress men. *"I need to experience being independent,"* she mimicked. The girl then poked her head into the hall and grinned back at her. "My deal stands; I'll start dating when you do," she finished, just before wisely disappearing into her room and closing the door.

"Okay, fine," Julia growled. "I'll start dating when it starts raining frogs."

Soaking up the weak but still surprisingly warm November sun, Julia sauntered home from the housekeeping facilities behind the second hotel segment, having indeed fallen back into her routine of cleaning cottages, hunting for a new source of pinecones, and trying not to worry about Trisha. Oh, and battling some persistent felines that weren't about to let two silly little lock pins keep them out of their old home.

Big Cat must have simply *leaned* on the door, because when Julia had gotten home that same afternoon, she'd found an explosion of feathers in the living room, a live frog — that she hadn't even been tempted to kiss — in the bathroom, and muddy paw prints on the *counters.* And Tuesday morning, she and Trisha had awakened to find they weren't alone in their beds again, even though Julia had replaced the pins with heavy nails and shoved a chair up against the cupboard as added insurance. Only that morning Big Cat had brought along a fat white buddy — apparently Nicholas had three cats, not two — and Julia had managed to slide out of bed before it could snag her pajama pants. She'd met Trisha in the hallway just as the girl had been coming to tell her their nocturnal visitors were back, and they'd repeated the food-luring trick using leftover tuna casserole.

There was now a piece of scrap plywood Julia had filched from the resort's maintenance shed covering the outside of the cat door, being held in place by a couple of heavy pieces of firewood she'd filched from the woodshed, because she hadn't quite dared to drive nails into the building's siding. In retaliation, she'd arrived home that afternoon to find their front pathway littered with enough bird feathers to stuff a pillow.

So other than her ongoing war with Nicholas's cats, the only unanticipated addition to Julia's plan to put her humiliating weekend behind her was that she had to *actively* avoid Nova Mare's director of security now that she was living at the resort. It seemed that every morning as she walked from her apartment to housekeeping, she narrowly escaped Nicholas coming in or out of the registration pavilion that also housed the resort's offices. Then, walking home yesterday afternoon, he'd been coming out of the barn leading a monstrous, scary-looking horse, and Julia had seen him just in time to scurry behind a tree before *he* saw *her.*

But she hadn't been quite so successful this morning, nearly running Nicholas over with her cart when she'd rounded a curve — she hadn't been speeding, since *her* cart was about as fast as a turtle — as he'd been coming back from an obviously long run on the mountain trails with four of his big, strapping security guards. Julia had nearly driven into a tree at the sight of all that naked chest and leg muscle glistening with sweat despite it being only fifty degrees out with a crisp wind. For crying out loud, it had taken her heart half an hour to quit racing and her cheeks at least twice as long to cool down, the amusement in Nicholas's sky-blue eyes as he'd given her a wink on his way by making Julia nearly wear out the wheels of her vacuum on her next cottage.

For a second there, she'd seriously thought about *becoming* the town slut.

That had actually lifted her spirits, though, when she'd realized Clay hadn't completely killed her interest in men, since there seemed to be a few sparks of what she suspected might be passion left floating around inside her somewhere. Still, she wasn't letting that welcome revelation override her common sense, and she sure as heck wasn't going to start daydreaming about Nicholas kissing her again.

So she daydreamed about being Inglenook's guest liaison instead.

In fact, Nicholas notwithstanding, over the last few days Julia had often wanted to pinch herself to make sure she was still alive, because it certainly felt like she had died and gone to heaven. The last time she'd left the mountain had been to pick up Trisha at the marina when Duncan had brought her across the fiord Sunday afternoon, and truthfully, Julia didn't care if she stayed up here until the day she really *did* die.

She hadn't even left to get groceries, instead leaving that chore to Trisha.

They'd actually started a ritual of nocturnal swims in the outdoor heated saltwater pool, in utter and complete awe to be floating on their backs staring up at the stars that seemed close enough to touch. And Trisha appeared to be embracing adulthood now that she truly felt free. Reggie was still being a brat, although Julia figured he was angrier at being stuck alone with their father than at having to load the cedar into his pickup and drive it clear up the mountain, even for *twice* what she'd been paying him.

When she'd called to check on Tom Sunday afternoon, she'd learned he hadn't pressed charges for the minor concussion he'd received, but Julia hadn't expected him to. Although her brother was just as tired of their father's drunken tirades, Tom wasn't about to bite the hand of the person who fed him. Not with a baby arriving in about six weeks and Jerilynn having had to quit waitressing at Angie's Bar in Turtleback when she'd started showing — because apparently men didn't like knocked-up barmaids serving them drinks at a stripper's club. Still, the fact Tom had rushed to their sister's rescue warmed Julia's heart, and like she'd told Trisha last Monday morning at five A.M., she wasn't quite ready to give up on the two boys.

Just exiting the cart path, Julia halted in surprise when she saw Jerilynn sitting on one of the wooden love seats on the common green. She looked around and saw Tom's old pickup parked in a visitor parking slot beside the registration pavilion, but not seeing Tom, she rushed down to the green. "Jerilynn, what are you doing here?" she asked, noticing her sister-in-law had on makeup and was wearing her Sunday coat.

"Oh, Jules," Jerilynn said in surprise, reaching up to clasp her arm. "I was hoping I'd see you. Come on, sit down," she said, tugging Julia down beside her. "My God, the view up here is amazing." She rested her hands on her protruding belly and nudged Julia with her shoulder. "I'd give anything to work up here looking at this all day."

"What are you doing here, Jerilynn?" Julia asked again, glancing over her shoulder before looking back at her sister-in-law. "Did you come up here alone, hoping to see me? Is Tom okay? Reggie?"

"Oh, no," Jerilynn rushed to assure her, her pixie face lighting with her smile. "Everyone's fine. I came up with Tom." She gestured behind them. "He's in talking to Nicholas, and when they're done Nicholas is taking us to Alus . . . Eellises . . . How do you say the restaurant's name again?" Jerilynn asked. She tugged on the edges of her coat, not that it came anywhere close to closing, her face turning pink as she leaned closer. "I don't want to embarrass Tom by sounding ignorant in front of his new boss."

It took Julia a moment to close her slackened jaw, not that it came any closer to closing than Jerilynn's coat. "Boss?" she whispered. "Are you saying Nicholas is Tom's new *boss*?"

Jerilynn nodded, her smile beaming again as her bright blue eyes sparkled in the low-hanging sun. "Nicholas came by our house early Monday morning before Tom left for the mill, saying he wanted to see for himself how Tom was doing. And they stood out in the driveway talking so long that I was tempted to take some coffee out to them." Her smile widened. "Mostly being nosy. But just about the time I worked up the nerve, Nicholas left and Tom came back inside and said he wasn't going to the mill that day and hopefully not ever again. He said Nicholas had just offered him a job as a security guard at Inglenook, only he'd have to start right away so he can be trained by May."

This time Julia actually used her hand to close her mouth and then sat her chin in her palm to keep it closed, utterly speechless.

"What's Nicholas's last name, Jules? I can't go around calling Tom's boss by his first name. And the restaurant? How do you pronounce it again?"

"It . . . um, it's *EE-uh-luss-es.* The *Ae* sounds like a long *E,* then *UH,* then *LUSS,* and then the apostrophe *S.* Aeolus is the Greek god of the winds."

"And Nicholas's last name?"

"He doesn't have one," Julia snapped. She took a deep breath. "Sorry. I'm just . . . Seeing you up here caught me by surprise. Um, don't take this wrong, okay, but why would Nicholas hire Tom as a security guard? I

133

mean, Tom's not . . . he can't . . ." Julia blew out a sigh. "Heck, Jerilynn, face it: Tom can't fight his way out of a wet paper bag, mostly because he *hates* violence. And Daddy knocked him out cold Saturday. So why would Nicholas offer him a job as a guard?" she repeated.

Jerilynn went back to smiling. "I asked Tom the same thing. And he told me Nicholas said he can teach a man how to fight, but that he can't teach him courage. He said he was impressed by how Tom hadn't hesitated to go up against a drunken man who outweighed him by over a hundred pounds." She touched Julia's arm and leaned into her again, even as she used her other hand to pat her belly. "And Nicholas said he's going to have Olivia waive the waiting period for the medical insurance, so me and the baby will be covered when Tom starts work tomorrow." Her hand on Julia's arm tightened. "Do you realize how much they pay their security guards here, Jules?" she whispered. "It's over three times what Tom was making at the mill, and it comes with a whole bunch of benefits, some I've never even heard of before. There's even a retirement plan. Tom said if we don't go crazy with all the extra money, we can probably get a loan to buy the house we're renting in about a year."

Julia turned to prop her elbow on the back of the wooden love seat so she could hold up her chin with her palm again. Nicholas had hired her brother?

"You don't have a problem with Tom working for the resort, too, do you, Jules? Or that he'll be part of what Nicholas called his elite team of guards, and that he'll be earning more than you do as a house-keeper?"

Julia pulled her chin out of her hand to give her sister-in-law a warm hug. "Are you kidding? I'm as excited as you are." She gave her an exaggerated scowl. "But he bet-ter not try to lord his position over me, because I'm still his big sister." She patted Jerilynn's belly. "And I intend to be this one's favorite aunt, but don't tell Trish —" Julia whipped her head around when she heard Tom's nervous laugh, and saw Nich-olas and her brother and another man com-ing out the side door of the pavilion. "Darn," she muttered, slumping down in the seat.

"Jules, what are you doing?" Jerilynn asked, gawking at her.

Julia kept her eyes trained on the men by peeking through the chair's slats, and started backing across the green the mo-

135

ment they turned away as Nicholas gestured toward the summit. "It's going to take me a month of Sundays before I can face Nicholas after what happened at the house," Julia explained as she darted a glance at where she was going before looking back at the men still facing the summit. "The guy lugged all my stuff out in *trash bags*," she growled, knowing Jerilynn would understand, since the girl's home situation had been even worse before she'd run off and married Tom. "Tell my brother I'm really happy for him. For both of you."

Julia straightened when she reached the trees and pointed at her still-gawking sister-in-law. "And you stop worrying about embarrassing Tom and enjoy your dinner at Aeolus's," she continued in a loud whisper. "You're beautiful, Jerilynn. You get flustered, you just shoot Nicholas one of your pixie smiles, and he'll forget what he was even talking about. Oh, and don't panic when you see they don't have prices on the menu. Get the surf 'n' turf. I hear it's delicious. I'll be in touch," she finished, giving a wave as she turned and disappeared into the trees.

CHAPTER SEVEN

Nicholas was quickly coming to the conclusion that it was easier to mount a war campaign than it was to romantically pursue Julia Campbell. The woman was living and working practically under his nose, and yet he couldn't seem to get close enough to even talk to her — the irony not lost on him that he wasn't exactly a conversationalist. Hell, he was seriously thinking of ambushing her while she was cleaning her cot—

The explosion of pain, followed by the realization more was coming, made Nicholas take a decidedly stupid swing in retaliation, only to have his legs kicked out from under him, sending him sprawling onto his back with a curse vile enough to make his opponent drop down beside him with a laugh.

"I've had more satisfying battles with *Henry,*" Mac said, also gasping for breath as they both lay staring up at the roof of the massive cavern. "Is there a reason you're fighting like a ten-year-old boy? Because I'm fairly certain the last time I was able to knock you on your ass so easily was . . ." Mac suddenly sat up, his eyes narrowing. ". . . was when your mind was back in bed with some . . . I believe it was that fair-haired Teutonic noblewoman. What was her name? Bertilda?"

"Bertilla," Nicholas growled, carefully poking the lump over his left ear. "And I was distracted because she'd just told me she was pregnant."

Mac flopped on his back again. "You barely escaped that one, did you not?" He turned his head and grinned. "Didn't the lady have the disposition of a . . . harpy seal?"

"First," Nicholas said on a hiss as he sat up, "she was no lady, as I subsequently discovered when *four* men claimed the child was theirs." He rolled to his knees and used a grunt to propel himself to his feet. "And secondly," he added, extending his hand down to Mac, "*you* introduced us."

Mac pulled his hand back in midreach. "I thought you two were perfect for each other," the wizard muttered, getting himself to his feet, then grinning as he straightened. "Seeing how she never shut up and you're quieter than all your cats put together." He sobered when Nicholas crouched in preparation to attack, and raised his hands. "Wait. I believe we should discuss *today's* distraction before I knock you on your ass again." He arched a regal brow. "What sort of lady trouble are you having this time?"

Nicholas straightened. "What makes you think I'm having lady trouble?"

"Do I look like I was born yesterday? The only times I've ever managed to best you without getting several of my teeth loosened in the process, a woman was involved. So what's this one's name? Do I know her?"

"There can't be a woman involved if I can't even get close to her."

"Who?"

"Julia Campbell."

"The Julia Campbell you *kissed* within half an hour of meeting her?"

"How do you know I — Olivia," Nicholas growled as he crouched again. "By the gods, women love to talk."

"Having someone to tell secrets to is one of the benefits of marriage," Mac said, "which you would know if you stopped being so damned self-contained long enough to find a wife." He sobered again. "Would you care for some advice, Nicholas?"

"Thanks, but I'd rather not hear advice

on women from a man who wanted his sister to marry an idiot."

"I wanted Carolina to be happy."

Nicholas straightened again. "Lina's so happy, she's glowing."

"She's glowing because she's pregnant," Mac snapped as he in turn crouched to attack. "And *unmarried.* And if MacKeage doesn't put a ring on her finger before she starts showing, I'm going to personally make sure this is the *only* child he sires."

"You know, I never realized what a sore loser you are," Nicholas said with a laugh, lunging without the prerequisite crouch when Mac straightened in surprise. He slammed into the wizard with the entire force of his weight, sending them both into the dark, subterranean pool of seawater.

"Poseidon's teeth!" Mac bellowed when he surfaced, which he followed with a wild swing — which found only air when Nicholas dove again. "What did you do that for?" the wizard growled when Nicholas resurfaced.

He shrugged. "I thought it was something a ten-year-old would do."

Mac scrubbed his face with his hands and, despite the water only being slightly above forty degrees, started floating on his back. "Mother will be impressed when she sees the mess you've made of us."

Not being a true Atlantean, Nicholas swam to the ledge and pulled himself out of the frigid water, then grabbed his shirt and wiped his face. "They're arriving over a week early, aren't they?" he asked, unbuckling his belt and peeling off his wet pants. "I thought they weren't coming until just before Olivia's Thanksgiving holiday."

Nicholas heard Mac sigh. "Olivia contacted them yesterday and asked if they couldn't come now, as she's in desperate need of Mother's help."

"Ah, yes," Nicholas said, crumpling up his pants to wring them out. "I guess Rana would be the one I'd call if my director of special events suddenly ran off to Fiji without warning." He grinned. "Do you suppose Olivia will give me a raise for not making her have to look for a new director of security as well?"

Mac lifted his head to glare at him. "Why would you want a raise if you can't even remember to *cash* your paychecks? As for that resort in Fiji, I hope the bastards know that stealing my wife's event planner just bought them a seven-year plague of sand fleas," he muttered, finally swimming to shore and climbing out of the water. "Back to your woman trouble. My *advice*," Mac said as he snagged his shirt off a ledge and started wiping down his chest, "is that you refrain from calling Julia a walking disaster." He grinned. "At least to her face."

Nicholas shook out his pants and started putting them on. "Is there nothing Olivia doesn't tell you?"

"Sorry, my friend, but apparently lying in bed sharing the high points of the day is considered foreplay to women." Mac stopped wiping and scowled. "And not talking is apparently the signal it's time to go to *sleep.*"

Nicholas stilled with his pants halfway up his thighs. "You're not serious."

The wizard shook his head. "Women equate communicating with intimacy, Nicholas. You're going to have to *talk* to Julia if you want to woo her. And when you do, try compliments instead of baiting her."

"I called her a walking disaster to get the defeated look out of her eyes — which worked, I might add."

"By the gods, you're a horse's ass. It's a short-lived victory, because all she'll remember is the insult."

Nicholas buckled his belt with a sigh. "It would appear I keep seeing Julia at her worst — or rather, what *she* sees as her worst."

"And what do you see?"

"A lovely lady who's strong and resilient, and who's also too proud to accept help from anyone."

"Sometimes pride is a woman's only defense," Mac said softly. "And judging from what Olivia told me after Saturday's little incident, Julia has every reason not to trust anyone — especially men."

"Why? What did Olivia say?"

Mac slipped on his shirt. "Do I look like a gossiping woman? If you truly are interested in Julia, then maybe you should stop approaching her like an opponent you wish to conquer. You're not running Genghis Khan to ground this time, Nicholas."

"I'm not trying to annihilate Julia; I'm merely trying to get her in my bed."

Mac arched a brow. "For *merely* pleasure?"

"I can't know that," Nicholas snapped, "if I can't even get near her." Since they'd stripped to just their pants to do battle, Nicholas sat down and pulled his socks from his boots. "For all I know, Julia is completely turned off men."

Mac sat down beside him and also started dressing his feet. "I've seen you take in defensively aggressive cats even a saint would walk past," he said quietly, "and turn them into pussycats. Was Solomon not such a wretch when you found him?"

Nicholas stopped lacing his boot and grinned. "Sol's no pussycat; he's a beast with an attitude."

"Like his mentor?" Mac said with a chuckle, only to sober again. "Then use your magic touch on Julia instead of seeing her as a conquest."

"And how do you know how I've been conducting my pursuit?"

"I know *you.* Except for being completely blind when it comes to my sister and your cats, you view everything as victory or defeat."

"This coming from a man who pursued women across every continent over tens of centuries," Nicholas drawled, "until a twenty-first-century mere slip of a lonely widow finally called your bluff by calling your *daddy.*" He got to his feet and grinned down at his scowling friend. "I was there when Titus got that call, by the way. And if I remember correctly, Olivia rattled *him* so badly that he had your poor mother standing on Inglenook's doorstep at the crack of dawn the very next morning."

Mac stood up, Nicholas presumed, to better glare at him. "Mother didn't mind using the magic to get here because she was anxious to meet Henry."

"She was suddenly more anxious to meet the woman her son was calling *marita,*" Nicholas countered, stifling a grin at the prospect that if he couldn't beat Mac today, he could at least prick his temper. "Even though you had yet to tell your *wife* you'd married her several days earlier."

Mac stepped closer. "At least I had the sense to pursue a woman who wasn't a walking disaster."

"No, according to your sister, Olivia was the mouse that roared," Nicholas said as he suddenly reached out and snagged Mac's shoulders. He dropped onto his back and sent the surprised wizard sailing over him, then lay grinning up at the roof of the cave as Mac's shouted curse ended abruptly with a splash. But Nicholas scrambled to his feet when the massive subterranean pool suddenly began frothing with geysers of seawater spewing several fathoms into the air, the noise drowning out his laughter when a metal behemoth lifted the once again cursing wizard out of the water as it surfaced.

"By the gods," Mac shouted as he scrambled to stand upright on the vessel now dwarfing its cavernous hiding spot deep inside Whisper Mountain. "I swear I will —" The rest of the mighty theurgist's threat

145

was lost to the jets of steam that suddenly shot out of several valves, one of which sent Mac scrambling to safety with a startled yelp before he could once again stand glaring down at Nicholas.

A small door opened on the giant underwater vessel with a hiss of pressurized air just before a gangplank emerged, followed by Titus Oceanus — making Nicholas rush over with a curse of his own when he saw the elder theurgist carrying Rana.

"I'm fine," Rana assured him as Titus stepped onto the ledge. "Or I will be as soon as I feel solid ground beneath me again." She turned and gave her husband a tight smile. "I swear I don't know whether to feel cherished or insulted when you start coddling me. You know I get a silly bellyache every time you use the magic to get us here in a hurry, and you know I'm fine within minutes of — Maximilian, what on earth are you doing on top of our ship?" she called up to her son. "And why are you soaked?"

"Nicholas was being a *sore loser*." Mac then slid down the curved side of the vessel, landed with a grunt when he bounced off the wall of the cave, and walked over and extended his arms. "Let me take her," he said to his father.

Nicholas shoved him out of the way. "You're wet. I'll take her."

Titus stepped back, giving them both a regal glare. "I believe I'm still capable of looking after my wife."

Rana leaned her head onto Titus's neck — Nicholas assumed to hide her smile. "Actually, I believe I'm still capable of looking after myself. Sweetheart," she added, her smile widening when Titus muttered something under his breath as he set her on a large rock — then immediately sat beside her and wrapped an arm around her shoulders.

"So," Rana said, smoothing down her shirt with a deep sigh as her gaze traveled over Nicholas's wet pants and her son's wet pants, shirt, *and* boots, "what were you two gentlemen discussing that ended with the both of you taking a swim?"

"I was trying to explain to our illustrious warrior here," Mac began before Nicholas could, "that kissing a woman within thirty minutes of meeting her and calling her a walking disaster to her face is probably not the best way to begin a romantic pursuit."

"*Now* who's acting ten?" Nicholas snapped, even as he felt his neck heat up when Rana's brows lifted in surprise.

"You've begun a romantic pursuit, Nicholas? Of a wo—" She suddenly smoothed down her shirt again. "Yes, well, how wonderful. Is she anyone I know?"

"He's dallying with the help," Mac answered before Nicholas could. "But you may know her, as she takes care of the cottages. Her name is Julia Campbell."

Rana shook her head, although she was still looking at Nicholas, her expressive brown eyes speculative. "No, I enjoy tending our cottage myself. So, Nicholas, you've finally found a lady who's lovely enough to pursue . . . romantically?"

Whatever Mac had intended to answer for him came out a grunt instead when Nicholas drove his elbow into the wizard's ribs and stepped forward. "As a matter of fact," he said, extending his hand to Rana, "I have. Which I wish to speak with you about," he continued, tucking her arm through his when she stood up, then leading her toward the large metal door in the side of the cavern. "As I prefer taking advice from someone who *knows* what they're talking about," he said over his shoulder, "rather than someone who needed magic tricks and an epic stunt to catch his lady's interest."

Rana pulled him to a stop when they stepped into the tunnel that ran from the fiord up to the summit of Whisper Mountain. "I must say, you've caught *my* interest." She looked in both directions, then up at him. "Are we riding or climbing a million stairs?"

Nicholas turned them toward the fiord. "You have a choice of riding the tired old horse your son brought you or the really fast boat I brought." He bent to whisper in her ear when they emerged into the sunlight as Mac and Titus came up behind them. "I'll let you drive."

"Oh, Nicholas," Rana said with a musical laugh, pulling him past the horses toward the fiord. "You always know the perfect cure for a bellyache."

CHAPTER EIGHT

Julia straightened when she heard the sound again, and even stopped breathing to listen as she looked around the sun-dappled old-growth forest. Did lynx hang out in pine groves? Or those curious, sneaky coyotes? Only it hadn't been a twig snapping or an animal grunting she'd heard, but more like a muffled *thwack.* Sort of mechanical, but muted. Distant. Yeah, it probably wasn't even nearby, Julia decided, knowing that sound traveled strangely on the side of a mountain riddled with cliffs and ravines. Or it might only be the breeze rubbing branches together.

Then again, it could be the wind turbines she'd heard about — but had never seen — that supplied most of Nova Mare's electricity. The turbines were rumored to be some fancy new design that didn't have to rise above the ridgelines to be efficient, and Julia had heard they were hidden on this side of the mountain someplace. The entire resort ran on wind and solar and geothermal energy, making it completely self-sufficient as well as eco-friendly — which, now that she thought about it, made heating an outdoor swimming pool all winter not such an outrageous luxury. It also explained the massive number of pipes running through all the granite corridors.

Julia went back to gathering the explosion of pinecones littering the forest floor, unable to believe her luck. Well, luck and a little reconnaissance. But she'd finally had time to really explore the facilities now that she was actually living up here, and she'd been blown away by the view from the gazebo that sat on the windswept ledge a short hike up from the conference pavilion. But where most of Nova Mare's buildings faced south and east overlooking Bottomless, the gazebo had a three-hundred-and-sixty-degree view, including all the way into Canada.

It had been from there that she'd spotted the stand of tall pines halfway down the western side of Whisper. And since she didn't have to be at work until ten o'clock, and she only had a three-minute commute now, she'd gotten up with the sun, grabbed a handful of sacks, and made the trek out here this morning.

It had been very kind of Nicholas to leave a note on her apartment door yesterday offering to take her to a pine grove that he knew of *across* the fiord on her next day off, but she'd sent him a note very politely declining via the front desk again, as she really didn't want to spend an entire day with a man being kind to her out of pity.

And besides, someone at the marina would see them together when she got in his boat, and that person would tell *everyone,* and before she knew it some busybody would feel compelled to tell the town's most eligible bachelor that he really shouldn't be seen in public with the town slut. "Oh, and did you know she's also the daughter of the town drunk?" Julia muttered as she stuffed a fistful of cones in the sack.

Nope, she'd already humiliated herself enough to Mr. No Last Name.

And if his stupid cats broke into her apartment one more time, she was going to shave them bald, which would certainly stop them from strolling around the resort like they owned the place, wouldn't it? Well, at least until their hair grew back. Yeah, and maybe she'd take all that shaved hair, add it to all the hair she was still vacuuming up, and make Nicholas a big fat pillow to rest his big *kind* head on. "Size matters," she growled, bending to grab the last of the cones in the immediate area. "Yeah, well, not everyone spends all their time day-dreaming about being pulled into your big strong arms and kissed until their toes curl. Some of us have better things to do, like earn a living any —"

Julia heard the sharp *thwack* at the same time something slammed into her backside with enough force to knock her to her knees. Her scream of surprise apparently drowning out the second *thwack,* she was hit again in the head hard enough to send her sprawling, this time the shock freezing her scream in her throat.

A hunter was shooting at her!

No, the entire mountain was closed to hunting, so it had to be a *poacher.*

"You're dead!" a man shouted — sounding way too happy about it. "But if you still don't think so, maybe a steel blade on your throat will make you a believer," he added, his voice moving closer.

Heaven help her, he *knew* he'd shot a person and was coming to finish the job!

Julia started to belly-crawl toward some bushes, but went perfectly still when she heard the man laugh at something another man said to him. There were *two* of them, and they were getting closer. Realizing she'd never make it to the bushes, Julia looked around for something to defend herself and reached for a rock the size of her fist — only to still again when she saw her glove covered in blood. It was then she realized the whole left side of her hair felt wet and sticky. She grabbed the rock and pulled it beneath her, reached for a branch and tucked it down along her right side, then closed her eyes and went limp just as the man spoke again — this time nearly to her.

"Give it up, Rowan," he said with a chuckle. "Your adage that old age and treachery overcome youth and — Sweet Zeus, it's a woman!"

Julia erupted the moment she felt his hand touch her shoulder, rolling over and striking the man in the face with her fist holding the rock at the same time she snapped the stick into his groin as he crouched over her. She continued rolling away as he momentarily froze before crumpling into a fetal position with a groan, and jumped to her feet and hurled the rock at the other man's shocked face.

Hearing the simultaneous *thunk* and shout of surprise as she spun away, she ran down the ridge toward the dense forest. For the love of God, she'd been shot! Twice! Having heard there usually was very little pain with trauma, which explained why her head and backside only stung, Julia figured she could keep going on adrenaline alone — assuming she didn't bleed to death before she made it back to the resort.

"Get her before she's lost," one of them said in a strangled hiss. "Or *we're* dead."

Julia heard footsteps racing after her. "Lady, stop," the man called out over the sound of snapping branches. "We mean you no harm."

Yeah, right. They'd shot her and intended to finish her off with a knife! She ran darting through the trees despite knowing every beat of her pounding heart was pumping out precious blood, until she was suddenly jerked nearly off her feet when a branch snagged the pocket on her fleece. She unzipped the light jacket and frantically shrugged free, then took off again at a ninety-degree angle for another hundred yards before ducking behind a large tree to look back. She saw the man stop and scan the woods to his left, and Julia realized he was expecting her to flee toward Nova Mare.

Not daring to even touch her wounds for fear she'd faint, despite the slowly oozing blood making her hair stick to her face and the sting in her backside making her want to rub them, Julia started running along the ridge *away* from the resort. She just had to hold on long enough to get behind them and head up the mountain to the summit, which should be the opposite direction they'd be looking for her. Then she'd find Nicholas and tell him that poachers were shooting employees in his supposedly secure woods — just before she humiliated herself again by bleeding to death at his feet.

Nicholas stared down at the three empty sacks in his hand, undecided if his heart was pounding so hard from having spent the last hour running through the woods trying not to be shot, or if he was having a heart attack at the thought of Julia believing men were actually trying to kill her. Micah finally staggered to his feet, carefully tugging on his pant leg as he straightened, and Nicholas stepped forward and drove his fist into the idiot's face, sending him sprawling onto his back with another black eye to match the one Julia had given him. "That was for taking a shot without identifying your target," he growled. "Now get up and let me show you what I think of your letting a woman bring you to your knees."

Micah wisely stayed on the ground.

Nicholas turned his glare on Dante, who

immediately stepped back with his hands raised in supplication, the cut on his cheek still oozing blood. "She can't be hurt badly, sir. She's obviously light on her feet to have slipped away so quickly, which is why I chose to find you instead of chasing after her." He used one of his still-raised hands to gesture east and actually grinned. "She's probably already back at the resort."

Rowan beat Nicholas to the punch with a powerful blow to the jaw, sending Dante sprawling beside Micah. "Terror overrides pain, you ass," Rowan growled, bending down to pull the idiot back to his feet.

"Leave them," Nicholas said, tossing the sacks at the two men. "I expect to see those full of cones and sitting in the woodshed in an hour." He then turned and headed in the direction the men said Julia had fled, determined not to roar. "Remind me again why I didn't send you all back to Atlantis after you let Alec MacKeage walk in and out of the resort right under your noses last year?" he said when his second in command fell into step beside him.

Rowan snorted. "Because you would have had to send yourself back with us, as I recall he rubbed *your* nose in it, too. Sir."

Figuring Julia didn't need to see a half-naked man running her to ground, Nicholas pulled his T-shirt off his belt without breaking stride, took off his rifle and slipped on the shirt, then slung the weapon back over his shoulder. Of all the places she could have found to collect pinecones, why in Hades here? Nobody ever roamed the west side of Whisper because the terrain was too rugged, which is exactly why he and his men used these woods for their war games.

And just how had she planned to carry four bags of cones back, anyway?

"Here," Rowan said, veering to the left just as Nicholas also spotted the pale pink garment hanging from a branch by its pocket.

He took it from Rowan and ran his finger over the red smears on the collar. "She was hit in the head or neck," Nicholas said roughly. "Damn, that had to have stung."

"Micah is certain he also hit her in the lower back," Rowan quietly added. He began studying the area. "It says a lot about Julia for how she kept her wits enough to surprise two . . . warriors. Here," he said, scuffing the ground with his feet. He lifted his gaze to the north, then looked at Nicholas and grinned. "Dante lost her because she headed *away* from the resort."

Nicholas felt his heart slowing to a steadier rhythm as he looked north and then up the ridge. "She's a lot smarter than people give her credit for." He sighed, trying to dissipate more of his anger — although it did nothing to stem the heat radiating off him like an erupting volcano. "I'll go it alone from here," he said, handing his rifle to Rowan. "I don't want her further terrorized by having two men coming after her."

"Once they've gathered the cones, I'll see that Julia's kindling is also split and stacked in the woodshed," Rowan said as he headed up the ridge. "Assuming our two elite idiots can manage a hatchet without maiming themselves. And maybe I'll give them a nice long lecture while I watch, on how *old age and treachery* — and one cunning woman, apparently — *always overcome youth and skill.*" He turned to Nicholas with a grin. "Which you would do well to remember when you catch up with your Julia."

"She's not mine yet," Nicholas muttered to himself, tearing off in the direction she'd gone the moment Rowan was out of sight. Hell, he'd be lucky to be in possession of his own manhood when Olivia learned what his warriors had done to one of her employees this morning.

Nicholas focused his senses on the desperate energy he was chasing and, although he was working himself back into a fine rage, couldn't help being impressed by Julia's cunning. And at her courage for defending herself against two powerful men with nothing more than a rock, a stick, and a quick mind. But having learned something about a woman's thought process during his years shadowing Lina, he had a worry this false victory might encourage Julia to be even more reckless should she find herself in a truly threatening situation in the future. Because the truth was, if Dante had gone after her instead of coming to find him, the man would have caught her within minutes.

Nicholas knew the moment Julia realized he was closing in on her, as he felt the desperation trailing in her wake turn to terror. He thought of calling out to let her know it was him, but understanding that terror played tricks on the senses, he feared her flight might turn frenzied and she'd run off a cliff. By the gods, Micah would be ready to *swim* back to Atlantis by the time he was through with the idiot.

Nicholas caught up with Julia just as she was trying to scale a waist-high ledge, his gut tightening at her frantic whimper when she glanced over her shoulder and spotted him, lost her grip, and tumbled down the steep incline below the ledge. But he couldn't help being impressed again when she sprang to her feet holding a stout branch and actually charged him.

Nicholas stopped and prepared to take the blow, only to see Julia suddenly toss the stick away and throw *herself* at him instead, making him have to sweep her off her feet when her legs buckled. "Oh, thank . . . God . . . it's you," she rasped between panting sobs, clinging to him. "Men chasing me. Two. Sh-shot me. Poachers. I'm . . . bleeding . . . to death."

Nicholas dropped to his knees, but it wasn't until he tried to smooth back the hair stuck to her face that he saw she'd fainted. He knelt cradling her, Julia's racing heart pounding against his, and sighed at the realization this likely wasn't going to help his romantic pursuit any. He rose to his feet, settled her comfortably against his chest, and started for home, his mood somewhat lighter when he remembered Julia's first instinct upon realizing who he was had been to run *to* him instead of away.

Julia slowly awakened to the kind of ache that suggested she remain motionless while she decided which hurt worse, her head or backside or legs, only to gasp and try to sit up when she remembered *why* she hurt.

"Easy, you're okay," a deep, calming voice

161

said as strong, gentle hands held her down. She opened her eyes to see Nicholas smiling at her. "Get your bearings before you sit up. You're okay, Julia," he repeated.

"No, I'm not. I was shot. Twice." She looked around and gasped again. "I'm not in a hospital," she said, struggling against his hold — only to go perfectly still when she realized she was . . . that there was nothing but *air* beneath her. "Wh-where am I?" she whispered, slowly bringing her gaze back to Nicholas — who was still smiling, still gently holding her down.

"You're in my home," he said, releasing her but leaving his hands hovering over her shoulders, "in my sleeping bag on the floor of my living room."

Julia turned just her head to look at his . . . floor again and realized it was made of glass. Granted, it appeared to be really thick glass, but the entire end of his house was jutting out beyond a jagged ledge with nothing but air beneath it for over a hundred feet. Add to that an entire two-story wall of windows, as well as the front third of each of the side walls also being nothing but glass, and Julia felt like she was literally floating.

Wait; instead of being blown away by his home, wasn't she supposed to be bleeding to death? "Um, did I tell you I was shot?

Twice?" Finally finding the nerve to touch the side of her head, she pulled her hand away and looked at the dried red flakes on her fingers, then held them out to him. "S-see, that's blood."

"No, it's paint," he said quietly, turning away and reaching for something beside her. She heard water dripping, like he was wringing out a cloth. "You were shot with a red paintball. Twice," he said with a grin.

"Why?" she snapped, deciding she needed to be angry so he wouldn't know how embarrassed she was that she'd fainted from . . . blood loss.

She wasn't sure, but she thought one side of his mouth twitched, like he was fighting a grin. "We were practicing," he said, as if that explained everything.

"Practicing what, shooting innocent people in the head with paintballs?"

Yup, that was definitely a grin trying to escape. "No, practicing how not to get *our-selves* shot." All hints of amusement vanished. "I'm sorry, Julia. Micah mistook you for another one of my men, as he wasn't expecting anyone but the four of us to be in those woods this morning."

Julia turned her head to look out at Bottomless so he wouldn't see what she thought of being mistaken for one of his men.

163

He gently clasped her chin and turned her back to face him. "I'm sorry," he repeated. "Do you have a headache? And your . . . backside?" He let a small grin escape. "I know how much those tiny paintballs sting."

"N-no, I'm okay. In fact," she said, pulling her chin free and trying to sit up again, "I feel so well, I think I'll go home."

His hand returned to her shoulder, but to help her sit up rather than hold her down, and then to steady her when she suddenly swayed. "Easy," he murmured. "You were run ragged by the time I found you."

"No, I'm dizzy because I'm dangling over a cliff," she growled, closing her eyes to see if that helped.

"Sorry," he said with a chuckle as he dropped the wet rag onto her lap. "Don't panic, I'm only going to pull you back."

Julia snapped open her eyes when she suddenly felt herself moving and grabbed his shoulder as he slowly dragged his sleeping bag — with her still in it — toward the center of the room, not stopping until she was over solid . . . rock. Okay, that was *slightly* better. At least now she didn't feel like she was about to fall hundreds of feet. She picked up the cloth and held it to her face so he wouldn't see her cheeks were about to blister, and didn't lower it again until she felt more than heard him stand up. He walked over to where she'd been sitting and picked up a . . .

Julia lifted the cloth to her nose and sniffed when she realized he was using what looked like a cat litter box for a wash basin. Okay, the cloth smelled of balsam, but she wasn't reassured enough to wash her face with it, so she gingerly started rubbing her head where she'd been shot . . . by a paintball.

Wait; hadn't her hair been braided?

"I undid your braid," he said when he saw her gather her tangled hair in her fist. He set the basin of soapy water down beside her. "I was worried it might be pulling on the bump on your head." He crouched down and grinned at her again. "The braid was mostly undone and full of leaves and twigs," he said, gesturing at the small mess of forest matter littering the floor hanging out over the cliff. "I'm afraid I may have created more tangles in the process."

He'd run his fingers through her hair? While she'd been unconscious?

Oh, she hoped this was a really bad dream.

Julia lifted the cloth back to her face, not caring if it was soaked in cat pee. She really, really needed to get out of here, preferably while she still had some dignity left. For crying out loud, had he carried her all the way here? His house must be at least a couple of miles from where she'd been collecting pinecones; wouldn't it have taken him at least a couple of hours to carry her that —

"Oh no," she said with a gasp. "I'm late for work!" Julia tried to get up, but was stopped by one of his big strong hands again.

"No, you're not. I called Bev and told her you wouldn't be in today."

She reared away. "You called Beverly? But she's going to wonder why you . . . Why I didn't . . . *You* called her?"

"She won't think it strange the director of security made the call, since I told her you'd had a small accident."

Julia found the cloth and started to lift it to her face again, but Nicholas pulled it away, sloshed it in the basin — turning the water red — then wrung it out and handed it back to her. She immediately pressed it against her face again even as she wondered where he bought his soap, because it smelled an awful lot like Regan's goat soap.

"Are you thirsty?" he asked as she heard him straighten and walk away.

She lowered the cloth, realizing she was pretty thirsty. "Yes, thank you," she said, only to flinch when something brushed up against her.

Big Cat folded itself around her as it rubbed its head against her raised arm, then settled the front half of its body down on her apparently too-small lap and curled its claws into the sleeping bag covering her thighs. Its two buddies made an appearance, the smaller eerie gray one — its eyes even more orange in the sunlight — deciding the indent in the sleeping bag between her calves looked like a really nice spot for a nap, into which it settled and started purring. White Cat — that Big Cat and Small Cat had brought along the second time they'd broken into the apartment — was apparently content to use the end of the bag for a bed and one of her feet for a pillow.

Julia flinched again, this time with a gasp, when two more cats — a delicate-looking spotted one and an everyday gray tabby — sauntered over as quiet as . . . cats, sat down on the glass floor at the very edge of the cliff, and stared unblinking at her.

Nicholas had *five* cats?

With the cloth still poised inches from her face, Julia slowly looked around to see if any others might be lurking nearby, and realized there wasn't any furniture — which likely explained why she was a cat magnet, since she was occupying the only soft spot in the entire house. Which was also probably why they kept breaking into what they still considered *their* apartment, ending up on her and Trisha's beds.

Five cats. Nicholas must own stock in several lint roller companies, she decided, as she'd never seen so much as a single cat hair on his clothes. Julia sighed and ran the cloth over her face again, guessing the man was only a *chick* magnet.

She heard an approaching chuckle. "I see you've met some of my friends," the devil himself said as he crouched down beside her.

Julia lowered the cloth to find him holding a tumbler — which looked exactly like the two in her cupboard — filled nearly to the brim with water. "Some?" she repeated, taking the water and looking around again. "There's *more*?"

"One more — Gilgamesh. Gilly must be out hunting." Nicholas took the cloth from her, then used it to gesture at the tumbler in her other hand. "Drink, before your muscles start cramping from dehydration."

Julia dutifully took a sip because she really didn't want anything else to hurt. "Um . . . so you guys were running through the woods this morning trying to shoot one another with paintballs?" she asked, just before taking another sip of water, because she really was very thirsty.

He nodded as he sat down on the floor beside her, which apparently was the signal for the other two cats to walk over and curl up on his lap. He grinned at her. "Tom told me he's looking forward to that part of his training, as he can't imagine getting paid to engage in a sport he used to pay money to play. Apparently there's a paintball course a few miles south of Turtleback Station that he and some of his high school classmates used to frequent."

"How come you hired Tom as a security guard?" she asked, staring down at the tumbler in her hand. "I mean, I love that he doesn't have to work at the mill anymore, and he's really proud and everything." She looked up. "But I don't understand why you sought Tom out. He's not exactly big and burly, like most of your security guards."

"Because I was impressed by his actions Saturday."

"You were impressed he got knocked out cold?"

"He *tried,* Julia. Tom ran upstairs to confront a drunken man nearly twice his size, even knowing that man was armed with a double-edged felling ax. And that told me he's someone I want on my team." Nicholas grinned again. "I was almost tempted to offer you a position as well."

Julia took a sip of water, uncertain if she'd just been complimented or insulted.

"You needn't worry," he continued. "Two months from now your brother won't be the one leaving an altercation with a concussion."

She frowned. "How does running around in the woods shooting one another with paintballs teach a guy how not to get knocked out cold in a fistfight?"

"Our war games are only a small part of our training," he said as he absently stroked the ecstatically purring, bronze-spotted cat on his lap — which sounded in stereo, as the gray cat wedged between Julia's calves was also purring. "Tom will also learn how to defuse a situation," he continued, "*before* it becomes an altercation."

Big Cat was starting to get a little heavy on her thighs, making Julia realize her legs were going to sleep. Then again, maybe it was the paintball-size bruise on her backside that was making everything below her waist numb.

Had Nicholas really carried her all the way here?

Did she dare ask?

"Um . . . what about the two guys who shot me?" she asked instead. She actually smiled. "Can I borrow one of your paintball guns and take some free shots at them — without them wearing any protective gear?" But then she frowned again. "Come to think of it, I don't remember them wearing much of anything despite it being frosty out. Not even goggles. Aren't you afraid somebody will lose an eye or something?"

"I believe that's the motivation not to get shot." He sighed when she refused to return his grin. "We're not playing a game, Julia; we're training. Ducking paintballs keeps us sharp." He turned away and dipped the cloth into the soapy water again. "As for letting you take some free shots at them, I'm afraid that when Olivia finds out what happened today, they'll both likely be dismissed."

"Are you serious?" she whispered.

He said nothing, merely wringing out the cloth.

"But it was a stupid mistake, and I wasn't really hurt." She shook her head. "I won't be responsible for their getting fired."

"You could just as easily have been a resort guest."

"We're not telling Olivia," she growled.

171

"It's half my fault for not wearing blaze orange in the woods in November." She gestured angrily when he merely looked at her, his expression unreadable. "Make them do a hundred push-ups every day for a month or something." She snatched the cloth away from him and pressed it to her cheeks. "Because if you tell Olivia, I swear I'll deny it ever happened," she said from the safety of the cloth — not stupid enough to threaten to call him a liar to his face.

And she wasn't quite brave enough to peek, either, when he remained silent for so long that she actually flinched when he stood up and said, "Works for me."

She lowered the cloth when she heard him walk away, and blew out a silent sigh of relief. She might want to pepper those two guys with stinging paintballs, but she really couldn't live with herself if they got fired.

Julia stared out the windows that made it appear as if she were in an airplane. Who built their home hanging out over a cliff, anyway? Didn't Nicholas know this area had *earthquakes*? Jeesh, the house would careen down the mountain like an Olympic bobsled if it ever shook loose — likely with its owner in it.

Had he really carried her all the way here? Heaven help her, she'd probably drooled all over his T-shirt — that she couldn't help notice clung to his muscles like a second skin. Julia pressed the cloth back to her cheeks, wondering if she couldn't have embarrassed herself any more ignobly.

And just when had she turned into a walking disaster?

Oh, that's right; it had all started when she'd come face-to-chest with a man who turned women — divorcées in particular — into chicks. Except *she* apparently turned into a walking disaster whenever she got within ten feet of Mr. Magnet.

Julia dropped the cloth when he suddenly spoke from right beside her, having walked up as quietly as his cats. "I started the downstairs shower running and hung one of my shirts on the door for you. There's a washer and dryer in the closet, so you might as well wash your clothes while you're at it."

For as much as she was . . . enjoying herself, that was definitely her cue to leave. "I'll take a shower at my apartment."

"Seeing the mess you made of my bed," he said, his sky-blue eyes crinkling with his grin, "I prefer you clean up before getting in my truck."

"I'll come back and wash your truck *and* your sleeping bag," she growled, pushing back the edge of the bag — effectively dislodging Big Cat with it — then sliding her legs from under Small Cat and slowly getting to her feet. "Better yet, make the guys who shot me wash them," she muttered, forcing herself not to rub her backside as she walked on numb legs toward what looked like an outside door as five cats rushed to get there ahead of her — only to have Nicholas beat all of them.

"Are you always this stubborn, Julia?" he asked, folding his arms on his chest.

"Are you always this bossy, Nicholas?"

"Yes. A shower will soothe the sting, and you need to get some heat on your muscles soon. Because if you think a paintball hurts, wait until your legs cramp up."

Well, the man probably did know something about preventing muscles from cramping, seeing as how he owned some pretty impressive ones. And honestly, she really just wanted to have herself a good cry, and a hot steamy shower was a pretty private place for something like that, wasn't it? Because she was fairly certain that once she was all cried out, she'd be able to walk home without *looking* like a walking disaster.

Well, except for the bright red splat of paint on her butt.

Nicholas watched Julia silently turn away and walk through the kitchen and down the short hall, surprised she'd given in without a fight. He dropped his gaze to see his cats staring after her until the bathroom door closed, after which they stared up at him. "I agree," he said softly. "The lady does look lovely in our new home."

Nicholas went into the kitchen with a sigh of relief, pleased that Julia hadn't wanted his men to get in trouble. He opened the fridge and grinned at the notion that she truly wasn't afraid of him, remembering how she'd boldly threatened to call him a liar if he told Olivia what had happened this morning. And she obviously liked his cats, inviting them to use her for a bed — including Sol, the heavy lug.

"Still, you better not make pests of yourselves to her," he told the small herd gathered at his feet to also peer in the fridge. He took out the fixings for an omelet, then closed the door and looked down with a threatening glare. "And our deal also applies to Julia; I'd better not see any cat hair clinging to her, either."

Bastet immediately gave one of her soft

chirps of agreement, Ajax stared up at him blankly, Eos tilted her head and blinked her round orange eyes, and Snowball rubbed up against his leg. Solomon, apparently not the least bit impressed by the threat, merely walked down the hall and sat facing the bathroom door.

Nicholas placed everything on the counter and went to work making Julia a large, nutritious omelet, deciding his pursuit was finally moving in the right direction. Despite its rocky beginning, he felt this morning had actually turned out well, as they appeared to have had a lovely conversation about . . .

Not about much of anything, he decided with a frown. Well, except for their short discussion about his hiring her brother, a little longer talk about not telling Olivia what had happened, and Julia apparently not being impressed that his house was hanging off a cliff. They'd discussed that amazing feat of engineering, hadn't they?

Nicholas set the large pan on the induction burner to start heating up. No, he guessed they hadn't had a conversation after all, as he didn't know any more about Julia than he had before. Well, except that she liked his cats — especially Sol — he thought with a grin as he broke eggs into a bowl.

But then Nicholas frowned as he pulled a

fork out of a drawer, wondering why Julia had answered his invitation to go looking for pinecones across the fiord with a note of her own politely declining. Not asking her in person had been Rana's idea, who had explained that, instead of putting a woman on the spot, giving her a chance to think about a fun day of boating and walking in the woods usually ended with an invitation being accepted.

Nicholas began beating the eggs. Rana might not be the person to seek advice from when he was trying to court a twenty-first-century woman, seeing how she'd been living in pre-prebiblical times when she'd first caught Titus's interest. Maybe he should be asking the younger Mrs. Oceanus instead, as not only was Olivia a contemporary, but she also knew Julia personally. Surely she could —

Solomon came tearing down the hall at the exact same time the other four cats raced toward the stairs leading up to the balcony. Nicholas set down the bowl of eggs with a heavy sigh and headed to his side door. "He was *joking,*" he called toward the balcony. "Theurgists don't make cats pull their chariots. And it's *Romans* who have chariots, anyway," he muttered, opening the door and glaring at Mac.

"It's nice to see you, too," Mac drawled as he walked in, followed by Titus.

Nicholas went back to the kitchen, which was separated from the living room by a large island counter, and poured the eggs into the pan. "You need to explain to my pets that you were joking about hooking them up to a chariot," he said, adding shredded cheese and then pulling a spatula out of the drawer — even as he wondered if Julia had noticed that some of her apartment's cooking utensils were missing.

Then again, she couldn't miss something she didn't know had existed.

"What are you doing home in the middle of the morning?" Mac asked, walking over and watching him carefully fold the eggs onto themselves.

"And why do I hear your shower running if you're out here cooking?" Titus asked, moving to Nicholas's other side to also watch.

"I'm home because I have company, and she's taking a shower while I cook us breakfast." He stifled a grin when that was met with absolute silence. "So if you gentlemen don't mind," he continued, nudging Mac out of the way so he could get down his two stolen plates, "I'd rather you left before she comes out wearing only my shirt and you set my pursuit back to the beginning by embarrassing her."

Mac moved up beside him again as Nicholas slid half the omelet onto one of the plates. "So you've given up on Julia Campbell?" the wizard asked.

Nicholas stopped with the pan poised above the other plate and glared at him. "Exactly who do you think is in the shower?"

Mac picked up the plate containing half the omelet and walked to the sink. "It can't be Julia," he said, gesturing out the window. "As I believe that's her running out your driveway. Although she is wearing your shirt over her clothes."

Nicholas shoved his plate at Titus and crowded Mac out of the way, then looked out the window in time to see Julia sprinting around a curve in his driveway. He closed his eyes and dropped his chin to his chest — his sigh drowned out by the sound of forks hitting plates as his uninvited guests ate his and Julia's breakfast.

"I'm sorry we interrupted your little . . . interlude," Titus said, sounding like he was still chewing. "But it's just as well, as we're here to discuss some trouble that seems to be brewing that might require your . . . expertise."

Nicholas turned to face them. "What's going on?"

His mouth full of omelet, Mac shrugged and swallowed. "We're not exactly sure, but there are rumblings coming from the Teutons."

"More specifically, from the Danube area," Titus added, setting his empty plate on the island counter. He looked around, then wiped his mouth on his sleeve. "It appears they're about to clash with the Romans."

"You're talking the second century BC," Nicholas said, being careful to conceal his surprise. "You can't think to interfere. That would change the course of history." He sighed when the elder theurgist merely arched a brow, knowing he was in for a long conversation, as both Oceanuses had a habit of talking in riddles. "What exactly do you want me to do?"

CHAPTER NINE

Julia turned from locking the door of Foxglove Cottage to find Nicholas standing at the bottom of the steps, his arms folded over his chest, looking . . . unmovable.

"Why did you run off this morning?" he asked quietly.

"You mean as opposed to hanging around to explain to our boss's husband why I was in your house instead of at work?"

His eyes lit up like sunshine reflecting off glacial ice — a sign Julia was coming to recognize meant trouble. "I could have said I invited you to breakfast at my new home."

Julia picked up her cleaning kit and headed down the steps. "Like he'd believe that."

Nicholas moved to block her from getting in her cart — another little habit he had of using his size to get people to . . . cooperate. "Mac heard the shower running and saw the two omelets I'd made, so I explained that you had —"

"Excuse me," she said, pushing past him and sliding into the driver's seat, utterly horrified. He'd told Mac *she* had been in the shower? "I'm already behind in my work," she muttered, shoving the key in its slot to Nicholas's shocked silence. "I'll see you around," she said, giving a wave as she zipped away at the speed of a fleeing turtle.

But once she'd gone far enough to feel certain he wasn't following her, Julia pulled into a scenic turnout on the cart path and dropped her head onto the steering wheel with a groan. Heaven help her, she was starting to feel *pursued,* almost as if Nicholas . . . liked her or something.

But the really scary part was that she was actually starting to like him back.

And that really couldn't happen, Julia decided with another groan. She couldn't be attracted to a man that handsome and confident and sexy, because she wasn't any of those things. Was the guy blind or what?

Julia suddenly sat up. Not blind — brilliant. Poor walking disaster Julia Campbell was the perfect solution to his chick magnet problem. Thanks to her father saying she should be grateful for *any* male attention the night Nicholas had brought her home — and gotten a free kiss without getting his face slapped — the guy knew she wasn't exactly a . . . What was the opposite of a chick? A rooster? Stud?

Yeah, she wasn't exactly a *stud* magnet.

Anyway, Nicholas must have decided they could be seen together having dinner or getting in his boat and disappearing for an entire day, and then he could tell everyone they were *dating* so the women would leave him alone. Because of course she wouldn't complain if he saw her only occasionally, since she'd be so *grateful* for his attention.

Oh yeah, she had his number, all right. Did the man honestly believe she'd let him just — no, wait. Wouldn't that arrangement work pretty well for her, too? It should at least stop Peg from constantly trying to fix her up with one of Duncan's cousins over in Pine Creek. And it wouldn't hurt her reputation any, either, since she'd go from being both stupid and a slut to . . .

Julia dropped her head onto the steering wheel with another groan. No, she really couldn't do that to Nicholas. For as much as he might deserve it for using her to avoid being chased by beautiful, confident, sexy women, she couldn't bring herself to elevate her reputation at the expense of his. And besides, there was still the danger of getting run down by a jealous female coworker.

Nicholas stood with his arms folded and frowned at Julia fleeing, undecided if he was impressed or really very disturbed that she had pushed her way past him as if he were nothing more than a recalcitrant child she no longer wished to deal with. Did the woman have no sense of self-preservation? Sweet Zeus, he'd had angry *gods* back down from him, and Julia had dismissed him with a cheery wave and driven off without a backward glance.

Nicholas shoved his hands in his pockets and started walking toward the common green, wondering if he hadn't completely misread the lady. It was possible Julia truly had no interest in a romantic relationship, even several years after her failed marriage. Which raised the question: Should he regroup and form a new plan of attack, or simply accept defeat and move on?

He stopped and turned to look back up the path. And just when had he ever walked away from a challenge? Hell, most battles — entire wars — were lost but for one final flat-out storming of the castle. And the last time he checked, he still had a full arsenal of weapons, not the least being his willingness to fight dirty. That could mean an ambush, or taking advantage of an opponent's weakness, or simply confusing them until they defeated themselves — and sometimes all three.

And hadn't Julia herself revealed a rather interesting weakness the night he'd eavesdropped on her and Trisha in the church?

Nicholas started walking toward the resort again, his step matching his suddenly lighter mood. It was decided, then; he'd give one final push to capture Julia, and if the lovely lady still rebuffed him after experiencing a much longer taste of passion . . . well, then he *might* concede defeat.

"Hallo, is mijn naam Julia," Julia repeated over the drone of the vacuum cleaner. She stopped in midpush and frowned down at the machine when it suddenly shut off — only to pivot with a yelp when someone called her name.

"Sorry," Olivia said with an apologetic shrug. "I thought pulling the plug would be less scary than walking up and tapping you on the shoulder."

"And getting punched in the nose?" Julia added as she pulled out her earbuds and stuffed them in her pocket beside her MP3 player. "What's up?"

"What were you listening to?"

"Today it's Dutch." Julia took a deep breath when her heart started racing again at Olivia's obvious surprise. "I thought it might be nice to greet Inglenook's guests in their native tongue, so I've been studying the basics of several of the major languages." She gave a crooked smile. "Only the couple from Spain staying in Pine Tassel last week burst out laughing when I apparently told them that a dried shoe was the best thing for starting fires in the hearth."

"Wow, it's obvious you're determined to get that liaison position." Olivia arched a brow. "I went looking for you at your apartment before coming here, because Bev told me Nicholas had called her to say you'd had a small accident."

Feeling her face heat up again, Julia turned away and started winding up the cord on her vacuum cleaner. "I . . . ah, I took a tumble down a hill while I was out looking for pinecones on the west side of Whisper this morning." She stopped and smiled at her frowning boss. "And lucky me," she said brightly, "Nicholas was out training with some of his men. He apparently saw me fall, then overreacted and called Beverly and told her I wouldn't be in to work." She held out her arms and let

186

them drop to her sides. "But as you can see, I'm fine. As soon as I got home and took a shower, I ran up to housekeeping and told Bev I was back in business."

"It's not like Nicholas to overreact."

Julia finished winding the cord with a snort. "The guy already thinks I'm a walking disaster, so he probably took one look at me covered in leaves and twigs and figured I'd broken my neck." She straightened with another smile. "I'm fine, Olivia."

Looking more suspicious than convinced, Olivia motioned for Julia to follow her outside. "About that Inglenook job," she said, making Julia's heart start racing again as she followed, "have you considered that there might be other positions here at Nova Mare where speaking several languages would come in handy?" Olivia walked down the stairs, then sat one step up from the bottom and patted a spot beside her, turning toward Julia when she also sat down. "Is that what you really want to do? Make this resort your career?"

Julia shook her head. "I hadn't really thought in terms of having an actual career. I'm only focused on earning a comfortable living right now, and making sure Trisha gets to pursue her dream of becoming a marine biologist."

"But what if I were to offer you a really comfortable living," Olivia said softly, "as my new event planner?"

Julia stilled. "Are you serious?" she asked just as softly.

Olivia gave a nod, then touched Julia's knee when she started shaking her head again. "Hear what I have to say before you dismiss my offer out of hand."

"But I don't know anything about planning events," Julia said, cutting her off. "I can't even throw a decent birthday party."

"Could I change your mind if I promised that you'd be mentored by a leading expert on throwing parties? Mac's mom, Rana, has hosted everything from intimate state dinners to royal balls with hundreds of attendees, and she's very kindly offered to share her secrets with you to get you started."

"But even with her help, you can't expect *me* to plan events for rich and famous people and . . . and *royalty,*" Julia said on a gasp, remembering some of the elaborate weddings and private functions that had taken place here last summer. Good heavens, several had had fireworks, and one couple had released a hundred doves. Where did anyone find a hundred white doves, anyway? "How would I know what a princess or billionaire or rock star wants?" Julia growled.

"You'll know by *asking*," Olivia growled back. "If you can make a young girl's dream come true, you can do it for a princess or billionaire or rock star. But only if you stop thinking like the daughter of the town drunk, Julia," she said softly, "and pursue your own dreams."

"But that's just it; I don't have dreams of grandeur because I *am* the daughter of the town drunk. I'm not like you, Olivia," Julia whispered, shaking her head again. "In a million years, I couldn't have conceived of building a resort like Nova Mare, much less running this place on a daily basis. You cater to the wealthiest people in the world."

Olivia leaned closer, the look in her eyes making Julia lean away. "Do you think I suddenly woke up one morning and decided to build a fancy resort on top of a mountain and cater to the rich and famous and *royalty*? Or that a foster kid from a three-car town down on the coast had dreams of grandeur?"

"But —"

"What I *had*," Olivia said, cutting her off, "was the same determination you have to make a better life for the people I loved. For you it's Trisha, where for me it was

Sophie and Ezra. This," she said, sweeping an arm to encompass the entire resort, "wasn't even a spark in my imagination." Olivia suddenly sighed, folding her hands on her lap and staring down at Bottomless. "But then I fell crazy in love with a man who only dreams big." She looked over and smiled sadly. "If we limit ourselves to our circumstances, Julia, we become our own jailers. You're a creative, energetic, intelligent person with the potential to be or do anything you want in life, and if I found the courage to build Nova Mare, you can find the courage to help me make it the best resort on the planet." She patted Julia's knee, then stood up and faced her. "Give me four months. And if you don't find yourself addicted to making people's wildest dreams come true, then you're welcome to have your housekeeping job back."

"But what about the guest liaison position?"

Olivia shook her head. "I'll have filled it by then, because I need someone to be trained and in place by the first of May."

Julia scowled down at her lap, undecided if she wanted to scream or throw up. Taking this job and not liking it — or completely sucking at it — meant she'd lose out on the job she did want. She looked up. "Does the planner position come with housing?"

Olivia's jaw slackened, and she dropped her arms to her sides. "Julia," she said on a strangled whisper. "With the salary I'll be paying you, you can *buy* a house. Hell, you can build one right on the shoreline if you want."

Julia felt her own jaw go slack. Within a month of the earthquake turning Bottomless into an inland sea, shorefront property had shot out of sight, and today even a falling-down shack on a dot of land cost a small fortune.

"If I'm charging exorbitant prices to fulfill people's fantasies," Olivia continued, her gleam returning, "then I have to pay outrageous salaries to hold on to the people making them happen — which I just recently learned the hard way, when some overpriced resort in Fiji stole my event planner right out from under my nose." The gleam disappeared. "You remember the single guy who left you that three-hundred-dollar tip last week? Well, the sneaky little weasel was head-hunting. Besides stealing Evelyn, he also tried to nab Nicholas."

Julia went back to gaping, then snorted. "Is that the real reason you're offering the position to me? Because you think a local will be less inclined to run off to Fiji?"

191

"I did say you were intelligent," Olivia drawled, even as she shook her head. "The fact that you can handle a Maine winter certainly doesn't hurt, but your talent for sizing up guests and anticipating their needs even before they know them themselves was the main reason for my decision. You also have a gift for decorating, which will come in handy when you're doing themed events."

"I do?"

"Julia, your cottages are so warm and inviting in such an understated way, I'm tempted to have you decorate the Inglenook cabins, from the furniture right down to the dishes in the cupboards." She took hold of Julia's hands and pulled her to her feet. "Be my new event planner, Jules. I promise that if you learn the ropes with Rana over the winter, I'll have to *double* your salary to keep you from being stolen right out from under my nose." Olivia gave her hands a squeeze. "Expand your dream from a comfortable existence to a magical adventure. But don't do it just because I'm desperate. And don't do it for Trisha, either. You've been protecting your sister since your mom died, helping her become the fine young woman she is, but isn't it time you *showed* her what the daughters of the town drunk can really do?"

"When . . . when did you become so wise?"

Olivia gave a laugh and pulled her into a hug. "When I started believing in the magic again," she whispered against her hair. She leaned away to look Julia in the eyes and nodded. "It's real, you know; as real as that inland sea down there and this mountain we're standing on. Say yes, Julia, and Rana and I will show you how to make your own kind of magic."

"You're not even going to let me think about this, are you?"

Olivia stepped away with a chuckle. "Did I mention I'm desperate? A bride and her mother are arriving from Germany tomorrow afternoon, expecting to go over last-minute details of a fantasy wedding that's *taking place in three days.*"

"But I don't have any details."

"Did I say the job would be easy?" Olivia shook her head. "There's a good chance it will turn you prematurely gray — which is why I believe I'm paying you the big bucks. I need a passionate, energetic miracle worker, Julia, who won't mind working fourteen-hour days and most weekends, who has a high tolerance for frantic brides and pushy mothers, and who thinks controlling chaos and thwarting disasters is the definition of fun. Say yes."

Julia scowled at the ground again, wondering what exactly was stopping her. Well, other than her very real fear of making a very big fool of herself. But then, hadn't she survived thirty years of being repeatedly humiliated? So what did she really have to lose? She blew out a very deep sigh and lifted her gaze. "Yes," she whispered — only to flinch when Olivia pounced on her with a shriek of delight.

"Ohmigod, thank you!" Olivia cried as she hugged her again. "Okay, come on," she said, grabbing Julia's hand — into which she slapped a key. She started dragging her to the four-passenger cart parked behind Julia's cleaning cart. "I'll take you to meet your staff, then come back and finish cleaning your cottage myself."

"My staff?" Julia squeaked as Olivia nudged her toward the driver's side.

"You don't expect to create high-priced fantasies all by yourself, do you?" Olivia slid into the passenger's seat. "You have two assistants who are miracle workers in their own right, two strapping young men for the heavy lifting, a talented carpenter, and a secretary who speaks practically every language known to man. Ariel is worth her weight in gold when it comes to dealing with foreign clients." Olivia patted the driver's seat. "Come on, Mac's mom is already at your office, anxious to meet you."

"I . . . I have an office?"

"Actually, you have the entire downstairs of the conference pavilion." Olivia waved in the general direction of the summit. "It's mostly storage for your props, but there's a beautiful office full of windows facing Bottomless, a workshop and design area, and a meeting room for you to consult with clients." She patted the seat again when Julia just kept gaping at her. "Evelyn had been working on the Rauch wedding since last spring, so your assistants are right now bringing Rana up to speed because it's happening in *three days,*" she growled, patting the seat more firmly.

"Um . . . why am I driving your cart?"

Olivia blew out a sigh. "This is *your* cart." She leaned over to point at the rear side panel. "See, it even has your name on it, as well as your title."

Julia stepped back and saw her name printed in gold lettering on the side of the forest green cart, claiming she'd just agreed to become Nova Mare's director of special events. "I have my own — Wait," she said with a gasp, snapping her gaze to Olivia even as she pointed at the panel. "Why is my name already on there if I said yes only two minutes ago?"

Olivia straightened, her eyes taking on a gleam again as she arched a brow. "Seriously, Ms. Campbell, do you honestly believe I was taking *no* for an answer?"

CHAPTER TEN

Ms. Campbell. Her entire *staff,* and every person who had walked through the door of the conference pavilion that afternoon, had called her Ms. Campbell. Julia had actually looked over her shoulder no fewer than three times, wondering if her mom had suddenly come back from the dead. The only exception had been Rana, although it had taken the patient woman most of the afternoon to get Julia to stop calling her Mrs. Oceanus. For crying out loud, she was on a first-name basis with — if rumors were correct — a real live *queen.* Queen of where, the rumors didn't know, but probably some defunct country no longer on the map. Still, there was no mistaking Rana was royalty — from her lavender turtleneck and royal purple chambray shirt right down to her Gore-Tex hiking shoes.

With only the moon shining through the floor-to-ceiling windows lighting her beautiful office, Julia slumped back in her plush leather chair and let her gaze wander over the trappings of her new job laid out on her beautiful cherrywood desk. The tote bag — made of the softest leather she'd ever touched — and matching calendar book had been personal gifts from Rana. The woman claimed they'd been crafted by a designer from her homeland — which appeared to be an island somewhere in the Atlantic Ocean, Julia had gathered from their conversations over the course of the afternoon.

She next slid her gaze to the thin black cell phone she didn't have a clue how to operate, although Olivia had assured her as she'd plopped the phone in Julia's hand that it was no more difficult than sewing balsam pillows. After which she'd then plopped a ring of keys, complete with an attached remote fob that went to the pearl white SUV parked outside with Julia's name written in small gold letters over the large Nova Mare logo on the door.

She would have to vacate the apartment she and Trisha were staying in, her boss had then gone on to tell her, but only so they could move into the event planner's cottage tucked down a wooded driveway beside the resort road's upper guard booth. A deliberately chosen location, Olivia had said with a familiar gleam in her eyes, because guards worked much better than small brass bells when it came to keeping frantic brides and pushy mothers from intruding on her private sanctuary. Julia was still free to buy a home of her own, Olivia had assured her, and only use the cottage when she needed to be close by for major events or if she simply didn't feel like navigating the mountain road late at night or in foul weather.

The thought of actually buying her own home made Julia slide her gaze to the legal-size envelope on the desk as she remembered having to sit down when she'd started reading the paperwork — already filled out with her name and all her personal information — that stated her outrageous salary, a medical plan that included eyes and teeth and probably splinters, an almost obscene retirement package, and the generous number of perks that came with the job.

Julia liked that she got free weekly massages at the resort's spa, but she couldn't really see herself paying even half price for a friend or family member to stay at the resort or taking advantage of free dining at Aeolus's Whisper. Well, okay; she wouldn't mind treating Trisha to a gourmet meal when the girl came home on leave from college. And Julia figured she'd know the menu pretty well by then, since she was expected to wine and dine clients there.

She was also expected to chauffeur both signed-on and prospective clients to town or down to Turtleback to visit all the artisan shops that had multiplied like bunnies since the earthquake had made the area a huge tourist draw. She was also, apparently, supposed to use either of the two credit cards she'd been issued to pay for and occasionally accompany clients who wanted to cruise Bottomless on one of the ever-popular whale watching and autumn foliage tours.

It was at that point that Rana had taken over explaining the full scope of Julia's new position, first by imploring her not to worry about spending money to make money, then stating that an effective event planner was really just an illusionist with battle skills. Julia's main goal, Rana had told her, was to always appear as if she had everything under control, *especially* when an event was imploding right before everyone's eyes. And then Olivia's regal mother-in-law had opened the Rauch file with an utterly feminine snort and stated that Julia was about to get her first lesson in creating miracles, since she really couldn't understand why anyone wanted an outdoor wedding on the top of a mountain in Maine in November.

Julia leaned forward and pulled her baby-soft leather tote in front of her, then laid her head on it on her desk. She hadn't really signed that contract, had she? Both copies? In indelible ink?

What in Hades had she done?

Julia sat up. Where had *that* come from? Hades? Really? For crying out loud, she'd spent one afternoon with Rana and already was sounding like the elegant woman!

Wait, wasn't that a good thing? Didn't she want to be as confident and collected and apparently as unflappable as Rana Oceanus? Wasn't that the point of having a mentor? The woman's influence had obviously rubbed off on her daughter-in-law, because when Olivia had been running Inglenook for the Baldwins, she'd been known as the town *mouse.* And now here she was running her own world-class resort and apparently taking no prisoners when it came to recruiting staff.

Julia smiled, trying to picture Olivia browbeating Nicholas into becoming her director of security — only to still in surprise when she saw the devil himself standing in the doorway of her office, smiling back at her.

Well, darn it to Hades; that should teach her to be careful who she thought about.

Julia laid her head back down on her tote. "Go away, Nicholas. I'm very busy."

Even though he walked quieter than his cats, she knew in her next heartbeat that he was standing on the other side of her desk. "Anything that I can help you with?" he asked, the deep timbre of his voice washing over her like a warm summer rain.

Speaking of which . . . "Can you make sure it doesn't rain this Sunday?" she asked without bothering to sit up. "And that the temperature is at least sixty degrees?"

"I'll see what I can do."

"How did you know I was here?" she asked, still without straightening. "All the lights are off and the doors *locked*." To which he had keys, she realized, seeing how he was the director of security.

"Your cart is still parked outside."

Oh, she'd forgotten she had a cart and probably would have walked right past it when she finally found the energy to go home. Odd that she'd spent the last three months bicycling to work because she didn't want to spend money on her old truck, and now she had a brand-new pearl white SUV *and* a personal cart with her name on them. And then there was the irony of having spent the last four years paying off credit card bills she hadn't run up, and now she had *two* cards — again with her name on them — that apparently had limitless funds.

"Where's Trisha? I checked, but she hasn't come through the lower gate yet."

Hoping that if she kept lying on her soft leather tote he'd get the message that she really wasn't in the mood for company, Julia said, "She's spending the night at her friend Kimberly's house because band practice was going to run late tonight." Which was just as well, Julia had already decided, because she really needed some time alone to decide if she'd just made the smartest decision of her life or the dumbest.

"I had planned to take both of you to Aeolus's for dinner," he said, "but it appears it will be just the two of us celebrating your new job."

Nope, he wasn't taking the hint. "That's very kind, but I really can't be seen having dinner with you at Aeolus's Whisper."

"Why not?"

Julia finally sat up and shot him a crooked grin. "You're kidding, right? I'd be found dead on a cart path tomorrow morning after being run over by an entire herd of female coworkers."

"Then we'll go into town and have dinner at the Drunken Moose."

She shook her head. "Same problem."

"We'll drive down to Turtleback," he said, a bit of an edge creeping into his voice.

Not really wanting to explain *why* they couldn't be seen in public together, Julia stood up and started placing all the trappings of her new job into her tote. "It's really very kind of you to want to celebrate my new position, but I think it would be better if you just sent me flowers."

"I'm not being *kind;* I'm trying to take you to dinner."

Nope, not only not taking the hint, but not backing down, either. "I'm not going out with you, Nicholas. It's nothing personal. I just don't date men."

"Why not?"

Julia slung her new tote on her shoulder, walked around her new desk, and headed out of her new office. "Because I prefer women."

"No, you don't."

She stopped at the door and shot him a smile. "Thank you for clearing that up for me. I've been so confused," she said, bolting down the hall on rubbery legs before that look in his moonlit eyes reached his brain and he chased after her.

Was she suicidal? Who in Hades tugged a giant tiger by the tail?

She made it all the way to the common green before he silently fell in step beside her, and Julia silently continued walking toward the guard booth, nearly reaching it before he finally spoke. "Is your cart not running properly?" he asked.

She came to a halt and blinked up at him, then looked back up at the conference pavilion with a shrug. "I forgot I had one." She arched a brow. "Where's your cart?"

He gave a soft grunt. "I can run faster."

She started off again, waved at the guard in the booth on her way by, and headed down the tree-shadowed driveway to check out her new home — Nicholas still silently walking beside her. Not that she minded all that much, she decided when they'd gone quite a ways and she still hadn't seen any sign of a cabin yet.

"You'll be perfectly safe back here, Julia," he said, making her realize she'd been inching toward him until they were almost touching.

She tried inching away, but apparently his big strong muscles were *magnetized.* "I'm not afraid of —" She bumped into him with a gasp and grabbed his hand when something scurried through the leaves beside them. "The dark," she muttered as she tried to let go, only to give up when his fingers gently tightened on hers.

"Do you like to fish, Julia?"

"I used to — when I was ten."

He stopped walking, and since he wouldn't let go of her hand, Julia also had to stop. "You haven't been fishing since you were a child?"

"No, I've been since. But it's so boring that I don't go unless I absolutely have to, like when I lost a bet to Vanetta while working for her at the Drunken Moose."

She felt his hand twitch, and there was enough moonlight streaming through the trees for her to see his eyes narrow. "Boring?" he quietly repeated.

"Well, yeah. Fishing is really just hours of sitting in a boat holding a long stick, interrupted by two minutes of a small tug-of-war with some angry little fish, followed by more hours of sitting in a boat, only now your hands are all slimy and smelly — and in some cases bloody — from having wrestled the hook out of the angry fish's mouth." She turned away to hide her smile and started walking again, having to all but drag Nicholas because he still refused to give up her hand. "So now that I think about it, fishing isn't only boring, but also messy and dangerous."

"That's what makes it a sport," he said,

the edge back in his voice causing her smile to widen as she glanced away — because she really didn't dare let him see how much she was enjoying herself.

She knew Nicholas owned a fast fishing boat loaded with fancy technology, because she'd heard more than one male employee mention it; their tones were more admiring than jealous as they'd wondered why he always fished alone.

She shrugged the shoulder of the hand he was holding. "It must be a guy thing. Oh," she said, halting when she spotted the two-story, log-and-stone cottage bathed in moonlight. "It's utterly charming. And bigger than I thought it would be."

She heard Nicholas sigh as he started off again, leading her up onto the porch but stopping two steps down as he turned her to face him, which put them at eye level — which was not a good thing, Julia realized when her gaze drifted to his mouth.

She really had no business wanting to feel those lips on hers again, because she really wouldn't know how to react. And anyway, town sluts — even if they had suddenly morphed into event planners — had no business kissing men like Nicholas, because . . . well, stuff like that only happened in fairy tales and romance novels.

"Come fishing with me, and I'll wrestle the angry fish off the hook," he said thickly, making Julia lift her gaze to find *him* looking at *her* mouth.

So she smiled. "Then I'll have to sit in a boat with a slimy, smelly man."

His eyes lifted to hers. "We won't use hooks."

"That would certainly help the boring par—"

He palmed her cheeks and touched his lips to hers, and Julia had to clutch his big strong arms when she felt herself melting into a puddle of pleasure. Holy Hades, now what was she supposed to do? Kiss him back? Kick him in the shin?

Wait for him to realize she wasn't participating?

But she was! In fact, Julia felt her lips parting and her body going boneless so that he had to wrap her up in his big strong arms before she really did seep through that crack in the porch. And she'd swear some crazy woman was making an unfamiliar little sound that she was afraid might actually be passion getting ready to explode.

Nicholas felt Julia's surprise turn to resistance, then briefly to acceptance before becoming fully engaged participation not a heartbeat later — a revelation that surprised him but certainly not enough to throw him off his game.

He deepened the kiss when she made a sweet little sound, letting his hand drop to her lovely backside to snug her up against him, her trembling body pressing into him as she suddenly . . . erupted. She clasped his neck and lifted herself to wrap her legs around his waist and canted her head and pushed her tongue into his mouth.

Okay then; it appeared Julia hadn't been boasting to her sister that night in the church, because she certainly did seem determined to knock his socks off. Nicholas finished walking up the porch stairs and pressed her against the cottage beside the door so he could free up at least one hand for a little exploring. But the lovely lady apparently had the same intention, her writhing body making him so hard, he thought *he* might erupt when she arched back to yank his collar, pulled her mouth from his, and started a fiery trail of kisses down his jaw to his neck.

So instead of following through on his intended target, Nicholas reached beside her and twisted the knob, his sigh of relief that the door opened turning to a groan of his own when he felt her teeth rake over the cords in his neck. "Hang on," he growled, splaying his hand across her lovely backside as he pulled her away from the cottage and stepped inside — the motion not slowing her passionate assault as her tongue soothed the spot she'd just nipped.

He made it as far as the rug in front of the fireplace, then merely dropped to his knees and lowered her to the rug. And since he no longer had to worry about holding her up, and she no longer had to worry about holding herself up, Julia immediately unzipped his jacket and pushed it off his shoulders, then headed for the buttons on his shirt, making him have to finally over-power her in order to undress her instead.

Nicholas had a moment's hesitation when he got her stripped down as far as her turtleneck, however, and fought to keep his wits about him, only to have the lovely lady reach down with crossed arms, grab the hem of the jersey, and pull it off over her head — her fingers apparently snagging her bra on their way by, making her totally naked from the waist up as she tossed the garments away. But before he could even catch enough of an appreciative glimpse in the stingy light, she caught hold of his neck and pulled him down as she strained up-ward, her mouth capturing his with another sweet little noise as he pressed her back onto the rug.

Settling between her restless legs, Nicholas once again fought for at least enough control to slow her down. But Julia was having none of it; her tongue going in search of his as she arched up with a soft moan when he cupped her small firm breast and gently raked his thumb across her hardened nipple.

He broke the kiss and settled lower, capturing her other nipple in his mouth, only to have her cry out as she planted her feet and lifted her pelvis into his. Her hands left his shoulders a heartbeat before he felt them wedge between them, and he was just about to stop her from pushing him away when he realized she was actually unfastening her pants and lifting her hips to shove them down.

He rose to his knees and finished stripping off her pants along with her shoes, then managed to unbuckle his belt and push down his own pants just as she reached up to pull him back to her. "Inside me," she rasped raggedly. "Now. Hurry." Her hands tightened when he once again hesitated, her legs wrapping around his thighs as the strength of her apparent urgency tugged him down. "Please, Nicholas, I really need to feel you inside me."

Reassured that she at least knew *who* she was exploding all over rather than just being in a passionate frenzy, he settled intimately against her again — closing his eyes on a groan when he felt the heat of her bare skin against his. He leaned away, unable to stifle a grin when her protest turned into an approving moan the moment he reached down between them and moved himself through her slickness. She suddenly stilled when he pressed into her slightly, then protested again when he retreated — which once again became a sweet little sound of pleasure when he in turn pressed deeper.

Feeling her trembling with building energy as her fingers dug into his, Nicholas captured her hands and pinned them above her head, resting his weight on his forearms as he kissed her again and slowly pressed deeper, retreated the moment he felt her resistance, then pressed forward again; gaining a bit more ground with each slow, gentle thrust until he was fully seated inside her.

He then stilled except to lift his head, enough moonlight streaming through the windows to let him see her eyes suddenly close with a long hum of pleasure. "Damn, that feels good." She looked at him and smiled. "It would feel even better if you . . . ah, moved," she said huskily, lifting her hips as if to show him what she meant. "I'm not fragile, Nicholas."

She wasn't subtle, either; her eyes suddenly widening when he still didn't move. "I'm sorry, am I scaring you?" she drawled.

He dropped his forehead to hers to hide his own smile, and retreated and pressed forward again, slowly increasing his thrust until he found a rhythm she seemed happy with — for some reason not surprised that it was somewhere near ninety miles an hour. That created a bit of a problem for him, though, as her body responded with shuddering bursts of unbridled energy and her vocally impassioned pleas to go faster brought him right to the edge of his control.

Sweet Prometheus, he couldn't believe how wild she became, having wrestled her hands free to rake her fingers up his arms to his neck, her heels digging into the back of his thighs to stop him from retreating too far before pressing him deeper with each surge. "Come for me, Julia," he tightly growled when he felt himself slipping.

"Nooo," she keened. "Later. Or . . . next time," she said in ragged pants. "Come, Nicholas. Show me . . . what I do . . . to you."

Despite realizing she wasn't even going to try, he might have been able to at least last longer if Julia hadn't brought one of her hands to her mouth, her eyes locked on his as she slipped two fingers inside and suckled them. Nicholas surged into her, his last coherent thought that of wondering when the last time was he'd flat-out stormed a castle and found not only the gate open but that the prize he'd been after had actually surrendered without his even asking.

Well, this was awkward, Julia decided as she lay staring up into the shadowed darkness, trying to catch her breath, uncertain if she'd just had the best sex of her life or the worst. She definitely felt more alive than she had in . . . forever. But then, that might be due to the fact she could actually hear her blood rushing through her head with every beat of her pounding heart. As for it possibly being the worst sex, Julia suspected Nicholas had just ruined all *future* sex for her, because she had never, ever felt so wild and out of control like that before. In fact, she was worried she may have left claw marks on his big strong shoulders. And he wasn't moving, so she may have also given him a heart attack. Well, he couldn't really be dead, because he was breathing as hard as she was, but he was still inside her and didn't seem in much of a hurry to move.

Wow, that had been fast. They had to have just broken a speed-sex record or something. One minute he'd been kissing her — or had she been kissing him? — on the front porch of her new home, and suddenly here she was, lying naked on the floor, staring up at her new ceiling with an almost complete stranger lying on top of her.

He was very kindly not crushing her, though, so *his* brain cells must still be firing. But hers must still be zinging out of control, because she couldn't for the life of her figure out how to extricate herself from this awkward position. Not the physical position, because she probably only needed to give him a nudge to get him to roll away, but how was she going to get up, find her clothes in the dark, and make her escape without his noticing she was utterly and completely mortified?

Then again, why wasn't *he* making the first move? Surely a chick magnet had more experience than she did when it came to this . . . after-wild-sex stuff.

Nicholas slowly began to stir, and Julia stopped breathing, only to have to start up again because she really needed to get some oxygen to her brain. But she stopped again when he smoothed her sex-tangled hair off her face and kissed her sex-dampened forehead with a — Wait; when had her hair gotten unbraided?

"I don't think I've ever been more pleasantly surprised," he murmured. He lifted his head to smile at her — at least she thought he was smiling. "Although I suspected you'd be an energetic lover," he continued thickly, "since you're always racing around at ninety miles an hour, I wasn't expecting you to explo—"

Julia covered his mouth with her hand before he could finish what she hoped to Hades had been a compliment. "Um, do you think you could . . . I really need to . . ." She flashed him a really big smile that he couldn't miss in a pitch-black cave and used her hand on his shoulder to give him a friendly little pat and then a slight nudge. "Could we continue this conversation after I make a quick trip to the . . . um, powder room?"

He hesitated, apparently having to think about that. So she tried a bit firmer nudge, then silently sighed with relief when he gave her forehead another kiss, gently pulled out of her, and moved away. Julia was on her feet before he'd fully straightened to his knees, and gathering up her shoes and clothes before he was standing and pulling up his pants — that he'd apparently pushed down only enough to . . . free himself.

Oh yeah, they'd definitely broken a speed-sex record.

Not wanting to spend any more time looking for her bra, Julia inconspicuously snagged her tote and hid it in the clothes, then forced herself not to run toward what looked like a hallway that she hoped led to a bathroom. "I'll only be a minute," she promised brightly, skirting an end table just before she smacked into it.

Julia breathed another sigh of relief when she stepped into a small powder room, softly closed the door, and even more softly locked it. She felt for a light switch and turned it on, then gasped when she saw the wild woman in the mirror. "I really don't remember unbraiding my hair," she muttered, dropping her clothes and then rifling through them for her panties. She stilled with one foot in one of the legs when she realized she was only wearing one sock — which had a hole in it.

How sexy was that?

She set another speed record dressing and putting on her shoes, then slowly opened the window, climbed up on the toilet, lowered her tote to the ground, and crawled out as quietly as one of Nicholas's *six* cats. She hiked her tote over her shoulder, looked toward the end of the cabin with another sigh of relief, then scurried toward the woods and ran straight into a big broad unmovable chest.

"Ready to finish our conversation?" Nicholas asked, a *definite* edge in his voice.

"No, actually," she said, tugging down the hem of her jacket as she inched away. "I was thinking we might finish it another time. Soon. Yeah, maybe tomor—"

He caught her face in his big strong hands and bent until his nose was only inches from hers. "Are you upset, Julia? Or disappointed?"

"Huh?"

"Maybe angry?" He brushed a thumb over her lips. "I'm sorry for not seeing to your woman's pleasure before I . . . well, I'm sorry."

Darn, she'd hoped he hadn't noticed that. "Oh no, I had a really pleasurable time. *Really,*" she assured him, nodding in his hands for emphasis. She gave his arm a pat and stepped back from his grasp, hiked her tote higher on her shoulder, and turned and entered the woods at a different angle now that she realized she had to go up the mountain to reach her apartment. "But I really need to get going, because I have to be in my new office bright and early in the morning," she said brightly, only to be gently but firmly pulled to a stop again.

Julia exploded — and *not* with sexual energy. "Okay, listen up, because I'm only going to say this once. I don't know who that was back there," she growled, pointing toward the cabin, "but it wasn't *me.* Contrary to popular opinion, I don't sleep around and I sure as heck don't *explode* like some sex-starved woman."

She poked him in the chest when he tried to say something, knowing if she didn't get a handle on this she was going to finish humiliating herself by bursting into tears. "I'm talking," she snapped, "and you're listening. As far as I'm concerned and *you* are concerned, this never happened. Everyone's entitled to one really dumb mistake in her life, and mine was tonight. And I swear, if you stop me again or try following me, I'm going to bludgeon you to death with my brand-new soft leather tote. Got that?" she finished with one final poke to let him know she wasn't bluffing.

And then she bolted into the woods, not waiting around to see if he believed her. Of all the stupid, outrageous, suicidal things she could have done, what had possessed her to have sex with Nicholas?

Talk about disasters!

Julia ran through the forest until she got a stitch in her side, then stopped and slumped against a tree and buried her face in her hands. But the really scary part was, hadn't her mom always said things came in threes? So if in just one day she'd been blindsided into accepting a position she knew absolutely nothing about and had had wild passionate sex with a man she knew even less about, what was next?

She suddenly straightened with a gasp. Holy Hades, what if she'd just gotten pregnant? That would definitely qualify as disaster number three, wouldn't it?

No. *No,* she firmly scolded herself, she wasn't going there. Having sex one time didn't automatically translate to *baby.* And she and Clay had had unprotected sex lots of times after they'd gotten married without her getting pregnant.

But really, what *had* she been thinking? Well, other than how good it felt to be kissed and touched and . . . Julia leaned her head back against the tree with a groan. At the time all she'd been thinking about was how feminine Nicholas was making her feel, how he was kissing her as if she were beautiful and sexy and desirable, and how he'd been pursuing her as if she were some wonderful prize.

It had been a close call afterward, though, but she'd managed to escape before he could get too carried away about her not having found her *woman's pleasure.* What was it with men, anyway? Did it threaten their manhood or something if a woman didn't have a stupid orgasm?

Julia started in the general direction of the apartments again, figuring she couldn't get lost if she kept going uphill. So she'd had sex with Nicholas — so what? She was a healthy thirty-year-old woman; wasn't it time she started acting like other divorcées and had herself a little sex once in a while? Yeah, maybe she'd even start carrying condoms in her beautiful new tote, just in case she felt like having sex *again.*

She'd go on the pill, too, for added insurance, remembering how she'd had really nice boobs when she'd been on it before. Nicholas hadn't seemed to mind that she was lacking some anatomy, but the next guy she went crazy over and had a one-night stand with might be disappointed.

But she couldn't ever have sex with Nicholas again, because that would really compound tonight's disaster. And now that she thought about it, she should probably make one-night stands a permanent rule. She might be able to bluster her way out of not experiencing the big O as nervousness the first time she was with a guy, but when it still didn't happen times two and three and ten . . . well, then it would turn into a problem.

And wasn't it programmed into men's DNA to *fix* problems?

And anyway, the director of special events couldn't keep having sex with the director of security, because they'd keep bumping into each other at work and she really didn't think she'd be very good at pretending there was nothing going on between them. And besides, Olivia probably had a policy that prohibited employees from getting sexually involved.

Yes, she would definitely have wild passionate sex again, Julia decided just as she caught sight of the barn, because she really couldn't remember ever feeling this wonderfully alive. And now that she knew what she'd been missing trying to prove to everyone that she *wasn't* the town slut, she was suddenly eager to explore her apparently passionate nature. Too bad, though, that it couldn't be with the mysterious man with no last name and compelling blue eyes and magnetic muscles, Julia thought with a sigh as she finally caught sight of her apartment, but she truly didn't want to be found dead on a cart path.

And now that Nicholas had caught her, he'd probably stop chasing her, anyway.

Because for sport fishermen, wasn't it all about catch and release?

CHAPTER ELEVEN

Julia was indeed up bright and early the next morning, but instead of sitting behind her new desk in her new office, she was sitting on Peg MacKeage's pontoon boat tied at the dock of the Nova Mare marina. Sipping her coffee and occasionally eyeing the bag holding the two still-warm cinnamon buns, Julia watched her friend waiting for the bus with her little tribe of heathens, along with Henry and Sophie and the horse wranglers' son.

Julia sighed, remembering how it had taken her half an hour to work up the nerve to actually get in her new pearl white SUV — with her *name* on it — this morning, then another fifteen minutes to figure out all the buttons that apparently did everything but make it fly. The steering wheel alone had more buttons than the entire dash of her old truck, and when she'd finally decided to just drive the darn thing, she'd expected the guard at the top gate to pull out his gun and accuse her of stealing it.

But the big, burly guard had merely asked her to make sure the resort radio mounted on the dash was on as he'd tapped some keys on a computer inside the booth, then given her a warm smile and waved her through. As for the SUV's dash, it was computerized, which is why Julia had gotten halfway down the mountain before realizing that instead of indicating how fast she was going, the display was stating she was getting nineteen-point-three miles to the gallon. And then that number had dropped to fifteen-point-eight when she'd sped up as the road had leveled out along the ridge.

Having absolutely no idea how fast she'd driven into Spellbound Falls, she'd parked at the post office so if anyone saw her they'd think she'd been given a company vehicle to get the resort's mail. Then she'd spent another ten minutes figuring out how to get her cell phone to display a keypad so she could call Peg and ask if they could meet at the marina when she brought her kids over to catch the bus, and have a little bun-fest on the boat and . . . chat.

Julia wasn't sure, but there was probably still an open line between her phone and

Peg's, since she never did figure out how to end the call because the screen had gone blank when her thumb had touched . . . something as she'd pulled the phone down from her ear. So she'd slipped it in her beautiful tote, gotten out of her beautiful truck, pushed the button with a closed padlock on the key fob — jumping when the vehicle beeped at her — and walked to the Drunken Moose as if this were just any ordinary day.

Thanking her lucky stars that Vanetta was busy out back in the kitchen, Julia had ordered two large coffees and two cinnamon buns to go, then sprinted back to her truck when she'd spotted Janice Crupp and Christina Richie barreling into town in Christina's now-classic red Impala. Knowing the octogenarians were headed to Vanetta's for their biweekly breakfast date, the last thing she'd wanted was for them to see her driving a resort vehicle. She wasn't ashamed of her new job or anything, but she would like to get used to the idea of being a director of *anything* before she shared that fact with the two biggest town gossips and they shared it with the entire world.

Still not hearing the telltale sound of a school bus laboring down the marina road, Julia set her coffee in the cup holder on the arm of the couch, then grabbed the bag with a sigh of defeat and pulled out one of the buns. She sank her teeth into it with a hum of pleasure as she watched Peg talking to the horse wranglers' son while her daughter, Charlotte, and Olivia's daughter, Sophie — both twelve-year-olds — hung on the teenager's every word. Peg's *almost*-ten-year-old, Isabel, was trying to interest Mac's ten-year-old, Henry, in a book she'd pulled out of her backpack, and Peg's eight-year-old twins, Peter and Jacob, were making a valiant attempt not to get their sneakers wet as they combed the shoreline of their old gravel pit for treasures the tide had left behind.

Nicely rounding out the domestic scene, the MacKeages' sappy canine mascot — aptly named Hero — was staring up at the two marina workers sitting in front of the office also wolfing down cinnamon buns. Yeah, well, if the bus didn't get here soon, Julia decided as she licked icing off her fingers and took another hum-inducing bite of her own bun, she was eating the one she'd brought for Peg, too.

Duncan had ridden across the fiord with his tribe this morning, met up with Mac when he'd brought his children and the wranglers' son down from the summit, and the two men had taken off with Princess Hugs-a-lot and Duncan and Peg's two-week-older son, Mur the Magnificent.

Well, Duncan called the boy Mur, but Peg called her precious little baby Charlie. The poor kid's official name was Murdoc Charles MacKeage, because, Peg had told Julia, that had been the only *important* argument she'd ever lost to her contrary, never-say-die husband.

Hearing the bus just moments before it pulled into the parking lot, Julia picked up the bag holding the second cinnamon bun, rolled it closed with a sigh of regret, and lobbed it down the boat onto the couch opposite the captain's chair. She then pulled out the fistful of napkins she'd stuffed in her pocket, licked one of them, and began wiping the icing off her mouth and chin.

It was really quite warm for seven o'clock in the morning in mid-November, she realized, even as she hoped this spell of weather lasted until *after* the wedding taking place up in the gazebo. Which she'd learned yesterday from her staff would be followed by an *outdoor* reception that included long sticks to cook hot dogs and s'mores over a roaring bonfire. Who came all the way from Germany to a five-star resort to have a hot dog wedding, anyway?

And then the new bride and groom planned to leave their international guests dancing around said bonfire while they took off on a weeklong hike through the wilderness in *late November.*

Was it security's responsibility to go find them if they got lost in a snowstorm?

Julia picked up her coffee and took a sip, remembering more than one discussion with coworkers and townspeople of how strange and unexplainable . . . stuff seemed to happen at and around Nova Mare, a good deal of it involving the weather. Like sudden deafening claps of thunder that actually shook the ground even without there being any clouds in the sky. The oceanographers and geologists who'd jointly built a permanent facility just south of Spellbound Falls kept assuring everyone the earth-rumbling booms weren't coming from the sky but from the mountain itself, and were aftershocks of the original earthquake.

But that didn't explain why the weather on top of the mountain and down on the fiord always seemed perfect for special events, even those planned months in advance. More than once, storms — affectionately known as nor'easters — barreling up the eastern seaboard heading straight for Maine would suddenly change direction and go out to sea. Or much to forecasters' consternation, cold fronts racing down from Canada would all of a sudden slow to a crawl before they just as suddenly swept through *after* some over-the-top event.

Like the epic earthquake *and* nor'easter that had hit simultaneously three and a half years ago — creating an inland sea, a twelve-mile-long fiord, and a couple of brand-new mountains that the scientists still couldn't explain — the area's unusually co-operative weather had become an equally baffling phenomenon. Some people — mostly from away — were calling it the work of the devil, and some — mostly locals — felt it was the handiwork of a benevolent God who wanted to bless the good folks of northern Maine for being such hardworking souls.

And a good number of locals and people from away, as well as the strange folks who'd started some sort of colony down near Turtleback, were calling it magic.

Julia still hadn't decided which camp she was in, but Peg was definitely rooting for the magic angle; her childhood friend claimed that if falling in love with a man who was powerful enough to break a five-generation black widow curse wasn't proof enough it existed, then how about that same man getting her pregnant even though she'd had her tubes tied after the twins had been born?

Oh yeah, Peg was definitely a believer, and she hoped Julia had the good sense to also believe in the magic — just like they both had in kindergarten, when a simple little pebble had mysteriously soothed their fears.

"You better not have eaten my bun, too," Peg warned as she untied the boat. She gave it a shove away from the dock and stepped on board, then stopped in the middle of the deck to point at Julia — although she was smiling as she did. "You missed some icing on your cheek."

"Five more minutes and your bun was gone," Julia muttered, licking her napkin and wiping her face again, only to stop in mid-wipe when Hero came barreling across the dock and lunged for the open door of the drifting boat — and missed.

Peg got down on her knees with a sigh, grabbed the flailing dog by the collar, and hauled him up onto the deck. She immediately scrambled to her feet and positioned herself in front of Julia just as Hero gave a body-length shake that sent several gallons of frigid seawater flying.

"Now that's true friendship," Julia said with a laugh, using her napkin to wipe some errant drops off her tote. "And why I would have done the same for you."

Peg walked back to the steering console, started the engine, and slowly turned the boat around, then idled toward the fiord. "Hey, leave that alone," she growled when she noticed Hero nosing the bag on the couch across from her. "Go on, go lie down and dry off," she added, pointing at a crumpled towel on the floor at the rear of the boat. Only then did she snatch the coffee Julia had set in the console's cup holder, sit down, take a sip, then lower it with a groan of pleasure. "Why does coffee always taste better if you drink it outdoors from a cardboard cup?" she asked, leaning back in the big plush captain's chair and taking another sip.

"I think it has something to do with the fresh air," Julia said, taking a sip of her own coffee as they idled through the opening in the old tote road that had been washed out when the earthquake had created the fiord — which had then poured in and flooded Peg's old gravel pit. "Indoors, coffee has to compete with too many smells."

Peg set her cup in the holder, leaned over and snagged the bag off the couch, then pulled out the bun and took a bite large enough to choke a horse — again giving a groan of pleasure, only this time muffled by chewing. "So," she said after swallowing, "to what do I owe this morning's surprise visit?" Her eyes danced in the recently risen sun as she clutched her chest. "No wait, I know; you wanted to see my reaction in person when you tell me you're coming with us to Pine Creek for Thanksgiving so you can — No, wait," she repeated, holding up the bun as she reached for the throttle with her other hand. "Let's go sit in the middle of the fiord so nobody will hear me shriek when I get all excited that you've finally come to your senses about having a simple, no-commitment date with Seamus Mac-Keage."

She pushed down on the throttle before Julia could respond, and the large boat surged through the gentle swells like they were merely ripples. Julia stared down at her coffee, using her thumbnail to make little indents in the cardboard sleeve. Peg was determined she'd go out with Duncan's nephew, Seamus, who also happened to be Alec MacKeage's younger brother. Seamus was home on leave from Washington, DC, Peg had offered in way of argument, so besides its being safe to be seen on an actual date because the good people of Pine Creek didn't know she was a slut, Seamus was leaving on Sunday, so she didn't have to worry about any long-lasting commitment.

Julia wondered if Peg had told Seamus he was being used for practice.

Once they'd reached the center of the fiord, her friend brought the motor to an idle, shut it off, stood up and ran her sticky hands through the water Hero had splattered all over the console, then wiped them on her pants as she walked forward and sat down opposite Julia. "We plan to leave early Thursday morning and come back on Sunday. What time are you expecting Trisha to get back from New York on Sunday?"

"They said not until sometime after six. But I'm not going to Pine Creek with you, Peg. I think I'll invite Reggie to come have Thanksgiving with me at *Nova Mare.*"

"I thought you said he was going hunting with Corey's family for the week."

Darn, she'd forgotten she'd told her that. "Oh yeah, that's right," Julia said, tapping her forehead with her palm. "And I completely forgot that Jerilynn invited me to spend Thanksgiving with her and Tom, because she knows Trisha will be gone. And I don't want to disappoint the girl, what with her being so close to her due date."

Peg leaned back and folded her arms under her breasts — *she* certainly couldn't sleep on her stomach — and arched a brow. "When I saw Jerilynn at the post office the other day, she told me that she and Tom were going to her grandmother's in Presque Isle for Thanksgiving *and* spending the night."

Julia rubbed her face with a groan, then lowered her hands with a snort. "Okay then, try this one on for size: If I provide the gun, will you just put me out of my misery?"

Peg dropped her arms and sat up. "Are you crazy? No!"

"Well, jeesh," Julia said with an exaggerated glower. "I'd put you out of your misery if you asked me to, because we're *friends.*" She grinned, nudging Peg's foot with the toe of her shoe. "But only if you promised to leave me the twins."

Peg gaped at her. "You really must be crazy if you want Peter and Jacob." She leaned back against her seat again. "I tell you what; you just go ahead and take them, and that'll put me out of my misery," she said with a laugh. "Because I swear, little boys turn into little snots the second they reach the age of reasoning, and suddenly arguing with everything Mom says is their new favorite sport."

Julia also leaned back and spread her arms out on the couch back. "I'd argue with them 'til the cows came home if I had those two precious little boys. But I'd settle for Charlotte and —" She shook her head. "No, you better keep Isabel, because I'm toast when she starts batting those long, girly lashes at me. So as a heads-up, I'll be your official babysitter when Trisha heads off to college."

"Why don't you start building your own little tribe of heathens, Jules?" Peg asked, suddenly serious. "Instead of changing sheets for rich tourists, crawl between them with some sexy . . . oh, some big sexy Scotsman."

Julia choked on a laugh. "You're biased, Mrs. *MacKeage*." But then she also sobered, blowing out a heavy sigh. "Okay, here's the thing: I'm afraid I did two, maybe three really stupid things yesterday, and I need someone to talk me off the ledge before I make an even bigger fool of myself."

Peg straightened, her eyes filling with laughter again. "*You* did something stupid? Are we talking about the same Julia Campbell here? The town Miss Goody Two-shoes who can't cuss worth a damn and who thinks men are God's punishment to women for eating one silly apple? That Julia Campbell?" She snorted. "What did she do, flip off Christina Richie?"

"No, we're talking about *Ms.* Julia Campbell, who just agreed to be Nova Mare's director of special events, and who —"

Peg jumped up with a shriek and hauled Julia to her feet in a fierce hug. "Ohmigod, Jules! That's wonderful!" She leaned back. "Wait, how can that be stupid?"

Julia stepped away and gestured toward Whisper Mountain. "Yesterday Olivia handed me an outrageous salary, the keys to a truck *and* a house, and an entire staff to make wealthy people's fantasies come true," she said, trying to disguise the tremor in her voice by turning to pull her cell phone out of her tote. "And I'm such a backwoods country girl, I can't even operate this stupid phone because it doesn't have any *buttons.*"

"I'll have you texting *God* in half an hour," Peg growled. "As for the rest of what you just said, I personally believe you'll make a kick-ass event planner."

Julia gaped at her. "Why would you believe that?"

"Gee, I don't know; maybe because you're the person who threw together a beautiful wedding in less than six hours when I came crying to you that Duncan was threatening to sleep in my bed that night with or without a wedding band on my finger?"

"You walked down the aisle carrying *pussy*

237

willows I cut off the side of the road."

Peg nodded. "And it was the nicest bouquet any bride could want, Julia, all wrapped up in gossamer ribbon. And not only did you fill the church with forsythia that you stole out of Christina's front yard, you somehow persuaded Reverend Peter to drop his counseling prerequisite, got Vanetta to close early and all the waitresses to decorate for our reception, and even talked Sam into being our photographer and Ezra into walking me down the aisle." She shook her head with a wince. "And I hope you know I worried for months what you used to blackmail Nick Patterson into leaving his precious bar in Turtleback long enough to deejay for us. And you did all of it in *six hours.* That sure sounds like one hell of an event planner to me."

Julia shoved her phone back in her tote. "I was helping a *friend,* not trying to create an over-the-top wedding for some billionaire wanting fireworks or a hundred white doves released. Who in their right mind expects the cleaning lady to suddenly morph into an event planner overnight?"

Peg sat back down, stretched her arms across the seat back, and canted her head. "Olivia obviously does. And so do I. And deep down you do, too, or you wouldn't have accepted the position."

"Will you please tell me when Olivia went from being the town mouse to the town matriarch?" Julia muttered. "And when did she start getting so bossy? Yesterday I was blindsided by a woman who used to run out of the Drunken Moose and hide in people's vehicles just to avoid *talking* to someone."

Peg gave a chuckle. "She got a bit pushy with me, too, and issued an unnamed threat if I didn't crawl out of Billy's casket and into Duncan's bed before she got back from her cross-country honeymoon." Peg sighed. "Olivia's always been assertive in that quiet way of hers, but I think falling in love with a man as big and scary as Mac makes her feel invincible. Trust that she knows what she's doing, Jules. But more importantly, trust *yourself.* Um, you said two or three stupid things, so what else?"

Julia walked to the front rail of the boat and hugged herself as she looked up at Whisper Mountain, realizing she could barely see the glass-fronted house — that she now knew also had a glass floor — since it blended into the trees as it dangled over the edge of a tall cliff. She took a deep breath in anticipation of Peg's reaction. "I had sex with Nicholas last night."

Stark, absolute silence followed, lasting two, three, four pregnant heartbeats.

Which reminded her . . . "And we didn't use any protection." Julia turned when Peg still said nothing, and saw her friend clutching her throat, staring at her in horror.

"*You* made love last night," Peg finally whispered, "to *Nicholas*?"

"We didn't 'make love,' " Julia said, her own eyes widening in horror as she waved toward the mountain. "We had *wild passionate sex* on the floor of the event planner's cabin. And then I ran into the bathroom and crawled out the window." She hugged herself again. "He was standing outside next to a tree, waiting for me," she continued softly. "And I . . . I got angry and told him that if he followed me, I was going to bludgeon him to death with my brand-new tote that was a gift from Rana." She looked up to find Peg's horror had turned to disbelief, and sighed. "I know threatening him was crazy, but I just wasn't up to dealing with the . . . with whatever it is people do after they've just . . . Darn it, Peg, I had sex with *Nicholas.*"

"I don't know which shocks me more," Peg said softly. "That you made love at all or that it was to Nicholas." She stood up, shaking her head as she walked over. "You might see it as having wild passionate sex," she said with a crooked smile, "but I doubt Nicholas sees it that way." Peg led her to the couch opposite the steering wheel, sat her down, then grabbed Julia's coffee and handed it to her before sitting down in the captain's chair. "Nicholas is . . . He's a lot like Mac and Duncan and Alec. You remember Alec, don't you, who I kept trying to fix you up with before he ran off with Mac's sister last year?"

Julia mutely nodded.

"Anyway," Peg continued, "what I'm trying to say is that those four men are really quite frighteningly alike."

"You mean big and scary?"

Peg nodded. "Yeah, they are that, but they're also overly confident, stubborn, protective, and so maddeningly noble and old-fashioned that you'd swear they were all born in some long-forgotten century." She shook her head again. "Nicholas has been here over a year now and hasn't once shown interest in any woman. In fact, he's gone out of his way to avoid them. And you're telling me that he just suddenly decides to have sex with you?" She canted her head. "Why is that, I wonder, and why with you?"

"I don't know," Julia snapped. "Maybe he heard I was the town slut and decided to relieve a year's worth of pent-up sexual frustration." She snorted. "I certainly proved the rumors right, didn't I?"

Peg jumped out of her chair, making Julia press back against the seat when her friend got right in her face. "You say something like that again and I swear I'm throwing you overboard. You've spent so long proving to everyone that you're the town *saint,* you don't even remember how to swear."

"Then what *in hell* happened last night?" Julia growled right back at her.

"I'll tell you what happened. A strong, handsome man tall enough to see past that nose you keep stuck in the air called your bluff, and you finally remembered that you're a flesh-and-blood woman."

"But I'm not," Julia whispered, looking away.

Peg pressed her hands to Julia's face. "Why do you say that, Jules? What did Clay do that turned you off men? There's something you're not telling me that goes way beyond the rumors. We've been best friends ever since we teamed up in kindergarten to teach Bobby Pinkham how to kiss, and I thought there wasn't anything we couldn't tell each other. So what really happened to my wild and daring best friend who left here ten years ago and came back six years later a hollow shell of a woman?"

Julia simply dropped her gaze and shook her head inside Peg's hands.

Peg straightened away with a sigh, then walked to the front of the boat where she silently stood staring out at the fiord they were drifting down. Julia set her coffee in the holder beside her, then bent forward and hid her face in her hands, wondering when she'd become such a mess.

No, a walking disaster.

"He may have let you run away last night," Peg said without turning around, "but don't for a minute think he'll let you pull that kind of stunt again."

"There's not going to be an again." Julia straightened. "I can't ever have s— I can't ever be with him again."

"And if you're pregnant?" Peg asked softly, still looking out at the water.

"Then I'm going to find a *real* friend to put me out of my misery."

Peg turned and surprised Julia with a lopsided smile. "Damn, Jules, you really are on a stupid roll, aren't you? Men like Nicholas don't make unprotected love to a woman and then shove their hands in their pockets and walk away whistling." She came back and sat in the chair opposite Julia again. "On that you can trust me, because I

243

found myself *married* less than twenty-four hours after making love to Duncan. And just before you moved back here, Olivia found herself standing in front of Reverend Peter within a month of first laying eyes on Mac."

"Men like Nicholas don't fall in love with women like me. Not the way Duncan and Mac fell madly in love with you and Olivia," Julia countered. "What you guys have is either a miracle or a fluke of nature."

Peg laughed, gesturing out at the water. "You're sitting smack in the middle of a fluke of nature, Jules, so apparently miracles are more common than you think." She leaned forward and touched Julia's knee. "And if it can happen to Olivia and to me, then why in God's name can't it happen to you?"

"Because just like I told Olivia yesterday, I'm not *like* either of you." Julia gestured at herself. "If I cut my hair I'd keep getting mistaken for a twelve-year-old boy, whereas you . . . you got boobs in the sixth grade. My eyes are plain old hazel, my hair is mousy brown and always out of control, I can't flirt my way out of a wet paper bag, and I'm about as sexy as a cow moose in heat."

"Then if you're so unattractive, why did

Spellbound Falls' most eligible bachelor make love to *you* last night?"

"Because he had a year's buildup of sperm!"

Peg gaped at her, then shook her head. "My God, Clay did a number on you," she muttered, only to suddenly straighten in her chair. "Okay then, do something about it. If you don't want to be mistaken for a twelve-year-old boy, then get your hair professionally styled, start dressing in more feminine colors, and buy yourself some really nice boobs."

"Buy some *what*?"

"Boobs; if you can't grow them, then buy them. You ought to be able to afford a really impressive pair on an event planner's salary."

"Now you're the one talking crazy. If I suddenly showed up with boobs, every Tom, Dick, and Harry would start groping me again like they tried to after my divorce."

Peg bobbed her eyebrows. "Grope them back."

Julia's jaw dropped, but then she suddenly burst out laughing. "Margaret Conroy, you're outrageous!" she cried, jumping up and pulling Peg to her feet. She hugged her tightly. "I knew you could talk me off the ledge. Thank you for being the best friend in the world."

Peg stepped away and brushed down the front of her jacket. "It's Margaret Mac-Keage now," she said thickly, but there was laughter in her eyes when she lifted her head. "And anytime you feel like talking stupid again, you just come see me."

Julia looked toward Whisper Mountain. "I'm still an event planner."

"Pfffaaa," Peg said with a dismissive wave. "You'll have that job nailed down within a month, tops. As for Nicholas," she drawled, turning away to step behind the wheel and start the boat's engine, even as she shot Julia what could only be described as a sinister smile, "I'm betting he'll have *you* nailed again within a week. Sit down, Jules," Peg said as she gripped the wheel and pushed the throttle forward. "You don't want to be late for your first full day on your new job."

CHAPTER TWELVE

Poor Julia. Nicholas couldn't decide which had made her more uncomfortable: that she had been attending a director's meeting, that she'd spent that meeting sitting across from the man she'd made passionate love to the night before, or that she'd had to simply *sit* for the entire hour. At least she hadn't been holding a long pole in her hand, he thought with a grin as he watched the clearly overwhelmed woman extricate herself from yet another one of the congratulatory hugs she'd gotten from several of the directors — one of them *not* being her former supervisor, Nicholas noticed.

Rana slipped into the chair beside him. "She's absolutely lovely," she said, also watching Julia bolt out the door. "But then, I've always known you had an eye for quality." She patted his arm with a sigh. "Although I'm afraid you have a challenge ahead of you. Julia has a bit of a . . . self-esteem issue — which truly baffles me, as she's really quite an intelligent, beautiful, and vivacious woman."

Nicholas slid his gaze to the window and stifled his own sigh when he saw Julia rush past her cart without even seeing it and start running up the path leading to the conference pavilion. "I'm not the one you have to convince." He looked over at Rana. "Will you be able to get the *lovely lady* to see she's all those things and more?" He shook his head. "Because I don't appear to be having much luck, as it seems that for every step closer I get to her, she shoves me two away."

Rana arched one of her regal brows. "But did your note inviting her to go pinecone hunting across the fiord not work out as we'd hoped?"

Nicholas stood up with a snort. "No, it did not. She sent me a note in return thanking me for the very *kind* offer, then hunted down her own stand of pines — which happened to be right in the middle of my training grounds." He reached a hand out to her. "I think you better chase after your protégé before she threatens to bludgeon anyone else with that bag you gave her. I believe she left you her cart," he drawled, gesturing out the window.

Once on her feet, Rana refused to relinquish his hand, her brow arching again. "But did Titus not tell me you were cooking *breakfast* for Julia yesterday morning?"

"Would that be the breakfast he and your son ate while she crawled out my bathroom window? After which, when I sought her out and asked why she'd run, she shoved past me as if I were a minor annoyance?" Nicholas started them toward the hallway. "What Julia lacks in self-esteem she certainly makes up for in recklessness." He stopped and grinned. "She likes my cats, though, especially Sol."

Rana broke into a broad smile. "Then by all means, use those little scoundrels to your advantage." Her eyes suddenly widened. "I know; get your lovely lady a kitten of her own. Yes," she said with a nod, "a soft and cuddly little ball of fur that will make Julia think of you every time she laughs at its antics. And have the carpenters install one of those tiny doors in her new home like you had in your apartment." She leaned closer. "Go to some far-off ancient land and find an exotic breed like your lovely Bastet, only be sure the kitten's eyes are the exact color of yours," she instructed, making Nicholas grin at the wistfulness in her voice. "And put a bow around its neck, so Julia will see it as a gift of *your* esteem for her."

She slipped her arm through his and started down the hall toward the outside door. "And when you do, also make sure you get down on the floor in front of a roaring fire you're going to build in her hearth and the two of you play with the kitten together."

Nicholas lost his grin when he realized Rana's wistfulness had turned somewhat . . . angry. They walked into the sunshine and she gave his arm one last pat before she slid into Julia's forgotten cart, set her hands on the steering wheel, and looked up at him with a tight smile. "Use your legendary patience to hold that equally infamous pride of yours in check, Nicholas," she continued, "and try not to take Julia's rebuffs personally. It really has nothing to do with you and everything to do with whom or whatever has stolen *her* pride." Rana's smile turned tender. "And I'll see what I can do to further your cause." But then it suddenly vanished completely. "Although I have no idea why any woman would want to saddle herself with a stubborn, overprotective, insensitive . . ." she continued, the rest of what she said being lost in her growl as she zoomed away.

Knowing not to take *that* personally, Nicholas turned and walked back inside, thinking he might want to ask Titus how long it had been since the old theurgist had given his wife something soft and cuddly and gotten down on the floor in front of a roaring fire to play like young lovers. But also thinking he might want a more modern opinion, Nicholas stopped at Olivia's open office door and knocked on the casing.

"What's up?" she asked, waving him in.

"I've come seeking advice on a personal matter," he said without preamble, sitting down and leaning forward to rest his elbows on his knees. "I'm trying to get a handle on Julia Campbell, and I thought with your having known her for some years that you might be able to help me. She's an intelligent woman, but my attempts to let her know I'm attracted to her seem to be going right over her head," he prevaricated, not about to mention last night's passionate step forward followed by two *large* steps back. "I've offered to take Julia to dinner and pinecone hunting and fishing, but she keeps turning me down. Do you think she might truly be afraid of men on some deep level, or merely reluctant to get involved in a relationship again — maybe with me in particular?"

Olivia gave a quick laugh. "Julia's not afraid of you or any other man. My first guess off the top of my head is that she's trying to protect you."

He straightened in surprise. "From *what*?"

"From being seen in public with the town slut and daughter of the town drunk." She sighed at his glower. "Okay, look; you might as well hear it from me, because you're definitely going to hear it from somebody. Before he headed off to Boston *with his new wife,* Julia's ex-husband started telling people in town that she'd slept with half the men at the fraternity house where she worked when they lived in Orono, so he wouldn't look like a jerk for divorcing her after she spent six years putting him through college. Since Julia moved back home, she's been going out of her way to prove those rumors wrong — all to no avail," she said with a shake of her head. "And since it's no secret you're considered Spellbound Falls' most eligible bachelor, my guess is she's trying to save your reputation."

"I couldn't care less about my reputation."

"But *she* cares." Olivia leaned back in her chair. "And there might be another reason she keeps turning you down. Remember when we were moving Julia out of her house and I explained how embarrassing it was for her to have you watch? Well," she said when he nodded, "that might also be why she doesn't want anyone seeing you together. Because no matter what century it is, gossip is every small town's primary entertainment. If Julia is attracted to you — and she'd have to be dead if she weren't — then she's probably worried someone will feel compelled to tell you her entire, sordid history, and she'll be even more humiliated."

Nicholas stood up to keep from growling in frustration. "Thank you," he said, turning to leave — only to stop at the door when Olivia called to him.

"Mac told me he saw Julia running from your home yesterday morning," she said, arching a brow. "Is there more to her little . . . accident I should know about?"

"No," he said succinctly.

"I was just about to resort to blackmail," Olivia continued before he could leave, "when I finally was able to get Julia to see past her circumstances long enough to agree to be my event planner." She shook her head. "But there's a very real possibility not even my dear mother-in-law's wisdom and patience will be able to break down Julia's defenses, and I'm afraid the first time she makes a mistake that she'll quit."

"Don't underestimate Rana. Or me," Nicholas said quietly as he turned with a wave and walked out the door. He slipped on his sunglasses when he stepped outside, then shoved his hands in his pockets as he headed toward the barn. Considering Julia was obviously *physically* attracted to him, he still couldn't figure out why she kept fighting his pursuit. At least he knew for certain she didn't prefer women, he thought with a grin as he remembered her reaction to his kiss last night. But then he scowled, remembering her whispered urging that he seek his own pleasure without seeing to hers, as if she hadn't wanted — or felt worthy of — anything in return for giving herself so openly.

In fact, Nicholas couldn't recall the last time he'd been so caught off guard — be it on the battlefield or in the bedroom — to be literally brought to his knees by such honest abandon, the likes of which he'd never experienced before. Yet when he'd caught her escaping afterward, Julia had told him she didn't know who that woman had been back in the cabin, but that it definitely hadn't been *her.*

So it appeared the lovely lady was equally perplexed at her reluctance to admit their mutual attraction; one moment responding to him quite passionately, and within the next heartbeat running away. After threatening to bludgeon him to death, he thought with a grin, even though standing on tiptoe her nose still hadn't reached his chin. She did have a powerful finger poke, however, to back up her beautiful temper.

Yes, he definitely liked an abrasive woman.

Nicholas walked into the barn, grabbed his saddle and bridle out of the tack room, and headed down the aisle, grinning again when he heard Phantom impatiently kicking his stall door. "You in need of a run?" he asked when the battle-scarred warrior shoved its nose between the bars and tried to take a nip out of his shoulder as Nicholas pushed on the door — that Phantom was still kicking — to open the latch. "Behave," he said with a laugh, stepping in the stall, "or you're only going for a slow walk."

The large, ghostly gray stallion gently nudged the same shoulder it had just tried to nip, then blew out a belly-deep equine sigh.

"That's better," Nicholas murmured, tossing the saddle onto its broad back, then positioning the bit in the stallion's mouth. "We'll ride out to see how our new guards are surviving their first day of Sampson's tutelage." He secured the bridle, repositioned the saddle and secured the cinch, waited several heartbeats, then finished tightening it when Phantom was forced to release the breath he'd been holding. "You haven't won that game in centuries, you old dog," he said with a chuckle, giving the warhorse an affectionate pat before leading it out of the stall.

"Nicholas," Sally said, walking in from the back of the barn. The female half of the resort's horse wrangler team gestured behind her with a frown. "Would you know who that kid is sitting on the paddock rail? I saw him back up a muddy old pickup to the woodshed and unload some firewood, but instead of driving off he walked over and hopped up on the fence. He's been sitting out there for half an hour."

Nicholas led Phantom partway down the aisle to look out the back door of the barn. "That's our new director of special events' youngest brother — Reggie, I believe his name is. He sells the resort cedar kindling. Have you had the pleasure of meeting Julia Campbell yet?"

"Isn't she the woman staying in your old apartment?" Sally asked as she reached out and respectfully gave Phantom's cheek a scratch. "I've met Julia," she continued when Nicholas nodded. She smiled. "Caught her in here a couple of days ago trying to work up the nerve to pat old Jeb," she said, gesturing at the horse with its head hanging out over a stall door, softly snoring. "Nice lady. She asked why some of the horses are behind bars and can't stick their heads out." Sally gave a soft chuckle. "When I told her they were the stallions and had a tendency to nip at anyone walking by, she said that figured. But I thought Julia told me she worked in housekeeping."

"She did until yesterday, when she took over Evelyn's position."

Sally scowled. "That's one woman I'm not going to miss." She gestured out the back door again. "So what about the kid? You want I should just leave him alone?"

Nicholas looked out at Reggie Campbell to see him rubbing the face of a mare he'd coaxed over. "Could I get you to saddle up old Jeb for me, Sally? Since the boy seems interested in horses, he might like to ride out to see his brother. Tom Campbell is training to be a security guard for Inglenook."

"Well, there's no question Olivia likes hiring entire families," the wrangler said, heading toward the tack room. She stopped at the door. "The day Peyton Jr. turned fifteen, she put him on the payroll part-time and plans to let him lead trail rides this summer." Her smile widened. "Ain't nothing Big Peyton has been enjoying more than getting to *officially* boss that boy around. I'll bring Jeb out all ready to go — assuming I can wake him up," she said as she disappeared into the tack room.

Nicholas led Phantom outside, then walked to the paddock and leaned his arms on the rail. Reggie glanced over, his eyes widening when he recognized him from their little meeting in the parking lot a week ago, and started to get down off the fence.

"Don't leave," Nicholas said quietly, stifling a grin when the boy stilled halfway to the ground. "You like horses?"

"I've never been around them much," the kid said, slowly settling back on the rail. He glanced over again when Nicholas said nothing. "That one you got is really big." He used his chin to nod at Phantom. "And all scarred up and sort of mean-looking."

"I'm a pretty big guy. And like his owner," Nicholas said, scratching Phantom's neck, "this old warrior looks a lot meaner than he is — sometimes."

The boy went back to watching the horses. "You hired Tom as a security guard."

"Yes."

"How come? He doesn't much like confrontations."

"That's why I hired him."

Reggie looked over in surprise. "But what

258

happens when a guest gets drunk and . . . turns mean or something?" He used his chin again, this time to gesture at Nicholas. "Julia told me how you knocked the wind out of our father last Saturday and carried him outside." He shook his head. "Tom won't be able to do that."

"He won't have to, because he's going to learn how to read a situation and not let it reach that point."

Sally came out leading Jeb, and Nicholas motioned for her to give the reins to Reggie. "What?" the boy asked in surprise when Sally held the reins out to him. He jumped off the fence and shoved his hands in his pockets, even as he darted a nervous glance at Nicholas before looking at Sally again. "I don't want . . . I can't . . . I don't know how to ride."

"That's okay," Sally said with a laugh, yanking one of his hands out of his pocket and slapping the reins in it. "Jeb knows what he's doing." She tilted her head. "You look about my son's age. You go to school with a kid named Peyton Knox?"

Reggie nodded. "I know him. I'm one year ahead of him."

"Then how come he's in school today and you're not?" Sally asked.

Nicholas saw the boy's face redden as he

darted another glance his way before giving Sally a shrug. "I was feeling sick to— earlier this morning."

Sally turned and headed back to the barn. "Sick of school, most likely," she said, giving Nicholas a wink on her way by.

Nicholas walked over to him. "Mount up and I'll adjust your stirrups."

"I've never ridden a horse before," Reggie said, even as he moved to stand facing the saddle. He eyed Jeb's big head, then squared his shoulders and grabbed the saddle, lifted a foot into the stirrup, and awkwardly pulled himself up — only to grab the horn with both hands when the old horse released a loud groan.

Nicholas took the forgotten reins from Reggie and looped one on each side of Jeb's neck before silently handing them back. He adjusted one of the stirrups, led his own horse around to the other side, and adjusted the other stirrup. "Squeeze with your legs to make him go," he quietly instructed. "Pull back easy on the reins when you want him to stop, and gently pull on the left or right rein for whichever way you want to turn. And don't fall off, because the last thing I want is your sister to come gunning for me."

Reggie's eyes widened. "Are you saying

you're *afraid* of Julia?"

Nicholas turned and mounted up. "For the record," he drawled, holding Phantom in check so Reggie could follow as he headed toward the resort. "I wasn't saving Trisha from your father last Saturday; I was saving your father from *Julia.*" He chuckled. "I have it on good authority that she's quite lethal with a stick when she's riled."

Reggie gave a snort, then fell silent as they passed the lower one of the hotel segments; Nicholas noticing the boy sitting taller in the saddle when several guests heading to or from their rooms stopped to watch them ride by. He also was pleased to discover that Reggie was a young man of few words, apparently content to simply be in the moment. Or else, just as Julia had the night Nicholas had hustled her into his truck and given her a ride home, the boy was silently waiting to see why the big man with the mean-looking horse had all but kidnapped him.

Nicholas turned once they'd passed the common green and started up the path that led to a high-mountain pond a couple of miles away, not even considering they'd be going past the conference pavilion until he spotted Julia getting in her cart with Rana and two women — her German bride and mother, he presumed.

Julia spotted them, her eyes widening when she recognized her little brother, and scrambled back out of the cart to stand gaping at them riding by. Nicholas glanced over in time to see Reggie give his sister a shrug, silently communicating that he didn't know what he was doing riding a horse through the resort, either.

They continued on in companionable silence until Nicholas saw the other half of Nova Mare's horse wrangler team returning from guiding a family of four on a trail ride. The tall, slim Canadian immediately cantered over, then sidled up closer and spoke softly. "We just passed three young men and a fairly young girl not half a mile down the fiord trail and . . ." He leaned closer. "I can't say I saw anything particularly wrong, but I sensed the girl was . . ." He blew out a sigh and adjusted his hat on his head. "Hell, I got the feeling she was uncomfortable to be out there with them. She had a look in her eyes that said she knew she'd made a mistake but didn't know how to get out of it." The wrangler glanced over to see his family continuing toward the resort on their own, then turned back to Nicholas and shook his head. "I told the girl she was looking a mite tired and offered to give her a ride back, but one of the boys caught her hand with a laugh and started leading her off down the trail, the other two assuring me they were all fine. I think the boys are guests, seeing how they had pretty heavy accents I didn't recognize, but the girl looked like a local."

"Where, again?" Nicholas asked.

"They were about half a mile down just fifteen minutes ago." Peyton dropped his gaze and shook his head again. "I got my phone wet the other day and haven't taken the time to replace it, or I would have called you or Rowan. And I couldn't start anything with those three boys while I had that family with me," he muttered, waving toward his four riders — two of whom were children. He lifted his gaze back to Nicholas. "I'm sorry. I cut our ride short and have been trying to hustle back to tell you or Rowan."

"I'll go find them now," Nicholas said. "But you stop and have my secretary give you a new phone. Sally can take care of your riders. And Peyton," he said quietly. "You don't go even an hour without a working phone again. And when you or Sally or your son takes riders beyond the five-mile range, you make sure you have a satellite phone and one of the GPS emergency beacons with you."

The wrangler's face reddened as he touched his hat with a nod. "I won't be caught with my pants down again," he said, cantering his horse after his guests.

"You up for a faster ride?" Nicholas asked Reggie as he guided Phantom toward the lower fiord trail. "If you start bouncing," he said, breaking into a slow trot, "just put more of your weight on your stirrups."

"Are we . . . going after . . . those guys and girl?" the boy asked as he bounced, grabbed the horn and righted himself, then bounced some more.

"Yes." Nicholas sighed when Reggie nearly fell off again. "Okay, look; you won't be able to keep up with me, so follow this trail until you come to my horse. Then wait there with him, staying completely silent, until you see me or hear my signal. Pull Jeb to a stop so he doesn't try to follow."

"What's the signal — *ohff!*" Reggie ended in a grunt, barely catching himself again when Jeb suddenly halted.

"You'll know when you hear it," Nicholas said, finally releasing Phantom when his intuitive old friend reared in response to its rider's urgency and immediately broke into a ground-eating gallop. Nicholas rode low in the saddle as the powerful warhorse raced down the narrow hiking trail with the same agility and confidence that had carried them into more battles than either of them cared to count. He finally pulled to a halt when he caught the first wave of desperation pulsing through the air, dismounting and tying the reins around Phantom's neck. "I'll signal if I need you," he growled to the horse, breaking into a run as he left the trail at a diagonal.

He wove through the steeply descending forest as the breeze pushing up from the fiord thickened with the smell of fear; the girl's pounding heartbeat growing louder as Nicholas raced toward what he realized had become a chase. Sensing frustration and anger coming from the men, he suddenly grinned past his own anger. The local women, it appeared, were damn good runners. He began slowing, now able to actually hear the chase he'd been sensing, and stopped beside a large tree and waited, then reached out and snagged the girl as she ran past.

Clamping his hand over her mouth and gently subduing her struggles, he spoke softly into her ear. "You're safe now. I'm resort security. I'm going to point you in the direction of the trail, and when you reach it, turn left. Understand?" he asked, removing his hand when she nodded and loosening his hold when she started breathing raggedly again. "There's a young man waiting a short distance up the trail. Tell him *Nicholas* said to take you back to the resort, but have him leave my horse. Can you do that?"

She nodded again.

"Good girl. Reggie will take care of you," he said, pointing her uphill. He then opened his arms, leaving them hovering nearby until he was sure she wasn't too winded to run — only to grin when she took off like he'd pinched her. He watched until she disappeared into the trees, realizing the pretty little thing couldn't be more than fifteen or sixteen years old. Hell, she was probably in Reggie's or young Peyton's class, and would likely think twice about missing school again or letting some rich tourist boys talk her into coming back with them to the fancy resort on top of the mountain.

He turned when he heard the men getting closer, their taunting petitions to the girl telling him that two were still together and one had moved farther down the mountain to drive their prey toward them. Nicholas's anger suddenly returned tenfold when he recognized that between their stilted cajoling English, the language they spoke to one another hadn't been used anywhere in the world in centuries.

And that was a game-changer.

There would be no call placed to deputy sheriff Jason Biggs this day, as the authority these three young men were about to answer to was big and mean-looking and far more ancient than they were.

CHAPTER THIRTEEN

Julia stood in the center of the gazebo pretending she knew exactly what she was doing, while also pretending Rana's eyes weren't shining with barely restrained laughter as *Mrs.* Rauch explained to *Miss* Rauch — for the fifth time in ten minutes — that no daughter of hers was getting married wearing jeans and hiking boots.

Well, that's what Rana had told Julia they were discussing, as the majority of the conversation was in German — which, thankfully, her mentor spoke.

"Frau Rauch," Rana said, stepping up to the mother of the bride with an utterly serene smile. "Ms. Campbell apparently shares your sentiment, as she told me just before you arrived this morning that she plans to have a wardrobe tent set up right over there," she said, pointing at the stunted pines on the western edge of the windswept ledge. Rana then turned all that regal serenity on the glowering bride. "She felt an experienced hiker such as you are, fräulein, wouldn't have any problem negotiating the granite ledge in heels. Is that not what you said this morning, Ms. Campbell?" Rana asked, turning that serene smile on Julia.

Was her mentor going to Hades for lying, Julia wondered, or was *she* going there for compelling the woman to lie on her behalf? "Yes," Julia quickly agreed with a nod at her two clients, also trying to exude serenity as she boldly compounded the lie. "Actually, I plan to set up two tents, so the groom and his men can also change out of their formalwear after the ceremony. Because," she further compounded, "I thought it quite . . . venturesome of you, Miss Rauch, to wear traditional wedding attire juxtaposed with such a rugged and powerful backdrop. In fact, I saw it as an even more defining statement than your reception," she added, gesturing at the surrounding landscape, "as I pictured your wedding portrait hanging over your mantel, showing everyone how your marriage embraces both the civilized world *and* the wilderness that you and your soon-to-be husband obviously love so much."

"Oh, but that was exactly my intention," the young woman said excitedly, even clapping her hands as she turned to her mother. "Is that not perfect, Mutti? Our portrait will say to everyone, 'This is who we are — civilized *and* wild.' " She turned back to Julia. "You may set up the tents, but please make sure they can't be seen from the gazebo and the bonfire, yes?"

"Not a problem," Julia assured her as she furiously wrote in her beautiful leather calendar book. She stopped and looked up. "And the horse?" she asked. "You still want to ride off into the sunset in the arms of your new husband?"

"A *gentle* steed," the girl said with a laugh. "As my dear Berdy is no horseman."

"Not a problem," Julia repeated, again making a note to ask their lady wrangler — Sally, she thought her name was — for the horse that Reggie was right now riding with . . . For crying out loud, what was her brother doing with *Nicholas*? "We have just the steed for your Prince Charming to whisk you away to the excited cheers of your friends and family." Julia looked up again, hoping she wasn't pouring it on too thickly, and released a silent sigh to find both mother and bride smiling dreamily. "And one of our people will be hiding in the woods to lead you to the campsite we'll have all set up waiting for you," she added, making another note to find a good spot not too far away. "All your hiking gear will be there, ready to go in the morning."

Julia squeaked in surprise when young Adeline Rauch threw her arms around her clueless event planner in a book-crushing hug. "Oh, Ms. Campbell, I knew the moment we met that you already shared my vision better than your predecessor just by seeing how you — and now your staff as well," she continued, waving one hand toward Rana before hugging Julia again, "are dressed in slacks and camp shirts instead of stuffy suits. Thank you for making my wedding day everything I've dreamed it to be."

Julia patted the bride's back, then slowly extricated herself from her grip, stifling an urge to tell the girl not to thank her until *after* they rode off into a warm sunset instead of a wind-driven rain mixed with snowflakes. "Well, you're only going to do this once," she said brightly instead, attempting to make her arched eyebrow appear regal. "So it needs to be memorable so you'll want to return to Nova Mare to *renew* your vows on your golden anniversary."

"One can only hope my dear Berdy will live to see that day," Adeline said with a laugh as she laced her arm through her mother's and headed off the gazebo. "Come, Mutti, let us hike back to our cabin on this beautiful afternoon, so I can try on the dress I suspect is in that large box I saw Papa sneak through baggage at the airport." She stopped and looked back at the gazebo. "Thank you, Ms. Campbell. And Rana," the young woman added with only a cursory nod at the *real live queen* before looking back at Julia. "I will see you tomorrow morning, then, for breakfast at Aeolus's Whisper so you can meet my dear Berdy?"

Julia nodded. "I'll be there at . . . Is eight a good time?"

"Oh, dear God, no," the girl said with a laugh, heading off again with her smugly smiling mother in tow. "Let us make it ten."

Julia walked over to the bench that ran along the inside perimeter of the large gazebo and sat down with a sigh. She opened her calendar book, smoothed out the pages that had been crushed in the hug, and jotted down her breakfast date at ten o'clock on tomorrow's page.

"Might I suggest you set an alarm on your cell phone for nine thirty A.M.?" Rana said, sitting down beside her, then leaning over and turning the page back to see what Julia had written. Her mentor took the book away and settled it on her own lap, pulled

272

the pen from Julia's hand, and added three words ahead of several of the notes. "And you might also wish to *delegate* these tasks," she said, sliding the pen into its leather sleeve and setting the book back on Julia's lap. She smiled, leaning in to nudge Julia's shoulder with her own. "As I believe that's why you have three assistants and two young men sitting in your design room furiously whittling hot dog sticks as they await to make your every wish their command."

Julia looked down to see that Rana had written *Ask Merriam* or *Anna* or *Ariel to* in front of whatever note she'd made to herself. "Sorry, I forgot I had them," she said, stopping short of nudging Rana back — figuring she probably shouldn't shoulder-butt a real live queen. So she shrugged instead. "I guess I'm used to just rolling up my sleeves and doing things myself, although I didn't mind delegating cutting and then whittling sixty hot dog sticks," she said deadpan.

But then Julia sighed again, staring off at the two women disappearing into the stunted pines. "Well, that was a big faux pas, mentioning their golden anniversary. Have you by any chance seen *dear Berdy?*" she asked, grinning at Rana's now familiar snort. "He must really, really love her," Julia

273

drawled, "because the distinguished, definitely forty-something gentleman I saw Adeline passionately kissing when they got out of the limo has never set foot on a hiking trail in his life."

"Love has the power to make men do amazing things to impress a woman," Rana said, leaning back against the rail with a dreamy smile of her own. "Sometimes even compelling them to slay dragons and move mountains."

Julia got a little dreamy at that notion herself. That is, until she remembered she had better things to do than wonder if anyone — oh, say, a man with sky-blue eyes and magnetic muscles — would ever feel compelled to slay dragons or move mountains for her. She started writing notes again. "Do you think I might persuade Adeline to leave that small boulder on her finger in the resort safe," she asked, "while she and dear Berdy hike through the wilderness for a week in late November?"

"Yes, that might be wise." Rana wrapped an arm around Julia and gave her a squeeze. "You, my lovely lady, are not only a quick prevaricator, but a natural at creating illusions." She leaned away to look Julia in the eye, her own eyes shining with laughter again. "You have *me* wanting to renew my marriage vows on top of this wild and rugged mountain." She patted Julia's knee and stood up. "But not in November. Nor do I have a wish to ride off into —"

Rana gasped and Julia flinched so badly that she dropped her calendar book when a sharp clap of thunder suddenly pierced the air at the same time a flash of light burst up from the woods to the northeast, immediately followed by a low rumble that shook the ground beneath the gazebo.

"Since when do aftershocks *flash*?" Julia whispered, staring at where she'd seen the light — which was the same direction Reggie had been riding, she suddenly realized. "Oh no, Nicholas and my brother are down there. That flash could have been the sun reflecting off dust from a huge landslide or something."

Rana caught Julia's sleeve when she started toward the stairs. "Your brother is perfectly safe with Nicholas." She waved in that direction. "Have you not heard any of these . . . aftershocks up here before?"

"Yes, several times, actually. In fact, there was a really long, rumbling one just a few days ago." She let Rana lead her back to the bench and they both sat down again. "I had to tell the guests whose cottage I was cleaning that the tremors are never violent enough to damage anything. But I've never seen a flash like that before."

"Our vantage point is likely the reason we saw it today," Rana said. "But you needn't worry about —"

"Mother!" Olivia's husband shouted as he broke through the trees running toward them. Julia recognized his father, Titus, running up the path behind him. "Where's Nicholas?" Mac asked as he drew near. "He's not answering his cell phone."

Rana stood up, her smile gone as she gave a worried glance in the direction of the flash. "He's out riding with Julia's brother. Reggie, isn't it?" she asked, looking back at her son when Julia nodded. "They may be out of range of the small phones, as the two of them rode past the conference pavilion over an hour ago."

Julia bent to retrieve her calendar book off the floor and also stood up. "We saw a large flash of light with this aftershock," she told Mac, pointing down the northeastern side of the mountain. "I thought it might be a —"

They all flinched this time, including Titus just as he was reaching them, when another crack pierced the air — the two men spinning just as the second flash faded and the ensuing boom rumbled the ground beneath them again.

"By the gods, what is he *doing*?" Mac growled, looking at his father. "He can't arbitrarily —" The rest of what he said was lost when Mac turned away and lowered his voice as he stepped closer to Titus.

Julia stared at them in confusion. The two men had run up here thinking Nicholas had something to do with the booms? What; had his training sessions graduated from paint-balls to *hand grenades*?

And Reggie was with him? And Tom?

"I have to go find Reggie," Julia told Rana as she picked up her tote. She shoved her calendar book inside and headed down the steps to find her baby brother even if it meant she had to ride a horse. But when she started past Mac, he suddenly moved into her path — quite like Nicholas often did, she realized.

Only she wasn't quite brave enough to push past this particular giant.

"I'm sure your brother is fine, Julia, if he's with Nicholas."

"Thank you, but Reggie's only sixteen, and I'd rather not have him around any training sessions that involve explosives." Although now that she thought about it — considering Mac was looking at her blankly, apparently trying to figure out what she was talking about — why would Nicholas need explosives to protect the resort?

Mac stepped to the side to stop her when she tried going around him. "I prefer you not run through the woods right now until we're certain —" He snapped his head up when another flash appeared, this time closer to the fiord, its piercing crack arriving half a second later, along with a ground-shaking rumble that was slightly subdued compared to the previous two. Julia shot around him and started down the path leading off the ledge again — only to be snagged around the waist and lifted off her feet. "Julia," Mac growled, making her go perfectly still, "I would ask that you not —"

"Oceanus!" a man shouted as he came through the stunted trees running toward them, an equally frantic woman struggling up the path behind him. "What in the name of Zeus is going on? I've spent the last hour searching for my sons, and suddenly there are *three* percussions?" He stopped in front of Mac's father. "By the gods, if anything's happened to them — where's your man who brought us here?" he asked, looking around before pinning his florid-faced glare back on Titus. "Nicholas. Where is he?"

"Mac," Rana said softly, having walked up beside him. "Give me Julia."

It appeared Mac had forgotten he was still holding her dangling off the ground, not that Julia had considered bringing that fact to his attention. Holy Hades, the man was big. And obviously strong. No wonder Olivia felt invincible.

And no wonder Peg thought her childhood friend was insane for threatening to bludgeon Nicholas — who was equally big and strong — with her tote.

Okay, that was another thing she couldn't ever do to Nicholas again.

Mac lowered Julia to her feet but didn't release her, his attention once again on the man glowering at his father. And she wasn't sure, but she'd swear Mac was . . . well, *growing;* like he was actually getting taller or something. She definitely felt the tension humming through him as the angry man — a guest as well as a personal acquaintance of the elder Oceanus, she gathered from the way Titus was trying to reassure him that his sons were probably just out hiking the trails — continued to rant and rail at him, only now in a language she didn't recognize.

"Rana, you have to help us," the angry man's wife petitioned in a panting, heavy accent, abandoning her husband to run to her friend — although the woman hesitated when she realized she had to go past Mac to get to her.

Rana, bless her unflappable heart, went to the woman and immediately wrapped an arm around her shoulders. "All will be well, Meleda. I'm sure your boys are fine."

Meleda gave her a hopeful smile. "They . . . they can be a handful sometimes."

"Julia! Hey, Jules!"

Julia gasped at the sight of Reggie waving at her from where the trail intercepted the cart path as he headed toward them at a run while all but dragging the horse he'd been riding — only now there was a young girl in the saddle. Julia struggled against Mac's hold. "Let me go," she demanded when he still hesitated, then started running the moment he released her — although Mac reached her brother before she did.

Reggie dropped the reins and turned to help the girl down, then protectively tucked her against his side. "This is Katy. She's in my class. Three men were chasing her through the woods," he said in a rush. "Nicholas went on ahead and got her away from them and sent her to me with instructions to bring her back while he . . ." Reggie looked at the woods behind him, his eyes turning troubled as he darted a nervous glance at Mac, then back to Julia. "He went after them," he whispered. "But then we heard some of those aftershocks and the entire forest lit up behind us. Three times." His hold on Katy tightened when the girl hid her face against him just as Titus and Rana and the angry husband and frantic wife arrived.

"Where are my sons?" the man snarled, reaching for Reggie.

Mac stepped in front of him. "That's enough, Perdiccas," he said, the look in his eyes making the man back away. "I suggest you take your wife to your cottage, and Father will bring word of your sons once we know their whereabouts."

"Please," Meleda said, tugging on her husband's sleeve. "Let us do as he says."

"Come, Perdiccas," Rana also gently petitioned, even as she embraced Meleda again and started for the resort — only to stop at the sound of hoofbeats.

Everyone turned to see Nicholas calmly cantering out of the woods, veering without changing stride when he spotted them. He brought his massive gray horse to a halt several yards away, then silently ran his gaze over the gathering.

Julia flinched when Mac's hand shot out to land on the angry father's chest when he stepped toward Nicholas. "Enough, Perdiccas," Mac growled in warning.

"Where are my sons?" the man in turn growled up at the man on the horse.

"I sent them home," Nicholas said quietly — although Julia doubted she was the only one who heard the dangerous edge in his voice as his unusually dark blue eyes bore into the man. And then he actually grinned when Mac had to shove Perdiccas back when he heard *that* news. "They should arrive in a . . . week," Nicholas continued rather provokingly, "if they're more successful at their little sport as prey than they were as predators."

Julia then saw Nicholas make eye contact with Titus and give a slight nod before urging his horse into a canter down the cart path toward the resort.

No, she was never, ever threatening him again.

Perdiccas — his eyes narrowed and his face nearly purple with rage — rounded on Titus. "I want that insolent bastard delivered to me in chains."

"I will afford you one hour to pack," Titus said calmly, contradicting the rage in *his* eyes. He turned with a slight bow to Meleda. "Although brief, it was nice seeing you again, madam." And then the elder Oceanus took Rana's hand and walked away.

282

"Wait," Perdiccas snapped, causing Titus to stop and look back. "I'm not leaving until we conclude our business."

"I suggest you gain authority over *your sons* before you consider ruling a nation," Titus said roughly, turning and walking away again.

"Please, *maritus*," Meleda whispered — Julia recognizing the Latin word for *husband* — as the woman reached out in petition. She dropped her hand when he still didn't move, then also turned and walked away.

"Will you and your wife be traveling home together or . . . separately?" Mac asked, the threat in his voice making Julia wrap an arm around Reggie, her heart swelling with pride as her baby brother still hugged the probably even more traumatized young girl, one of his gangly teenage hands holding her head against his chest as if he could stop her from hearing any of this.

Not that Julia knew what any of *this* was.

The man they were calling Perdiccas — why did that name sound familiar to her? — stared into the woods where his *three sons* had been chasing the girl and the light had flashed *three times,* and out of which Nicholas had ridden *alone,* then finally turned and strode toward the resort, his anger and frustration palpable.

Okay then; their impromptu little gathering was down to four — two of whom were apparently scared speechless, and one . . . well, Julia couldn't decide if she was scared or utterly and completely . . . spellbound.

What in holy Hades had just happened?

And what could Nicholas have meant when he'd said *I sent them home*?

How, by lightning bolt?

"Is Nicholas in trouble, sir?" Reggie asked Mac, making Julia wonder whose strong and confident voice her brother had stolen. "Because from my point of view, and Katy's," he said, nodding down at the girl he was still protectively holding, "Nicholas is a hero. Katy met those guys down in Turtleback, and they lured her up here by promising to take her swimming in the outdoor pool and then to dinner at the restaurant. But once they got here, they talked her into going for a hike first." Julia saw Reggie's jaw tighten. "She managed to get away when they tried to rape her," he growled, "but they were gaining on her when Nicholas caught Katy and sent her to me and then . . . went after them," he said, darting a look at the woods before he turned back to Mac and lifted his chin. "They deserved whatever he — they deserve to spend several cold nights lost in the woods

284

trying to get home, and I don't think anyone should go searching for them."

Mac's eyes softened, and he reached out and gently cupped the girl's head. "Did the boys harm you, Katy?" he asked.

"Th-they tore my blouse," she said, pulling the jacket Reggie must have given her more tightly around herself. She shook her head and hid her face in Reggie's chest as he tightened his embrace again. "But they didn't hurt me."

"Still," Mac said, dropping his hand, "Olivia and I will see that your parents take you to a doctor when we bring you home."

"No!" Katy cried on a gasp. She looked at Julia and then Reggie, her eyes filled with renewed fear. "Don't let them call my parents, Reggie," she pleaded, apparently deciding he was her best bet. "You know what my mom's like."

Julia knew exactly what Shirley Angstrom *was like,* as she'd had a few go-rounds with the holier-than-thou woman herself concerning Katy's older sister spreading vicious rumors at school about Trisha. "Come on, you two," she said, even as she looked at Mac for approval. "We'll go back to my apartment and make some hot cocoa."

Mac reached out again, this time his large hand clasping Reggie's shoulder. "I can see why Nicholas didn't hesitate to send Katy to you. On behalf of my wife, Nova Mare appreciates your actions today." He then gave the three of them an actual bow and walked to the horse Reggie had been leading.

Her arm still around her brother, urging him forward and effectively bringing Katy with them, Julia started off again — only to have Reggie pull to a stop. "Mr. Oceanus?" he asked. "You didn't answer my question. Is Nicholas in trouble?"

Mac turned, holding the reins. "Trust me, Mr. Campbell," he said with a grin. "Nicholas has made a very long and illustrious career of getting *out* of trouble."

On that note, Julia hustled the two teenagers up the path to the gazebo where her cart was parked, deciding she would have to think long and hard, and maybe stretch her imagination really far, about what had happened this afternoon on this mountain overlooking the fiord — neither of which had actually existed four years ago.

CHAPTER FOURTEEN

Nicholas felt the footsteps stop at his side door, then heard a soft knock. Finding himself caught off guard again but nevertheless immensely pleased, he remained sitting leaning against the two-story-tall windows staring out at Bottomless and simply waited. Sensing his visitor peering inside, he then heard the footsteps continue along the side porch, and took another sip of beer just as Julia stopped at the corner of his house.

When several heartbeats passed and she said nothing, Nicholas extended his hand without looking at her; partly to see if she'd walk onto the exterior continuation of his home's floor, but mostly to find out if she would approach despite there being a six-pack of beer sitting on the glass deck beside him. Several more heartbeats passed until he heard a sigh, followed by stilted footsteps before her hand slipped into his. He set down his beer and moved the six-pack to his other side, then steadied Julia as she slid down the window she was keeping herself pressed against and settled beside him.

"Would you like a beer?"

"Yes, thank you, I believe I would."

He pulled a bottle out of the cardboard pack, twisted off the top, and handed it to her, stifling a grin when she took a long guzzle, wiped her mouth on her sleeve, and relaxed back against the window with another sigh. "Aren't you supposed to have a railing on a deck that's over a foot off the ground?" she asked, also staring at the uninterrupted view of Bottomless nearly two thousand feet below.

"The carpenters are still trying to figure out how to attach one. Is the girl okay?"

Julia gave a soft snort. "She's more than okay; Katy thinks she's in heaven. That's her name, Katy Angstrom. She turned sixteen just a week ago. And the poor clueless girl either doesn't realize how close she came to this day ending very badly, or she honestly believes having a man swoop in and save her is how these things work." She tapped his leg with the toe of her sneaker. "I'm sorry, but Reggie has stolen your thunder and is now officially Katy's hero. She was still holding his hand when I left."

"Thank you for coming to tell me . . . assuming that's why you're here," he said, just before taking another sip of beer.

He lowered his bottle to see Julia worrying the label of her own bottle with her thumbnail. "Between Trisha showing up with her friend Kimberly and Reggie and Katy and *six* cats, the apartment was getting a little crowded. Well, five cats now, because Big Cat escorted me here."

"Big Cat?"

"The long-haired Maine coon or bobcat or . . . something on steroids."

"Ah," Nicholas said with a chuckle. "That would be Solomon."

"Any particular reason you named him after a very wise Old Testament king?"

"Because Sol is a very wise old cat."

Julia lifted her bottle, giving another soft snort just before taking a sip.

"So you came to my home to escape the chaos in yours?" he asked, turning to stare out at Bottomless again.

"Partly. But also to thank you for what you did for Reggie today."

He looked over in surprise. "For taking him horseback riding?"

"Well, that, too. But mostly for treating him like the intelligent, capable young man he is." She looked down, her thumbnail worrying the bottle's label again. "Folks around here have a tendency to visit the sins of a father upon his sons, and to a lot of people Reggie is . . . well, at best he's invisible and at worse he's a loser. But he's not," she softly growled, looking up. "He just needs a chance to prove himself." She reached over and touched his arm. "You can't possibly understand what you did today by sending Katy to Reggie and saying that he'd take care of her. My brother has never known what it's like to be treated with respect, or ever had anyone simply . . . expect him to do something really important." She gave his arm a pat, then dropped her hand with a soft chuckle. "You should have seen him after you cantered away and those boys' father stormed off. Reggie actually defended you to Mac, basically saying you better not get in trouble because those boys deserved it."

Nicholas looked out at Bottomless. "What does Reggie believe I did to them?"

"He thinks you scared them so badly they won't dare return to the resort, and that they're going to spend several cold nights lost in the woods trying to . . . get home."

He looked at her again. "And what do you believe I did to them?"

She hesitated, lifting her bottle to take another drink, then lowering it and resting her head against the window. "That's the story I'm also going with."

She fell silent at that, and Nicholas was content to also drop the subject and simply sit with her, the two of them watching the shadows stretching across Bottomless finally fade to nothing as the sun disappeared behind the mountains, blending the world below into varying hues of gray.

"I believe your French-Canadian neighbors to the west have a saying for this time between daylight and dark," he said quietly into the deep silence. "*Entre le loup et le chien;* between the wolf and the dog."

"Don't you mean *our* neighbors, or are you just . . . passing through?"

"Yes, our neighbors."

"I also came here tonight to apologize for *last* night."

Nicholas stilled with his beer halfway to his mouth and lowered it back to his lap.

"First for turning into a madwoman and attack —"

He captured her hand worrying the bottle label again and gave it a squeeze. "Do not finish that sentence, Julia."

She took a shuddering breath. "And also for running away after. And then for threatening to bludgeon you with my tote." She looked up. "But I don't want you to think . . . because I'm not . . ." She blew out a heavy sigh. "We can't ever do that again, Nicholas," she said, shaking her head. "Not ever."

"Why?"

She stilled except to blink in surprise, her cheeks suddenly darkening. "Because we can't," she snapped. "Because I don't sleep around."

"I don't remember either of us sleeping," he said, stifling a grin when her jaw slackened. "In fact," he continued, taking the bottle out of her hand and setting it on the other side of her as he leaned closer. "I haven't been able to sleep since."

Her response was a startled squeak when he lifted her around to sit straddling his thighs, at which point she threw herself against him. "We're dangling over a cliff!"

"You'll always be safe in my arms, Julia," he growled, capturing her braid to tilt her head back to look at him. "Now, would you care to come up with another answer as to why we can't make love again, other than because you 'don't sleep around'?"

Her fingers dug into his shoulders. "You have a bad habit of using your size to control people, you know that?"

He nodded. And grinned at her glower, unable to remember the last time he'd been so turned on. Well, except for last night. "It works well, too — on *most* people."

"You admit to intentionally using your size to get your way?"

He arched a brow. "You prefer I should use my strength?"

"You mean like you are right now?"

"Oh, sorry," he said, letting go and holding his arms out to show she was free.

"Hey!" she yelped, throwing herself against him again. "We're dangling over a cliff and you don't have a *railing.*"

She clasped his face and leaned back just enough to look him in the eyes, and Nicholas knew the game was up when she saw the laughter in them. So, considering his success the last time he'd full-out stormed the castle, he kissed her.

And just like last night, the lovely lady initially resisted, then accepted, then began fully participating with all the fire and heat of an erupting volcano.

"Okay, one last time," she muttered after breaking the kiss, but only so she could trail kisses along his jaw as she provocatively slid her hips forward. "And *then* we're never doing it again."

And that was when Nicholas realized the price of victory might very well be his heart — not that the prospect worried him nearly as much as he suspected it would Julia.

Damn, she wished the guy would stop pulling her into his big strong arms and kissing
her. *Safe in them,* he'd said. Yeah, well, she
felt more like a deer caught in headlights.
How was *any* woman — slut or saint —
supposed to resist magnetic muscles, laughing sky-blue eyes, and warm and really
talented lips that made a girl feel sexy and
desired and . . . and . . . God, he smelled
good.

Yeah, they could have sex *one* more time.

"Ohmigod, you smell good," Julia whispered as she pulled his shirt collar away to
kiss the heated skin of his neck — only to
pop a couple of his buttons when his big
broad hands slipped under her jacket *and*
fleece *and* blouse, blazing a trail of fire up
her back. Popping another of his buttons
when she felt her bra unhook, Julia leaned
away just enough to reach down and pull all
her tops off over her head in one fell swoop.
And then she thoughtfully *unbuttoned* the
rest of his shirt, tugged its tails out of his
pants, and pushed it down over his shoulders — which he then cooperatively finished
shedding before pulling her back into his
warm embrace and kissing her again.

Forget breaking last night's speed-sex

record — Whisper Mountain was about to experience another sonic boom when they broke the sound barrier. She wasn't sure how he did it, but the next thing Julia knew, her sneakers and jeans were gone, his jeans had also disappeared, and just that quickly he was easing up inside her and she was making that strange but now familiar little noise of wild, passionate pleasure.

Oh yeah, she *needed* this one last time.

"Wait, don't move," she whispered once he was fully inside her and she melted against him in utter contentment, feeling really quite powerful when he turned as still as a stone. "I want to savor this a moment."

Well, his body stilled, but his talented lips started kissing her face, completely ruining her contentment by creating an urgent need to *do* something.

"Okay, you can move now," she softly growled, flexing her fingers into his big strong shoulders and arching forward to rub her nipples across the soft hair on his big broad chest — only to have him duck and capture first one of those nipples in his mouth and then the other. And there was that sound again, only it kept escaping on ragged pants as Julia felt that madwoman inside her suddenly . . . well, *explode.*

"Ohmigod, that feels good. Don't stop,"

she moaned when he pressed upward even as he guided her hips forward and back along the length of his shaft. Except he was doing it so maddeningly slowly, her moans grew more frustrated than salacious. So taking advantage of the fact that she was on top, Julia simply increased the rhythm while varying the depth and angle of her movements — giving only a fleeting thought that she hoped the window she was driving him against didn't crack under the strain.

She was also peripherally aware a breeze had come up, although Nicholas — who she was pleased to note was also making salacious but very manly groans — was radiating enough heat to cause her to break into a sweat. And his big broad hands felt like molten embers against her skin as one of them splayed across her back with its fingers threaded through her hair and the other one cupped her thrusting backside — she assumed to keep her from flying off the deck.

And that, Julia realized in some distant corner of her sex-fogged brain, left her completely free to further explore her new-found passionate nature. And since this was their *last* one-night stand, she wanted to make it really memorable; for her because she probably wasn't ever going to find another guy who could make her feel this wild and alive and completely free, and for Nicholas because . . . well, because she really was starting to like him. Really a lot.

Oh yeah, they definitely couldn't ever do this again.

The hand on her backside suddenly put a stop to her thrusts, and the hand on her back suddenly came around to her front and copped a feel of first one breast and then the other, its thumb worrying each of her dampened nipples before it continued down to where her pelvis was pressed into his. And then that fire-hot thumb found its way between them and started rubbing her intimately.

"Come for me, Julia," he whispered thickly, the edge in his voice sounding more urgent than dangerous.

Julia closed her eyes and dropped her forehead to his chest with a shudder even as she reached down and stilled his hand. Well, she guessed nothing lasted forever, but she'd been enjoying herself so much. The question now, however, was did she simply fake it or try to . . . redirect his focus?

Considering she really didn't know him all *that* well, Julia straightened and gave him a smile that she hoped looked sultry in the waning light, opting for the latter because she wasn't quite brave enough to outright lie to him — not even with her body. "How about," she whispered, hoping she *sounded* sultry as she pressed two of her fingers past his thumb into her slickness. She lifted her hand and then slowly ran those fingers over his lips, even as she just as slowly moved her hips against him. "If we let it build awhile longer?" she continued, slipping her fingers in his mouth. She gave a hum of pleasure when he suckled them, then leaned down and replaced the fingers with her lips. "Damn, Nicholas, you turn me on. I didn't sleep last night, either, remembering your hands on me, everywhere, making me hot and shivery at the same time." She brushed her lips over his jaw. "Make me feel that way again."

Both his hands went to her backside with a definite male growl, and Julia had a moment's worry that she may have just tugged a tiger's tail when he twisted enough to lay on his back, then started directing her movements. As fast as she'd left, that sex-starved madwoman returned, and Julia braced her hands on his chest and threw her head back on a moan. "Oh God, *yes,*" she cried out. "That's the spot. Don't stop."

His answering grunt was accompanied by a slight bucking, and Julia cried out again as she slid one hand down between them, moistened her fingers, then locked her eyes on his. "Come for me, Nicholas," she pleaded raggedly, lifting her fingers to her own mouth and suckling. She closed her eyes on another moan of pleasure as she straightened, running her hand down her throat as she brought her other hand up and cupped her breasts, even as she took over the rhythm again. "Damn, that feels good."

She felt the tension humming through his straining muscles as he suddenly stilled, his hands on her hips holding her tightly against him as he gave a groan of pleasure. Julia locked her eyes on his, feeling his release in every cell in her body before she collapsed forward, trembling against the rise and fall of his chest as they both gulped in ragged breaths.

"Oh . . . my . . . God," she said in a panting shiver. "That was wonderful. Am . . . am I too heavy for you?" she asked, although she didn't make any effort to move despite feeling more alive than she had in forever — even as she wondered if she couldn't get away with *one* more one-night stand in the near future.

His answer was a half grunt, half snort as he stirred, just before Julia felt his shirt settle over her. He had to tuck her arms in its sleeves because she really wasn't up to doing it herself, then smooth it down over her backside before folding his arms around her and releasing what she hoped was a sigh of contentment.

Because *she* certainly was content to simply lie here feeling safe and cherished and desirable in his big strong arms as his heart pounded against hers. That is, until the breeze blew up her sweat-dampened legs and made her shiver again, which made Nicholas sigh again. He slowly sat up, lifting her as effortlessly as if she weighed no more than one of his cats, then turned her so she was sitting across his thighs. "I'll light a fire in the hearth," he said, ducking to look her in the eyes as he threaded his fingers through her hair to brush it off her face. There was just barely enough light for Julia to see his smile. "You go on inside, and I'll bring your clothes," he added, nodding toward . . . something.

Julia looked in the direction of his nod to see her jeans lying on the glass deck just a few feet away — one of her socks peeking out of one of the legs dangling over the edge — the breeze every so often causing them to slide closer to falling off. She looked around and saw one of her sneakers near the window and one about ten feet down the deck toward the side porch, her balled-up jacket and fleece and blouse also only inches away from taking flight. She saw her panties but not her bra, and hoped it was inside her balled-up jacket and fleece.

She was wearing Nicholas's shirt and, remembering he'd been barefoot, she wasn't expecting to see his boots, but . . . "Um, where are your pants?" she asked, leaning over slightly to peer down through the glass deck, only to quickly lean back into the safety of his embrace.

He chuckled. "Probably halfway to the fiord."

Julia blinked up at him, caught him running his tongue over his lower lip, and immediately felt her cheeks heat up. Had she really stuck her sex-dampened fingers in his mouth? Really?

No, it had been that madwoman inhabiting her body; the one who exploded the moment she got kissed and who cussed like the town slut all through sex.

Yeah, that woman.

"Okay then," Julia said, gathering his shirt closed and standing up and pressing against the window while holding down its shirt-tails against the breeze. She started to bend over to pick up her nearest sneaker — being careful not to look at Nicholas because he was still naked and she really didn't want that madwoman to attack him again — but straightened when he snatched it away before she could reach it.

"I'll get your clothes," he said, a bit of a dangerous edge back in his voice.

"Thank you," Julia said brightly, making sure not to look down as she walked to the set of sliding doors in the middle of the wall of windows, slid one open, and stepped inside. She continued walking through the darkened living room, past the kitchen area, then down the hall to the bathroom. She softly closed the door and locked it — which was a tad difficult because for some reason her hands were shaking — then felt for the light switch and turned it on.

She didn't gasp because she was expecting the wild woman in the mirror, but she did frown as she gathered up her tangled hair. Was her alter ego pulling the elastic off her braid every time she had wild passionate sex, or was Nicholas the culprit? She looked up at the ceiling when she heard footsteps overhead, then dropped her gaze back to the mirror as she held the huge shirt closed — only to pull the collar away from her neck with a gasp. Holy Hades, he'd left his mark on her.

And now he was holding her clothes hostage, Julia realized with a steadying breath as she slowly looked around the bathroom. Well, except for the one really sexy wool sock she was still wearing. She opened the double doors to find a linen closet with a sum total of one towel and facecloth — only to realize they were identical to the towels she restocked in the resort cottages. She opened the door on the washer-dryer combo stacked beside the shelves, hoping he might have left clothes in the dryer, only to find more towels and a plush bathrobe that was also identical to the ones in her cottages.

She closed the dryer with a snort and turned to the window, wishing she could disappear into the woods again — in the opposite direction he'd expect her to go this time — but she really wasn't up to explaining to Trisha why she was returning from her walk wearing only a really oversize men's shirt and one sock.

Julia stilled when the window she was quietly opening stopped after only a few inches, and lifted her gaze to the top of the sash with another frown. She reached up to touch the narrow piece of scrap wood to find it nailed into the track just above the sash, then looked over and saw an identical slat on the other side. She backed away, staring at the sticks that allowed the window to open only six inches, undecided if she was very disturbed or really quite amazed that Nicholas had — Wait; did nailing his sash closed mean he'd been expecting her to crawl out his bathroom window again?

Because that would mean he'd been *expecting* them to have sex again.

Julia plopped down on the toilet and hid her face in her hands. She'd certainly lived up to his expectations, hadn't she? Heck, *she* had sought *him* out this time; not to thank him for what he'd done for Reggie today, apparently, but to have wild passionate sex with him again.

"Everything okay in there?" the devil himself said from the other side of the door.

Julia bolted upright. "Just peachy," she snapped.

He hesitated, and she wasn't sure but she thought she heard him softly chuckle as he walked away. She hid her face in her hands again with a groan. Now what was she supposed to do? Go out there and sit in front of the fire in his hearth and . . . chat?

About what? When they were going to have sex again?

Or about the sex they'd had tonight — specifically why she hadn't *come* for him?

Julia stood up and glared at the window. She might be skinny, but she wasn't that skinny. She grabbed the washcloth out of the linen closet, filled the vanity sink with hot water, and plucked what was left of the obviously once tree-shaped balsam soap out of the china dish embossed with the Nova Mare emblem.

Okay then, maybe now would be a good time to let Mr. Magnet know she was wise to his little habit of helping himself to anything that caught his eye — including the new director of special events, apparently.

CHAPTER FIFTEEN

Nicholas set out two unopened bottles of beer, then rearranged the large pillows on the fourth-century Persian rug he'd rolled out only this afternoon — fortuitously, it now seemed — in front of the hearth. He added a log to the crackling fire, walked over and flipped on the wall switch that gently flooded the granite ledge under the floor with light, then looked around to see if there was anything else he needed to enhance the scene.

Well, other than the lovely lady.

Hearing the water running in the bathroom sink, Nicholas stretched out on the rug and reclined back on one of the colorful pillows, absently scratching his bare chest where he distinctly remembered lovely feminine claws digging into him — only to sit up when he heard the cat door open.

"Psst," he whispered, making Sol stop in midstep as the cat silently exited the cupboard. He pointed outside. "This is not a spectator sport, so scram."

Being a very wise cat, Solomon silently reversed direction, his paw curling to pull the door closed behind him. Nicholas waited several heartbeats before softly growling, "All the way out," then grinned when he heard the exterior door close with a soft thud.

He reclined back on the pillow and laced his fingers behind his head, gazing up at the pine ceiling being illuminated by the lights beneath the floor as he wondered yet again about Julia's reluctance to find her woman's pleasure — twice now. Thinking she may have been overwhelmed by his size last night, he'd reversed their positions tonight in hopes she'd feel more in control. He grinned, remembering she certainly *had* taken control, again with glorious abandon. But then he frowned as he remembered how he'd once again realized she had no intention of even seeking fulfillment, instead artlessly trying to entice him into moving on without her. And guessing it hadn't exactly been the time to discuss the matter, he had once again conceded to her wishes.

But they had plenty of time now, he thought as he looked over at her clothes stacked in the far corner of the living room.

Well, he hadn't found her bra — not that he knew why she bothered with one. He recalled Duncan telling him, during a camping expedition they'd taken together to lay out a carriage path along the fiord last spring, how the highlander had had a woman move in with him one bra and panty at a time before he'd met and married Peg. Nicholas softly chuckled, figuring he could have Julia moved in here in about a week if he hiked down the cliff tomorrow and found her missing bra, then tucked it in his bureau next to the one he'd picked up off the floor of the event planner's cottage last night.

Assuming she ever came out of the bathroom. He used a bare toe to scratch his leg through the jeans he'd gone upstairs to put on, worried they wouldn't have *any* discussion if she came out and found him still naked. He probably should also broach the subject of contraception, seeing how they hadn't talked about it *before* they'd stormed each other's castles — twice now. But last night all he'd really been looking for was a little kissing and maybe some exploratory touching, whereas tonight the lady had once again surprised him by seeking him out on her own. And considering he was a healthy, hot-blooded male, he hadn't even considered defending himself against a full-out passionate attack.

Yes, poor Julia; she wasn't having much success ignoring their mutual attraction, and it appeared she still couldn't decide how to deal with the problem. He wondered if she'd even comment on finding his bathroom window nailed halfway closed. He sat up again when he heard the door open, and made sure to hide his grin when Julia came striding down the hall looking as if she were primed for battle, wearing one wool sock and his bathrobe that all but swallowed her up.

She stopped suddenly and blinked down at the glass floor that began at the kitchen island. "Oh, wow," she whispered, stepping out over the lighted ledge and slowly turning around. "It's beautiful." She looked up, beaming him an equally beautiful smile even as she shook her head. "Okay, I get it now. But aren't you afraid the house will shake loose during an aftershock and go sliding down the mountain with you in it?"

He shrugged. "Even an earthquake like the one three years ago wouldn't shake the house loose, as it's anchored by over a dozen steel rods the size of my arm running deep into the ledge." He patted the rug beside him. "Come sit down, Julia."

Her smile disappeared and she looked

around again, her gaze stopping on her clothes sitting over gently illuminated air that dissipated into nothingness. She looked back at him. "Um, I should probably head home." She smiled again. "Before security is forced to evict four teenagers and five cats partying like there's no tomorrow."

"Bastet will chaperone them," he said, patting the rug again.

"Bastet?" she repeated, not moving.

"The bronze spotted lady named after the Egyptian cat goddess." He reached over and grabbed the two bottles of beer, then held one out to her. "The evening's still young, and I thought we might have a . . . conversation," he said, lowering his hand when she glanced at her clothes again.

She looked back at him, and Nicholas watched her add another knot to the belt on the robe as she pulled in a deep breath and finally walked over and sat down — at the far side of the rug, he couldn't help but notice. She then stretched out her hand for the beer, making him have to lean over to give it to her after he twisted off the top.

She took a long guzzle and then glanced around his home again before giving him a rather direct look. "You do know there's a small warehouse of furniture under the third hotel segment, don't you, and that Norman probably wouldn't even notice if a couch and dining table happened to . . . go missing? In fact, when I was there getting an end table for one of my cottages, I saw boxes full of tumblers and wineglasses." She smiled rather smugly. "Maybe you should blackmail those two paintball-happy idiots into helping you *help yourself* to enough stuff to furnish your new home."

Nicholas also took a long guzzle of beer. Yes, he definitely liked an abrasive woman who was determined to keep fighting even after the castle had been captured. "Thanks for the idea. Maybe I'll have Tom stay late Monday night and help me help myself. I'll tell him breaking into the facility director's warehouse and lugging off furniture without being caught is part of his training."

That wiped away her smugness.

He shook his head. "I had several pieces of furniture custom-made that should be delivered next week, but my mother suggested I let my wife pick out the dinnerware and kitchen furnishings," he said — only to jerk upright when Julia suddenly scrambled to her feet.

"Your wife," she whispered as she backed away, her face having gone deathly pale. "You're married?" But then she flushed deep red. "You jerk! You're *married*!"

Nicholas jumped up when he realized she was about to hurl her beer at him and grabbed the bottle with one hand and snagged her around the waist with the other. "There is no wife," he said with a laugh, having to lift her off her feet when she tried to punch and kick him at the same time. He lugged her back to the hearth and sat down, set the beer out of her reach, then tucked her beneath him and tossed a leg over hers to pin her down. He brushed her riot of curls off her scowling face. "Much to my mother's dismay," he said gently, "I'm not married." He grinned. "Yet."

Her eyes widened. "Does that mean you're *looking*?"

He nodded.

She started struggling again, forcing Nicholas to capture her fist when she took another swing. "Then what are you doing messing around with me? *Practicing?*"

He closed his eyes and dropped his head beside hers with a heavy sigh. "Please tell me you don't really believe that," he muttered into the pillow. He lifted his head to glare down at her. "I'm trying to *court* you."

She stilled again, all the blood draining from her face as her jaw slackened. But then she suddenly exploded, her flailing elbow jabbing him hard enough to make him grunt as she somehow managed to slip out from under him. Only instead of running, the woman grabbed one of the pillows, then threw herself on top of the pillow on top of his face as *she* held *him* down — but only because he was trying so hard not to laugh that he wasn't fighting her.

"Are you insane?" he heard from the other side of the pillow, sounding like she was also fighting laughter. "Or so desperate that you — oh!" she yelped when he slid his hands under the robe and grasped her bare bottom.

Nicholas gave another grunt, jackknifing to protect his groin when she scrambled off him, and just barely managed to catch the hem of her robe as she twirled away. He grinned up at her flushed face and slowly pulled her toward him.

She burst out laughing and hurled herself at him again, and Nicholas wrapped his arms around her when the lovely lady landed with her nose inches from his and suddenly sobered. "Nicholas," she whispered huskily, "you're barking up the wrong tree, because I'm never getting married again. Not ever."

"Why?"

She blinked, her jaw going slack again. "Because I don't want to," she snapped.

He pulled her head down beside his with another heavy sigh.

"Try courting Wanda Beckman. She definitely wants to get married again."

Nicholas involuntarily shuddered.

"What part of 'I don't date' didn't you understand the other night?"

"The part where you exploded in my arms not twenty minutes later."

She lifted her head. "Please don't take it personally, because it really has nothing to do with you." She patted his cheek and straightened to sit straddling him, smiling sadly as she pushed her hair back over her shoulders. "It's just that I'd like to think I'm intelligent enough not to make the same mistake twice."

"And if you became pregnant last night or just now?" he asked — only to jackknife again when she pushed off him and ran across the room before he could snag her robe.

"If I am," she said tightly, sweeping up her clothes and heading down the hall, "I promise you'll be the first to know."

Nicholas waited until he heard the bathroom door close, then scrubbed his face in his hands with a curse. Wonderful; he'd taken another two steps forward tonight and *ten* back. What was the woman's problem?

It obviously had something to do with her ex-husband, but had the bastard hurt Julia badly enough to *never* want to get married again? Despite what she'd told Trisha in the church about it only being teenage lust, could Julia truly have loved her husband and felt her heart was irrevocably broken? Or had something else happened between them that had stolen her confidence in . . . what? Marriage itself? Or her ability to hold on to a man, as her father had claimed?

The lies her ex-husband had spread around town before he'd left — with his new wife — didn't bother her, as Nicholas had decided that night in the church that Julia considered her tarnished reputation nothing more than a nuisance. And she certainly didn't fear men in general, and definitely not him in particular, judging by her seemingly eager willingness to openly spar with him, almost as if she needed a good rousing battle to burn off some of that overload of energy she had.

Nicholas got to his feet and stood staring toward the bathroom, trying to reconcile Julia's obvious enjoyment of sex with her reluctance to enter a relationship that would provide her with all the lovemaking she could handle. He walked to the outside door and picked up his boots, then went back to the hearth and sat down, pulled out the socks he'd stuffed in the boots, and dressed his feet. He finished tying the laces, then rested his arms on his knees and stared down at the illuminated ledge. No, if he had to take an educated guess, he believed Julia's reluctance to remarry — or even enter into a relationship — had something to do with the act of making love itself.

Why did she explode so passionately at his touch, yet brush off his attempts to bring her to fulfillment? He had some experience with women who were shy, simply uninterested, and even frigid, but he'd never known one who turned to molten lava in his hands only to then balk at taking her pleasure. And that made him wonder if it might be a control issue, with Julia being afraid to give a man that kind of power. Or, considering how quickly *she* lost control, maybe she was merely determined to hold on to that final piece of herself.

Nicholas stood up when he heard the bathroom door open and walked across the room to get the shirt he'd brought downstairs off the banister, shrugging it on and buttoning it up as he intercepted Julia walking to the side door. He put on his jacket without bothering to tuck in his shirttails, followed her outside, and fell into step beside the silent woman as she headed out the driveway.

But once they reached the road and started toward the resort, he felt Julia slowly inching closer until her arm brushed against his. He gently clasped her hand, relieved and immensely pleased when her fingers closed around his. Not wanting to break the mood, Nicholas continued on in companionable silence, the low-hanging half-moon doing little to light their way as it winked in and out of the clouds.

"How come you have six cats?" she asked when Sol stepped out of the ditch and began walking up the road ahead of them. Nicholas knew without glancing down that Julia was looking up at him, and he knew she was smiling because he could hear it in her voice when she said, "Don't you know dogs are supposed to be man's best friend, and little old spinster ladies have six cats?"

"Dogs are noisy and demanding and always tracking in mud," he said, hearing the lightness in his own voice, "whereas cats are quiet and clean and take care of themselves. And I have six," he drawled, "because I'm a sucker for a good sob story."

"They're all rescued cats?" she said in surprise.

Nicholas nodded. "Ajax was the first of

them to find me."

"Ajax?"

"The black and gray tabby that always has a blank look on his face," he said with a chuckle, "named after a Greek hero who was big and dumb but always meant well — which perfectly described the ten-month-old kitten that unwittingly caught Lina's tent on fire when we were traveling through Scotland . . . some years ago."

"Lina?"

"Carolina Oceanus." He grinned. "Soon to be Lina MacKeage, if she knows what's good for her."

Julia smiled up at him. "Olivia told me you were Carolina's bodyguard from almost the minute she was born." But then she frowned. "Only she also said you were just a kid yourself at the time."

He went back to watching the road. "I was seven when Lina was born, but almost fifteen when Titus and Rana finally let her run loose on the island."

"Which island would that be? I can't even figure out what nationality you all are, because none of you have any sort of accent."

"The Oceanuses are Mediterranean. Then came Bastet," he continued. "I found her starved nearly to death wandering the Sa-

318

hara and figured she'd gotten separated from a caravan. Then came Eos, the little gray with the orange eyes; I woke up to find her sleeping on my chest one morning in northern France."

"Carolina did a lot of traveling, apparently."

"Yes," he agreed, wondering what Julia would think if he told her that all his cats came from different centuries, since his travels with Lina had traversed *time* more than distance. "Then came Solomon," he continued, using his free hand to gesture ahead of them when Sol glanced back at the mention of his name. "But instead of finding me, I actually went looking for the unusually large cat I'd heard was in town. I suspect there's some Asian leopard in him, as they're about the size of your lynx. Sol's owner had him displayed in a cage in the town market and was trying to entice the locals to place wagers by pitting their dogs against him in battle."

Julia pulled him to a stop. "Their *dogs?*"

Since the moon was behind a cloud at the moment, Nicholas ran a finger down one of her cheeks, confirming his suspicion that she was flushed with anger. "I named him Solomon," he said soothingly, "because the big guy wisely didn't battle *me* when I took him out of his cage so I could stuff his owner in it." He started them walking again. "Although it did take me the better part of a year to get Sol to step foot inside a house." He sighed. "Only now I have to all but push him outside to do his business if it's even threatening to snow."

"You don't have a litter box?"

Nicholas looked down, wondering at the relief in her voice. "Why would I want to deal with a litter box if everyone is healthy enough to go outside? Then came Gilgamesh," he continued with a chuckle. "He's the fat yellow tabby. And I should have expected he'd cause me nothing but trouble, considering what I went through sneaking him away from that small gang of street urchins."

She pulled him to a halt again. "You stole him from *kids*?" she growled, trying to shake off his hand, then just glaring up at him when he refused to let go.

He gave her a small tug to get her moving again. "They were in the process of fattening him up to *eat* him."

She suddenly skipped ahead as far as his hold would allow and began walking backward. "They were *starving* street urchins?"

He maneuvered Julia around to walk beside him again, deciding that if he wanted to have a conversation with the lovely lady, he merely needed to take her for a walk. Because even though she still became passionately engaged, there appeared to be a better than even chance they wouldn't both end up naked in under ten seconds. "You needn't worry," he assured her, giving her hand a squeeze. "The next morning they found a small bag of money tied to the rope they had tied around Gilly."

She in turn gave his hand a squeeze — he assumed to let him know she approved. "Um . . . I'm almost afraid to ask, but what about the white one that's missing half its tail? Where did you get him — or her?"

Nicholas hesitated. "Snowball has been with me three years," he finally said, "although he spent most of the first six months in a pouch on my father's back as Dad tended his gardens." He stopped and turned Julia to face him. "I can only speculate on what he'd been through, which is why I decided to name him Snowball."

"W-why?"

"Because he'd obviously been through hell and survived."

She went silent at that, staring at his chest, then leaned in as she slipped her hand free and wrapped her arms around him. "Oh, Nicholas," she sighed against his jacket.

"You're nothing but a bighearted sap, aren't you?" She tilted her head back to look up at him just as the moon emerged to reveal her smile. "You've spent your whole life protecting a princess, running around saving women from their drunken father and clueless girls from guests, and rescuing cats." Her arms around him tightened. "You do know you can't save the whole world, don't you?"

He threaded his fingers through her hair to hold her looking at him. "I am aware of that. But I see nothing wrong with trying."

"And while you're trying, who's watching out for you?"

Nicholas felt his own jaw slacken. "Why would I need anyone watching out for me?" He bent and gave her forehead a kiss, then took her hand from around his waist and started walking again. "If the day should come that my back needs guarding, it will be too late because I'll already be dead."

He looked down when she snorted. "You're not one of those ancient gods you've named your cats after, you know. Even *they* weren't invincible."

He watched the road again. "Are you sure about that, Julia?"

"You see any of them walking around today? I took some world mythology classes

322

when I lived in Orono, and near as I can tell, all the gods — of every mythology — were so busy fighting one another that they didn't even notice when they became extinct."

"Why?" he asked in surprise.

"Because they were all power-hungry idiots."

"No, why did you study world mythology?"

He glanced down to see her shrug. "One of the brothers at the fraternity house I worked at was majoring in anthropology, and one day I picked up his book on European mythology and got sucked in. Once I got through the Celtic and Norse gods, I started sneak— I started taking classes on the various deities and legends." She gave another soft snort. "All the ancient gods had more drama going on than soap operas do today. And the sex," she said, smiling up at him. "Who needs romance novels when we can read about all those horny gods and goddesses?"

Nicholas brought them to a stop and stared down at her, undecided if he was amazed by her interest in mythology or really very disturbed. "You think the gods are —" He stilled, looking toward the hairpin turn to see Sol suddenly scurry into the woods. "Someone's coming," he said, leading Julia off the road. He swept her into his arms when they reached the ditch and carried her up the steep bank into the trees, then sat down with her on his lap. "I assumed you didn't want anyone seeing us together," he offered in explanation when she finished sputtering.

She settled into him with a sigh. "There you go being a hero again," she said, patting his chest. "Which brings us back to your needing someone to watch out for you. I wasn't talking about anyone actually trying to kill you when I said that; I was thinking about Wanda Beckman."

Nicholas didn't quite manage to stifle another shudder.

"She's really not that bad, you know. I think Wanda's just lonely. And probably tired," she added as she snuggled into his embrace. "Garret Beckman wasn't exactly up for any husband of the year awards before he ran off with his best friend's wife, leaving Wanda to raise three children all by herself with *no* financial support." She tilted her head back and smiled up at him. "And since there haven't been any rainstorms of frogs for women to kiss hoping they'll find Prince Charming, you're the next best thing."

Headlights arced through the darkness just as the sound of an engine laboring against the weight of a vehicle descending the steep incline broke the nighttime silence, and Julia sat a little straighter. "That's Reggie's truck," she said when it came into view around the curve, giving a snicker when it drove past them. "And that would be Katy cuddled up next to him." She in turn cuddled up against him again. "Sorry, I guess you can't be *everyone's* hero."

"I'd settle for being yours," he said quietly.

All that declaration got him was another pat on the chest. "Again, sorry," she murmured with a yawn. "But I don't need a big strong man to swoop in and save me."

"Are you falling asleep on me?"

She nodded against him. "I tell you what; tomorrow I'll take your men out for a little paintball hide-and-seek and *you* deal with my bride and mother and dear Berdy."

"Why didn't you drive your cart down?"

She tilted her head back again. "I was afraid the battery would die on my way back home and I'd have to call somebody to tow it back up the mountain, and I didn't want to explain why I'd driven my cart down the resort road in the first place."

"Then why not use your truck?"

She sat up. "And have the guard at the

bottom gate decide I must have driven off a cliff when I didn't eventually show up, and have him send out a search party?"

Nicholas lifted her to her feet to keep from growling in frustration, then stood up and took hold of her hand. "You just had to tell the guard at the *top* gate that you were only going as far as my house," he said, leading her out of the trees and then helping her across the ditch.

She shrugged free and shoved her hands in her pockets as she headed up the road at a brisk pace, making Nicholas wonder when their conversation had driven off a cliff. "You don't have to walk me all the way home," she said when he fell into step beside her again.

"Yes, I do. I'll just ride Phantom back. I have a stall for him in my garage."

He sensed her relaxing, apparently glad to have the conversation back on safe ground — not that he was letting it stay there. By the gods, he was finding out *tonight* why she refused to get married again, even if he had to toss the lady over his saddle and kidnap her. He suddenly grinned, thinking he may have been spending too much time around the MacKeage men, as the highlanders' fondness for stealing their women appeared to be contagious.

And according to Julia, he did have a bad habit of helping himself to things.

"That's your horse's name — Phantom?" she asked, slowly inching closer as her breathing increased with the steepness of the road. "Because he's gray, like a ghost?"

"No, because he's really a figment of the imagination."

That got him a glance, and a sigh, and then her hand slipping into his.

Yes, the poor woman was definitely waging an internal battle.

And to Nicholas's delight, *he* appeared to be winning.

They continued on in companionable silence again, and by the time they reached the upper guard house, Nicholas realized Julia's energy truly was flagging when she didn't bother to let go of his hand as they walked past the grinning guard. And not being one to pass up an opportunity, he justified taking advantage of her fatigue by deciding a little persistent questioning might be less upsetting than being kidnapped — although probably not as much fun.

He did, however, wait until they'd passed the common green in deference to the guests sitting out under the stars enjoying what he suspected was only one of a few more warm evenings for a while. But as soon as they entered the wooded path running past the barn, he asked, "Could you explain something to me, Julia?"

"Mmmm, what?"

"The two times we've made love, why did you insist I move on without you?"

She stopped walking and dropped her hand from his as she continued staring straight ahead and said nothing.

"I need to understand."

"There is nothing to understand, because it's no big deal."

"Of course it is. A man's greatest pleasure is sharing it with someone."

She finally turned to face him and looked up, but there wasn't enough light for him to read her expression — although he did hear her pull in a ragged breath. "Let me put it another way, then. Don't *make* a big deal out of it. Please, Nicholas, don't spoil the most beautiful, most mind-blowing sex I've ever had."

"Mind-blowing?" he repeated, even more confused. "Julia," he quietly growled, "make me understand."

She dropped her gaze to stare at his chest. "You want to know the real education I got while I lived in Orono? It wasn't from any textbook or class, but what I learned from the frat brothers. And that's that men want to fix stuff." She looked up. "Anything and everything, even if they know nothing about it; they just want to fix it. And that's why we can't . . . That's why this won't work between us." She smiled sadly. "If you were one of those selfish men who only worried about what's in it for him, then we might stand a chance. But you're not, are you? You're one of the nice guys who insist on giving a woman pleasure. And if it's not happening, you only get more determined. And the more you try, the more pressure it's going to put on me, and the less likely it becomes that it's ever going to happen."

"You didn't even give me a chance, Julia."

"Would you prefer I had faked it? Because I swear you never would have been the wiser."

"Then why didn't you?"

"Because I won't ever lie to someone who treats me with respect, and who makes me feel beautiful and sexy and more alive than I've been in forever."

He touched one of her wild curls. "It's probably just a matter of your becoming comfortable with me."

"I'm not broken, Nicholas. But this . . . thing between us soon would be, because you would keep trying." She laid her hand on his chest. "Why is it so all-fired important that I come, anyway? I can give myself an orgasm anytime I want. But what I can't give myself is the warmth, the intimacy, the feeling of being cherished, of knowing I turn you on. I can't wrap myself up in big strong arms and shiver at the feel of you moving inside me. And from where I stand, that's way more important than some stupid old orgasm. Please, Nicholas," she whispered, dropping her hand, "let it go. Better yet, let *me* go."

"I can't, Julia." He gently embraced her when she rested her forehead against him with a heavy sigh, and pressed his lips to her hair. "It became too late last night." He tilted her head back and smiled down at her. "So that's it? That's the reason you've been fighting my pursuit?"

"What do you mean, *that's it*? From where I stand, that's a darn *good* reason."

"Why?"

She reared back as far as his embrace would allow, and there was more than enough moonlight for him to see her scowl. "Because you're a damn *hero,*" she snapped. She wiggled an arm free and waved at nothing. "You run around trying to save the world one woman and cat at a time. But for your information, I don't need Prince Charming to come riding in on his big gray horse and fix me, because *I'm not broken.*"

Nicholas got right down in her face. "For *your* information, I'm no prince, and I'm definitely not *charming.* And you know what else I'm not?" he asked more softly, tightening his embrace when he felt her trembling again. "I'm not trying to save you, Julia, but hoping you would have the courage to save me."

He kissed her then, gently, tenderly, maybe even desperately, then released her and stepped back, and turned and walked away. He was halfway to the barn before he knew she was no longer staring after him, and turned to see her walking toward her apartment — Solomon walking beside her.

Nicholas folded his arms over his chest, undecided how he felt about Julia's little revelation. Of all the lovely lady's real or imagined demons he'd been prepared to battle to win her heart, he'd never once considered he might have to fight *himself.*

Because she was right; he would become fixated if not obsessed with giving her pleasure. But not because he wasn't one of those selfish men she'd spoken of, but because he was; because he very selfishly wanted *all* of her.

CHAPTER SIXTEEN

Julia sat at her large cherry desk with her head lying on her baby-soft tote and wondered if weddings might be contagious. Not halfway through Adeline and dear Berdy's boisterous bonfire reception, two separate parties of curious resort guests had wandered up to the summit and eventually approached Nova Mare's semihysterical director of special events, wanting to book their own . . . venturesome Maine woods wedding — complete with hot dogs and s'mores and cases and cases of the state's various microbrewery beers.

One of the parties had very sensibly asked if there were any openings for next June, but a twentysomething couple from Texas — with a recently inherited trust fund apparently burning a hole in the woman's pocket — had asked Julia to please make it happen *tomorrow.* That way they could have an abbreviated honeymoon *hiking the wilder-*

ness before they had to fly to California so the woman could be a bridesmaid in her friend's plain old boring beach wedding next weekend.

And since it was too short of a notice for family and friends to drop what they were doing to attend, the couple wanted to invite *all* the resort guests so their bonfire would be just as boisterous as the one going on now. And could Julia please find a local artisan to design them a pair of unique folk-artsy wedding bands? Oh, and also make sure they left with an album of photos that juxtaposed them with the rugged surroundings, the bride-to-be had gone on to ask, so she could show everyone at her friend's wedding how *her* marriage was going to *embrace both the civilized world and the wilderness.*

It appeared that Adeline Rauch — now Frau Altbusser — had been trumpeting that little axiom all over the resort yesterday, and would probably have it engraved on their wedding portrait hanging over their mantel on the off chance no one *got it.*

Julia didn't bother to lift her head when she realized someone had silently walked up to her desk, as she would recognize that wonderfully delicious smell from her grave. "Go away, Nicholas. I'm very busy."

"I can see that," he said, the deep timbre of his voice washing over her like a warm gentle rain.

Which reminded her . . . "Thank you for arranging the nice weather and beautiful sunset." She finally sat up to give him a smile. "And for the extra security. The team leader you sent — Dante, he said his name was — was very kind. Somebody must have told him it was my first event, and he spent most of the reception by my side while directing his men." Seeing Nicholas's sky-blue eyes suddenly light with amusement, Julia laid her head back on her tote. "Anyway, I appreciate your guards' not letting any of the boisterous guests get lost in the woods or tumble down the mountain and then making sure everyone got back to their rooms okay."

"You say his name was Dante?" he asked, the amusement she'd seen in his eyes reaching his voice. "Did he happen to be sporting a small cut on his cheek where a well-aimed . . . rock may have struck him four days ago?"

Julia bolted upright. "You sent one of the idiots who shot me to guard my event?"

"I told him to leave his paintball gun at home," he said, that amusement finally escaping on a chuckle, "and suggested he might want to make sure tonight went smoothly for the one person standing between him and a long swim home."

Julia hid her face in her hands and slumped down on her tote again. "And to think I was going to send you a letter to put in his file saying how kind he was," she muttered, "and he was just sucking up to keep his job."

She peeked past her fingers to see one of Nicholas's big strong hands press down on the desk beside her and felt him bend closer. "Dante is no more *kind* than I am," he said, a distinctly *not* amused edge in his voice. "And if he'd gone after you instead of coming to get me, he'd have caught you within minutes."

Julia rolled her chair back to slide out from under him and stood up. "Yes, well, it was very ki— thoughtful of you to hang around to walk me home. But I'm driving my cart, since Trisha managed to get us all moved into the event planner's cottage before she took off for New York."

He folded his arms over his chest. "Actually, I'm here to take Rana home."

Julia spun away to hide the heat rushing to her cheeks and walked over to grab her jacket off the chair. "Oh, I forgot she mentioned that Titus and Mac are away on business," she said brightly, facing the windows as she put on her jacket and took her time zipping it up, wondering if she shouldn't throw herself off the mountain. "Rana should be right along. She's in the bathroom helping one of our assistants fix her hair from where a flying, flaming marshmallow singed it." She snatched her tote off her desk and headed for the door. "Thanks again for the extra security. Oh!" she gasped, stepping back to avoid bumping into one of her staff — only to bump into Nicholas as he'd apparently been trying to beat her to the door again. "Everything secure on the summit, Greg?" she asked, smacking Nicholas with her tote as she swung it onto her shoulder, then stifling a smile when she heard him sigh. "You guys made sure the bonfire is *completely* out?"

The twenty-year-old vigorously nodded even though his widened eyes were looking behind her, his face flushing as he finally lowered his gaze. "Um, yeah. We put enough water on it to drown a whale. And we made sure the wardrobe tents were all closed up like you said. And a couple of security guards," he added, his gaze lifting to Nicholas again, "helped us search the woods with flashlights to make sure we didn't miss any guests who might have wandered off."

"Where's Paul?" Julia asked, drawing the boy's attention again.

"He's putting the leftover beer in the storage room."

And probably a couple of cases in his locker, she silently added.

Holy Hades, she didn't know which was more exhausting, the three days of prep work or sweating bullets through the actual event. Because she really wasn't sure she could have pretended all was fine if everything had suddenly imploded around her. Heck, she'd nearly had a heart attack when the groom — apparently needing a little liquid courage to ride in and whisk his bride off into what ended up being a moonrise instead of a sunset — had actually mounted the steed *backward.*

No, dear Berdy probably wasn't going to see his golden anniversary, because he was going to die trying to live up to Adeline's expectations.

"Okay then," Julia said with more enthusiasm than she was feeling, since it was nearly one in the morning. "I officially call the Rauch-Altbusser wedding a wrap. One of the security guards is waiting to drive you guys down the mountain to your cars, and I don't expect to see any of you back here until eleven — no, make that *ten* A.M." She turned her smile up a couple of notches and aimed it at Ariel and Merriam when they came walking over with Rana. "Because as of ten tomorrow, we are officially on the Petty-Ringwood wedding. And that means we're going to need at least a hundred and fifty new marshmallow sticks and another bonfire lit by five P.M.," she said excitedly to her gaping staff, Paul also having walked up. "Because we did such an amazing job tonight, we get to do this all again tomorrow night. Isn't that *wonderful*?"

"Are you serious?" Merriam whispered.

"A hundred and fifty?" Ariel squeaked, touching her singed hair.

Julia's smile faltered, however, when she noticed her unflappable mentor also looking a little . . . flapped. "Hey, everyone," she continued brightly. "Other than making the sticks and hunting up another forty cases of beer, most everything is already in place, so it's going to be really *easy.*"

Assuming she could find wedding bands — although they'd probably cost more than Adeline's big fat diamond now safely tucked in the resort safe, because she was going to have to bribe a local artisan into making them in less than . . . sixteen hours.

"But what about the hot dogs and rolls and the s'mores stuff?" Paul asked, shaking his head. "I completely wiped out the Trading Post's stock of chocolate and marshmallows Friday afternoon, and Ezra said the next time we don't give him at least a week's notice he's going to charge us *triple*."

Julia closed her eyes and dropped her head with a silent groan.

"We'll figure everything out in the morning," Rana piped in, sounding surprisingly bright, and Julia looked up to see her mentor herding their staff toward the outside door as the woman pulled her phone out of her pocket. "Meanwhile, we're going to give you people a couple of rooms for the night, so you can spend the next eight hours sleeping instead of traveling all the way home and back." Rana stopped and looked at Julia, her smile once again calm and confident and unflappable. "And after a big hearty breakfast at Aeolus's, we will be here at *nine* sharp, ready to work our magic all over again."

Julia slid her tote off her shoulder, stepped around Nicholas, and headed back to her desk — only to stop with her jacket half off when she saw him still standing there with his arms folded over his chest, frowning at her.

"Go away, Nicholas. I'm very busy," she said as she finished taking off her jacket before sitting in her big leather chair and rolling up to her desk. "You're welcome to use the cart to take Rana home."

"And then I'll come back and get you."

Deciding to ignore the threat in his voice, Julia pulled her calendar book out of her tote. "That's very ki— Thank you, but just leave it at registration," she said, leafing through the pages to find tomorrow — no, today's — date. "I'll grab it on my way home."

Two big broad hands pressed down on her desk on either side of her book. "I'll pick you up in ten minutes."

Julia leaned back in her chair and said nothing, simply looking at him with all the serenity she could muster, considering she was so tired she wanted to cry.

"Ten minutes," he said quietly as he straightened and walked away.

The moment she heard the outside door close, Julia dropped her head onto her calendar book with a groan. Oh yeah, she couldn't ever have sex with Nicholas again, because she really didn't want to get used to having a big strong *kind* hero constantly swooping in and saving her.

Nicholas reached down to turn the key on the cart, only to have Rana stop him.

"You're not going to win any points by try-ing to intimidate her, Nicholas."

He looked over in surprise and then at where she was nodding, and saw that Rana had had a clear view of Julia's lighted office through the windows. He turned the key. "She can barely stand without swaying, yet intends to keep working," he said, pressing down on the accelerator and heading for the Oceanuses' private cottage. "I was merely explaining that I'd be back in ten minutes to take her home."

"There's nothing wrong with throwing herself into her work. Or are all you men so needy that you feel threatened by a woman who gets passionate about anything other than yourselves?"

Nicholas frowned at her tone, wondering if they were still discussing Julia.

"If Titus should ask, which I'm sure he will, you brought me home at ten."

No; definitely no longer about Julia.

"And if Maximilian *suggests* you ac-company Olivia and me and Sophie to Bangor this Friday, I want you to tell him you're busy." She nudged him with her elbow. "As it's always been, Nicholas, you don't answer to the Oceanus men."

Just the women, he silently added, stifling a smile. "Are you *trying* to get me banished to the underworld for lying to Titus and Mac?"

She gave a soft laugh, as was her ritual every time he voiced that worry when she asked him to lie for her. "You wouldn't be there a day before Hades sent you back to us." She sobered when he stopped the cart in front of her cottage. "I mean it, Nicholas; the Oceanus women are climbing in the RV early Friday morning for a *ladies only* adventure." She just as suddenly smiled again. "Minus Ella, because Olivia said the shopping malls on Black Friday are no place for a cherub."

Nicholas stopped partway out of the cart. "Why on earth would you go shopping on Black Friday?" he asked, although he had to raise his voice because she was halfway to the cottage steps, making him scramble after her. "I've been led to believe it's complete chaos."

"Which is precisely why I asked Olivia to take me with her and Sophie this year. I want to feel that amazing energy for myself instead of watching it on the news," she explained, the porch light revealing her excitement. But then she sighed. "Although Olivia said even she isn't quite brave enough to be at the stores when they first open their doors, which means we're going to miss all the best sales."

"Rana," Nicholas growled. "Titus is not about to let you go anywhere near that chaos without protection." *He* sighed, dropping his chin to his chest. "I'll go with you."

"No, you will not," she growled right back at him. "It's *ladies only.* So make sure you're busy Friday. And Nicholas," she said more softly, touching his arm to get him to look at her. "If you become overprotective of Julia, you're going to send her running in the opposite direction. Like Olivia, Julia Campbell is a twenty-first-century woman and quite capable of taking care of herself." She arched a regal brow. "Which, I assume, you consider one of her more attractive qualities, just as I suspect that's what attracted Maximilian to Olivia."

Nicholas felt a grin tug free. "A quality that has given him nothing but fits for the last three and a half years."

That got him a laugh. "Yes, I do believe that's what I most admire about my daughter-in-law." Rana walked up the steps and opened the door, but then turned back to him, the porch light revealing her scowl. "And when you do catch Julia, I suggest you *encourage* her to follow her passions without trying to *direct* them."

She disappeared inside, and Nicholas

stared at the closed door for several heart-beats before finally getting back in the cart, wondering if he shouldn't warn Titus that the queen of *his* castle was preparing a rebellion — one that Nicholas suspected had the potential to make the wars of the gods seem like minor skirmishes.

He drove toward the conference pavilion, undecided how to handle Julia if she wasn't ready to go home, since he agreed that her abrasive independence was what had first attracted him to her. Well, along with her seemingly endless energy. Only that energy was obviously flagging tonight, and Julia's stubbornness — as well as her apparent need to prove to *herself* that she had what it takes to be a good event planner — could very well end up being her downfall.

For every warrior knew that more battles were lost from sheer exhaustion than lack of planning, which meant he wasn't being overprotective by insisting she go home and get some sleep, but merely giving her the benefit of his experience. Nicholas stopped in front of Julia's darkened office windows and strode to the door, only to find it locked. He pulled down the note taped to the glass and stepped out into the moonlight to read it. *Thank you, but I took myself home.*

He slowly folded the note, undecided

whether he was impressed by Julia's own little rebellion or disappointed, as he had planned to kiss the lovely lady *without* their both ending up naked in under ten seconds.

He stilled when he suddenly caught the scent of what felt like desperation coming from the general direction of the event planner's cottage, then shoved the note in his pocket and tore off at a run. He cut across the common green and ducked into the trees without breaking stride, trying to discern if it was coming *from* Julia or aimed *at* her, only to pull up short when he reached her cottage and saw the porch and interior lights on, everything looking peaceful. His attention was drawn to the edge of the clearing when he heard muttering and saw Julia half-buried in a thick stand of bushes — his pounding heart skipping a beat when he realized she was cutting long thin branches and tossing them out into the driveway.

Tomorrow, he decided with a silent growl, he would encourage Julia's passion for her job *after* she got some sleep. He silently walked up and caught the next branch she tossed out and tossed it past her deeper into the woods.

"Oh!" she gasped as she whirled toward him. "Darn it, Nicholas; *whistle* when you

345

approach someone." She turned back and cut another branch, but tucked it under her arm instead of tossing it out. "Please go away. I'm busy."

"You have five healthy young assistants to do that."

"No, I have four healthy assistants," she said, tucking another branch under her arm. "Anna ran out of the office to — yesterday with a bad case of morning sickness," she growled, continuing to hack off more of the bushes. "And the four I have left will be busy hunting down food and beer and wedding rings and flowers and a marriage license and a bunch of hiking gear, all while trying to figure out how to invite a resort full of the wealthiest people in the world to attend a bonfire on top of a mountain in November to cook friggin' *hot dogs* on a goddamn *stick*."

Nicholas stopped her by clasping her arms from behind, then gently turned her around and silently folded her into his embrace.

"I . . . I can't do it," she whispered hoarsely, burying her face in his shirt. "I can't make everyone's dreams come true."

"Yes, you can."

"It's supposed to s-snow."

"It will hold off until after midnight."

"Reverend Peter said he won't marry

anyone who won't sit through his classes."

"One of my men, Rowan, is also a . . . man of the cloth."

He felt her wipe her eyes on his shirt just before she tilted her head back. "You can't just swoop in and fix everything. You're the director of *security;* it's not your job to do mine."

"I am aware of that." He brushed back her hair — that had been elegantly styled with two seashell combs he recognized as belonging to Rana — and kissed her forehead before clasping her to him again. "I'm merely pointing out that for every problem you encounter there's a good chance someone working here might have or be a solution. Like your rings; did you know Sally does all the horseshoeing, and that she also forges the iron and silver jewelry sold in the gift shop?"

Julia tilted her head back again. "She does? For real?"

Nicholas bent and scooped her off her feet and started for the cottage. "And did you know Aeolus's pastry chef makes marshmallow hearts every Valentine's Day?"

"From scratch?"

"From scratch." He walked up the porch steps and set her down. "Giselle makes them by the hundreds every year. Now, are you going to bed and not setting foot outside again until at least nine A.M.?"

She immediately beamed him a huge smile and nodded — making Nicholas reach in his pocket and pull out his phone. He slid a finger across the screen, tapped an icon, and lifted it to his ear — all without taking his eyes off the lovely lying lady. "Micah, dress warm and come to the event planner's cottage," he said into the phone, twisting slightly when Julia gasped and made a grab for his hand. "And bring Dante. You're both on guard duty until nine A.M."

"You can't do that!" she cried when he shoved the phone in his pocket.

"Ah, but I can," he said softly, crowding her up against the door and palming her flaming cheeks in his hands. "Because I'm the director of security."

"I . . . I'll stay inside. All night. Until nine A.M."

"Yes, you will."

"You can't really expect me to get any sleep knowing those men are sitting out here in the cold. They're predicting *snow.*"

"Would you feel less guilty if I told you that Micah is the one who actually shot you — twice?" he murmured just before he kissed her, sweeping his tongue inside her lips the instant she went from resistance to acceptance, only to lift his head the moment he felt her eager participation. He reached behind her and opened the door, gently backed her inside, and kissed her again. But apparently having caught her second wind, not only did she go straight to eager participation, she popped the top button on his shirt.

Nicholas broke the kiss, wondering if *he* wasn't the idiot, and leaned his forehead against hers. "Remember the feel of me moving inside you when you pleasure yourself tonight before you go to sleep," he softly growled, stepping back and grinning at her slackened jaw, then closing the door on her gasp.

CHAPTER SEVENTEEN

Julia's nose woke up first, her eyes blinking open two seconds later to see a tall cardboard cup waving just inches above her. She reached for it with a thankful moan.

Peg straightened away, not relinquishing her prize. "You're not getting this perfectly brewed black tar I cajoled Vanetta into making until you tell me why the guard at the upper booth wouldn't let me in your driveway. Which, I might point out, forced me to park at the barn and sneak down through the friggin' woods, only to be stopped at your porch by *another* guard, who told me he's under strict orders to, and I quote, 'not let Julia step so much as a toe outside until nine A.M.' "

Julia sat up and brushed her hair off her face, positioned the pillow behind her, and reached out again. "So how did you get in here — drop-kicked him, I hope?"

Peg still refused to hand over the coffee.

"No, I gave him and his buddy out back the *four* cinnamon buns I'd brought and asked if their orders included *me* not going *inside.*" Her big blue eyes lit with laughter. "So what's up? Why is the director of special events under house arrest? Did you finally lose it and bludgeon your bubbly little bride to death with your tote?" She gasped, her eyes widening as she clutched her jacket. "Nicholas! He tried to nail you again and you really did smack him."

Julia grabbed the second pillow from beside her and pressed it to her face. "No, I nailed him first," she muttered. "Friday night, outside on his deck hanging over a cliff, right in front of God and probably some poor scandalized eagle sitting in a nearby tree."

Julia tightened her grip on the pillow when she felt it being tugged, only to have Peg finally just give it a yank and pull it away. Then she wisely replaced the pillow with the coffee. "Wow, you're not on a stupid roll anymore, Jules; you're actually smartening up."

Julia took a long guzzle of the tepid coffee, glaring over the cup at her too-happy friend, then wiped her mouth with her pajama sleeve. "Yeah, I'm so smart now that I've decided to go with you to Pine Creek."

She took another sip, then shook her head. "But I'll follow you in my truck so I can come back Friday morning. Some executives from an Italian technology firm are here for their annual meeting, and my predecessor promised them a small, elegant cocktail party in the conference pavilion." Julia halted her coffee halfway to her mouth when she saw Peg clutching her jacket again, looking horrified. "What? Why aren't you jumping up and down and shrieking with excitement? I thought you wanted me to go to Pine Creek."

"Are you crazy?" Peg whispered. "You can't have drinks with Seamus now; you had sex with Nicholas. Twice."

"But that's exactly why I have to go. I need to *stop* having sex with Nicholas, and that's not going to happen unless I start seeing other men."

Peg sat on the bed with a sigh. "Damn, Jules, did you hear anything I said on the boat Friday morning? These big strong scary men — Seamus MacKeage included — are atavists." She shook her head. "I know you know the definition, but do you know what it *really* means?" She held up her hand when Julia tried to say something. "It means you could strip naked in front of Seamus and dance a jig, and all he would do is throw a blanket over you, toss you over his shoulder, lug you back here, and drop you at Nicholas's feet — along with the suggestion that Nicholas keep better tabs on you."

"Are you serious? Wait. How would Seamus know to lug me back to . . ." Julia reared back, pointing at Peg. "You told! You told Duncan I had sex with Nicholas."

"No!" Peg said, jumping to her feet. "I wouldn't do that to you. But Nicholas and Duncan are friends. And that means if you go with us to Pine Creek, Nicholas will ask *his friend* to keep an eye on you for him, and *that* will tell Duncan you two had sex."

"Are you serious?" Julia repeated.

Peg waved at nothing. "One of the first things I learned when I married Duncan is that there's an unwritten code of honor between all these big strong scary men. They band together if there's trouble, and they look out for one another's women." She nodded when Julia went back to gaping at her. "It's true. Even though Mac initially wasn't real . . . happy when he found out Alec was courting Carolina last year, and even though Nicholas and Duncan both sided with Alec, those four men still would have laid down their lives for one another — and for one another's women."

353

"But what's any of that got to do with me? I'm not Nicholas's woman; we just had a couple of one-night stands. We aren't even dating. And I told him I don't ever want to get married again, so he knows better than to ask Duncan to keep tabs on me."

Peg went back to looking horrified. "You said . . . you actually told Nicholas you're never getting married again? Wait — he *asked*?"

"No!" Julia sucked in a deep breath and started pressing her thumbnail into the sleeve on her cup. "The subject just sort of came up . . . after. He mentioned something about his mom wishing he'd hurry up and get married, and I . . . um, wished him luck."

Peg sat on the bed again and took hold of Julia's free hand. "Does Nicholas have to bludgeon *you* before you get the hint, Jules? There's not a man alive — big and strong and scary *or not* — who would ever bring up the dreaded *M*-word in the presence of a single available female unless he's already picturing her wearing his ring."

"Now who's talking stupid? We haven't even gone on a *date*."

"No, you've just had wild passionate sex. Friggin' *twice*." Peg stood up and headed for the door. "Go on and get dressed while

354

I put on some coffee to replace the one I gave the guard in the booth." She stopped in the hall and looked back. "The jerk had the nerve to take it and *then* tell me the only way he was letting me in your driveway was if I got Nicholas to personally call and say it was okay." Her eyes suddenly started dancing with laughter again. "You poor clueless child," she said, shaking her head. "You don't even realize what just happened, do you?"

"Oh, please enlighten me, dear older wise one," Julia drawled.

Peg just as suddenly sobered and walked back into the room. "Ohmigod, you truly don't know. Julia," she whispered, "last night Nicholas flexed his *real* muscle."

Julia stilled at her friend's seriousness. "What do you mean? All he did was . . . he just locked me . . . Ohmigod," she whispered on an indrawn breath.

Peg nodded. "He ended the chase."

"But . . ."

Peg sat on the bed again and took hold of her hand. "There are no buts when it comes to men like Nicholas. Last night he declared — publicly, by involving his guards in your little battle of wills — that he's bigger and stronger and more stubborn than you, and that he will always have the final word. And you either have the courage to love him *because* he's so old-fashioned you want to smack him, or you walk away before it really is too late. But that means you walk away completely, Julia; no more maybes or what-ifs or mixed feelings, and no more one-night stands."

"But that's what scares me; that I *could* love Nicholas."

Her friend smiled warmly, giving her hand a squeeze. "But isn't it a wonderful scary? Doesn't it make you feel really alive? When you're with Nicholas, doesn't your mouth go dry and your insides clench and your heart beat faster?" Peg set Julia's coffee on the nightstand, then wrapped her in a hug. "Be the girl I grew up with," she whispered. "Be that brave and daring woman you were becoming, and believe in the magic again. It really is that simple, you know." She leaned away and reached in her pocket, then lifted Julia's hand and pressed something warm and smooth into her palm.

Julia felt her eyes start to sting as she closed her fist over the small stone.

"This is what I really came here to give you this morning," Peg continued thickly, her own eyes welling with moisture. "So that whenever you start feeling scared, you can remind yourself how brave and invincible we both were when we believed." Peg pulled her into another hug. "I love you, Jules. Now please love yourself enough to love Nicholas."

"Dammit, Peg," Julia muttered, hugging her back fiercely. "Don't make me cry. I don't have time for a tear fest this morning."

Peg pulled away after wiping her eyes on Julia's pajamas and stood up, smiling smugly. "Wow, was that another cuss I just heard, Ms. Campbell?"

Julia threw back the covers and got out of bed. "You'd cuss too if you were facing my day." She slapped her forehead with her palm. "What am I saying? You don't need an excuse."

"I've quit," Peg said, following her down the hall. "With the kids gone to school all day, I've gotten sloppy and forgot Charlie has ears. But I had to clean up my act when I heard him say *friggin'* at our campfire Saturday night."

Julia stopped in the middle of the kitchen and swung toward her. "You've already corrupted that beautiful little boy? He's only *two.*"

Peg winced, giving a sheepish shrug. "That's the scary part; he used it perfectly. Hero was trying to steal the charred marshmallow off Charlie's stick, and my sweet baby shook his finger at the dog and said, 'No, Hero, it friggin' hot.' " She hung her head. "I'm such a bad mother. I don't think I should have any more babies."

"Um . . . didn't you tell me that because Duncan was sort of an only child that he wants a big family? And that you agreed, because you're also an only child?"

"We have *five*." Peg hopped onto a stool at the island counter and rested her head in her hands. "And I'm not going to survive their teens." She looked up. "Charlotte is twelve but acts sixteen — which, if I remember correctly, was the hardest year on *our* mothers. And Isabel's only a tween and she's already giving me attitude. Belligerent boys I can deal with, but what if I have another girl?" She suddenly straightened. "I know: Let's you, me, and Olivia all have babies together."

Julia actually dropped the scoop full of coffee grounds on the counter. "What!"

Peg nodded. "That way we can do what Olivia and I do with Ella and Charlie; we'll throw them all together and raise them up like a little pack of wolves."

"I don't have a *husband,*" Julia cried when she realized Peg was serious.

Peg waved that little detail away. "Pffft, I

give you one month, tops, before you're planning your own wedding instead of other people's." She canted her head, her smile turning cheeky. "But this time around you might want to rethink the theme. I mean, really, Jules — Cinderella?" She snorted. "I hate to break the news to you, but that particular prince turned into a frog."

"Margaret Conroy, stop talking." Julia swept the spilled coffee into her palm and dumped it in the filter. "And for once hear what I'm saying: I am *never* getting married again."

Apparently undeterred, Peg kept right on talking. "I suppose you can just live with Nicholas, if you don't mind disappointing his mother and having to figure out how to tell your children why you won't marry their father."

"I'm not falling in love with him, either."

Peg arched a brow. "Need I remind you the chase ended last night? Publicly? How much are you willing to bet that by noon today it's all over Nova Mare, and by supper tonight it's all over town?"

Julia set her hands on the counter and hung her head with a groan. "And by nine tonight Nicholas will know he just caught the town slut."

Peg was standing behind her in half a

heartbeat and turning her around, Julia assumed to make sure she didn't miss her glare. "Nicholas caught the town *princess.*" She suddenly went back to smiling smugly. "And *I'm* planning your wedding."

"I give up," Julia growled, spinning away and marching down the hall. She turned inside the bathroom. "And thank you for the friggin' coffee!" she shouted, just before she slammed the door.

"You're friggin' welcome!" Peg shouted back.

Only Julia had barely stripped off and was just about to turn on the shower when she heard a soft knock. "Ah, Jules? The guy out front said he's not letting me step any of *my* toes outside until nine A.M., either."

Julia walked over and pressed her forehead to the door. "What time is it now?"

"Eight. And he asked me if you want the half cord of branches I saw stacked on the porch to be taken up to the summit or dropped off at the conference pavilion."

Julia straightened. "There's a bunch of branches on the porch?"

"Yup. All with whittled pointy ends. There must be over two hundred. So where do you want him to take them?"

"To . . . I guess to the summit. Peg?" Julia whispered.

"Yeah?"

"I'm sorry."

"Sorry for what?" Peg whispered back — although there was a smile in her voice. "For cussing at me or for being my stupid-talking best friend?"

Julia rested her head on the door again. "Yeah, for that."

"I wasn't really leaving just now, you know." There was a soft thud on the door, as if Peg had also rested her head on the opposite side. "In fact, I'm staying the day so I can help you make some crazy bride's fantasy come true."

Julia straightened again. "Nicholas called you?"

"No, Rana did. She said you were in need of reinforcements. I cleaned Vanetta out of graham crackers when I picked up the cinnamon buns. Ezra said his meat guy is due this morning, and he'll get several cases of hot dogs off him. But I'm afraid we're out of luck on the marshmallows. Jules?" she asked when Julia didn't say anything. "You do know this is how the magic works, don't you? Everyone pulling together to help someone in need?"

"Even when that someone is acting like an ass?"

"*Especially* then," Peg said with a soft

laugh. "So okay, Ms. Campbell, say something . . . bossy to me."

Julia felt herself smiling. "Two eggs over easy, toast — not too dark — and a big mug of *hot* coffee brewed the way the boss likes it."

Julia heard a loud and definitely not regal snort trailing down the hall, then turned her back against the door and slumped forward to hide her face in her hands. Oh yeah, she was on one hell of a stupid roll, because she'd swear that last night she really had felt Nicholas moving inside her before she'd fallen asleep, and it had been . . . explosive.

And honestly? The more she thought about it, the more she liked the idea of being caught by a big strong scary atavist. Well, not so much that she was going to let him get away unscathed for *publicly* flexing his *real* muscle.

The director of special events and her entire staff — including a real live queen and a real best friend — not only survived Nova Mare's second boisterous bonfire wedding in two days, they'd been grinning worse than the drunken revelers as they staggered off the summit at two A.M. Tuesday morning just as the first snowflakes fell from the sky. As for the bride and groom . . . well, the juxtaposed Ringwoods were likely holed up in a tent with the dear Altbussers someplace in the nearby wilderness, waiting for the three inches of snow to melt so they could hike back to the resort, no doubt with SD cards full of pictures, anxious to tell all their plain old boring friends about the huge Maine blizzard they'd survived.

If she didn't hear from either party by noon tomorrow, she was asking the director of adventure to send out a search party, Julia decided as she sat on Nicholas's deck with her new best buddies, watching the shadows lengthen across Bottomless. An appropriate ending to Thanksgiving Day, since she'd shared the traditional dinner she'd brought to her cottage from Aeolus's with them.

"You guys tell anyone that I sat you at the table and served you on bone china," she said, causing six heads to turn to her, "I swear I'll deny it."

Julia looked out at Bottomless again, remembering making her first executive decision at two A.M. Tuesday morning, giving her staff the following three days off and instructing everyone not to step foot on the mountain until Friday morning. Well, except Rana, since she lived here. Julia had instead politely asked her mentor to please stay away from the conference pavilion, then generously given her four days off when the dear woman had actually *asked* for Friday, too.

Julia, however, had spent the last three days practically living at the conference pavilion — which had felt eerily silent after the frenzy of the previous four days. But it wasn't until this afternoon, as she'd strolled down the resort road with her stuffed-to-their-whiskers buddies, that Julia realized she had spent the last three days nesting, putting her personal touch on her beautiful new office, making it *hers.*

It had all started when she'd wandered into the prop room and been blown away by all the over-the-top . . . stuff. Some of which, she had realized upon closer inspection, were authentic antiques. As for the marble bust of the big scary horse she'd lugged to her office to display on her desk, she hoped to Hades *it* was a reproduction. Because if not, that meant she had an ancient Greek artifact dating from around the reign of King . . . Perdiccas.

Oh yeah, she'd gone on the office Internet and Googled *Perdiccas* just for the fun of it, and found a couple of kings going by that name ruling Macedon around the fifth and sixth centuries BC. And after reading up on them, she'd decided the angry man and his three sons were just as bad as kings Perdiccas I and II.

No, not nice men, any of them — ancient *or* modern.

Julia looked down at her hands, one holding the note she'd found on Nicholas's kitchen counter this afternoon and the other holding her cell phone. She had no business feeling bummed that he hadn't said good-bye before he'd left Tuesday — with one of his men, she'd since learned — to go . . . somewhere on some sort of business. After all, it wasn't like they were dating or anything. But he could have at least called to ask if she wouldn't mind babysitting his cats while he was gone, which could be anywhere from a few days to a few *weeks,* he'd said in his text.

Julia pressed the button on her phone and slid her thumb across the screen, then went to her messages and scanned down through the list of texts she'd exchanged with Trisha in New York City, and Peg and Olivia and Rana and all her assistants, only to wince when she saw all the texts she'd sent accidentally — to God, for all she knew. She finally spotted Nicholas's name and tapped it.

Keep an eye on our little herd while I'm away, he'd said, not asked. Our herd? And just when had she inherited six cats? *Had to leave unexpectedly on business, and will be gone from a few days to a few weeks.*

With his *horse*?

Because when she'd stopped by the barn Wednesday morning to once again thank Sally for making the elegant, folk-artsy wedding bands, Julia had noticed that Phantom wasn't in his stall. When she'd asked where he was, having brought a couple of carrots for the big scary figment of the imagination — that looked a lot like the big scary bust sitting on her desk — Sally had shrugged, saying Nicholas had ridden off Tuesday around noon with one of his men on another one of their stallions, and when they hadn't returned, she'd assumed the horses were staying at his house. Which wasn't unusual, apparently, since several of his men were familiar with Phantom and often took care of him whenever their boss left on business.

But the only thing in the garage was Nicholas's big scary truck. And Julia distinctly remembered hearing a distant . . . aftershock shortly after noon on Tuesday.

Be good while I'm gone and I'll bring you back a surprise.

That ominous little text had cost her a couple of sleepless nights. Darn Peg for putting the idea in her head that Nicholas really was seeing her as wife material — which had her all worried that he was bringing back a friggin' engagement ring.

How in Hades was she supposed to react to that?

Maybe she should start carrying a brick in her tote — although she suspected it would take a ton of them to knock some sense into him.

As they'd worked together Monday, Peg and Rana and Olivia (when she'd dropped by to lend a hand for an hour) had all offered their own little tidbits of advice on dealing with big strong scary contrary atavists — Rana introducing *contrary* into the growing list of . . . qualities. But what had really scared Julia was that all the women had been acting as if she and Nicholas were a done deal.

And judging by the note he'd left her on his kitchen island, so did Nicholas.

I gave the men delivering the furniture your number. If it arrives before I return, go ahead and have them place it where you think it works best. There should be linens delivered at the same time to fit the custom-made mattress if you feel like making up the bed. I didn't have time to clean out the fridge, so take what you can use. The house is designed to look after itself, but if any problems arise, bring them to Duncan's attention. Also, if you find you have to return to your father's house for any reason, I would appreciate it if you took Duncan, Mac, or Rowan with you, or Dante or Micah.

Sorry I had to leave without a proper good-bye, but duty is often an inconvenient taskmaster. I shall make it up to you when I return. Until then, the memory of me will have to do.

— Nicholas

Julia pulled in a shuddering breath as she slowly folded the note and slipped it in her pocket. She'd tried texting him back Tuesday, but now knew why she hadn't gotten any response. She hadn't been snooping or anything; he'd left his cell phone right there in plain sight in a basket on the counter, along with his wallet, some loose change, and his watch — almost as if he'd wanted her to see them.

Like he *wanted* her to question why a man — who didn't have a last name — went on a business trip that could last anywhere from a few days to weeks without taking his personal belongings; on his big scary horse that had a lot of scars, which had disappeared with him right around the time of another rumbling aftershock.

Oh, and with one of his elite guards. Sampson, Sally had said his name was; another big strapping guy who had shown up at Nova Mare with Nicholas last year, along with Rowan and Micah and Dante. All, apparently, from the same mysterious island the Oceanuses were from — which Sally had heard was "somewhere in the friggin' Atlantic."

Oh yeah, it would take more than courage to fall in love with Nicholas, as Julia was beginning to suspect it would also take believing in magic again.

She pulled the small, jet-black stone Peg had given her out of her pocket and slowly rubbed her thumb over its shimmering, polished surface. Bastet suddenly stood up and walked over, touched her nose to the stone, then blinked up at Julia and gave a soft little chirp. Julia gave her a pat, remembering also looking up the Egyptian goddess online and discovering that Bastet had been the patron of love, sex, and fertility.

How interesting, Julia decided as she pulled in another shuddering breath, considering her highly dependable biological clock meant she should have started her period two days ago. Except not only hadn't she, but she also didn't have any of the telltale signs of tender breasts and slight cramping that usually preceded it.

She wasn't quite in panic mode yet, still holding out hope that running around like a crazy woman trying to make two brides' fantasies come true was the reason she was late. Mother Nature was allowed to skip a beat once in a while, wasn't she?

Yeah, she'd get her period any day now.

Julia held the little stone out when the other five cats all got up and crowded around, insisting she let each of them touch it. Well, except Ajax, who kept looking at everyone blankly, as if trying to figure out what was so interesting about a rock.

Solomon gave her arm a less than gentle nudge after he'd taken his touch, then walked around the side of the house, giving a loud, growling meow as he headed down the side porch — which apparently was some sort of signal for the other five to follow. But when Julia didn't immediately follow, Bastet stopped at the corner of the house and looked at her, then gave another chirp, this one rather demanding.

"Okay, I'm coming," Julia said with a

chuckle, slipping her phone and the stone in her pocket and standing up — making sure she stayed pressed up against the glass. "Hey, where do you all think you're going?" she asked when she rounded the corner and saw the parade continue past the cat door. "The whole point of this trip was to bring you guys *home.*"

Julia dropped her head with a sigh, knowing exactly where they were going, which was back to *her* house — the one with the big soft bed they'd all spent the last two nights crowding her out of. Only instead of heading up the resort road when they reached it, Sol led his band of merry followers across the pavement and into the woods.

Julia stopped at the ditch. "Ah, guys? It's getting dark."

Bastet stopped just before disappearing into the trees and gave another loud chirp, which apparently signaled Sol to come back to see what the problem was. Could cats glare? Because she'd swear the big lug was looking at her through narrowed, impatient eyes. Julia sighed again, pulling her gloves out of her pocket and slipping them on. "Okay," she said, scrambling across the ditch and up the bank on the other side, "but if this isn't a shortcut, you're all sleeping *under* the bed tonight."

CHAPTER EIGHTEEN

Julia sat in her big leather chair watching out the office window, about to make an executive decision that if her escorts didn't show up in the next ten minutes, she was leaving without them. Once Nicholas's business trip had passed the six-day mark, the cats had started walking her to and from work every day — although she couldn't figure out how they always knew when she was ready to head home every evening. The ritual had been ongoing for three weeks now, making it a sum total of twenty-eight days — not that she was counting — since anyone had heard from Nova Mare's director of security.

Which made Julia glad she'd caved in and installed a cat door after five nights of repeatedly having to get out of bed to let Ajax outside, then wait and let him back inside, because he couldn't seem to hold his bladder longer than a few hours. But not wanting to cut a hole in a perfectly good wall, she'd had her staff carpenter replace one of the window sashes with a flapping door.

Well, the cats walked her to and from work when it wasn't snowing — spending their days only *they* knew where — and rode in her enclosed cart during foul weather. The new cart had actual doors and a heater and even windshield wipers, but the really cool part was it had a track system instead of wheels that supposedly made it able to maneuver through really deep snow like a Sherman tank — not that she'd had a chance to find out if that was true yet.

Every day Julia grew more amazed at the lengths Olivia was willing to go to make Nova Mare one of the most exclusive and unique resorts in the world. And she didn't care what the woman claimed; the former town mouse had some pretty outrageous dreams of grandeur. Although Julia did recall the gondola across the fiord was really Mac's idea, which had actually been discussed at a couple of directors' meetings.

Four days to Christmas and still no Nicholas. Julia really hoped he was back by then, because she had a really exciting present to give him. One she hadn't even had to shop for; she'd only had to stop having periods.

Oh yeah; she'd gone past panic a couple of weeks ago after peeing on three home pregnancy sticks, and was now at the *how in Hades do I tell him?* stage. Hopefully she'd have it figured out and be well into resigned acceptance by the time he got back. Because if how much she missed him was any indication, she was pretty sure she was utterly and completely in love with the tall, blue-eyed, maddeningly handsome man.

Except how was that even possible, considering she'd known him exactly a week and a half? And considering she'd actively avoided him four of those days, how could she possibly be missing and wanting and loving the muscle-flexing atavist with every fiber of her being?

Granted, they'd had two one-night stands, so she not only must have trusted him on some innate level from the very beginning, she must still be trusting that little inner voice she *hadn't* listened to when she'd had doubts about marrying Clay. And those hadn't been last-minute doubts, either; she'd started catching small glimpses of Clay the jerk within a month of losing her virginity to him.

Getting pregnant her senior year had obviously muffled that voice, but losing the baby only six weeks along should have had it *shouting* that was her chance to smarten up — especially when Clay had said it was probably for the best, and it was a good thing he'd persuaded her not to tell anyone. And she really wished that voice had found a tote full of bricks and smacked some sense into her when the jerk had suggested they get married anyway and keep to their plan of putting each other through college.

No, it hadn't been teenage lust that had made her think Clay had been her best shot at happily-ever-after, but rather the deadly combination of wanting to leave town, the zinging hormones of pregnancy and loss, and plain old teenage stupidity.

So . . . if her inner voice had been right ten years ago but she hadn't listened to it, what if it was right about Nicholas and she didn't listen to it this time, either, and she walked away from the real deal?

It would be nice if the man were actually *here* to help her decide, but no one — not even Olivia or Mac or Rana — had heard from Nicholas in twenty-eight days. Julia's growing anger at his not even calling had turned to worry, however, when she'd discovered that her unflappable *mentor* was worried.

Several mornings ago, when she'd been digging through the prop room looking for inspiration for Nova Mare's annual New Year's Eve bash, Julia had overheard Rana and Titus talking in the hall, the couple obviously believing no one was at work yet. Well, it had been more of an argument than a discussion, with Rana threatening to go find Nicholas herself if her almighty husband or son wouldn't, and Titus threatening to have her back on the island in the blink of an eye if she stepped even a foot off the mountain.

"In the blink of an eye or *clap of thunder?*" Julia had muttered to herself when the conversation had at that point turned ominously silent. Not wanting them to know she'd overheard their private discussion, Julia had left the prop room via the rabbit warren of corridors and run down to registration, then gone outside and run back up the path and strolled in the front door as if she were just coming to work . . . without her coat.

But apparently even queens had to defer to *real* muscle being flexed, because Rana hadn't stepped foot off the mountain, her mood had been anything but serene for the last several days, and Rowan was now walking her home every evening.

Julia stood up when she spotted Sol in the path lights racing to the door with the rest of the herd valiantly trying to keep up, and she rushed out of the office to let them in. "Okay, okay," she said with a laugh when Sol ran inside and down the hall without even looking at her. "What's all the excitement about?" she asked, following when the other five also ran past. "Were kids throwing snowballs at you?"

Julia stepped into the design room to find all six cats standing stiffly, staring at the side wall as their tails twitched back and forth. She stilled when her skin prickled and her hair stirred with static electricity, and saw that even Sol's hair seemed to stand out from his body like he'd been vigorously rubbed with a balloon.

She slowly became aware of a sharp buzzing growing ominously louder, until it became so piercing that Julia started to raise her hands to her ears — only to still again when Sol suddenly gave a loud guttural growl. The other cats immediately shot toward the hallway as Solomon turned and charged directly at her. The huge cat leapt up and slammed into her chest, the force sending Julia stumbling back with a shout of surprise when she fell, Sol landing sprawled over her just as the wall beside them exploded.

Debris flew into the design room, and Julia's scream was lost in the deafening percussion as a wave of heat and blinding light filled the air with the acrid smell of what she was afraid was detonated fireworks. She rolled over, pulling Sol beneath her as wood and plaster and small chunks of granite rained down, then had to bury her face in Sol's fur because of the dust, only to snap her head up when she heard an unmistakably human scream. "Ohmigod," she cried, rising to her knees. "Someone's in there."

Julia stumbled to her feet, nearly tripping over Sol as he rushed past her, and followed him through the gaping hole in the wall. She stepped into a narrow cave, only to stop when she realized the granite was . . . glowing, the walls actually giving off enough light to see that the sloping tunnel made a sharp turn twenty yards away.

"No, come back," she called out, picking her way over small rocks when Solomon disappeared around the curve. "More fireworks might explode —"

Another pained shout echoed toward her, and Sol came rushing back around the turn, his tail swishing in agitation as he gave an urgent growl before he disappeared down the tunnel again. "Okay, I'm coming. Hang on, mister, I'm coming!" Julia shouted when she heard cursing — only to stop again when she didn't recognize the language.

Oh God, what if that angry man, Perdiccas, had come back for revenge?

Julia rushed forward when she just as quickly decided Sol's urgency meant it had to be *Nicholas*. She rounded the curve and saw him lying half sprawled against the cave wall, mostly naked and covered in blood. But it wasn't the sight of the man — *completely* covered in blood — Nicholas was clutching to his chest that made her hesitate, but rather the bloody sword lying beside him.

Spotting her, Nicholas shouted something she couldn't understand, although she was pretty sure he mentioned both Mac and Titus somewhere in the tirade as he weakly gestured at her. It was then Julia noticed the large, deep gash in his side, which meant a good deal of that blood was *his*.

"Ohmigod, Nicholas," she cried, rushing to crouch down beside him. "Let me see where you're hurt," she said more gently, trying to move the obviously dead man she assumed was Sampson.

Nicholas reached out with surprising speed and shoved her away. "Don't fucking touch him!" he shouted, cradling the man back against him. "Do as I say and get Mac. *Now,*" he snapped, his hand reaching for the sword.

Julia scrambled to her feet and ran back up the cave — passing Sol watching from the safety of the turn — ducked through the gaping hole, and ran into the hall, slamming open the outside door and racing down the path only illuminated by occasional lampposts. She nearly fell on some ice when she made the turn that led to Mac and Olivia's lodge, but righted herself just in time to run straight into Mac.

He caught hold of her shoulders. "Where is he?"

"In a cave . . . behind the design room," she said in gulping pants. "Covered in blood. Sampson . . . I think he's dead. Nicholas won't let him go. He told me to come get you."

"Henry," Mac said as the boy ran up beside them. "Father is likely on his way, so head him off and tell him Nicholas is at the conference pavilion. Also call Rowan and tell him the same thing." Mac started leading Julia back down the path. "Have Rowan bring Dante and Micah to the pavilion. And Henry?" he growled, stopping just as the boy started off, making him turn back. "Then you come there, too."

His entire countenance looking fifty instead of ten, Henry gave a silent nod, then ran into the woods in the direction of the elder Oceanus's cottage.

"Is Nicholas also hurt?" Mac asked as he started down the path again, his pace making Julia have to run to keep up.

"Yes. I saw a deep gash in his side and one on his head. And his pupils were really dark, and . . . and he's really angry."

Mac came to an abrupt halt. "Did he hurt you?"

"No," she quickly assured him as she started walking, only to start running when Mac quickened his pace again. "But the man — Sampson. I think . . . I think he's dead."

"He might not be," Mac said quietly. "How did you enter the tunnel?"

"The side wall of the design room blew out and Nicholas's cat, Solomon, ran inside when we heard a scream," she ended on a whisper.

Mac stopped again, although it was too dark for her to read his expression. "I must rush on ahead, but I would ask that you also come back to the pavilion. We may need your assistance."

"Yes, of course."

He pulled his sweater off over his head and handed it to her. "You're shivering." And then the moment she took it, he turned and disappeared into the darkness.

Realizing she *was* shivering uncontrollably, Julia slipped on the sweater and started running again as she tried *not* to speculate on how Mac had known the loud, earth-trembling explosion had been Nicholas. And likely Sampson — who was definitely dead, she decided, remembering he'd been hacked nearly in half by a . . . sword or something.

Julia felt all her pockets as she ran before finally remembering her phone was in her tote, even as she wondered if someone should call 911, only to decide Mac probably had already.

She reached her office just as Titus and Henry ran inside, the elder Oceanus turning in surprise when she ran in behind them. "Julia," he said, moving to block her way. He shook his head. "You shouldn't be here."

"I found Nicholas and went after Mac," she told him, pressing a hand to the stitch in her side. "Your son asked me to come back and help."

Titus swung around at the sound of a bloodcurdling scream and ran into the design room with Henry not two steps behind him. Julia followed, but stopped just inside the gaping hole in the wall when she realized Nicholas was still really angry.

"Bring him back!" he roared.

"It's too late, Nicholas," she heard Mac say calmly. "He's gone."

"Fucking bring him *back.*"

"You know I can't," Mac snapped. "Not if he doesn't *want* to. He's already chosen, Nicholas," he continued more calmly again.

"Then send me to him. I'll make the son of a bitch change his mind."

"You need to give him up, Nicholas," Julia heard Titus say softly, "so we can see to your wounds."

"Back off, old man," Nicholas growled. "The fucking idiot took a blow meant for *me;* I'll damn well not abandon him now."

"Enough," Mac snarled. "Henry, run to the infirmary and get the triage kit. Micah, Dante," he said just as Julia heard footsteps echoing up the tunnel from the opposite direction. "Take Sampson while Rowan and I control Nicholas."

"Could you not simply heal him, sir?" Julia heard Rowan ask.

"Sweet Zeus, you want to deal with him in a rage at *full strength*?"

Henry came running up the tunnel and stumbled to a halt when he saw her, making Julia realize she'd dropped to her knees and was bent over, hugging herself. The boy turned and said something back down the tunnel in a language she didn't recognize, then stepped past her and ran into the design room.

And that was that, apparently; because with a succinctly explicit curse from one of the men, the conversation resumed but in the same foreign language. It was rooted in Latin or ancient Greek, though, so Julia caught a word or phrase often enough to know that instead of kneeling in a tunnel she hadn't known existed, silently sobbing at Nicholas's anger and pain, she probably should be running for her life.

She flinched instead when something brushed her side and Sol gently butted his head against hers. She gathered him in her arms and buried her face in his fur, sucking in a shuddering breath when she heard Nicholas roar again, followed by sounds of a scuffle laced with more curses and grunts just as something metal — like that sword she'd seen on the floor — struck the granite with enough force to make her flinch again.

Julia stilled when everything suddenly turned silent but for the heavy breathing of the men, and quickly scrambled to her feet holding Sol when she heard footsteps coming up the tunnel. She ducked into the design room and ran across the hall to her office, where she found the other five cats huddled in her leather chair behind her desk, all staring at her with huge, unblinking eyes.

"I'm in my office," she said when Mac called out to her.

He strode in, the front of his shirt smeared with blood and his eyes unusually bright. Titus walked in behind him.

"Father?" Henry said, skidding to a halt at the door, a large backpack in his arms.

"Take it to Rowan," Mac said, nodding across the hall. He looked back at Julia and started to say something, but then looked at his father.

Titus actually managed something resembling a smile. "You needn't worry, Julia; Nicholas's wounds are not life-threatening." He also hesitated briefly, then said, "But we wish to ask if you would be willing to spend the next few days being his nursemaid."

Mac frowned at his father. "Are you sure that's wise?"

Titus looked directly at Julia when he answered. "She's the only one who will be able to handle him."

Was he serious? It had taken five men to wrestle Sampson away from Nicholas, and Dante and Micah were probably right now holding him down so Rowan could tend his wounds. "You mean after he gets out of the hospital, right?" she whispered, hugging Sol more tightly. "Someone did call an ambulance, right?" *And the sheriff,* she refrained from adding, remembering there was an honest-to-God dead man in that tunnel.

"Nicholas won't hurt you, Julia," Mac said, not answering her question. "Father's correct; you're the only one he won't fight." He smiled tightly. "Not physically. But I'm afraid you should be prepared for verbal attacks."

"*After* he gets out of the hospital," she repeated.

"There will be no hospital," Titus said. "Rowan and the others will take him home and . . . settle him in."

"The fewer people who know what went on here tonight, the better," Mac added, drawing her attention again. He held up his hand when she tried to speak. "I would ask that you trust us, Julia, for Nicholas's sake. There's a good chance he's still in danger, and the safest place for him is right here on this mountain." He stepped closer. "I must have your word that you won't speak to anyone about any of this."

Or what? she wanted to ask. She nodded instead, tucking Sol under her chin.

"And you'll stay with Nicholas while he

mends?"

She must have nodded again, because the next thing Julia knew, Mac was taking Sol from her and setting him on the floor, then leading her out of the office. "I will allow you to go home and gather enough clothes for a few days," he said as he opened the door and ushered her outside. He stopped beside her cart and turned her to face him. "I suggest you tell your sister that . . ." He stopped, looking past her shoulder in thought. "No, instead of going home, call Trisha and tell her the resort doctor believes you may have contracted a benign illness from one of your clients. Explain you're being quarantined as a precaution and Olivia decided you should stay at Nicholas's house because of its isolation." He reached in his pocket and pulled out his phone — that she couldn't help notice had a fingerprint of blood on it. "Ask her to pack your clothes because you can't be in contact with anyone, and one of our guards will pick them up."

He waited while she made the call, Julia forcing herself to sound perturbed and inconvenienced for Trisha's sake, then handed the phone back. Mac opened the door on her cart, but Julia didn't get inside.

"Um, I know this probably isn't the time, but has anyone . . . Do you think Phantom might be hurt and wandering around the resort someplace?"

Mac looked back toward the pavilion, then lifted his gaze toward the summit and shrugged. "That old warrior has managed to find his way back to Nicholas before, despite being given up for dead."

As in this has happened before? Julia wanted to shout, instead sliding into the cart.

Mac held the door from closing. "I would have your word that you will go directly to Nicholas's house and stay there."

She nodded, then looked toward her office. "Would you make sure the cats are put outside before you leave?"

"I will. And don't worry about the mess. We'll clean it up."

"Oh, wait; we have the employee Christmas party tomorrow night. That's why I was still here when . . . when . . ."

"Mother will see to it. And Julia?" he said when she straightened from turning on the headlights. "Once he calms down, Nicholas will answer all your questions."

He closed the door on that ominous promise and walked back inside, and Julia glanced at her office windows to see Titus pick up Sol and hug the cat to his chest.

She pressed down on the accelerator,

snapping back against the seat when she forgot about the more powerful motor, and headed toward the guard booth, even as she reminded herself that her inner voice was *sure* she trusted Nicholas with every fiber of her being, even though she had absolutely no idea who — or what — he was.

CHAPTER NINETEEN

It took Julia longer than she cared to admit to finally realize the cooking range was induction, so only the pots and ultimately their contents heated up. But needing to keep busy, she was making soup from two cans of vegetables and a couple of bouillon cubes she'd found in the mostly empty cupboards while Rowan and Micah and Dante were upstairs getting Nicholas . . . settled in.

She didn't know how they'd gotten here ahead of her since no one had passed her on the road, but Julia had arrived to a heated discussion — in that same foreign language — going on upstairs. Most of the heat was coming from Nicholas, although Rowan occasionally gave back as good as he got in between impressive stretches of amazing patience. Even the cats had beaten her here and were now lined up like little soldiers sitting on the couch as they also listened to the goings-on upstairs, their huge unblinking eyes fixed on nothing. Well, except Sol, who was up on the balcony facing the hallway leading to the bedroom, apparently prepared to do some damage of his own if he decided Nicholas needed his help.

Cussing, Julia was discovering, was unmistakable in any language.

And so was anger, especially when rooted in guilt. She remembered their discussion walking home the Friday night they'd made love on the deck and Nicholas saying that if he ever needed anyone guarding his back, they'd be too late because he'd already be dead. Only no one had told Sampson, apparently, as he had stepped in front of the fatal blow meant for Nicholas.

Yeah, she supposed she'd be acting crazy, too, if someone *died* saving her.

Julia set the lid back on the pot of simmering soup, then turned and braced her hands on the granite island counter as she looked toward the living area gently illuminated by beautiful wrought iron floor and table lamps. The lamps had arrived three weeks ago with several end tables, an eight-foot-long dining table that opened to *twelve* feet — making her wonder who Nicholas intended to have over to dinner — two bureaus and the huge, extra-long bed upstairs, and a beautiful desk and credenza that she'd had the deliverymen place in the room off the downstairs hall.

She'd learned from one of the men that all the furniture had been made right here in Maine from native cherry and had been ordered over a year ago. Then a few days later she'd gotten a call from Rowan, saying he'd signed off on a delivery of leather furniture and could she please come tell him where to place everything.

It had been after Rowan and Micah and Dante had left that Julia had stood in the middle of Nicholas's amazing home and realized the mysterious man from an island *somewhere* in the Atlantic had completely immersed himself in the elements of wood, water, earth, fire, and metal. He'd also managed to include the element of air by literally suspending himself over it. No plastic in sight, not even cladding the window casings. Heck, the only truly man-made material in the house was glass, and that was made mostly of sand. That little revelation had gotten Julia curious enough to snoop, and she'd found that all the clothes hanging in his closet were made of natural fibers; hemp, cotton, leather, and even silk.

Julia stopped breathing to listen, realizing that after hearing the shower running and footsteps going back and forth from the bedroom to the en-suite bathroom upstairs for nearly an hour, everything had suddenly gone quiet.

Maybe, she hoped, they'd found something in the triage kit for pain that had finally knocked him out, because she really hadn't been looking forward to babysitting a big strong *angry* man. She walked into the living area to see Rowan descending the stairs, rolling down the sleeves of his more wet than bloody shirt.

He stopped at the bottom when he saw her. "You shouldn't be here, Julia," he said, his cheeks darkening as he glanced up at the balcony before giving her a forced smile. "Come back in a few days, when he's . . . more like himself."

"Titus asked me to stay with him," she said, feeling her own cheeks heating up. "Because he believes Nicholas won't get . . . that he won't fight me."

Rowan looked back upstairs just as Dante and Micah appeared on the balcony, Dante carrying the triage bag and Micah picking up Sol and holding the cat to his chest.

"Will you tell me what his injuries are?" Julia asked, drawing Rowan's attention again. "Is he going to be okay?"

"We stitched a deep gash on his side and

wrapped his ribs on the chance they might be cracked, and he has a nasty bump on his forehead and a bunch of minor cuts and bruises." He shrugged. "Knowing the commander, he'll be hobbling around as early as tomorrow and probably back at work in a week," he said, smiling tightly again.

"Are you sure he shouldn't be in a hospital?"

That smile vanished and he shook his head. "Until we know more details of what happened, he's safest right here at Nova Mare."

Julia looked away. "No one's calling the sheriff, are they?"

"No."

"And . . . Sampson?"

"I imagine Titus and Rana will personally take him back to — back home." Rowan looked upstairs. "Which won't lighten Nicholas's mood any, I'm afraid, as he'll feel that is his duty." He looked at her, his cheeks darkening again. "It's not my place to say any more, Julia. Nicholas will answer any questions you have."

"Yeah," she said on a sigh, "that's what Mac said." She turned away and walked to the kitchen. "Is he asleep? I made some soup."

"You should wait until morning to try

feeding him anything," he said, following her. "Men's bellies won't accept food so soon after battle."

She stopped with the lid half off the pot and stared at the wall behind the stove so Rowan wouldn't see what she thought of that little piece of information given so nonchalantly, as if he were as well acquainted with battle as Nicholas apparently was.

"Would you prefer one of us stays the night?" he asked, just as she heard the other two men walking down the stairs. "There's much that needs to be done at the conference pavilion before morning, but I can leave Dante or Micah here."

"Did you give Nicholas something for the pain?" she asked, not turning around.

"We tried," he said with a humorless chuckle, "although I don't know how much we actually got into him or how effective it will be. But just coming down off the rush should knock him out." She barely stifled a flinch when he set a hand on her shoulder and gave her a gentle squeeze. "I completely agree with Titus; Nicholas would never hurt you, Julia, as his inherent nature is protective — especially of women."

"Yeah, the man's a hero," she softly muttered, finally turning around. "Thanks for the offer, but I'll be okay with him." She gestured at Micah setting Sol down on the floor before unrolling his own wet and bloody sleeves. "And anyway, I have Solomon. The big lug's been hanging around Nicholas so long that he saved me when the wall exploded." She shook her head at the three men's obvious surprise. "He must have sensed what was happening, because he knocked me to the floor and even covered my head with his body."

They all turned to watch Sol walking back upstairs, the other five cats following.

"Well, if you're sure you'll be okay," Rowan said tiredly, "we'll be going."

"Um, that door seems to be stuck," Julia said, motioning at the front door. "I tried to go get something out of my cart earlier, but the door wouldn't open."

Micah reached out and turned the knob and opened it, then looked at her and grinned — also tiredly. "It appears to be fine now."

Julia followed them and stood in the doorway as they walked down the two steps off the porch. "How did you guys get here? I didn't see a truck."

"We . . . ah, came down the shortcut," Rowan said.

"You can take my cart back," she offered.

"We'll walk," Dante said with a wave over

his shoulder. "The shortcut is quicker."

Julia watched them head out the driveway, then stepped back inside and closed the door. She went over and shut off the burner, put the soup in the fridge, then turned and looked around the silent house. She could sleep on the couch, she decided with a tired sigh as she walked back to the door to make sure it would open — only to find it was stuck again.

She pulled and tugged, then pressed her shoulder into it while turning the knob, but it wouldn't budge. She rushed over to the double doors leading onto the deck, only to find they wouldn't open, either. She went to the windows behind the dining table and tried each one, slowly backing away when they wouldn't open, then headed to the downstairs office only to find those windows wouldn't friggin' open, either.

Julia walked back into the main room and stood hugging herself. What was going on? How had the men been able to leave but she couldn't? Did the house have a secret male handshake or something? But she'd come here a lot over the last month and hadn't had any trouble. So why in Hades couldn't she leave now?

"Rowan!"

Julia snapped her gaze to the balcony, then

ran up the stairs, worried Nicholas might try to get out of bed. "Rowan and the others have left," she said, stopping in the bedroom door when he gave a foul curse in good old English. She gave him a tight smile as she approached the bed. "I'm afraid you're stuck with me."

He turned his head away. "I don't want you here."

"Too bad," she growled right back at him, knowing if she didn't get a handle on him now, even half dead he'd start flexing his *real* muscle. "I promised Mac I'd look after you. So what did you want Rowan for? Is there something I can get you?"

He looked back at her, his narrowed eyes almost jet-black. "Yes. Since it doesn't seem to require participation on my part, you can take off your clothes and crawl in bed with me. If that's not a service you're offering, then leave."

Okay, that hurt. "I tried to," she snapped right back at him, turning and walking away. "But it appears all your doors and windows are *stuck.*" She stopped in the hall and shot him an equally threatening glare. "And even though I'm skinnier than a twelve-year-old boy, I can't fit through your cat door. Oh, and for future reference, you might like to know that it takes more than male posturing to scare off the town slut."

Julia turned away when he simply lay there glowering at her and wondered what had possessed her to say *that*. She walked past the cats lying on the balcony facing the bedroom and felt their large unblinking eyes following as she descended the stairs. She walked to the wall of windows facing Bottomless and hugged herself on a shuddering sigh, then simply stood staring down at the lights of Spellbound Falls.

And why, she also wondered, had she thought finding the courage to fall in love with Nicholas would be her biggest hurdle? Because if she had considered him way out of her league before, then tonight's little . . . event put him an entire world away.

Or should that be *centuries* away? She might have caught only pieces of the conversation in the tunnel — in a language she wasn't even sure still existed — but she'd certainly recognized *Atlantis,* and several words such as *mythical, trap* or *ambush* or *trickery,* and something to do with someone's *birthright.*

And then there was Nicholas himself, bleeding all over Sampson cradled in his arms, demanding that Mac bring the man back to life. And Mac saying it was too late, because their friend had already chosen to move on. Move on where, exactly? And if Sampson hadn't already chosen, did that mean Mac *could* have brought him back from the dead?

Nicholas certainly seemed to think so. Because why else would he have nearly died himself carrying Sampson all the way back here from . . . wherever they'd been in that hellacious fight dressed like . . . gladiators. No, the armorlike leather and metal skirt both Sampson and Nicholas had been wearing had been more northern European, if she remembered her stolen classes on ancient civilizations correctly.

Another word she was pretty sure she'd recognized had been *warrior.* And she was fairly certain those had been sword wounds on both men, as she couldn't imagine what other weapon would leave that kind of gouge. For the love of God, Sampson had been hacked nearly in —

Julia stilled on another shudder when she heard the heavy, stilted footsteps in the upstairs hallway.

"I'm sorry."

"It's okay, Nicholas," she said, not turning around. "I'm well aware that angry, hurting men say and do things they don't mean."

"That's not me. I don't lash out at people I care about."

"I know," she said softly, finally turning and looking up to see him standing on the balcony with nothing but a sheet wrapped partly around his bandaged torso and trailing behind him. She smiled sadly. "And I also know you cared very much for Sampson and feel responsible for his dying. Please go back to bed before you fall down." She turned her smile crooked. "Because I really can't carry you there."

"Come with me."

Julia felt her smile turn sad again. "I don't think so."

She saw his grip on the balcony rail tighten as he swayed slightly. "I'll let you keep your clothes on. Just come lie with me, Julia."

"That's very kind of you, but no."

"I am not *kind.*"

"Sorry. I forgot. I seem to keep confusing you with someone else. Go to bed, Nicholas. I'm not going anywhere, apparently," she said with a soft snort. "So if you need anything, just give me a shout."

"I need you to come to bed with me."

It took her only a heartbeat to realize he had every intention of standing there until either he dropped or she complied. Then again, maybe feeling a warm, *alive* body after carrying Sampson all the way here was what he was asking of her. So with a sigh of defeat, Julia walked back through the living room and up the stairs, then stopped in front of him, gathered up the trailing sheet, and carefully slid her arm around his waist — surprised when he actually leaned some of his weight on her.

"You roll over and crush me in your sleep," she muttered as they started down the hallway together, "and you're going to get that other eye blackened."

Nicholas woke up to find Julia cuddled up against his side, her riot of hair — that he'd managed to set free once she'd fallen asleep — draped over his arm and chest, her pliant body warm and inviting, and her feminine scent stirring his senses as he remembered anticipating this moment. The only problem was he hadn't planned on being half dead when it finally happened.

And he sure as Hades hadn't planned on Julia's ever seeing him covered in more blood than clothes, much less having her witness the full force of his dark side. He was still amazed she hadn't run screaming in terror the moment she'd spotted him in the cave holding a dead man. But not only had she stayed calm, she'd agreed to nurse him back to health. And instead of panicking to find herself trapped in his house, even after he'd brutally tried to send her away, she'd come to bed with him and fallen asleep as if she hadn't just learned there was more to Nova Mare and the Oceanuses — and him — than met the eye.

He wasn't surprised Mac had locked Julia in the house, considering all she'd witnessed last night. The true question, however, was how the wizard intended to proceed with her from here. Because the one thing Nicholas *did* know was that they couldn't have modern mortals running around knowing their secrets.

He felt Julia's breath suddenly hitch. "Good morning," he said quietly. "Did you sleep well?"

Keeping her head down, she tentatively tried sliding away from him. "Uh-huh," she murmured when she didn't make it very far. "A-and you?"

Undecided if she was embarrassed to find herself waking up plastered against a mostly naked man or if her voice was merely husky with sleep, Nicholas predicted some long stretches of silence in the upcoming days. He suddenly remembered he needed to respond when she tried sliding away and failed again — apparently unwilling to hurt him by struggling free. "I slept like a well-fed cat curled up in a sunbeam." He actually felt a grin trying to form when she put a bit more effort into her bid for freedom before she went limp with another sigh of defeat. "We need to talk, Julia."

"O-okay," she said, drawing out the word as she gently patted his chest above the bandage around his ribs. "We'll talk right after I have a cup of coffee," she said, once more attempting to leave only to still again. "Please tell me you have coffee."

"Tea."

"What about wine?" she growled. "Because no offense, but the last time a man said 'we need to talk,' I found myself divorced, living at home with a drunken father, and paying back a small mountain of credit card debt."

He smoothed her curls off his chin, then cupped her head against him. "I find myself concerned that you haven't mentioned all that you witnessed last night." He held her still when she tried to look at him. "Why aren't you asking a thousand questions?"

"Because I really don't want to know the answers," she said, a hint of fear in her voice — or maybe that was barely restrained anger?

"You have to be curious."

She snorted against his chest. "Not if

curiosity is what killed the cat."

"You have to at least be wondering what happens . . . now."

She scrambled back so quickly that she landed on the floor, then crab-crawled away when he lunged onto his side and tried to snag her arm. "Don't run," he growled, collapsing with a curse at the screaming pain that spiked through him.

"If your windows are bulletproof glass," she growled right back at him from the far wall, "then I'm taking an ax to the door." He remained motionless facedown on the bed as he heard her get to her feet. "Do you hear me?" she continued, her voice moving toward the hallway. "Nothing's happening *now,* because I just got a bad case of amnesia about what happened *last night.* Nicholas?" He heard her mutter an actual curse of her own, her hesitant footsteps moving closer. "So the only thing happening *now* is that I'm breaking out of this house and stealing your truck and driving as fast and as far away from here as I can get." He heard her creep closer. "And I swear, if your guards try to stop me, I'll run them over without even honking the horn. You got that —"

He captured her hand on its way to giving him a nudge and, ignoring the pain spiking

406

through him as well as her yelp of surprise, rolled onto his back while using his other hand to make sure she landed on the mattress instead of on him. He then rolled half on top of her, pinning her hands beside her head and pressing a leg over hers. "I'm tempted to invite you to our next war games," he said with a pain-laced chuckle, using his stubble-roughened jaw to move her tangle of hair off her face. He turned serious. "Mac won't do anything worrisome to you, Julia. And even if he wanted to, he'd have to go through me first."

"Um, no offense," she said, the apprehension in her eyes reaching her voice, "but even if you weren't a battered mess, I . . . I'm pretty sure Mac and his father get the final word."

"Oh, I believe I have some sway with the Oceanuses," he drawled. "And besides, Providence forbids them from harming an innocent. Ask me anything and I will answer you honestly."

She shook her head. "I really don't want to know anything. *Honestly.*"

"Too late," he said with a heavy sigh, followed by a stifled hiss as he rolled onto his back — keeping a firm grasp on her hand so she couldn't slip away. "Like Pandora's box, you can't undo last night. So ask me something."

"Um, if I promise not to take an ax to your house, will you let me go make a cup of . . . tea?"

He sighed again and opened his fingers, releasing her. "Are you still going to be this stubborn when you're ninety?"

She immediately jumped off the bed — carefully, he noticed, so as not to jostle him — then turned with a glare only to suddenly spin away with a gasp, although not quickly enough for him to miss the sudden flush in her cheeks.

Nicholas pulled the blanket over his waist.

"I probably won't live to be ninety," she muttered, walking out of the room with all the dignity of a scandalized virgin.

He looked up at the rafters with another heavy sigh, deciding a gentleman wouldn't point out that the town slut probably wouldn't blush at the sight of a naked man — not that he'd ever considered himself a gentleman. *Or kind,* he thought with a snort. Why did Julia keep insisting he was kind? And who in Hades was the bastard she kept confusing him with?

He heard the downstairs toilet flush and realized a good part of Julia's urgency to get away probably had more to do with her need to use the bathroom than with her desire to avoid their little talk. Not that they *had* talked; and by the looks of things, not that they would anytime soon.

But should they finally get around to discussing the magic, he did intend to tell the lovely lady she definitely was reaching the age of ninety. He might, however, hold off mentioning she'd be celebrating that birthday with *him.*

Nicholas slid his feet over the side of the bed and carefully pushed himself into a sitting position. The pain quickly propelled him to his feet with a snarl, which in turn had him grabbing the bedpost to keep from falling. He stood trembling like a newborn foal and took shallow breaths, then leaned his forehead against the post with a curse.

Sampson was about as dead as a man could get, Phantom was also probably dead, whoever had ambushed them was determined Nicholas not live to claim his birthright — despite his still not knowing what that birthright *was* — and this wasn't over.

The one glimmer of light, however, was that Julia was carrying his son.

CHAPTER TWENTY

Julia stepped out of the downstairs shower, dried off, and dressed in yesterday's clothes, then stopped in the act of fingering the tangles out of her hair when she realized she smelled coffee. She threw open the bathroom door and ran down the hall to find Olivia and Rana in the kitchen.

"Julia," Olivia said, giving her a hug. "Please tell me you're okay." She leaned back, her eyes going to Julia's forehead. "Mac told me you were standing in the design room when the wall exploded, and that you looked dusty and rattled but not hurt."

Julia touched the small bump on her forehead and smiled, looking over to include an equally concerned Rana. "Solomon knocked me to the floor just in time. I didn't get hurt," she assured them, stepping free only to have Rana pull her into a fierce hug.

"Oh, honey," Rana whispered. "You must

have been . . ." She leaned away. "Not scared, certainly. Not you. Let's go with shocked."

"Yeah, shock works. Is that coffee I smell?"

Rana walked to the counter and got a mug out of the cupboard. "No, it's tar."

"Even better." Julia went to the island and peeked in the boxes, only to groan as she started pulling out food. "Oh man, thank you, guys. Wait," she said, stepping back and eyeing the five boxes. "There's enough food here to last two people a couple of *weeks,*" she said, turning to the women — who both suddenly turned away. But not quickly enough to miss their glances at each other before becoming very busy pouring coffee and stirring something in a pan on the stove.

Julia immediately ran to the side door and tried to open it.

"Don't waste your energy," Olivia muttered, walking over to take Julia's hand and guiding her to one of the leather chairs by the fireplace. "The doors and windows won't open . . . ah, for you."

"But *you* can open them?"

Olivia smiled, shaking her head. "Not to let you out, I can't." She sat down on the hearth with a sigh. "We can't . . . You see . . ." She looked at Rana for support.

"Maximilian feels it's better if you stay

411

inside," Rana said, handing Julia a mug of coffee. She sat down on the hearth beside Olivia. "At least until you and Nicholas have had a nice long talk."

"About?"

"The magic," Olivia said.

Rana reached over and squeezed her daughter-in-law's hand. "We've given our husbands our word to let Nicholas explain it to you," she said with her signature serene smile. "Which is as it should be."

Julia shook her head. "I really don't want to know. Really."

Olivia snorted. "Too late." But then she also smiled. "You *already* know."

"I believe a lot more than you're willing to admit," Rana added.

"It's okay, Julia," Olivia continued, touching her arm. "There's nothing to be afraid of. In fact, you're going to be amazed."

"Yeah, well, *the magic* killed Sampson and nearly killed Nicholas last night."

"No," Rana said. "It likely saved Nicholas's life. As for Sampson, he —"

The door opened and Carolina Oceanus came rushing inside. "Where is he?" she asked, not slowing down as she headed for the stairs, scooping Bastet off the third step. "Oh, baby, you must be so worried," she continued, scooping Ajax off the top step

412

and disappearing down the upstairs hall.

Alec MacKeage caught the closing door with his foot and walked in carrying two boxes, which he set on the island beside the others before heading to the living area as he took off his gloves. He glanced up at the balcony, then turned and shook his head with a grin. "Remind me never to let her drive if she's been told Nicholas is hurt." He turned serious. "How is he?"

"Well enough to still pose a threat," Rana said with a sigh, "but sore enough to be off his feet for a while."

Alec started to look back up at the balcony only to stop his gaze on Julia, his eyes widening in surprise. "*You're* Nicholas's lovely lady?" He grinned again. "Let's not tell him that Peg kept trying to fix us up before I met Jane, okay?"

"Jane?" Julia repeated.

Alec gestured toward the balcony. "My nickname for the princess."

"Julia's our director of special events now," Olivia interjected.

Alec's smile widened as he nodded and took off his jacket and tossed it on the couch. He glanced toward the balcony again and sobered, then walked to the windows and stared out at Bottomless. "What about Phantom?" he asked quietly.

"He's been known to show up several days later when Nicholas was forced to leave without him before," Rana returned just as softly. "That ornery beast is as tough as he looks and smarter than most men."

Sort of like his owner, Julia silently added as she blew on her coffee and finally took a sip. But then, she supposed figments of the imagination were hard to kill.

A loud snort came from the balcony. "Make that ornerier than most *men,*" Carolina said, walking down the stairs now holding Solomon. "Particularly those three in there," she added, nodding toward the bedroom. "I rush all the way from Pine Creek in a panic to see Nicholas, and they kick me out." She stopped in front of Julia, her scowl turning into a smile. "Hi. You must be Nicholas's lovely lady." She set Sol down and held out her hand. "I'm Lina, his favorite princess."

"Julia Campbell," Julia said, also extending her hand — which she didn't get back as Carolina squeezed herself onto the hearth between Olivia and Julia's chair.

"So," the beautiful woman continued as she darted a quick glance at her mother and Olivia before shooting Julia another smile, "I guess this means welcome to our magical little family."

Julia choked on the coffee she'd nervously taken a sip of and got her hand back by jumping to her feet. "Thank you. I . . . If you'll excuse me, I have to go do something with my hair before it dries this way."

"What?" Carolina said, also standing up and looking at her mother.

"I don't believe Nicholas and Julia have had the talk yet," Rana explained, also standing up. She walked over and picked up the small suitcase by the door and held it out when Julia set her coffee on the counter. "Here are your things Trisha packed."

"Thank you," Julia said, forcing herself not to run down the hall. She softly closed and locked the bathroom door, then turned and leaned against it with a silent groan. *Welcome to our magical little family?* Really? That would have been scary enough without the magical part. Because if even half of what she'd read in Nicholas's library these last three weeks was true, the Oceanuses shouldn't . . . exist.

Oh yeah; missing the big strong guy with every fiber of her being and wanting to feel closer to him, Julia had spent her spare time here in Nicholas's home, sitting in his giant leather chair suspended over nothing but air and slowly working her way through his collection of veritable tomes — some of them positively ancient, she couldn't help but notice — that filled the floor-to-ceiling bookshelves taking up an entire wall of his office. Well, she'd read the ones she *could,* because many of the ancient books were in Greek and Latin. But the more she'd read, the more she'd realized the college classes she'd stolen had barely brushed the surface of the various mythological deities.

Julia jumped when the door rattled behind her. "Jules, let me in."

She opened the door, then staggered back when Peg rushed in and threw her arms around her. "Ohmigod, are you okay?" Peg said, hugging her fiercely. She reached up and touched the small bump on Julia's forehead. "Tell me you're okay."

"I'm fine."

Peg hugged her again. "Well then, welcome to the magic."

Julia reared away. "Ohmigod, you, too?" She narrowed her eyes. "How long have you known?"

Peg dropped her gaze, her cheeks darkening. "Um, since I married Duncan." She looked up with a crooked smile. "And his mountain patted me on the ass." She hugged Julia again. "Damn, I've been dying to tell you. I was so excited that morning on the boat, I nearly peed my pants when you said

416

you'd had sex with Nicholas," she whispered, "because I knew it was only a matter of time before there wouldn't be any secrets between us again."

Julia leaned her forehead against Peg's. "Okay, then I guess I better tell you mine," she whispered back. "I'm five weeks pregnant."

Peg stepped away with a squeal — only to slap her hands over her mouth as she looked down the hall and closed the bathroom door with her hip. "Ohmigod," she said behind her hands, her big blue eyes bright with excitement. "Oh, Jules," she squealed, hugging her again. "*Finally.* Um, you want to know another secret?"

"N-no."

"I'm pregnant, too."

Julia stepped back to gape at her.

Peg nodded. "Five or six weeks. Our little wolf pack is growing; Carolina, you, and me." She bobbed her eyebrows. "Now we just need to get Olivia pregnant and all our big scary men can walk around with their chests puffed out, proud of themselves for being such studs." She snorted. "But when this one pops out, I'm having my tubes tied *again,* getting an IUD put in, making Duncan have a vasectomy, and buying stock in a condom company. And if I still get pregnant,

I'm going to —"

Peg stopped talking and they both looked up when they heard Nicholas very succinctly tell Mac exactly what he could do to himself.

And near as Julia could tell, the discussion was heading downhill from there. "Excuse me," she said, pulling open the door. "I have some housecleaning to do."

"Wait," Peg said on a gasp, chasing her down the hall. "You can't — Olivia. Rana. Carolina. Dammit, *Duncan,*" she continued frantically when Julia ran up the stairs. "We have to stop her."

Striding along the balcony, Julia saw Carolina pull Peg to a stop then beam a huge smile up at her. "Come on," Julia told Solomon standing in the hall, his tail twitching in agitation. "If things get nasty, just think of them as dogs." She walked into the bedroom without knocking, causing the two big scary men beside the bed to pivot around and the big scary man in the bed to snap his mouth shut in midgrowl, his eyes also widening in surprise.

"Excuse me, gentlemen," Julia said as Sol jumped up on the bed and straddled Nicholas's legs. "But the next person to cuss is getting a mouthful of balsam goat soap," she said specifically to Nicholas before sliding her gaze to the two obviously stunned Oceanuses. "I'm sorry, but you'll have to come back when he's feeling less combative — say, in about a *week.*"

"Do you have any idea how serious this is, Ms. Campbell?" Titus asked. "It's imperative we discover who was behind the attack and why."

"Today," Mac snapped, "because a week could be too late."

"Do you honestly think he doesn't know that?" Julia said, gesturing at the bed as she fought to hold on to her serenity. "If you're not getting the answers you want, it's either because he doesn't *have* them or doesn't want *you* to have them. Either way, this is an exercise in futility." She stepped to the side, opening a path to the hall. "Give him time to catch his breath, and he'll be more cooperative once he's had a chance to *decide* what happened."

Both men stood stiffly, the elder Oceanus looking like he'd just swallowed a lemon and Mac eyeing her speculatively.

"I believe the door will open for you," Nicholas said into the silence. "Gentlemen."

Titus walked out without looking back, but Mac swung to the bed. "For the love of Zeus, Nicholas, you're putting us all in —"

"I know where my loyalties lie," Nicholas

said quietly. "Do you?"

Mac hesitated, then finally turned and silently walked out of the room; Julia just as silently following him.

"Julia."

She stopped at the door and looked back, saying nothing.

"Don't ever do that again."

She nodded. "I'll try not to," she said, pulling the door closed on the sound of his heavy sigh, which she seconded as she slumped against the wall.

Holy Hades, she was going to need another shower, she was such a ball of sweat. Because honestly, she'd been half expecting Mac to send *her* somewhere in a clap of thunder. She stayed leaning against the wall staring at five cats staring back at her as they all listened to the hushed murmurs downstairs, then the outside door open and footsteps on the side porch. Several vehicle doors closed and engines started, and in less than three minutes the house was silent again.

Julia went downstairs, turned the burner on low to reheat the home fries Olivia had been cooking, then headed to the bathroom. Seeing her hair had dried a mess, she sprayed it with leave-in conditioner, worked her large comb through the tangles, then braided it — even as she wondered if half the reason Titus and Mac had left without an argument was because she'd looked like a wild and crazy witch getting ready to turn them into toads or something.

"Welcome to the magic," she muttered, digging through her cosmetic bag for her toothbrush. "Yeah, well, Miss Margaret Conroy, now I don't feel so bad about keeping my pregnancy a secret our senior year, seeing how you never told me you'd married a friggin' . . ." What? Wizard? Sorcerer? Magician? And what in hell had Peg meant, his *mountain* had patted her on the ass?

Julia sat down on the toilet. So what did that make Nicholas?

Well, other than the father of her baby.

Then what, exactly, did that make their child? For crying out loud, she was just getting used to being in love; now she had to get used to loving a magical . . . warrior?

No, not magical — mythical.

Even better — from friggin' *Atlantis*.

And what did that make Titus and Maximilian Oceanus? The bosses, apparently, since everyone seemed to be deferring to them.

Well, except for Nicholas, because they couldn't seem to get the information they wanted from him, so he couldn't be all that

421

afraid of their magic.

Oh yeah; she really didn't need to ask him anything, because several very old, hand-written books she'd found in Nicholas's library, surprisingly — or magically? — written in good old English, had mentioned Titus Oceanus in great detail. More a series of journals than actual history books, they had chronicled Titus's rebellion against the gods, from his building Atlantis to hide the Trees of Life he was cultivating to hold all knowledge and ensure mankind's free will, to his sinking the island into the sea when the gods had discovered what he was doing.

Julia didn't doubt the magic Titus — and his son — appeared to command was *good;* it's just that some of the accounts in that book, showing what lengths he was willing to go to in order to protect the Trees, had been downright . . . chilling.

And although not mentioned by name, there'd been no mistaking *who* the infant was who had washed up on an Atlantis beach, eventually becoming the warrior Titus often sent on missions as his . . . enforcer.

Yup, she'd fallen deeply in love with a big strong *mythical* hero.

Julia stood up with a calming breath and began brushing her teeth. So what if Nicholas thundered through time on his figment of the imagination to keep mankind safe? Even heroes needed a soft place to land, didn't they? A hearth to come home to, children to bounce on their knees, and a madwoman to make wild, passionate love to?

Julia went to the kitchen, pushed the home fries to the side, and broke several eggs into the pan. No, the question wasn't could she be that safe place for him to land, but could Nicholas fall deeply and madly in love with her? He might *say* her not having an orgasm when they made love didn't matter, but how long before he started getting frustrated and eventually resentful that she couldn't respond to him like a normal woman? Four or five years, maybe, before he went looking for someone who could, considering it had taken Clay only three?

But then, Nicholas hadn't exactly ever spoken of love, had he?

Julia slid the eggs and potatoes onto a plate with a snort. No man was going to declare undying love to a woman he'd known a sum total of ten days. She poured a glass of orange juice, cut an apple and an orange into wedges, slathered a couple of slices of bread with peanut butter, and made a mug of tea. Looking around for something to carry everything, she emptied one of the boxes and refilled it with Nicholas's breakfast, then headed upstairs hoping a full belly might stop him from growling at *her.*

Except when she crept into the room — followed by five equally hesitant cats — she found Nicholas sound asleep with Sol tucked into his armpit, his head resting on Nicholas's shoulder. The big lug just barely opened his eyes when the other five cats silently jumped on the bed and proceeded to find their own comfortable spots along the length of Nicholas's legs.

Julia took everything out of the box and set it on the nightstand, hesitated, then gently picked up his hand and sat down on the bed. She pulled in a shuddering breath, her gaze roaming over his pronounced cheekbones and stubble-shadowed jaw, his lips relaxed in sleep and his . . . She'd never noticed his long lashes — likely because she'd always been too mesmerized by those striking sky-blue eyes. Running her thumb over the back of his battered hand, she gently laid her other hand on his chest.

"Oh yeah, you've definitely got the heart of a hero, big guy," she whispered. "I missed you so much," she continued, reaching up and brushing a lock of hair off his forehead, deciding she liked how the longer length softened the chiseled planes of his face. "And I was afraid that just as I'd found the courage to love you, you might not come back." She pulled in another shuddering breath. "Promise me you'll always come back, and I'll promise not to mind your old-fashioned muscle-flexing."

Wanting to support his bruised shoulder, Julia reached past Sol for the second pillow, only to have a piece of jewelry slide out of the case as she lifted it. She carefully tucked the pillow under the arm of the hand she'd been holding, then reached past Sol again and picked up what appeared to be a masculine-looking brooch that spanned the width of her own hand.

The piece was heavy even for its size, made of what she suspected was bronze, with inlays of tarnished silver and three large gemlike stones she couldn't readily identify. The top stone might be a sapphire, as deep blue as Nicholas's eyes; the middle one could be an emerald, she supposed; the third stone was solid black, although it appeared to shimmer in the sunlight.

She was tempted to call the piece ancient rather than simply old, except the metalwork was amazingly intricate. Julia frowned at the inlaid silver tree spreading across the top half, then traced its roots winding around three distinct circles on the bottom half — the shorter of the roots running into the blue stone set just below the trunk, one root running into the green stone in the middle circle, and the longest root winding down to the black stone.

She knew this tree, having seen it — or one very similar to it — just recently.

In one of Nicholas's books, maybe? The piece appeared to be northern European. And if she remembered correctly, the tree was . . . "Yggdrasil," she whispered as she ran a finger over it, "the Norse rendition of the world built by Odin and his brothers, Vili and Vé, from the body of some evil frost giant the three gods had murdered."

Julia turned the brooch over to find a raised slot for a wide leather strap, except the strap would run up and down, as if diagonally across a man's chest. The top two gemstones were set all the way through the piece and faceted to catch the light, but the bottom black stone, even though it also came through, was smooth. She studied the word etched into the metal in an arc across the top of the back, but stopped tracing the inch-high letters when she realized they were filled with dried blood.

SALOHCIN. That was it; the only writing on the entire brooch.

Julia sighed and started to set it on the nightstand, but stopped in midreach when she remembered having seen the brooch sitting there last night. And she was pretty sure it had been there this morning. She looked at Nicholas, his features softened in sleep. Had Rowan found the piece when they'd undressed him and had washed off the blood and set it on the nightstand before he'd left, and Nicholas had slid it inside the pillowcase this morning to hide it from the Oceanuses?

Did *he* know what Salohcin meant? Was it someone's name or a place?

Julia carefully slid the brooch back inside the pillowcase tucked under Nicholas's arm, then pulled the blanket up as far as she could without disturbing the cats. She stood up and kissed his cheek, then softly whispered next to his ear, "I hope you handle surprises as well as you apparently handle a sword, big guy, because I've got a couple that are going to knock your socks off."

She kissed his cheek again, gave Sol a pat, then straightened. " 'At a girl, Eos," she said, moving down the bed to give the little gray curled up between Nicholas's legs a scratch. "And Snowball," she added, tickling the white one's chin. "You go on and purr him a lullaby. And you others keep sending him your healing vibes, because there's no better medicine in the world than unconditional love."

Julia quietly walked out of the room and closed the door to a crack so Ajax could get out — which he'd likely have to do within the next hour or two. She went downstairs and stopped beside the island, but then continued on to Nicholas's office, figuring the boxes of food weren't going anywhere anymore than she was. She went to the wall of bookshelves and started searching for the books she remembered seeing on Norse mythology — which she hadn't bothered to read because for some silly reason she'd been more curious about the *Greek* gods.

Nicholas watched the bedroom door closing to a crack, guessing that solved one mystery. Julia wasn't asking any questions about what had happened last night because she was slowly piecing together most of the answers on her own.

He grinned, wondering why that surprised him, considering he'd left her complete access to his house. And knowing her propensity to dive into any book left lying around, he'd taken the time to pull the *modern* translations of his more interesting journals out of their hidey-hole in his cellar before he'd left and randomly tucked them into his library.

He'd watched through slightly open eyes as she'd studied the medallion he'd taken off the ambushing bastard who'd been sent to kill him — the blow killing Sampson instead. And just as he had, Julia had obviously recognized Yggdrasil, the Norse Tree of Life. Nicholas grinned again, sensing Julia in the office below going through his books, and decided it was going to be a very interesting next few days, indeed. He dislodged Sol and carefully pulled himself into a sitting position with a pained hiss, then took the medallion out of the pillowcase and set it on the blanket beside him before picking up the plate of eggs and potatoes.

No, make that a very interesting next few *thousands of years.*

CHAPTER TWENTY-ONE

"I'm sorry you're going to miss your Christmas holiday with your family."

Julia lifted her gaze from the book she was reading and looked up the bed at Nicholas leaning against the headboard, propped up by four pillows and five cats — Ajax being outside at the moment. "No one will even notice I'm missing because they'll all be too busy fighting over who gets to hold baby Tom-Tom." She smiled at his surprise. "Reggie started calling the poor kid that the first time he held him, and it stuck. Everyone's going to Tom and Jerilynn's for dinner, even Daddy."

He closed his own book — which was in Latin — and set it on the bed next to the others he'd been scanning, already having gone through the pile on the floor that she'd lugged up over the last three days looking for clues as to who or what Salohcin was. "Have you seen your father since you moved out?" he asked.

Julia rolled onto her back to stare up at the ceiling. "Twice." She quickly glanced over. "But before you start flexing your muscles at me, we met at the Drunken Moose — nice and public neutral ground." She looked back up at the rafters. "He hasn't had a drink since Trisha and I moved out, and the second time we met for lunch he brought along a woman he met at the AA meetings he started attending down in Turtleback."

"AA?"

Julia rolled back onto her stomach. "It's a support group for alcoholics. Mom got him to go a couple of different times years ago, but it never lasted." She brushed the blanket smooth in front of her. "Dad actually drank less after she died, only going on a bender every couple of months instead of every few weekends." She shrugged. "Maybe having a woman friend who understands what he's fighting will make it stick this time." She looked up with a chuckle. "Dad was all spiffed up and smelling like a bottle of cologne, and Deloris — that's the lady's name — was acting like he hung the moon. They're going to Tom and Jerilynn's for Christmas as a couple."

"I'm sorry you're going to miss it," he

repeated.

Julia shrugged again. "It comes around every year. And besides, I've been so busy, I didn't have time to go Christmas shopping and I missed the deadline for online ordering." She looked down at the blanket again, this time nervously plucking at it. "I did manage to get you something, though. And I didn't even have to go shopping because I made it. Well, *we* made it," she said, finally looking up, only to scramble upright when she saw him staring at her belly. "Ohmigod, you know."

He lifted his gaze to hers and nodded.

"But *how*?"

"My mother is a midwife, so I grew up surrounded by pregnant women. I could probably spot one across the room at only a few weeks along." He raised his arm, gesturing with his fingers for her to move into his embrace — which she did without hesitation. He stroked a finger down her cheek as she melted into the crook of his shoulder. "The glow of your skin, the hint of a secret in your eyes . . ." He lifted her chin to look at him. "Plumper breasts," he said with a chuckle when she hid her face in his shoulder. "You've also slowed down. A month ago I couldn't have pictured you lying around in bed for three days just reading."

432

He lifted her chin again. "Thank you. I can't imagine my son having a more beautiful, intelligent, loving mother."

Julia tried to hide her face again, but suddenly leaned away instead. "Son? You know we're having a boy?" She narrowed her eyes. "As in you magically know?"

He shook his head. "No magic involved. I've merely decided I'm not having daughters." She saw him actually shudder as he looked toward the hall. "Just sons," he growled, looking back at her and grinning again, albeit arrogantly. "You'll be thanking me in the years ahead, Julia. Or have you not spent any time around Sophie and little Ella? Or Peg's girls, Charlotte and Isabel?" he continued, his eyes shining with laughter. He pulled her back to his shoulder and kissed the top of her head. "We'll get married New Year's Day."

Julia scrambled away again to gape at him, but then sighed. "Peg warned me you guys don't *ask.*" She got off the bed and walked to the window. "But I . . . I'm afraid, Nicholas," she softly confessed, staring down at the driveway.

"Of the magic?" he asked in surprise.

As in the magic they'd been tiptoeing around for the last three days instead of actually discussing? "No, I'm pretty sure I

433

can deal with that part of you." She took a deep breath and continued staring out the window. "But I'm not so sure I could handle your coming to resent me when I can't . . . I would probably still be married to Clay if it weren't for . . ." She took another deep breath. "What's going to happen when I don't respond to your lovemaking like a normal woman?"

Julia dropped her head when he said nothing and fought the tears stinging her eyes. "I love you," she whispered past the lump in her throat, "with every fiber of my being." She finally turned to see him looking down at his lap, sitting as still as a stone. "It would kill me if you started taking my lack of response . . . personally."

"What I take personally," he said quietly, still looking down, "is being judged by the same measuring stick as your former husband and lovers."

"Lover, as in *one,*" she growled. "I don't, nor did I ever, sleep around."

He snapped his head up, his eyes widening — that is, until they suddenly narrowed in . . . Oh God, he looked thunderous. "You're basing all your beliefs about lovemaking on *one* man? And from that you've decided we *all* need to prove our manhood in bed?"

Julia spun back to the window. "I'm not broken."

"*I'm* not the one you have to convince." She heard him pull in as deep a breath as his bandage would allow. "I would ask that you trust me on this, Julia, since it appears I'm the one with any real experience. So all you need convince me of before we marry is that *you* won't take it personally when I don't even try to make it happen."

She turned to gape at him. "Huh?"

He shrugged his unbruised shoulder, his grin sudden and irreverent. "Near as I can tell, our entire lovemaking is one long orgasm for you."

Julia slapped her hands to her slackened jaw and turned back to the window so he wouldn't see the sheen in her eyes at the realization he might actually *get it.* She *loved* making love to him. And yeah, it was one long orgasm.

"New Year's Day, then," he softly repeated.

Considering Mac had given Olivia a week and Duncan had given Peg less than twelve *hours,* she supposed nine days wasn't so bad. "Well," she hedged just to bug him, "I might be able to throw together a hot dog and beer wedding on such short notice, except we'll have to use the fireplace in the —"

435

Julia grabbed the window casing with a gasp. "Oh, Nicholas," she whispered, her vision blurring with tears again. "A figment of the imagination just came galloping into your driveway."

He threw back the blankets with a shout, scattering the five cats, and swung his feet off the bed with a growl. Julia rushed over and tucked herself under his arm as he used the nightstand to leverage himself to his feet. "Son of a bitch," he whispered, pulling away from her to lift the sash. "Phantom!" he shouted out the open window as Julia ended up having to kneel down and squeeze past him to see. "What took you so long, you old dog?" he continued when the horse stopped in midprance and looked around the dooryard. "Up here!" Nicholas pulled Julia to her feet. "Go call Rowan to come let him in the garage."

"I think Mac took your phone. I didn't see it in the basket when I wanted to use it to call Trisha yesterday."

"There's a resort phone in the oak box on my bookshelf," he said as he braced his hands on the window ledge and gave a sharp whistle.

Julia ran off just as the cats all headed to the window, except for Sol, who raced down the stairs ahead of her. She saw him slide to

436

a halt at the cupboard door and open it with his paw, then heard the cat door flap as he shot outside. She continued into the office, found the box and took out the phone, then turned it on as she rushed to the window. She found Rowan's number and pushed SEND, then slid back the curtain just in time to see Sol skid to a stop in front of Phantom, making the horse rear up excitedly.

"Sol, you idiot!" she heard Nicholas shout. "You know what he's like after he's —"

"Rowan, Phantom's back," Julia said when he answered. "He's standing in Nicholas's driveway. Can you come down and — yes," she said when he cut her off, "he's covered in dried blood and is still wearing a saddle and bridle without any reins, but he doesn't seem to be limping or anything." She headed back upstairs at a run. "Yeah, he's shouting out his bedroom window at him. Please hurry. I don't know if I can keep him inside, and he's still too unsteady to go near that horse."

She ran in the bedroom to find Nicholas pulling a pair of sweatpants out of his bureau drawer and rushed over to try to snatch them from him only to end up in a tug-of-war — which she lost when he merely raised his hand over his head.

"The only way you're going out there," she said, backing to the door and grabbing the casings, "is through me."

He actually grinned. "I suppose we might as well start setting the ground rules," he said as he leaned against the bureau and slowly bent to slide a leg into the pants, "before you say *I do.*"

"I'm warning you," she growled. "Don't make me flex my real muscle."

He slid his other foot in the other pant leg, worked the pants up over his boxers, then straightened with a soft hiss. He looked around and grinned again. "I don't see your usual weapon of choice. Where's your tote bag?"

"Nicholas," she softly petitioned when he opened another drawer and pulled out a sweatshirt. "Please don't go out there."

He started to lift the shirt to his head, but hesitated. "Unfair. No pleading."

"How about if Rowan brings Phantom to your office window and you can sit in a chair and fawn all over him? I have some carrots in the fridge you can give him."

"We need to make him a hot oat mash with molasses and diced carrots," he said, putting on the shirt.

"Show me how, and you can give it to him from your office window."

He was utterly serious when his head emerged from the shirt. "Do you have any idea the hell he went through getting back here on his own?"

"No, I don't," she returned just as quietly, walking up and placing her hand on his chest. "But I have a pretty good idea of the hell you went through. Please, Nicholas; you're just starting to — Wait. That night in the tunnel, I heard Rowan ask Mac if he couldn't simply heal you. Can he?"

He wrapped an arm around her with a snort and slowly started toward the door. "Mac knows better than to even try."

"But if he can heal you, why wouldn't you let him?"

He lifted his arm away to brace his hands on both banisters. "Because I can damn well heal myself," he said on a hiss of pain as he slowly started down the stairs.

Julia stood glaring at his back. "Then why *damn well* don't you?"

"Because I choose not to."

She rushed down the steps when he reached the bottom and tucked herself under his arm again. "Are you going to be this stubborn when you're ninety?"

"Yes." He gave her a squeeze. "Assuming you don't bludgeon me to death before then." He stopped and lifted her chin to look up at him. "My body is doing a fine job of healing itself, Julia, on its own schedule, using its own magic."

"But I don't understand why you don't just —"

"I'm buying myself time."

"Can't you just *pretend* you're not healed instead of going through all this pain?"

She saw the light go out of his eyes. "I'll not dishonor Sampson's memory by walking away unscathed as if it never happened."

Julia tried to turn away, but he gently folded her into his embrace. "He should have been the one carrying *me* back," he said on a heavy sigh. "And at the very least, I should be the one taking him home right now instead of Mac." He tilted her head back and grinned sadly. "Are you ready to talk about the magic now?"

"I might be, if we were to talk in your office while Phantom eats his mash."

"Deal," he said, using her as a walking cane again as he headed to the office.

Darn it to Hades, he hadn't had any intention of going outside.

Just like she hadn't had any intention of having *the talk* until they were ninety.

They stopped at the office window and Nicholas lifted the sash as if it had never been stuck, and Julia wheeled his desk chair over — only to scramble back when Phantom suddenly skidded into the side of the house, stuck his head inside all the way to his chest, and tried to bite Nicholas's shoulder.

"Yeah, I missed you, too," Nicholas said with a laugh as he grabbed the bridle before those teeth made contact. "Easy," he murmured, stroking Phantom's huge dark gray nose crusted with blood. "I knew I wouldn't be able to get rid of you that easily."

Julia ran to the kitchen, grabbed a fistful of carrots out of the fridge, and ran back into the office to find Phantom standing quietly with his forehead resting up against Nicholas's chest as Nicholas stood with his hands pressed to the horse's jowls. But it wasn't the fact they both had their eyes closed that made her go perfectly still; rather, it was the shimmering green light spreading over the horse's neck in soft, pulsing waves.

Okay then; they weren't going to have to talk about the magic because she was *seeing* it in action. Phantom released a long, deep-bellied sigh as Nicholas continued murmuring to him, that pulsing green light now covering the horse's entire body.

"Come here, Julia," Nicholas said softly, not opening his eyes. "Come feel this."

Utterly and completely mesmerized, she slowly walked over to them.

"Touch him," he whispered. "Touch his neck and feel the energy."

She nervously rubbed her hand on her thigh, then slowly reached out, barely stifling a gasp when the green light — which felt as if it were vibrating like a tuning fork — enveloped her hand with heat intense enough to make her hesitate.

"Keep going," Nicholas quietly urged. "Touch him."

She pressed her palm to Phantom's sweat-soaked neck and felt his muscles gently convulsing to the rhythm of the pulsing light. The huge beast let out another groan that ended in an equine sigh as the green light slowly began fading, and Julia looked over when Nicholas also softly groaned to see him drop his hands and stagger back, then carefully lower himself into the chair.

She stepped away when Phantom backed out the window, then recoiled when he gave a loud squeal and reared up, his front hoofs pawing the air as he pivoted on his haunches and took off. She rushed to the window to see him galloping and bucking around the dooryard, sparks flying off his metal shoes as they struck the frozen gravel.

"Are you serious?" she whispered as she

turned to see Nicholas slumped back in the chair, his eyes closed and his complexion ashen. "Oh, Nicholas," she said, getting on her knees next to him and touching his cool, pale cheek. "Please heal yourself."

"Too late," he murmured, his eyes opening slightly as he grinned weakly. "At least for another few days."

"You . . . you were saving your energy for Phantom?"

He nodded, then slowly sat up to see out the window, his grin disappearing. "This wasn't the first time I've had to leave him behind," he said as he watched Phantom prancing in circles. "And yet not only does he always manage to find his way back to me, he's always eager to head out again." He touched her cheek. "It's far more than loyalty that brings him home; it's unconditional love. And that is what you will always have from me, Julia, until the end of time." He lifted her chin to keep her looking at him when she lowered her gaze. "I am aware that notion may frighten you, especially considering what you've learned about me these last few days." He grinned weakly again, pressing a finger to her lips when she tried to speak. "So let's see if we can remain locked in a house together for nine more days before you agree to spend eternity with me." He stopped her from speaking again. "You need to be completely certain, Julia, because once we pledge our troth, it's *forever.*"

She smiled against his finger. "Too late," she whispered, gently clasping his face in her hands. "Forever started five weeks ago when you kissed me on the porch of the event planner's cottage."

One of his brows arched. "Not the first time I kissed you?"

"No, that one didn't count because you were just trying to escape. But no one was holding a gun to your head the second time," she said with a shrug, "so I decided to see if I couldn't scare you away by blowing your socks off."

He rested his head against hers with a snort. "You definitely blew my pants off."

"Yeah, I did, didn't —" Julia reared away at the sound of a throat clearing.

"Excuse me," Rowan drawled through the open window, standing with his arms folded on his chest and grinning at them, Dante and Micah peering past his shoulders, also grinning. "But could you not have waited until *after* we got that cantankerous beast in his stall before you healed —"

All three men scrambled away just in time to avoid being run over when Phantom came charging up to the window and slammed into the house again as he drove his head inside and gave an ear-piercing whinny.

"Maybe I should have waited," Nicholas said with a chuckle. He braced his hands on the arms of the chair, and Julia scrambled to her feet and steadied him as he slowly stood up. "Can you boil some water for the oat mash?" he asked as they started out of the office. Only instead of turning to the kitchen, he lifted his arm from around her and grabbed the bathroom door casing. "I'll just be a minute, and then I believe I'll find out how comfortable my new couch is."

He stepped into the bathroom and looked around, softly chuckling when Julia rushed in behind him and started pulling her underwear she was letting air dry off the top of the shower stall. "I was beginning to wonder if I would ever get a woman to move in with me one panty and bra at a time," he said as he picked up her hair conditioner.

"Huh?" Julia said, plucking the bottle out of his hand.

He picked up her toothbrush and handed it to her with a grin. "You might as well move your things upstairs." He turned serious. "Because you live here now."

"But where's Trisha going to live?"

445

"With us." He went back to grinning when her jaw dropped. "I had intended to set up the small room behind the office for my parents when they came to visit," he said with a shrug, "but Trisha can have it until she heads off to college and when she comes home on holiday." He gave a tired sigh. "It appears we'll have to start the bedroom phase of construction sooner than I was anticipating."

Julia backed out of the bathroom and looked up the hall, which led . . . nowhere, just like upstairs. "Is that why both of your hallways stop at the back wall of the house?"

He nodded, his grin widening as he dropped his gaze to her belly.

She glanced toward the large dining table sitting just off the kitchen under the balcony, then looked at him again. "H-how many bedrooms are you planning to build?"

He lifted gleaming eyes to hers. "I was thinking . . . six."

"You want *six* kids?" she squeaked.

"Sons — six *sons.*"

"Well, good luck growing a uterus," she snapped, bolting down the hall.

Holy Hades, that should teach her to be careful what she wished for!

CHAPTER TWENTY-TWO

Julia stilled in surprise as she stared down at the notepad she'd been doodling on, then slowly set it on the couch and got up and walked to the hearth. "Will you explain to me why you don't have a last name?" she asked, grabbing a log off the wood rack. "I mean, what about your adoptive parents? You said their names are Maude and Mathew, but don't they have a last name?"

Having opted for his giant recliner instead of the couch, Nicholas closed his book with a tired sigh and set it on the table beside his chair, still looking drained from healing Phantom — who was now happily munching hay in his stall in the garage. "Their surname would translate to *White-Cloud,*" he explained, sounding as tired as he looked.

Julia set the log on the fire, then straightened in surprise. "But that's . . . Are they Native American?"

He nodded. "And since I don't look

anything like them, Titus suggested I go by only Nicholas to avoid constantly having to explain myself." He snorted. "Mom's real name is Lomahongva, which is Hopi for *beautiful clouds arising,* and Dad's name is Chavatangakwunua. You can see why they settled on Maude and Mathew."

"But how come — wait. Hopi are a southwestern desert tribe. How did your parents end up in Atlan— on an island somewhere in the middle of the ocean?"

"Atlantis," he said quietly, "is populated with peoples from all over the world, each of the original settlers hand-chosen by Titus."

Julia set the screen back into place, glanced toward her notepad on the couch, then walked over to stand beside his chair. "Do you know who named you Nicholas? Was it your parents?"

He appeared surprised by her question. "I seem to remember Mom saying Titus suggested it when he agreed to let them raise me. Why?"

Julia shrugged. "No reason in particular. I was just wondering," she said as she returned to the couch and sat down. She picked up her notepad again. "Can you tell me how you went from being Carolina's bodyguard to your . . . other profession?"

Keeping the footrest elevated because it was also holding three cats, Nicholas brought up the back of his recliner and grinned, apparently deciding they were finally having *the talk.* "Since I was growing bigger and stronger than any of the other boys my age, Titus began training me right alongside Mac. Then later, whenever Lina was tucked safely at home, he began sending me out as his . . . peacemaker. Our unspoken deal was he never asked how I got things done and I never volunteered any particulars. He trusted my discretion, and I trusted that he'd have my back if I ran into anything I couldn't handle."

"So how come he didn't have your back this time?"

He shook his head. "I didn't have time to contact him. But the day you climbed out my bathroom window with a splat of red paint on your backside, Titus and Mac had come to the house to tell me trouble was brewing between the Teutonics and Romans, and wanted to know if I might be willing to go rescue someone who was in harm's way if it became necessary."

"A woman?" Julia whispered.

"No," he drawled, "a child."

Julia returned his grin with a sheepish smile. "Of course. Um, you said Teutonic.

Do I dare ask what century?"

He lifted a brow. "Let's just go with BC, okay?"

"Works for me. So you went to save a kid who wasn't even in trouble because it was really an ambush? Do you think you were the target, or Titus? Does he ever go himself?"

Nicholas nodded, reclining his chair back and closing his eyes. "He and Mac handle most problems personally." He shrugged again without opening his eyes. "But when they prefer to remain anonymous, they send me."

"So what's your best guess after spending the last three days studying the brooch and reading the books that I can't?" she asked, jealous of his ability to read so many languages, knowing those books might have the proof she needed to confirm her suspicion — which she was reluctant to share with him until he got his strength back. Because if what she'd discovered was true, Nicholas would hop on his *healed* horse and go galloping off to only God knew where. No, make that *when.* "Were you the intended target?"

He cracked open one eye when he apparently heard something in her tone, then sat the chair up again. "I've seen that look before, Julia; specifically when you're wanting to bludgeon someone. What's going on in that intelligent — and may I remind you, *pregnant* — head of yours?"

"What?" she said in surprise. "I can't even *want* to smack someone who tried to kill you?" She turned to stretch out on the couch, clasping her notepad to her chest as she stared up at the ceiling. "Trust me; I'm not about to do anything to jeopardize our child." She took a deep breath, deciding she might as well be as forthcoming as he was being. "I was pregnant once before," she whispered, "my senior year of high school. I didn't tell anyone — not my mom or even Peg — that that was why Clay and I were planning to get married right after graduation."

"What happened?" he asked just as softly.

"I worked at the cedar mill every day after school, and one afternoon when I was about six weeks along, the pallet of shingles I was stacking shifted. I scrambled out of the way in time, but one of the bundles knocked me into the log feeder." She turned onto her side to look over the arm of the couch. "But a little later I started . . . spotting, so I drove myself to the hospital in Millinocket because Clay was at a baseball game out of town. I didn't think I had hit the log feeder that hard, but I lost the baby," she said, pressing a hand to her belly as she shot him a sad smile. "You have no idea how much I've dreamed of having my own little tribe of heathens, so you don't have to worry; I'm going to take very good care of this one."

"I intend to see that you do," he said, returning her smile with what she recognized as his muscle-flexing grin. But then he frowned. "You still went ahead with the marriage."

Julia turned onto her back again. "Clay had been accepted at UMO, so he talked me into sticking to our plan of putting each other through college." She snorted. "And I was still desperate to leave Spellbound Falls and just dumb enough to believe he'd keep his end of the bargain." She let out a big, loud yawn. "I vote we have a nice long nap before you get to watch me cook supper."

"Works for me," he murmured, making her smile up at the ceiling when she heard his contagious yawn. "If you're still looking to get out of Spellbound," he murmured, "I happen to know a pretty little island somewhere in the middle of the ocean we can visit, where we'll have our own private quarters in a beautiful palace."

"For real? Wait — in what century?"

"In whichever century you want, although

Atlantis has changed little over the course of its existence."

"You'd really take me to Atlantis?" she whispered.

"We can honeymoon there if you wish." He yawned again. "If you don't mind being within earshot of your in-laws when you . . . explode."

"Aren't there any hotels or fancy resorts on Atlantis?"

There was a long pause, then a heavy sigh. "A myth can't be a tourist destination, Julia, if it's not supposed to actually exist."

"Oh. Yeah. I forgot."

The house fell silent after that, except for the stereo purring of Snowball and Eos on the recliner's footrest. Gilgamesh and Ajax were outside, Bastet was curled up on the hearth soaking up the fire, and last she'd seen, Sol was stretched out the length of Nicholas's legs with his big fat head on Nicholas's belly.

Julia must have also fallen asleep to the purring lullaby, although she didn't know for how long, but it was still daylight when she came awake with a start to see a bank of dark clouds was obscuring even the closest treetops, and it was snowing. She flinched again when a series of flashes turned the clouds a brilliant white, and held her breath waiting for the thunder — which she assumed meant Mac and the others were returning from taking Sampson home.

Except the boom never came.

Just another plain old weather anomaly, she guessed, watching the snowflakes swirling in every direction as she tried to decide how she felt about what she'd discovered earlier. Because she truly would have to stretch her imagination to wrap her mind around the fact she was deeply and madly in love with the illegitimate son of the biggest bad-assed Norse god of them all.

Which once again had her wondering what that made Nicholas.

Which also had her wondering how much Titus knew.

For instance, had the elder Oceanus known who the infant found on the beach was? Nicholas must suspect that he did, because why else was he reluctant to show Titus the brooch? And who had made the brooch, anyway? The Norse dwarves were supposed to have been amazing metalworkers, reputed to have made Thor's hammer and other magical objects and jewelry, so she guessed they could have made the piece.

But that didn't explain why it was showing up only now. Had the person who had ambushed Nicholas been given the brooch as a means to find him?

Julia stopped breathing. Oh God, what if it *was* some sort of magical homing device and was right now leading them straight to Nicholas? Darn it to Hades, they'd spent the last three days hiding that stupid brooch from the two people — no, the two *wizards* — who likely had the power to overcome its magic.

Julia got up and walked over to Nicholas to gently shake him awake — only to stop in midreach. Just what did she expect him to do with this wonderful piece of information? Try to reverse the brooch's energy and . . . what? Jump out of his chair, leap onto his trusty steed, and charge back through time to kill whomever was trying to kill him? Yeah, well, the man might have the heart of a hero, but at the moment he had the body of an invalid.

Julia went to the side door to see if it would open, but when it wouldn't budge she ran in the office and got the resort phone, deciding to call Rowan. Except she couldn't get through, not to anyone she dialed. She tossed the phone on the desk and stood staring out the window at the snow that seemed to be picking up in intensity, then walked to the hall and eyed the wall opposite the office door.

When she'd turned on the hall light on one of her trips to get more books to lug upstairs two evenings ago, she'd happened to see a faint boot print on the hall floor that she hadn't noticed before; the problem being that half of the bloody print was *behind* the wall. And since everything else about the over-the-top house was as mysterious as the man who owned it, she hadn't been surprised to eventually discover the wall actually opened. But when she'd crept down into the softly glowing basement carved out of the ledge under the back half of the house, she had been surprised to find a small arsenal of weapons that not only appeared to be from all parts of the world but also various centuries — from samurai swords to medieval crossbows to modern pistols.

A fact that had really driven home the definition of *mythical warrior.*

But it had been the small, upward-sloping tunnel that had really caught her attention, realizing it was probably the real shortcut Rowan and the other men had used the night they'd brought Nicholas home.

Julia looked toward the living area to make sure Nicholas was still asleep just as Solomon lifted his head. Sucking in a deep breath, she slowly opened the panel just as

Sol came padding over and stopped between her and the descending stairs, emitting a low, warning growl.

"You don't even think of flexing your muscle at me," Julia growled back at him in a whisper. "Somebody has to go tell Titus what's going on." She went to the pegs by the door, slipped on her coat, checked to make sure her gloves were in the pocket, then walked to the couch and sat down. She picked up her notepad and tore off a new page, figuring she'd better tell Nicholas what she was doing so he didn't panic when he woke up and couldn't find her. She thought a minute, then smiled, and had just started writing when lightning flashed again — again not followed by thunder, although she'd swear she felt the house softly shiver.

Julia continued writing, succinctly telling Nicholas what she'd discovered as well as why she'd left to go tell Titus. She stopped the pencil, smiled again, and added a little muscle-flex of her own before tossing the pad on the couch and picking up the book she'd been reading.

She walked over and gently brushed a lock of hair off Nicholas's forehead. "I guess we're going to find out if you meant everything you said about loving me, big guy," she whispered, bending down and kissing his cheek, "because I'm pretty sure I'm about to put that unconditional part to the test." She folded the letter, tucked it inside the book she'd found the answer to their mystery in, and gently set it on his lap. She took one last glance toward the windows just as another silent flash lit up the swirling snow, then ran to the hall, took another deep breath, and followed Sol down the stairs.

Julia hesitated before starting into the tunnel she assumed led to the summit, instead eyeing the small arsenal of weapons. She really didn't think she should show up at Titus's cottage brandishing a sword or crossbow or gun, but she wouldn't mind having something in her hand if she ran across a rat or fox or some other animal calling the tunnel home.

She dug a peppermint out of her pocket and popped it in her mouth, grabbed what appeared to be a short lance, and headed into the softly glowing tunnel — once again following Sol. Only she hadn't gone more than a few hundred yards when the tunnel forked off in *three* separate directions. "Lovely," she muttered around her candy, staring into each tunnel. She looked down at Sol looking up at her. "Any suggestions?"

The cat sat down, lifted a paw, and started

washing himself.

"Hey," she said, nudging him with her leg — which made him stop in mid-lick. "You want to be a hero like Nicholas, man up and pick a tunnel."

Sol gave a bored yawn, flopped down, and rolled onto his back, stretching out to expose his big white belly as he gave another yawn.

"Fine, I'll pick one," she snapped, heading down the center tunnel. "I know they're supposed to be secret, but is there a reason they're not marked?" she muttered, glancing over her shoulder and not seeing Sol. "Dammit, where'd you go?" she called in a whisper, walking back and reaching the fork just in time to see a big fat hairy tail disappear around a curve in the right-hand tunnel.

She ran to catch up, then once more fell in step behind Sol, walking ten or fifteen minutes before the tunnel forked *again.* Julia unzipped her jacket when she realized she was starting to sweat. "Okay, I choose left," she said, taking several steps down the left-hand tunnel before looking back to see Sol had disappeared down the right one. She gave a growl of frustration and raced after him.

Not ten minutes later, however, Julia realized they were descending instead of walking uphill, and half an hour — and four friggin' intersections — after that, she decided it was time to backtrack. But she didn't feel the first twinge of alarm until she arrived at an intersection she hadn't been to before — having started leaving peppermint candies to mark the tunnels she'd come up.

An hour later Julia finally had to admit she was lost. Honest to God, none of the tunnels seemed to lead anywhere. She should have stumbled onto something by now; a door, an opening in the side of a cliff — something.

Julia stopped at a four-way intersection and sat down right in the center of it. Solomon, the useless big lug, flopped down beside her and started washing himself. "Some hero you turned out to be," she said with a sigh, laying her lance across her folded legs. "Yeah, well, you're just as lost as I am. And Nicholas is going to panic when we don't show up by suppertime, and he's going to save whoever wants him dead the trouble when he kills himself coming after —" Julia stilled when she felt the faint stirring of a breeze coming from the tunnel to her left, the air slightly cooler and . . . salty. "Oh, God," she said, scrambling to her feet. "We're all the way down by the fiord."

At least they were *somewhere*. "Come on," she said, heading down the tunnel at a run. "Even a snowstorm beats wandering around in here until we starve."

The air grew cooler and more salty as the breeze became an actual wind, until Julia was forced to stop and zip up her jacket and put on her gloves. She continued on, finally noticing flashes of light intermittently overshadowing the glowing walls, and started running when she spotted snow blowing into the tunnel — only to slide to a stop when she realized that instead of a tree outside the opening, that tall dark blob was the outline of a man.

She started running again when she recognized Titus's white hair sticking out of the wide-brimmed hat. "Oh, thank God. You're not going to believe this, but I was looking for — Oh, crap," Julia muttered, sliding to a stop again when he turned.

Nope, not Titus — unless he'd grown a foot-long beard in the last four days and recently poked out an eye. Oh, and unless the one eye he did have — which was widened in surprise — had suddenly turned a vivid Nordic blue.

Nicholas woke up to a dark house just as lightning flashed through all the windows, revealing the blinding snowstorm raging outside. He straightened the back of his recliner and turned on the floor lamp beside the chair, stilling in surprise when he didn't see Julia on the couch. Bastet was sitting there instead, flanked by everyone but Solomon, the five of them blinking their eyes to adjust to the light.

He looked around the silent home, then back at the cats. "Where are Julia and Sol? Julia," he called out, closing the footrest to stand — only to catch the book sliding off his lap. He finished standing and opened the book to the page marked by a piece of yellow paper, then turned toward the light as he unfolded the note and started reading.

It's you! We didn't see it because it was hiding in plain sight. Salohcin is Nicholas spelled backward. (I could point out that gods always have only one name, but let's save that little talk for when we're ninety, okay?) Anyway, I don't know if Titus knew who you really were when he gave you that name or if he merely suspected, or even if the brooch was made after the fact. But I do think the obscure reference in this book about a rumored affair between the Norse god Odin and some starry-eyed Roman goddess might really be true. I assume the legend was discounted because two separate mythologies shouldn't actually be able to . . . intersect, so the resulting child — um, that would be you — shouldn't actually exist.

But you do, for which I am very glad.

Anyway, knowing you have a bad habit of charging headlong into a problem, and knowing you might forget you can barely stand much less fight this freaky storm I'm afraid might be coming for you, I tried calling Rowan. But the energy flashing through the air must be interfering with the phone signals, so I decided to go find Titus myself and let him know who we think is trying to kill you. Don't worry; I'm just going to very sweetly ask that he deal with this particular problem personally, since it's mostly his fault for not telling you what I believe he's suspected since you washed up on his island.

I promise I won't take any foolish

chances, and I'll come right back after. And if you still want to marry a woman who apparently is no more afraid of the magic than you are, we can pledge our troth on New Year's Day.

I love you. Unconditionally. (In case you forgot what that means, I don't care who or what you are, big guy, just so long as you're mine.)

Try not to worry, okay? I'm not going out in the storm, but instead using the tunnel shortcut in your basement — that I guess you forgot to tell me about. I'm taking Sol with me (okay, he's pretty much insisting on going), and we'll be back by suppertime. No climbing the stairs and stay away from the garage, and if you're good, I'll give you a really nice surprise when I get back.

Love, Julia

Hey, will I not have a last name, either?

Nicholas lifted his gaze and released a heavy sigh, staring at the snow slapping against the windows. That should teach him to want a lovely *intelligent* lady to spend the rest of his natural life with — although *natural* might be a relative term if Julia's conclusions were correct. He lifted the book he was still holding, quickly scanned the pages she'd marked with her letter, then closed the book to read its title — snorting at the realization they'd completely discounted Roman mythology.

He looked back out at the snow now being illuminated by more frequent flashes. Yes, Titus had definitely known who the babe was that Leviathan had deposited on that Atlantis beach thirty-eight years ago, and had decided the best way to control a potential threat was to channel the unusually strong and astute child's energy into serving mankind — as well as the old theurgist's *personal* agenda.

But then, anyone else would have simply killed the babe.

Nicholas tossed the book and letter on his chair and scrubbed his face with another heavy sigh, then dropped his hands with a grin. He wasn't afraid Titus would do anything worrisome to Julia, but he did wonder if she'd taken her tote.

Yes, he definitely should consider bringing her to one of their war games, if for no other reason than to let her work off six years of frustration trying to prove to everyone she was *not* the town slut. For the life of him, he didn't know how Julia had managed not to explode all over some poor unsuspecting schmuck before now — either sexually or with a big stick. Sweet Prometheus, the woman was practically a virgin; if not physically, then at the very least emotionally.

Yet she'd certainly sounded sure of herself this morning when she'd said she loved him — even declaring it again in her letter *after* discovering who his father was.

Nicholas walked to the hearth and flipped the switches to illuminate the floor and outside deck floodlights, then sat down when he felt his legs threatening to buckle. He looked toward the hall, not only *not* surprised Julia had found his secret entrance to the basement, but that she'd also realized it was the one way she could bypass Mac's selectively locking doors. He just hoped she didn't get lost in the labyrinth of private tunnels, although knowing Solomon was with her was reassuring.

He looked back out at the snow blowing past the floodlights, not happy but also not worried that Julia had left the house. As long as she stayed in the tunnels or on the resort grounds, who or whatever the storm was bringing in couldn't touch her, thanks to the powerful magic Mac had securing Nova Mare.

So the only real question was how to proceed with Julia when she returned. On the one hand he didn't want to squelch her sense they were a team, but on the other he couldn't have her running off on her own every time she felt compelled to guard his back. He rested his arms on his knees with a snort. If Julia wished to feel the beating heart of a hero, she need only press a hand to her own chest.

In fact, he knew very few women who would have accepted the magic as readily as she had, and he certainly didn't know many who were brave enough to waltz into a room and kick out two powerful — and obviously angry — wizards. "I'll try not to," she'd said when he'd told her never to do that again.

Yes, it was a good thing he wasn't having daughters, especially with Julia as their mother, because he really didn't think he would make it to ninety. As for —

Nicholas straightened when something slammed against the secret panel, then sprang to his feet with a growl of pain when Bastet tore off toward the hall as the panel slammed again.

Nicholas opened the door and staggered back when Sol lunged up at him. "Son of a bitch," he snarled as he caught the bleeding cat in midair. "What in hell happened? Julia!" he shouted down the glowing stairway. He stepped back and turned on the hall light, then dropped to one knee to hold Sol looking at him. "Where's Julia?"

Sol twisted free and ran to the outside door with another urgent growl, making Nicholas rise back to his feet. But he hesitated, looking down the stairs again, then finally went to the kitchen. "Come on, you need to take me to her. Is she lost in the tunnels? Is she hurt or did you run into someone?"

The cat paced in a circle in front of the door, blood oozing from a small gash in his side and his tail whipping in agitation as he emitted low rumbling growls.

"No," Nicholas snapped, turning back to the panel. "The tunnels are quicker." But he had to stop and brace his hands on the counter when his legs buckled again, taking deep breaths against the screaming pain in his ribs — only to have Sol leap onto the counter beside him.

The cat made a different sound, and Bastet suddenly jumped up, followed by Eos, Snowball, Ajax, and Gilgamesh. The six of them crowded around Nicholas, butting their heads into his arms and neck as they all began softly purring. "Damn. Okay," he murmured, closing his eyes at the feel of the gentle energy pushing into him. "That's it, little ones. Give me enough to heal, so I can bring Julia back to you."

He pictured the gash in his side, his mind's eye watching it knit back together, then directed the pulsing energy throughout his body, willing his muscles to strengthen and flex with renewed vitality. One by one the weakened cats dropped away until only Sol was left pressing against his shoulder.

"Now you," Nicholas whispered, straightening to clasp Sol's huge head and sending some of the healing energy back to the trembling beast. "That's it, my wise little friend, suck up all you need."

Sol suddenly nipped at Nicholas's hand with a snarl, then scrambled off the counter and started circling in front of the outside door again.

"I need to dress," Nicholas said, tearing off upstairs. He quickly stripped off, took off the bandage from around his ribs, and put on heavy wool pants and a thick wool sweater. He grabbed the brooch off the nightstand and shoved it in his pocket, then went into his closet and got his sword. He ran downstairs and dressed his feet, tossed on his jacket, slipped his sheathed sword onto his back, and stepped outside just as lightning flashed, the silent percussion making him stagger against the house.

"Okay, now I understand," he said as he followed Sol to the garage. "I can sense she's down at the fiord." Which meant aboveground was quicker, as he'd have to take the tunnel up to the summit before he could head down to the fiord.

He opened the garage door to the sound of Phantom kicking his stall in between rearing up and pawing the air. "Easy now," Nicholas crooned as he grabbed his saddle and two lead lines off the wall when he realized the bridle didn't have reins, all the while fighting to tamp down his urgency in order to calm the horse. He opened the stall door. "We're off again," he told Phantom as he tossed the saddle onto his back, "but we're staying in this century — I hope." He tightened the cinch, Phantom not even trying to bloat, then clipped the leads to the horse's halter.

"Sol, come," he said, patting his chest. He caught Sol in midlunge, unzipped his jacket and settled the cat inside, then led Phantom out of the stall and mounted up. "Four of us return or none of us are coming home," he growled, spurring the horse into the storm.

No, *five* were returning — including his son.

CHAPTER TWENTY-THREE

Forget that she'd fallen in love with Spellbound Falls' most eligible bachelor; if just six weeks ago someone had told Julia that she'd go up against a mythical god with nothing more than an ancient — and obviously puny — lance only to find herself being dragged off to only . . . that god knew where, she'd have called them insane.

But here she was with her hands tied together by a big fat rope, being led down to the fiord through a nearly blinding snowstorm. She assumed she was to be used as bait to lure Nicholas off the resort, because a deity from one mythology couldn't get past another mythology's magic, apparently.

Odin wasn't anything like the romanticized god in all the poems and sagas. In fact, this guy was downright nasty. He would have *killed* Solomon for merely trying to protect her if Julia hadn't started poking the jerk with her lance — using the blunt end, because she really hadn't wanted to piss him off.

She hoped that lance didn't hold any sentimental value for Nicholas, because it was now six very short sticks. And she really hoped a lot of the stuff she'd read in the ancient tomes about Odin were more myth than fact, because she really didn't want the sins of this particular father to be visited upon his son.

Speaking of which . . . "Why are you trying to kill Nicholas?" she asked, despite knowing most of the ancient gods had a bad habit of killing their offspring. And their siblings. And parents. And anyone else who rubbed them the wrong way, it seemed. "It's not like he's threatening your position or anything. He didn't even know you were his father," she muttered. "If you had just left him alone, you both could have spent eternity in blissful ignorance."

Odin stopped walking, making Julia scramble back when she bumped into him. "I'm not trying to kill him, those Roman bastards are. I came here to warn Salohcin that his conniving, thieving, ugly hag of a mother," he growled, spitting on the ground in disgust — apparently forgetting he'd had sex with the ugly hag — "has sent her brothers to kill him before he discovers his birthright."

"Which is?"

Odin started walking again, the rope making Julia have to run to keep up. "It's none of your business. What was that?" he asked, stopping again when she muttered something. "What are you caterwauling about?"

"I said I don't care if you are trying to help *Nicholas;* you're a nasty man."

"You're still breathing, aren't you?" he snapped, turning and heading off again. "I'd say that was nice of me."

"You tried to kill a poor, defenseless cat."

He snorted, rubbing the three deep scratches on his face. "That cat's about as defenseless as a dragon. Now are you going to stop talking anytime soon?"

"Do you have a last name?"

He turned to her, his one good eye narrowed menacingly. "Again, that's none of your business. Or is it?" he said quietly. He clasped her face in one of his big strong hands. "Exactly what are you to Salohcin? Are you his —"

They both turned at the sound of muted hoofbeats racing toward them, and Julia gasped when the giant figment of the imagination came galloping out of the swirling snow, Nicholas riding low on his back like the giant hero he was, and Solomon, bless his giant heart, riding in front of him on the saddle.

Julia drove her knee into Odin's groin, used her bound hands to punch his one good eye when he doubled over with a grunt of surprise, then tried to scramble out of the way when she realized Nicholas was charging straight toward them.

Only she hadn't taken two steps before she was plucked off her feet and hauled up against a big broad chest, catching sight of Solomon landing on Odin's back before she found herself straddling Phantom as the giant beast slid to a halt and Nicholas dismounted before she could even work up a good scream.

"Stand," Nicholas growled at Phantom. "Stay put," he then growled at her as he reached up and sliced the rope binding her hands. He turned away, pulling the giant sword out of the sling on his back as he strode toward Odin — who was now trying to pull Solomon's claws out of his beard as the cat bit his hat.

Okay then; wanting to think she was as smart as a warhorse, Julia stayed put. Besides, Nicholas looked like his big strong self again, and she was really quite eager to see this whole mythical warrior thing in action.

Well, that is until that warrior suddenly stopped in midstride just as Odin dropped his hands and stiffened and Sol also went perfectly still on Odin's shoulders.

"Julia," Nicholas said quietly, not looking at her.

"Y-yeah?"

"No matter what you see or hear, don't get off that horse."

"I'll —"

"Do *not* say you'll try."

"I'll stay on Phantom," she agreed, definitely as smart as the horse — that was also standing perfectly still, its ears perked toward the fiord.

"Well, son, I hope you're better with that sword than you are at picking women," the old Norse said, his one bright blue eye also trained on the fiord as he slowly lifted Solomon off his shoulder. "Because it appears you're about to meet some of your *maternal* relatives."

But when she looked at where they were looking, it took Julia several pounding heartbeats to realize that wasn't a shoreline of snow-covered boulders being illuminated by constant flashes of lightning, but a *legion* of Roman warriors in full battle gear.

She immediately changed her mind about wanting to see Nicholas in action.

"Um, Nicholas?"

"Not now Julia."

"You do know they can't enter the tunnels, don't you?"

"Neither can he," Nicholas said, still facing down an entire friggin' army as he nodded toward Odin walking over to stand beside him.

"You couldn't have found yourself a less talkative woman?" the Norse drawled, pulling an even bigger sword out from under his thick fur cloak.

Nicholas shrugged. "She's an acquired taste."

Where in Hades were the Oceanuses? This was their turf; they should damn well be guarding it. Julia looked around for something to use as a weapon, because she really didn't think she'd be able to *stay put* while an entire legion of Roman warriors was trying to kill the man she loved. But the best she could come up with was the rope that had been tied around her hands, which was now draped over Phantom's neck. Then again, maybe *he* would make a good weapon. Weren't warhorses trained to attack the enemy?

"Salohcin!" someone called from the

shoreline, making Julia grab the rope and lift her head to see three dark figures break away from the line. "Your mother has been searching for you since she lost her infant son overboard in a terrible storm."

Julia silently snorted; more like the ugly hag had *tossed* him overboard before anyone could discover she'd given birth to a rival mythology's child.

"We've already sent word that we may have finally found you," the middle of the three men continued, lowering his voice as he drew closer — only to reach his arms out to stop the other two when he obviously recognized the unmistakable one-eyed Odin standing beside Nicholas. She saw the man whisper something to his cohorts before taking another step forward, still holding his hands away from his sides. "She's very excited to finally meet you, Salohcin, as she's never given up hope of finding you." The guy briefly slid his gaze to Julia, then gestured toward her. "Is that your wife? You're welcome to bring her along if you wish, so she can meet her mother-in-law."

Like that's going to happen, Julia thought with another snort.

"Maybe another time," Nicholas drawled, his tone provoking. "For me as well, I'm afraid," he added with a loud sigh, "as I have obligations here at the moment."

"Speaking of which, where in Niflheim is that old son-stealing bastard, anyway?" Julia heard Odin softly mutter — recognizing the Norse equivalent of Hades.

"I'm right here."

Julia snapped her gaze to the outcropping of ledge behind Nicholas and Odin to see Titus and Mac standing — Holy Hades, talk about being larger than life! They had to be over ten feet tall!

She dropped the rope back on Phantom's neck with a sigh of relief. No battles of mythical proportions taking place here today, as Titus wasn't going to — Hey, wait. She was seeing *three* distinct mythologies in the same place all at the same time!

Well, three and a half counting Nicholas, as he was a completely new . . . hybrid.

"I suggest you go back to your sister," Titus said, his quiet voice reaching the three Roman bastards as the one who'd stepped ahead of his buddies slowly backed up to them. "Tell her you were mistaken, and that Titus Oceanus told you the infant she threw overboard did indeed drown." He gestured toward Nicholas, who, Julia noticed, was standing utterly motionless, still looking at the fiord — as was Odin. "This mere mortal is powerless but for what energies I give

478

him," the wizard continued, "and is the illegitimate son of a down-on-his-luck traveling minstrel and a naive island girl."

Then why in Hades didn't you name him Elroy or Bob or Sue or something, Julia wanted to shout, *instead of* Salohcin *spelled friggin' backward?*

"I started the rumor of an infant washing up on our beach," Titus continued as if he'd read her mind, his eyes flaring brightly with anger, "so that your sister would spend the rest of her days fearing the child she murdered would come looking for her. Our oceans are not a dumping ground for life's problems, and mankind and deities alike must learn that what goes into them will someday return with a vengeance."

Bummer. She wasn't pledging her troth to a real live deity on New Year's Day.

Wait — could mythical gods *lie*?

Was that a slight grin she saw on Nicholas's face?

Now what in Hades was he so happy about? Titus had set him up as a friggin' *target,* wanting the ugly murdering hag to worry that her son would rise up from the dead and come gunning for her.

So she'd sent her brothers to murder him — again.

Julia eyed the Romans eyeing Titus as they

appeared to be trying to decide whether or not to believe him.

"Do you gentlemen need help getting home?" Mac added when they didn't move.

The lightning revealed the middle Roman's hand going to the sword on his side, his narrow-eyed gaze on Nicholas — who made a *tsk*ing sound and shook his head.

"What did you expect?" Odin drawled. "They're Romans."

Julia hoped she did live to ninety years old, just so she could tell her great-grandchildren about the epic mythical event she had witnessed today. Because no sooner had the three Romans drawn their swords than a collective shout rose up behind them, and they spun around in time to see their legion of warriors disappear when the shoreline they were standing on sank into the frigid waters of the fiord. The massive landslide continued moving inland — eventually overtaking the three men scrambling to reach firm ground, until they also found themselves swimming — only to halt just a few feet short of Nicholas and Odin.

But Julia immediately stopped being excited about what she was seeing when a long series of flashes revealed the unmistakable dorsal fins of what seemed like hundreds of sharks moving in on the floundering army of men. She pulled her hood up over her head and bent forward to hide her face in Phantom's thick mane, fighting not to scream right along with those caught in the feeding frenzy.

Oh yeah, all the bone-chilling accounts she'd read about the Oceanuses were vividly, memorably true, and she was *never* kicking them out of anywhere ever again.

Julia flinched when Nicholas suddenly vaulted onto Phantom behind her and lifted her to sit crosswise in front of him, then turned her so she could bury her face in his sweater as he folded the edges of his jacket around her. She did peek through her fingers, however, when she felt him reach into his pants pocket, and saw him hand the brooch to Odin, now standing beside Phantom.

"You ever come back here again," Nicholas said quietly, "I will kill you."

Julia saw Odin's single eye narrow just before he grinned, gave a curt nod, and turned away.

"Meanwhile," Nicholas added, making Odin stop and look back, "you might want to be more careful about the company you keep, especially wolves," he finished. Julia remembered that Loki's son, a wolf named Fenrir, would eventually eat the mortal

Odin in the battle of Ragnarok — which signaled the end of the world.

Nicholas tightened his arms around her and spurred Phantom into an easy lope through the trees straight up the mountain, giving Titus and Mac a slight nod as they passed the two once again normal-size wizards. Only he brought the horse to a halt once they were well out of earshot of the horrific bloodbath taking place in the fiord. "Come, Sol," he said, patting his knee.

The big cat made a running leap up Phantom's side, then burrowed inside Nicholas's jacket on Julia's lap, giving a warning growl when Nicholas tried to pull Odin's mangled hat out of his mouth.

Not really sure of Nicholas's mood, since he didn't seem to be paying any attention to her except to make sure she didn't fall off, and not really eager to discuss how she'd ended up in the middle of a mythical battle, anyway, Julia decided a really smart woman would probably keep her mouth shut.

In fact, she was so determined not to cause the man she loved any more trouble, and felt so warm and safe in the arms of the muscle-flexing atavist, that she simply melted into him with a sigh — only to be lulled to sleep by the steady beat of his big strong hero's heart.

Julia woke up to find herself being carried into the house — through the magically one-way door — and up the stairs without Nicholas even bothering to stop and take off his boots. She looked over his shoulder to see the cats sprawled on the hearth soaking up what was left of the dying fire, barely lifting their heads when Solomon walked over still carrying his mangled prize in his mouth. He jumped up beside them and used the hat as a pillow.

Still not saying anything even though he obviously knew she was awake, Nicholas set Julia on her feet beside his oversize bed and silently started undressing her. Only he didn't stop with her coat and boots, but took off her fleece and pants and socks in between shedding his own clothes until they were both completely naked.

Still not quite sure of his mood, Julia still didn't dare say anything as he ran his gaze over her, his bright sky-blue eyes seeming to glow in the muted light shining down the hall from the blazing floodlights in the peak of the house.

He reached out and palmed her cheeks to tilt her head back, then kissed her.

Julia sighed into his mouth, slipping her

arms around his wonderfully healed ribs as she started to melt into him, only to feel one of his arms move around her shoulder as he tucked her head in the crook of his arm to continue kissing her and his other hand slipped behind her knees to lift her off her feet. He laid her on the bed, following her down without breaking the kiss, and settled himself intimately over her.

His mouth left hers to move across her cheeks, his hands roaming over her body as he appeared to be giving her a tactile inspection to confirm his eye's assessment she was okay. And so Julia started doing the same, reveling in the feel of his wonderfully strong, hard muscles shuddering beneath her fingers.

"Don't ever do that again," he quietly growled, his lips capturing her earlobe.

"I'll —"

He reared up just enough to glare down at her.

"I will try really, really hard not to," she said, pulling his mouth down to within an inch of hers. "I love it when you try flexing your muscle at me. It makes me . . . hot."

He touched his forehead to hers. "It's supposed to make you behave."

"Like that's ever going to happen," she said on a laugh — which ended abruptly when he flexed several really interesting muscles and gently slid inside her, and the madwoman who'd patiently been waiting an entire friggin' month for him to come home suddenly . . . exploded.

She had a wonderful time, too, now that she didn't have to worry about anything other than enjoying herself. Well, and making sure he was enjoying *himself.* But not ten minutes into her one long lovemaking orgasm, he rolled onto his back so that she was sitting straddling him.

"Come for me, Julia."

She suddenly stilled, certain she must have misheard him — only to realize she hadn't when he reached for her hand. "But . . . but you said I didn't have to," she cried hoarsely, pulling her hand free. "That you weren't even going to *try.*"

The directness of his gaze made her stop breathing as he took hold of her hand again and moved it down between them. "Come for me." He began working her fingers through her slickness. "Let me feel your pleasure."

Julia closed her eyes to escape the intensity in his, only to shudder again when he arched his hips as he continued to . . . assist her. "I'm sorry," he softly drawled, "am I scaring you?"

Julia snapped open her eyes to his provocative grin, realizing she'd said those exact words to him the first time they'd had wild passionate sex on the floor of the event planner's cottage. The muscle-flexing atavist; he was calling her bluff.

She shrugged his hand off hers, then closed her eyes again on his chuckle and continued what he'd started. He clasped her hips in his big strong hands to anchor her down over him as she felt the tension slowly build inside her. The heat of his hard body, hearing his labored breathing as he strained to hold himself still, the very idea that he would be the first man to see her lose it completely; it all grew so overwhelming that Julia suddenly, gloriously crested, the power of her orgasm tearing a sob from her throat as Nicholas joined her passionate explosion with his own shout of pure masculine pleasure, the salacious tremors going on and on for what seemed like forever.

She finally collapsed, utterly and completely boneless, against his heaving chest. "Ohmigod. Ohmigod," she got out between ragged pants. "Oh . . . my . . . God."

He brushed the hair off her face and kissed her forehead, then slid a hand down her trembling body to weakly pat her bottom as he gave an even weaker chuckle. "I think you might have just loosened some of those rods holding the house to the ledge," he thickly rasped as he also gulped in air. He kissed her again, leaving his lips against her forehead. "Thank you, Julia, for sharing that with me."

She gave his shoulder an equally weak pat. "You . . . um, you don't mind I had to . . . that I . . . helped?"

He shrugged, shrugging her with him. "I'll admit to being a goal-oriented man, but I've never worried much about *how* something should happen." He gently lifted her off him and spooned her into the heat of his body as he splayed a hand across her belly. "I was beginning to wonder if I'd ever get to make love to you in a bed. All we're lacking to fulfill my fantasy are the cats."

Julia snorted. "We're going to need a bigger bed."

He rested his head to nuzzle her shoulder with a sigh. "So tell me," he continued. "If you fell in love with me the night I kissed you at the event planner's cottage, why did you continue to fight my pursuit?"

Julia smiled at the opposite wall, wondering if Nicholas even realized he was a chatty-after-sex lover. "I fell in *like* with you that night."

"But this morning — no, yesterday morning — you told me that's when —"

"I told you that was the beginning of our *forever*," she said, cutting him off. "I didn't fall in love with you until later."

"When, later?" he asked, a bit of an edge creeping into his voice.

"When I read the journals you *deliberately* left for me to find and realized that I had to save all the poor unsuspecting women in Spellbound Falls by taking you off the market." She turned inside his embrace to cup his jaw. "Because," she whispered, "true atavists are rare even out here in the middle of nowhere, and I really wouldn't wish you on my worst enemy." She patted his scowling cheek, beaming him a big bright smile as she gave a shrug. "So I figured your chances of finding a *lovely* lady willing to love you even after learning why you don't have a last name are even rarer." She snorted. "And finding one who's willing to live with six cats would be nearly impossible. So," she said, rolling onto her back with a sigh, "I guess that means you're lucky I'm not easily intimidated, or you'd be rattling around alone in this beautiful house for at least a couple of more . . . centuries."

"Or instead of being lucky," he whispered, rolling to settle intimately between her legs, then gathering her hands and pinning them to the bed, "maybe I'm merely better at storming castles than you are at defending them."

She suddenly sobered when she felt the evidence of what was nothing short of a *magical* recovery pressing against her as she recognized the look in his . . . yes, those were definitely *Nordic* blue eyes. "Nicholas, is . . . is Odin your father?"

"I'll tell you in about eight or nine years," he murmured against her mouth as he slipped inside her again. "The day you give me my sixth son."

Epilogue

Julia sat on the bench in the gazebo in the early March sun and furiously filled the pages of her beautiful calendar book with notes to herself, because she really didn't want to screw up the most important event of her four-month career — especially after just telling Olivia she was permanently accepting the position of Nova Mare's director of special events.

That is, if she survived the Oceanus wedding, since this was her first major event without her unflappable mentor holding her hand because, as the mother of the bride, Rana had to be holding her daughter's hand.

And already mother and daughter and *father* were at odds as to the wording on the wedding invitations — which should have been sent out over a week ago. Daughter wanted *Jane;* Father was insisting on *Carolina;* and Mother was suggesting they go with *Carolina/Jane.*

At this point, Julia was tempted to get the bride alone and suggest she elope.

"What about leaving the reception in a hot air balloon?" Olivia asked, sitting down on the bench beside Julia. "I don't believe we've done that before."

Thank heavens Peg spoke up, since Julia was too busy gaping to say anything.

"Alec will never go for it," Peg said, sitting down beside Olivia. "Not with Jane being almost nine months pregnant by then. I say we stick with the horse and have them ride off into the sunset."

"But that's been done so many times now that it's becoming clichéd," Jane said, sitting down on Julia's other side. "The irony being that Alec and I are the *original* wilderness hikers." She glanced over at Julia's calendar book, then tapped the top of one of the pages. "Don't forget that Trace Huntsman in Midnight Bay has agreed to provide the lobsters. Oh, and I've decided to have Gabriella Killkenny play solo instead of getting a singer. She's really quite a talented violinist."

Feeling dumb for forgetting that Trace was a lobsterman, Julia crossed out the note to have Aeolus's chef order the lobster and started furiously writing again.

"Well, this is certainly a sight," Rana suddenly piped up, standing in the middle of the gazebo smiling at them. "Four beautiful women glowing with the promise of new life," she continued as she pulled a camera out of her pocket. "I believe this calls for a picture. Tighten together," she said, waving one hand. "Peg, give me a smile."

"We just learned we're having *twins*," Peg growled. "And they couldn't find even one penis on the sonogram. I'm having two friggin' *girls*."

Julia stared down at her calendar book to hide her smile. Peg talked the big talk, but Julia knew her friend was over-the-moon excited. Peg just didn't want Duncan to know she was, because the guy was already strutting around with his chest puffed out like a big strong proud stud.

"Come on, ladies," Rana said with a sigh as she held up the camera. "Smile."

"I'm having all the wells checked," Olivia grumbled. "Does anyone know if there's such a thing as naturally occurring fertility minerals that might be in the water? Because I have no idea how I got pregnant."

Peg snorted. "Need I remind you that you share a bed with a friggin' wizard? You think some silly little IUD is gonna stop his boys from reaching your girls?"

"Ladies," Rana sputtered. "Behave. Those

scowls are ruining your beautiful glow." She lifted the camera again and clicked the shutter without warning, then set up for another picture. "On the count of three — smile!"

She took several more pictures, even making them smooth down their jerseys and place their hands on their bellies — although Olivia was only two months along, and Julia was just barely starting to show. Peg, however, already looked as if she'd swallowed a small basketball, and Carolina was . . . well, she had a very elegant, regal-looking baby bump sitting on top of those really long legs.

Rana walked to the opposite side of the gazebo, propped the camera up on the rail, pushed a button, then rushed over and squeezed in between Julia and Olivia, throwing her arms behind them to encompass all four women. "Say cheese, ladies."

They all gave varying degrees of smiles, holding them until they thought they heard the shutter snap, then Rana dropped her arms to her lap with a sigh. "I've been thinking it might be a good idea to invite Nicholas's mom, Maude, to come midwife for us. What do you think, Olivia?" she asked, looking at her daughter-in-law. "Would you have a position on your staff for a royal gardener if the White-Clouds were to move to Spellbound Falls?"

"Oh, I'd love to have Mathew working his own special magic at Nova Mare. Your palace grounds are absolutely gorgeous."

Which Julia knew personally, since Nicholas had kept his promise of taking her to Atlantis. And yeah, she wouldn't mind having her in-laws around, since they absolutely adored her for loving their big strong scary son.

"Oh, that would be wonderful," Jane piped up. "I've been trying to figure out how to broach the subject with Maude about coming for an extended visit near my due date."

"That's good to hear," Rana said, leaning back with a smug smile. "Because I've already asked if she'd be interested in setting up a small clinic in town, and she's already agreed." She shot Olivia an apologetic smile. "And Mathew is already studying up on Maine's indigenous plants and planning an alpine children's garden." Her smile went back to being smug. "In fact, the White-Clouds should be arriving any day now.

"So, ladies," she continued, standing to turn and face them. "What do you say we throw ourselves one all-inclusive baby shower? The spring equinox would be a good day to celebrate the little miracles created with wonderfully feminine magic, don't you think? I'm sure we could get the weather to cooperate, and we can have a bonfire down on the beach of the beautiful home I've just purchased."

She was met with stunned silence.

"You bought a house?" Carolina whispered, eyeing her mother suspiciously. "On Bottomless? But I thought Daddy refuses to live off the mountain."

Rana looked down and brushed a speck of lint off her royal purple chambray shirt. "Oh, I'm sorry; did I not mention that I'm leaving Titus?"

And that, Julia decided, was one of the big scary dangers of loving a big strong *contrary* man — not that she'd trade hers for all the kissable frogs in the world.

LETTER FROM LAKEWATCH

MARCH 2013

Dear Readers,

You're the best! Romance readers are unrivaled as fans, I think because authors *and* readers *and* the fictional characters we come to love all share the same dreams, desires, and passions. (I know I've said this before, but some things are worth repeating.) Real and imagined people are optimistic or pessimistic, easygoing or easily offended, heroic or cowardly — all of which are traits that can and often do get in the way of happily-ever-afters.

So for those of you who have been following the ongoing trials and tribulations of my larger-than-life and sometimes over-the-top men and women, my question is: Do you believe in the magic yet?

If you're not sure what I'm talking about, then let me put it another way: Has anything ever happened that you couldn't really explain but that made you stop and think: Hey, *this* could be what that crazy lady in Maine is writing about! Have you ever experienced something amazing that should have been totally improbable if not downright impossible, and found yourself running around telling everyone you know (and sometimes total strangers) about it because you want them to be utterly amazed, too? Well, that's what I've been doing to you. I've discovered that magic really is real, and I hope to make you believe it's real, too.

But there seems to be a problem with the way I'm going about it. Based on some of your e-mails and letters, many of you think you have to come to Maine to find all this wonderful magic I'm writing about. (And all those big strong handsome highlanders, although that's a whole other *Letter from LakeWatch*). But I promise that you don't have to travel anywhere, because the magic is *everywhere.* In fact, I saw another example of it just the other day you might be able to identify with; proof positive that miracles are always waiting to bless the unsuspecting.

I have two grandchildren who, at the time of this writing, are seven and five years old, boy and girl. Besides being pretty neat little miracles themselves, Alex and Abby are . . . well, let's just say that at times they're less than angelic. With a few years separating them and being opposite genders, they aren't always interested in playing nicely together. But last Sunday, after everyone in my family returned to their respective homes, I realized we had all witnessed a daylong miracle.

"Did you notice," I asked my husband as we crashed onto our recliners, utterly exhausted, "how well Alex and Abby played together today? Not one argument that turned to fisticuffs, no huge crocodile tears or even any tattling on each other. They spent a good hour of collaboration lugging monstrous rocks to the beachfront to build a castle, and actually *took turns* using the frog-catching net. Heck, they even helped each other lure those poor unsuspecting frogs with pieces of hot dog. They didn't use the fishing poles as weapons, and they rushed to each other's rescue when Jaden (my son's exuberant chocolate lab) tried to climb into the kayak with whichever one of them was having a turn." I smiled in contentment. "When was the last time we had such a picture-perfect Sunday afternoon?"

Robbie got a familiar look in his crinkled blue eyes. "The first Sunday we finally had an empty nest."

Not that our sons moved very far. I could probably throw a rock and hit either of their homes. But Sunday family gatherings, especially once grandchildren and puppies arrived on the scene, became more a study in chaos than a Norman Rockwell painting. (Note to impending empty-nesters thinking of downsizing your homes: Don't! You're going to need those bedrooms for sleepovers and a *bigger* kitchen and living room and dining table, because your family is going to grow exponentially.)

Sorry, I seem to have a bad habit of digressing.

So back to the magic being everywhere and happening all the time; some might say that Alex and Abby are merely growing up, but I'm old enough to be a grandmother and I *still* torment my brothers and sister. (I do not, however, intentionally cast my fishing lure on top of theirs so they can't catch the big fish that just swirled.)

But I think I should warn you, dear readers, that sometimes the magic makes its first appearance in what you and I might see as disasters — or setbacks, terrible timing, or just plain bad luck. Sometimes it's only when we're looking back at an event that we see it for the blessing it was. And sometimes several *years* pass before we can say, "Oh, I guess that was actually a *good* thing."

In the very first book I published, *Charming the Highlander,* I originally had Podly, Grace

Sutter's beloved little satellite, crash into Tar-Stone Mountain — which was the reason Grace was kidnapped and Greylen MacKeage had to go save her from the bad guys. But my editor was worried that crashing Podly on that particular mountain at that particular time was too convenient to be believable. So despite being confounded and more than a little dismayed, I changed the reason for the kidnapping and rewrote several scenes even though my original idea was how it really happened.

But eight years later there was Camry MacKeage, a rocket scientist like her mother, needing her very own story. How . . . convenient that dear little Podly was still quietly orbiting Earth. Thus, *A Highlander Christmas* was born, because that long-ago rewrite had kept the door open for the next generation.

Oh yeah, the magic works in many mysterious ways. But then, I suppose that's the very definition of a miracle. What fun is there in knowing everything, anyway? Who doesn't love wonderful surprises? Just as long as you remember that even if something first shows up as a disaster, it usually and eventually will end up a blessing in disguise.

Bad stuff happens — to you, to me, to my characters. But it really can't be taken personally; no one or no thing is out to get us. I believe I've had more than one of my characters — usually one of my old and wise magic makers — mention that life is neither fair nor unfair, but simply *is.* The difference is often between letting bad stuff turn us into victims and moving through it with . . . well, with the heart of a hero.

Yes, we can be our own heroes if there's no big strong handsome highlander rushing to our rescue. Or we can be someone else's hero, which often requires nothing more from us than a smile, a shoulder to cry on, or a big strong hug.

There's powerful magic in those smiles and hugs.

But best of all, they are the harbinger of hope for happily-ever-after.

We are the magic makers.

But if you aren't quite ready to believe me yet, don't worry; there are many more stories rattling around in my head, just waiting to be told.

Until later from LakeWatch, you keep reading and I'll keep writing,
Janet

ABOUT THE AUTHOR

Janet Chapman is the author of twenty contemporary and paranormal romance novels, all set in the state of Maine, where she lives with her husband, surrounded by wildlife. Best known for her magical Highlander series (a family saga of twelfth-century warriors rebuilding their clans in modern-day Maine), Janet also has several contemporary series set on the coast and in the mountains. With more than three million books printed in six languages, her stories regularly appear on the *New York Times* and the *USA Today* bestseller lists.

When she's not writing, Janet and her husband are camping, hunting, fishing, and generally rubbing elbows with nature. Visit her on Facebook and at www.janetchapman.com.

CPSIA information can be obtained
at www.ICGtesting.com
Printed in the USA
FFOW05n0642050913
1727FF